LYNN-PHILIP HODGSON
ALAN PAUL LONGFIELD

CAMP X
THE FINAL BATTLE

Lynn-Philip Hodgson, Alan Paul Longfield

Copyright ©, Blake Books Distribution, 2001
Cover Design and Page Layout
© Peter A. Graziano Limited, 2001

Editor: Barbara Kerr

Distribution by:
Blake Book Distribution
467 Fralicks Beach Road
Pory Perry, Ontario
Canada, L9L 1B6
905.985.6434

lynniso@idirect.com

National Library of Canada Cataloguing in Publication Data
Hodgson, Lynn-Philip 1946
Inside-Camp X : Camp X, The Final Battle

Includes bibliographical references and index
ISBN 0-9687062-3-1

1.World War, 1939-1945 - Fiction.
2. Britain, Battle of, 1940 - Fiction.
3. World War, 1939-1945 - Aerial operations - Fiction.
4 World War, 1939-1945 - Military intelligence - Canada -Fiction.
I. Longfield, Alan. II. Title.

PS8565.O324157 2001   C813'.6   C2001-930462-5
PR9199.4.H62157 2001

Design and Production
Silvio Mattacchione and Co.

Peter A. Graziano Limited
pgraziano@sympatico.ca

Printed and bound in Canada
by Friesens, Manitoba

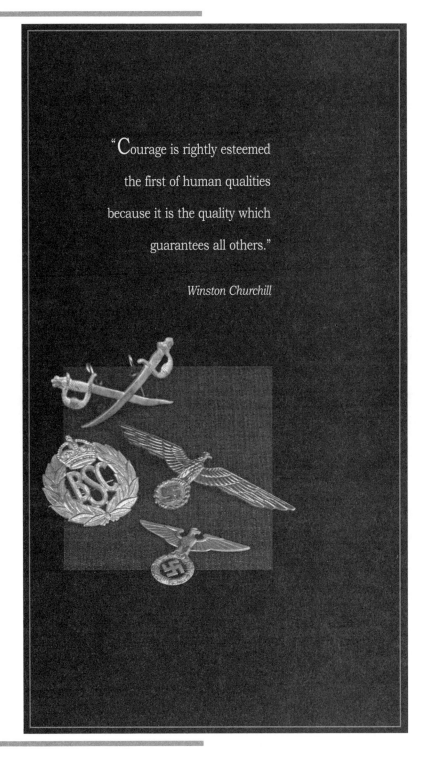

" Courage is rightly esteemed
the first of human qualities
because it is the quality which
guarantees all others."

Winston Churchill

To

Bill Hardcastle,

Mac Mc Donald,

Hamish Pelham Burn,

Joseph J. Gelleny,

and the late

General C.F. Constantine,

Eric Curwain, and

Andrew Durovecz:

a sincere thank you.

By telling your stories,

you have all helped to pre-

serve our history and have

ensured that the many others

who took their secrets

to the grave

will be remembered.

TABLE OF CONTENTS

ACKNOWLEDGEMENTS

Lynn-Philip Hodgson and Alan Longfield wish to express their gratitude to the following people for their contributions to the success of the **'Inside-Camp X'** series of books:

Bill Collier, J. Norman Donnelly, RCAF (Ret.), Elizabeth Ginn, Larry Grasby, Peter Graziano, Bill Hardcastle, Karen Hodgson, Marlene Hodgson, Roger Lee, Judi Longfield, Michael Longfield, Silvio Mattacchione, Mac McDonald, Hamish Pelham Burn, Richard and Janet Skilbeck, the late Harry Smith, Christine Tully, Janet Tully, Jim Tully, Frances Webley, Verdun Webley, David White, Jane Wilson, Brian Winter.

A special thank you to each of our readers who, by purchasing a book, have helped to bring the story of Camp X to light, and honoured the stories of the brave Canadians who served as members of British Security Co-ordination and Special Operations Executive.

INTRODUCTION

Sir Winston Churchill, the Prime Minister of Great Britain during World War II, was acutely aware that an imminent invasion by Adolf Hitler's Nazi Germany presented a very real, and ominous peril. Contingency plans, therefore, were put in place in the event that the threat became reality.

The following story is "faction": a compilation of documented evidence and anecdotal accounts blended into a riveting tale of suspense, treachery, and intrigue.

'Camp X The Final Battle' is a story of what might have been were it not for the sorely outnumbered and heroic Allied flyers who fought valiantly to win decisive victory in The Battle of Britain. Of these men, Winston Churchill said,

"Never in the field of human conflict was so much owed by so many to so few."

(August 20, 1940)

Collectively, the authors have accumulated more than fifty years of in-depth research, photographs from both the past and the present, and taped interviews with individuals who served the Allied cause, at home and abroad.

This is the story of the unthinkable and what might have been...

'Dodgy plots, half-baked schemes, and yesterday's crackpot theories!' Admiral Cunnington closed the report he had been reading, and angrily threw it onto the floor. It landed with a dull thump, ironically coinciding with the window-rattling shockwave of a bomb blast near by. 'And less than three hours until the meeting with Winston, dammit!'

Sir Willson Cunnington's desktop, in an unusual state of disarray, was littered to overflowing with heaps of secret intelligence estimates, military journals, and dry, academic papers. Unsettled, and still searching for answers, he had arrived at his office at five that morning, settled into his armchair, and hadn't moved since.

Even more agitated now, he rose and began pacing. 'Our country, hell, the Empire and all of Western Civilization, are facing extinction. Perhaps old Sun Tzu has something to say....' He picked up the well-worn, leather-bound 2400-year-old masterpiece, *The Art of War*, and flipped to Chapter XIII, 'The Use of Spies'.

Hence it is only the enlightened and wise general who will use the highest intelligence of the army for purposes of spying and thereby they achieve great results. Spies are the most important asset, because on them depends an army's ability to march.

"Thank you, master; that we know," he muttered impatiently, and then continued to read.

Whether the object be to crush an enemy, to storm a territory, or to kill an enemy general, it is always necessary to begin by finding out the names of the attendants, the aides-de-camp, and door-keepers and sentries of the general in command. Our spies must be commissioned to ascertain these.

He paused, '...*to kill an enemy general.* What about the general's commander-in-chief? How very un-British...and appealing. But how to get an assassin, man or woman, close enough to Der Führer? Read on...' A half hour later, he knew what must be done. "Miss Glover, please come in here straightaway, with a pot of strong tea and your steno pad. We have a report to write and reproduce, in...under two hours!"

Big Ben's Westminster chimes sounded the quarter hour, their reassuring cadences muffled by the dense fog, as Sir Willson Cunnington arrived at his destination. A Royal Marine guard held open the massive oak door for him, saluting as he passed through. Will acknowledged the greeting absentmindedly, glancing at his wristwatch. 'Eleven-fifteen', he noted. 'Right on schedule.'

"Good morning, Admiral." The assembled members of the top secret

London Controlling Committee (LCC) looked up, acknowledging the Chairman's arrival.

He addressed those gathered. "Good morning. We'll begin as soon as the Prime Minister arrives." They resumed chatting quietly among themselves regarding the latest gossip from the Whitehall tearooms overhead.

This room, unobtrusively hidden beneath Whitehall's corridors, had a nondescript appearance. There was little to indicate that it served not only as Prime Minister Churchill's refuge from officialdom but as his communications centre and command post as well. To Will Cunnington, it bore more than a passing resemblance to the cramped wardroom of his first ship. It was a small room, dimly lit, and furnished in what might charitably be described as 'Government Standard Issue'.

A floor fan chattered temperamentally in the far corner, a concession to visitors who found the pervasive odour of Churchill's cigar smoke offputting. On the panelled walls hung an outdated 1924 Royal Navy map of the Empire, a painting of Lord Nelson's battleship Victory, and two Union Jacks symmetrically draping a sepia photograph of His Britannic Majesty, The King.

'How like Winston,' reflected Cunnington, 'to carry on his secret plotting in a dingy crawl space. It's so typically Navy.' Approvingly, he noted the tray of sandwiches, the tea service, and the decanters of brandy on the sideboard, and smiled wryly at the conspicuous absence of the PM's usual cigar humidor.

At forty-nine, the Commander-in-Chief of Great Britain's Secret Intelligence Service, SIS, Willson Cunnington, code named 'G', was certainly one of the ablest if not the youngest of men to have ever been head of 'The Service' since the 1570's, when Sir Francis Walsingham placed his spies in foreign courts to report upon the 'knavish tricks and treacheries' of the enemies of Her Majesty Queen Elizabeth I, notably her cousin, Mary Queen of Scots.

Cunnington's rise had been rapid, almost meteoric, by all historical measures. His sterling record of distinguished service originated as a cadet. With the outbreak of the First World War, he was awarded his first command, the battleship 'dreadnought' HMS Prince Regent, in 1916. It was commonly known at that time that the Sea Lords had marked him for rapid promotion. He was brought 'inside' in 1917, ostensibly to modernize the Royal Navy's archaic wireless signals capabilities.

His intuitive grasp of tactically combined land and sea operations, blended naturally with his deep appreciation for the subtle teachings of the ancient warrior/philosopher/emperor, Sun Tzu: "(To)...undermine and subvert the enemy first; destroy him without fighting him...." This was considered not only revolutionary but worse, 'ungentlemanly', by many of the most powerful traditionalists in the appropriately named 'senior' service, which had changed its strategic thinking little since Admiral Horatio Nelson's decisive victory at Trafalgar in 1805 had shattered Napoleon's dream of invading Britain.

Undaunted, Cunnington quietly set about to develop a sophisticated signals encoding system for the capital fleet. His plan, 'Operation Woodwind', proposed an electronic 'cover' of deceptive radio messages supported by false but believable intelligence reports, and 'planted' by British agents throughout the Middle East. They were designed to mislead the Turkish and German defenders in the weeks leading up to a massive Allied amphibious landing, which was to be launched on the Dardanelles peninsula in 1917.

Woodwind was so watered down by the deans of naval intelligence, over First Sea Lord Churchill's strong protests, as to be virtually pointless, and, therefore, died on the table. The ensuing calamity known as Gallipoli resulted in the slaughter of thousands of British, Canadians, Australians, and New Zealanders. Characteristically, Winston Churchill assumed full responsibility for the debacle and was sacked ignominiously from the Admiralty. Before his departure, he had taken note of the brilliant and personable young officer, an Oxford-trained mathematician, and a gifted linguist, fluent in Hebrew, Russian, and several dialects of Arabic.

Willson Ewart Cunnington accepted the rank of Commander with His Britannic Majesty's Admiralty in 1919 where he was assigned the near-hopeless task of sorting out the Byzantine post-war politics of the eastern Mediterranean. Recommended to MI-5, military counter-intelligence, Cunnington was made Desk Officer in charge of monitoring the growing signs of Zionist activity in 'The Mandate', Palestine. Increasingly frustrated by the dithering, filtering and re-interpretation of his agents' intelligence reports by the Service's career bureaucrats, Cunnington secretly flew to Rome to meet with David Ben Levy, the shadowy head of the Haggannah, the illegal Jewish guerrilla army. Certain 'Agreements in Principle' and a 'working relationship' resulted, with mutually beneficial outcomes.

When Prime Minister Churchill assumed office, he wasted no time in tracking down Cunnington to offer him the position of Deputy Director,

SIS. Freshly knighted for unspecified 'services to the Empire' in Syria, Sir Willson inherited the corner office as Commander-in-Chief almost overnight; within the month, his predecessor, SIS head, 'V', was lost in a tragic airplane crash in central Russia's Ural Mountains.

Churchill entered the room and took his seat at the circular table. 'Winston's expression is even more grim than usual this morning,' reflected Cunnington.

The Prime Minister leaned toward Will, and growled, "My apologies for the delay. The House was somewhat more fractious than usual today. That fool Boothby hasn't even the most elementary conception of Adolf Hitler's wanton eagerness to commence the destruction of Europe."

"Lawrence unfortunately is not blessed with a deep grasp of foreign policy matters," Will concurred. The Right Honourable Lawrence Boothby, MP, was the national Labour Party leader. He was noted in the House of Commons and in the press, for his ceaseless appeals for time, patience, and understanding, and above all else, for sportsmanlike conduct in Britain's dealings with Herr Hitler.

Taking out his pocket watch from his vest, Winston Churchill glanced at it then raised his eyebrows and asked, "Shall we proceed, Sir Willson?" Will knew that it was not meant as a rhetorical question, nor was it open for debate.

Obligingly, the group of twelve quickly came to order. The members of the London Controlling Committee represented all branches of the military and intelligence services. It also included assorted talented civilians, each of whom was appointed by Winston Churchill to represent such diverse fields as communications, finance, industry, academia, and transportation.

At the centre of the gleaming mahogany conference table stood a small, elegant bronze statue of Diana, the Roman Goddess of the Hunt, holding her arched bow, and wearing a quiver of arrows on her slender back. Two eager wolfhounds preened patiently at her side. Diana, the Hunter, the sprightly symbol of the LCC, thought Will, was fast becoming the quarry.

"Thank you, Prime Minister. My Lords, Lady Jane, and gentlemen: my sincere thanks and appreciation, as always, to you for juggling your schedules and making the necessary arrangements in order to be here this morning, again, on short notice. But you all are quite practised, of late," Will smiled apologetically. There was restrained, polite laughter. "The situation report, which you are about to receive from Lady Jane, is of such urgency that it could not be kept back until our next scheduled briefing, as I'm sure you will agree.

"Lady Jane, if you would please be so kind. You may begin to read upon receipt."

Lady Jane Longchamps, Special Secretary to the LCC, distributed copies of a seven-page document on whose blue cover was marked: "This Document is the Sole Property of His Majesty's Government. Most Secret. Not To Be Removed," all underlined in red. Each person followed Admiral Cunnington's direction. After a suitable waiting period, allowing each member to read the report, he turned to the Prime Minister, seated to his left. "Sir? Do you wish to comment at this time?"

"I do, thank you, Will. We do indeed face a number of mortal threats, which, taken individually, would each be a challenge of the first magnitude, but would be surmountable. Coming all together as they do at this juncture, however, they conspire to overwhelm us and to under-mine the very existence of this nation. Will's proposals are, may I say, uniquely crafted to address this crisis, and reflect its magnitude that we now face. As such, they should not be dismissed out of hand. He and I invite your frankest appraisals and opinions. No minutes will be required, my Lady, thank you. An executive summary only. Admiral, please excuse me for usurping your role."

"Thank you, Prime Minister, not at all. Cyril, the RAF perspective, please?"

The LCC, Winston Churchill's inspired creation, was among the most carefully guarded secrets in Great Britain's wartime arsenal. Known only to its members as the 'The Shadow Cabinet' or, the 'XII Committee', it was the repository of twelve of the country's brightest and most extraordinary minds. All were charged with creating and putting into operation a bewildering host of clandestine, special warfare opera-tions and security measures. It reported only to the PM, and served both as a clearinghouse for classified information and as a special operations executive.

By mid-September 1940, it had become acutely clear to the LCC that the security of many of the Committee's most secret stratagems and their special means for unconventional warfare had been compromised.

Intelligence, counter-intelligence, espionage, infiltration of secret agents, spies and subversives into Nazi-occupied or 'listening post' countries, as well as the pipelines to the anti-Hitler clique of informants in the German High Command, the Schwarze Kapelle (Black Orchestra); all were in jeopardy. To what extent, how, when and by whom, the report was ambiguous.

Bletchley Park Manor

Fortunately, Allan Turing's brain trust at the General Code and Cipher School (GC&CS) at Bletchley Park, had cracked Germany's 'Ultra' military and diplomatic code, thereby unlocking the secrets of Germany's 'Enigma' coding machines. MI-5 had employed 'special means', after uncovering a bundle of letters penned by a love-struck GC&CS steno clerk, 'Alice'.

The contents of these letters hinted, with alarming naivety, at the very nature of the GC&CS' top-secret activities in Hut 6. The letters followed an amorous one-night tryst at a Brighton bed and breakfast late in December 1939, and were addressed to a 'Mr. Stefan Bedford', a.k.a. the 'naughty sausage', who was well-known to MI-5 as the handsome and charming Abwehr V-Mann, (secret agent) 'Oscar'. 'Alice' and 'Oscar' were swiftly placed 'out of harm's way', the report noted dryly, 'in a manner befitting the facts and each subject's particular circumstances', rendering the intelligence 'secure, if only by a heartbeat'. The exact fate of 'Oscar', was unspecified.

MI-5 counter intelligence had also successfully identified and neutralised all other known German Abwehr, SD and Italian SIM intelligence agents on British soil. Of these, a select few had been spared a sentence of life at hard labour or execution, and were successfully 'turned' by a 'Double Cross System' (XX) to be used as double agents, conduits of deceptive, seemingly authentic but nonetheless fictional radio intelligence messages sent to the Fatherland. All, that is, but one elusive Italian or German known only by his Axis secret services code-name, 'Tedesci'.

Air Marshall Fairchild's report minced no words: the military situation was becoming ever more critical. Statistically and quite likely,

Britain's RAF was facing defeat by the Luftwaffe, if the appallingly high rate of losses of aircraft and trained crew were to continue unabated. The stream of domestic and Commonwealth replacements, both in man-power and matériel, had slowed to a trickle as a result of aggressive U-boat attacks, and the incessant bombing of the aircraft manufacturing centres in the north.

If Marshall Göring's aircrews attained control of the skies over Britain, German domination of the sea-lanes would inevitably follow. Then, a full-scale assault across the Channel would be but a factor of time and weather.

Each member in turn spoke of the need to consolidate, regroup, and plan for the withdrawal of the Armed Forces to safety, before irrevocable harm was done. All agreed that the integrity of 'Ultra' would be key to survival and victory. Also, a safe and secure redoubt, from where the government-in-exile could continue the battle, was absolutely essential. The first stage would begin to move men, matériel, and command centres to the most remote parts of northern Scotland which remained, to date, impervious to Luftwaffe attacks. Then, there was always Canada. The report continued.

Across the submarine-infested waters of the Atlantic Ocean lay the Dominion of Canada, arguably the most secure and steadfastly loyal of the industrialised nations in the British Commonwealth. Strategically located on the world's longest undefended border with a potential, power-ful ally, the United States of America, Canada's role as a 'fair dealer' and 'honest go between' was an invaluable factor in relations between Britain and the U.S.A.

Canada's staggering mineral wealth, agricultural riches, and her large and skilled work force, had contributed immensely to the Allied vic-tory during the First World War, by providing a continuous flow of arms, food, and equipment. Moreover, the LCC brief commented, the impres-sive contributions and extremely high quality of Canadian men who had fought with valour and distinction in Flanders and France, as well as Canadian women, who had served in support roles, were major factors in the Allied victory.

Winston Churchill had visited Canada as a young army officer and was impressed with the vitality of its people, and its grandeur. Churchill had not one, but two aces up his sleeve in the event that it became nec-essary to convince his Cabinet of Canada's strategic importance: British

Security Operation (BSO) and its Canadian-born chief, Erik Williamson. Williamson, a wealthy electrical engineer/inventor/businessman, was Churchill's first and only choice to head MI-6 for North and South America. Code-named 'Stalwart' by Churchill, Erik Williamson was given the mandate to create an agency, BSO, which would be responsible for all British intelligence, counter-intelligence, and security operations west of the Atlantic.

Stalwart's reputation as a pioneer in the field of high frequency, short wave radio technology, was believed essential to BSO's success, were it to become the communications linchpin between Great Britain and the Americas. With headquarters established in New York City and Toronto, Williamson set about to forge alliances with key figures in The United States and Canada, cultivating leading academics, industrialists, publishers, government Crown Corporations, and policy-makers. His special relationship with the chiefs of both the Canadian and American domestic security services, the RCMP and FBI, earned him privileged access to their information bases and senior officials.

Williamson's bold plan for a North American Special Operations Executive (SOE) unconventional warfare training base, or Special Training School, 103 (STS 103), had been unanimously endorsed, and designated as 'Most Urgent' by both the War Cabinet and the London Controlling Committee, at the Prime Minister's insistence.

STS 103, or 'Camp X', was located in Canada, on a remote stretch of Lake Ontario farmland, within an hour's drive of Toronto (approximately an hour by high-speed motor launch, and less than half an hour by air-craft, from New York State). Since its opening, the base had graduated dozens of highly trained secret agents and spies representing target ethnic groups for clandestine operations in Occupied Europe and South America. Its proximity to the officially neutral USA made the Camp an ideal 'demonstration school' for training the future leaders of the young but burgeoning American Bureau of Security and Information Services (ABSIS) in the arts and skills of covert warfare.

'Canada...Camp X... of course! A ready-made school for assassins!' Will reflected excitedly. 'And far from Nazi prying eyes and ears.'

The Prime Minister cleared his throat, summing up the thrust of the reports. "A thousand swords are being held to our struggling nation's throat. We are bleeding our life's blood. I, and indeed the people of Great Britain, need your counsel and best advice, before we haemorrhage to death. Your recommendations will be forwarded to the War Cabinet with all dispatch for consideration. What we decide here today may well be the genesis of our island nation's salvation, and I pray that it will. Godspeed."

CHAPTER 1

WAR AND RUMOURS OF WAR

He glanced through the window just as three Royal Air Force Hawker Hurricanes in tight formation burst from the cloudbank overhead, a stream of white smoke trailing from the engine of the middle aircraft. 'Damn, another cripple!'

Air Marshall Cyril Fairchild tapped on the glass partition and signalled his driver to stop. The grey Air Force Humber limousine glided to the curb. Without waiting for his equerry to come around, Fairchild opened the rear door himself, alighted, and picked his way along the debris-strewn street, pausing only to glance up at the still-intact statue of the first Earl of Beaconsfield, Prime Minister Benjamin Disraeli, presiding solemnly over Parliament Square. 'Your beloved Empire is facing a fight for its very existence, My Lord. Any suggestions?'

It was September 15, 1940. The air war, which would come to be known as The Battle of Britain, had been raging without letup for five days and nights. After an exhaustive four-hour meeting with the Air Ministry's senior staff, department heads, scientific advisors and aides, and following the shockingly sudden resignation of the Deputy Minister, it was Fairchild's unenviable task to relate the Air Ministry's bleak conclusions to the Prime Minister's War Cabinet.

By some miracle, or, he thought, perhaps due to perverse German foresight, Whitehall, and the Houses of Parliament, though damaged, had not yet been completely destroyed in the constant rain of carpet-bombing. Fairchild entered No. 2 Great George, and began his descent of the steep, narrow and winding, wooden stairwell. The familiar, damp odour of mildewing paper mingled with the musty air rose in his nostrils as he neared the basement. The dankness reminded him of the hundreds of not-entirely-unpleasant hours he had spent together with Tilley Myers, a captivating Canadian Rhodes Scholar, and his future wife, in the murky, subterranean Archives when reading the Law at Regis College, Oxford.

Threading his way through a maze of underground corridors and cubicles, he crossed a marble lobby and nodded to the Royal Marine sentry at the sandbagged entrance to the Prime Minister's chambers. Cyril

Fairchild had struggled all night to formulate his report, in the full realisation that, no matter how carefully he might couch his dismal predictions, a crisis was inevitable. His report to the LCC had been a carefully worded warning of the possibility of a German victory. This time, he was bringing more than a statistical risk analysis; defeat was an odds-on probability. The PM would have no choice but to go to BBC Broadcast House and declare a national state of emergency.

'God help me, I mustn't agitate him to the point that he imposes war measures, or martial law. At least not yet,' Cyril reflected.

The Royal Marine Warrant Officer snapped to attention and saluted as he held open the door to the Prime Minister's inner sanctum. Late the previous evening, Prime Minister Churchill had telephoned Cyril at the Air Ministry to ferret out his situation appraisal. Following a terse exchange, Churchill ordered his

War Cabinet Room

Secretary, Basil Hall, to convene a meeting of the Cabinet citing 'extraordinary urgency', for ten o'clock the next morning. The electric wall clock indicated nine fifty-five as Fairchild entered.

The Sergeant-At-Arms ushered Fairchild to a chair immediately to the right of the Prime Minister's, and a white-jacketed Royal Navy ensign poured him a cup of tea. Fairchild set his overstuffed briefcase on the carpet, at his left side, and scanned the faces of the seven Cabinet Privy Councillors.

Winston Churchill's personal quarters in the underground War Cabinet Bunker.

Introductions were not required. He knew each one of these latter-day knights of the round table: Sir Malcolm Anderson, Lord Privy Seal; Sir Neville Kingsford, Chancellor; Anthony Burrows, Lord President of the Council; Lord Arthur Clarke, First Sea Lord; Sir Will Cunnington, Chief of the Secret Intelligence Service; Sir Harold Binnington, Army Chief of

Staff; Sir Edward Harris, Foreign Secretary; and Basil Hall, Esq., Privy Council Secretary.

As Fairchild contemplated how he would possibly manage a sip from the delicate Spode china cup without spilling its contents, the Prime Minister entered the room. "Good morning," growled the familiar, resonant voice. "Welcome Cyril. Thank you, gentlemen, that will be all for now." The Sergeant-At-Arms and ensign exited, silently closing the massive oak door behind them.

"Gentlemen, Air Marshal Fairchild has something to say to us this morning. This may not be what we wish to hear, but listen we must, nonetheless. Cyril, if you would be so kind."

Cyril Fairchild took a deep breath. "Thank you, Prime Minister. Good morning, My Lords, and gentlemen. I speak plainly: what I am about to say is of the utmost gravity and the highest degree of confidentiality. In brief, my Ministry's people have concluded that we are in danger of forfeiting the air war. It has become apparent, barring an act of God, that the Luftwaffe stands to achieve numerical superiority in our skies within the fortnight." The room was silent. "Both Fighter and Bomber Command are in complete agreement, which is a highly unusual precedent." He paused; there was no laughter. "I could have presented you with the statistical charts and graphs to support this conclusion, but thought it redundant.

"My predictions reflect neither upon the courageous efforts of our British and Commonwealth servicemen and women, nor upon the superb quality of our aircraft. Sheer numbers are simply threatening to overtake us. Replacements are unable to keep up with our losses. We must devise a plan that would see us maintain sovereignty and construct a bulwark against the inevitable attempted German occupation, codenamed 'Sea Lion'. The battle for Britain has taken a severe toll on the Luftwaffe's resources, as would be expected, and Sir Will has informed me that German Chancellor Hitler has decided to allow his Air Marshall time to replace and reposition his forces. Thus, the expected 'Operation Sea Lion' invasion will, in all likelihood, be postponed until October first. Gentlemen, if this all holds true, we have exactly sixteen days to prepare our response. I defer now, Prime Minister, to Sir Will."

"Thank you Cyril. I have asked Sir Will Cunnington to devise a comprehensive plan for the temporary evacuation from Britain of our top military people as well as our country's leaders in the event of an invasion and defeat. He will also tell us, in broad strokes, mind you, his intentions in the theatre of retaliatory warfare. Admiral Cunnington?"

"Thank you Prime Minister. Gentlemen, Cyril's presentation indicates that we have a massive, perhaps superhuman, undertaking before us. Just months ago, our Prime Minister called for the establishment of a 'Special Operations Executive', or SOE, designed to become a potent weapon in the critically important 'secret war' through the use of 'ungentlemanly' warfare. As originally conceived, SOE would, through Commando-style training coupled with advanced intelligence-gathering techniques and counter-intelligence methods, prepare so-called secret agents and spies for unconventional warfare in selected target countries. No quarter asked, none given. In dire times such as these just described by Cyril, it is imperative that we be able to rely upon admittedly cold-blooded unconventional modes of warfare. Forgive me, but is it too much of an exaggeration or overly dramatic to imply that the future of western civilisation is in danger of extinction?

"We have at this time several fully-operational top secret SOE bases known officially as 'Special Training Schools', both in Great Britain and the Dominion of Canada, three of which I will now describe, but only enough to give you the blank canvas and then to merely sketch a picture. Please withhold any requests for more colourful details.

"First, Baron Montagu's estate, Beaulieu, is our top-drawer finishing school. We have been sending out graduates from here since early this year. So far, these agents have largely been deployed in France, with mixed levels of success. This is not a reflection upon their calibre, or the resolve of the French people, but the situation is extremely volatile and unstable, because of...well, I'm sure that you know the details. Beaulieu's graduates provide a majority of the administrative and instructional staff cadre to the other special training schools.

"Secondly, Morar, in Northern Scotland, trains a variety of subversives and saboteurs for specific and often highly technical undercover assignments. These agents are intended to penetrate more deeply into occupied countries for special intelligence and critical sabotage missions. As you might imagine, contact before entry, as well as liaison on the ground with the existing resistance groups, is not uncommon. Otherwise, we might unwittingly be funnelling our people into the waiting arms of the Gestapo and SD as has happened far too often, particularly in France.

"The German operators and their radiolocation equipment are very skilled, too damned skilled, at intercepting our transmissions and rounding up our circuits, the underground networks. As an aside, one of our field agents who returned recently from Lyons remarked to me that the

Sicherheitsdienst, their SS security service chaps are reputedly able to pinpoint a contraband radio transmitter to within fifteen feet! He added, ironically, that they could likely also count the fillings in your teeth simultaneously!

"Thus, it is not always possible or desirable to confide our plans to any individual or group in hostile territory for a number of reasons. As a result, our agents must sometimes be parachuted in to fend for themselves by means of 'blind drops'. Also, close to Morar is the large Commando-training base, Arisaig. More, however, about that later.

"Thirdly, the Canadian base, Camp X, or officially STS 103, is situated on a remote stretch of lakefront in the small rural town of Whitby, the seat of Ontario County, in the Province of Ontario. This training school is the only one of its kind in North America. It was set up jointly with the assistance of our Canadian British Security Operation colleagues earlier this year for the purpose of special warfare training with an emphasis on infiltrating political warfare specialists and subversives into Eastern Europe.

"The location, although secluded, is within an hour's drive of the second-largest Canadian city, Toronto, an Indian name that apparently means 'meeting place', and for good reason. Toronto is relatively rich in its ethnic eastern European make-up, which, of course, makes it decidedly easier to recruit potential agents for the Balkans. Furthermore, most of these people are determinedly anti-fascist with a minority who are openly members of the perfectly legal Canadian Communist Party and ripe to settle scores against the Nazis for the occupation of their homelands. Toronto offers further benefits as well, which for a number of reasons will not be discussed at this time," he chuckled.

"Now, here is the plan. Beaulieu will be closed down immediately and all agents-in-training and instructors, as well as the required equipment, will be shifted north to Morar and Arisaig and several ancillary locations. No trace will be left of the school; Beaulieu and Beaulieu Abbey will be restored. The Montagu family will be relocated to Canada, as they would surely pay a heavy price for their war effort were they to stay behind. Herr Hitler is reportedly more than a little distressed by the antics of SOE's artful dodgers; the mere mention of Beaulieu sends him into a foaming frenzy.

"Arisaig and Morar will immediately be expanded. In addition, several other remote locations in the vicinity, and elsewhere in the Highlands and coastal islands, are to be developed as staging points for guerrilla operations, air raids and combined operations Commando attacks on southern enemy strongholds. The army and our other forces will be repositioned as dictated by events. Our redoubt is definitely to be Scotland. I assume that the Prime Minister will invite the Imperial General Staff to expand on this shortly.

"Lord Clarke has granted me permission to mention that contingency planning is well underway by the Admiralty should we successfully negotiate the temporary relocation of a large proportion of our strategic naval forces in Halifax, Canada. As well, opera-

Camp X from the air, 1943

tions are proceeding to strengthen and enlarge certain tactical bases in Northern Scotland.

"From Arisaig and Morar, selected SOE personnel including key Beaulieu instructors and senior staff, as well as several Arisaig officers and trainees, will be gathered and will sail to Canada via the most northerly route across the Atlantic." He paused to drink from a water glass. "Prime Minister, may I disclose the next part?"

"Pray do so, Will. We must all share the burden of the truth."

"Very well. With them will be some special passengers, including the Prime Minister and others, many of you among them."

"Excuse me, Cyril. Prime Minister," interrupted Malcolm Anderson angrily, "would that not appear to be an outright act of abandonment to our people? How are they to be expected to cope with a bloody-minded army of occupation if, to all appearances, we're seen to have deserted them?"

"A very good and most important question, Malcolm. Bear with us a little longer," responded Churchill. "All will become clear."

"Thank you, Prime Minister. Once they have arrived in Canada," continued Cunnington, "all SOE instructors, officers, support staff and trainees will be transported immediately to the Farm, or Camp X, STS 103. I should mention that Camp X is the popular name for the site. The 'X' reflects well on the security surrounding it, as the Commandant assures me that no one outside of the school seems to have the foggiest notion about its function. Even the Canadian Prime Minister may not have yet been told of its very existence! That will have to be rectified in due course.

"Prime Minister Churchill will be secretly and securely housed in a rather unusual location in Toronto called Casa Loma. As the name implies, it has the appearance of a fourteenth century castle. It was a folly, constructed in the eighteen hundreds by a Canadian industrialist. Casa Loma will be our primary headquarters; it is not far from either Camp X or the United States. The Canadians, that is Erik Williamson's British Security Operation, and SOE, are currently training fifty élite Special Air Service and Commando specialists at Camp X for the task of guarding the Prime Minister, his Ministers, and top government officials.

"It is imperative then that the Prime Minister set up his government-in-exile immediately and take control of Britain from outside of the British Isles. The people of Britain must know that they will not be forgotten, that they will be liberated. Nevertheless, we must have their total understanding and support! At this point, may I suggest that we take a moment to digest this information, Prime Minister? Perhaps some will have questions."

"Capital! Five minutes, and no longer, please. The WC's are on your right, directly across the lobby. What the...?" Suddenly, the delicate statue of Diana the Huntress began to tremble. Sir Edward Harris

Casa Loma, Toronto, Ontario. The site of the U.K. Provisional Government – in – exile.

grabbed the table to steady it. There was an urgent knock on the door.

"Enter!"

"Prime Minister, bombs are droppin' again on central London and one 'as apparently landed close by. I was wondering if you might require assistance," inquired the Sergeant-At-Arms, in broad Cockney.

"Good of you to look in, George. All present and accounted for. We're taking a short recess, so perhaps you and young Charles could look after replenishing the teapot. Kindly bring in more sandwiches and, of course, those delightful cinnamon buns. Also, if you would see to the maps, please, George." He nodded, indicating the wall opposite. "After, of course, attending to His Majesty."

The portrait of the King and the ageing wall maps, which had been listing heavily, were soon restored to their vertical positions and the meeting reconvened. "That gentlemen, is an example of British resolve", chuckled Churchill. "What was topsy-turvy moments ago is now back the way God intended. *Semper Britannicus.* This is what must be done at every turn in the road ahead. Now, Will, please continue. We'll not let the Nazi *sturm und drang* interrupt you further."

"Thank you, sir. Sir Neville, a question?"

"I believe that I express the concerns for all present, Prime Minister. Specifically, what arrangements have been made, or are being made, to ensure the safety, security, and well being of the Royal Family? Are they to remain in England or go into exile as well?"

"Allow me, Will," Churchill replied. "Thank you, Lord Chamberlain. I have had daily discussions with Their Majesties. They have made it patently clear to me that it is their fervent wish to remain here, in London, at Buckingham Palace, for the time being. The Princesses have already arrived safely in Ottawa, Canada. Beyond that, I am not at liberty to speak about the finite details of the arrangements for Their Highnesses or members of the Royal Household. Trust that all will be made clear, in due course."

"How did the Royal couple respond to your proposal for conducting the affairs of state, or, should I say, the affairs of war, from afar, Winston?"

"Lord Burrows, they were the first to suggest it, and they browbeat me for two hours into seeing the wisdom of their position. I should add that the King and Queen are confident that their presence on home soil will do much to bolster national confidence and help strengthen our valiant peoples' resolve to toss the invaders into the Channel. Please keep firmly in mind that our armed forces are to be re-assembled in Scotland; the country is not being stripped bare of resources. Their Majesties expressed faith in their own personal safety, given the examples of their brave royal relatives in Scandinavia, and Hitler's awe-struck attitude toward royal blood in general. He knows very well that the British people would take to the streets and fight to the last man and woman if anything were to befall their Royal Highnesses. Please continue, Sir Will."

"Thank you. Prime Minister, I was saying that once the first ship sets sail, another, carrying support personnel as well as the families of the training staff from Arisaig, Morar, and Beaulieu, would follow. All will be housed at STS 103. Camp X currently accommodates one hundred military and associated staff. When the instructors, families, agents, and support personnel arrive, STS 103 will grow to the size of a small village of six hundred or more. There are currently steps being taken to see the Camp's capacity immediately grow three fold.

"Gentlemen, if I may now turn your attention to this aerial photograph. This is Lake Ontario. The area outlined in blue is the perimeter of the existing base. The red section shows where the Canadian Army's engineers and construction battalions are building barracks and Quonset huts on the north side of the Sinclair farm road, exactly here. The expansion will continue up to the border of the Canadian National Railway line, shown here, which because of its elevation, forms a perfect physical boundary."

"Sir Will, what are those towers on the shoreline?"

"High frequency short-wave radio masts, Lord Clarke. The Canadians have come up with a first-rate transmitter/receiver. As I understand, it is immensely powerful. It's our principal link with our North American operations. For you technical types, it's known as a triple diversity rig. The chaps there characteristically christened it with a nickname, 'Hydra', for its multi-headed diamond shaped antennae..."

"After the snake-headed lady in the Greek myth, I presume?"

"Correct, Prime Minister. Gentlemen, these, albeit brief, are our plans. If there are no further questions I will turn it back to you, Prime Minister."

"Thank you, Admiral, for a job very well done, as expected. I hasten to add, that other reliable intelligence sources, to which I am privy, as are some one or two of you, share the same perceptions as those presented in Air Marshall Fairchild's report.

"Gentlemen, I will spare you the obvious rhetoric. In plain language, we are faced with a frightful predicament. Britain has withstood her enemies' blows and assaults for 1,000 years. Now, she is hovering on the brink of a calamity. Our friend, Mr. Roosevelt, states that his great democracy inches closer daily to becoming an ally, but Congress is not yet ready to join the game. "We must ask ourselves, as history assuredly will do: 'Have we, as Britons, done everything possible and, if not, what more can we do to prepare for the gathering darkness of an inevitable Nazi onslaught?' Please prepare your summaries and have them in the Admiral's hands ASAP, no later than 0900 this Friday. On Monday next, I must address the House of Commons.

"Our friends in Fleet Street are showing unusual patience and forbearance, but that will change as the situation becomes more critical.

The lead article in this morning's Courier chides me, saying that my silence is deafening, when the British people deserve to know what His Majesty's Government intends to do to turn the tide, et cetera, et cetera. The clock is counting down the precious seconds, minutes, and hours to zero hour, as we endeavour to ensure Great Britain's very survival. We shall not surrender to this gang of Nazi thugs, but rather, we must use all of our cunning and resourcefulness to put their head into the noose. Someday, all of Europe will rise against its oppressors and be done with Herr Hitler and his despicable lot. However, it will take considerable time and a great national, or, dare I say, international effort. Good day, good luck and God speed you in your deliberations."

At Camp X, in Canada, fifty Army and civilian workers were erecting barracks and facilities to accommodate the influx of new residents. The design and drawings had been entrusted to a Toronto firm of engineer/architects, headed by an associate of Erik Williamson, the Canadian chief of British Intelligence (SIS) in North and South America. With offices in Toronto and New York City, British Security Operation (BSO) was Williamson's cover name for SIS operations.

Each of the labourers, tradesmen, and army engineers, including their officers, had undergone rigorous background investigations followed by a forensic interview with the RCMP. Upon his approval at the gatehouse, each man was informed that the work site was a special weapons testing installation, and then ordered to sign *The rolling fields of Camp X, 1943.* The Official Secrets Act before stepping on the property. Army transports brought the crews to and from the Camp daily.

Erik Williamson rose at 5:15. Without waking Leah, he donned his workpants and favourite plaid shirt, then crept downstairs to be greeted warmly and wetly by Murphy, the family's Yellow Labrador. Later, returning from a rambling, fifteen-minute expedition with Murphy, he showered then dressed in his customary navy blue three-piece suit. Following a cup of tea with two slices of toast, leaving the crusts for an ever-appreciative Murphy, Erik left the modest two-story home (by Rosedale standards) at 6:15. The stroll through the peaceful, tree-lined streets of impressive residences was Erik's morning therapy, he had told Leah. At 6:45, Erik arrived at his office at the base of one of Casa Loma's towers. As he reached for the humidor of Cuban cigars, he smiled, recalling how he had initially been amused by London's suggestion that he locate his Toronto bureau in this picturesque and draughty old replica, as though it might somehow lend a certain cachet to his role. Pausing for a moment to relish the lingering aroma, he reluctantly closed the lid of the fragrant wooden container.

RCMP Commissioner Ted Reynolds continually harped on the security, or lack thereof, which Erik's habits presented to the Mounties' Security Service, detailed to safeguard him. Erik, code named 'Stalwart', shrugged off Ted's pleas. A chauffeured, government limousine was at BSO's disposal, but if a vehicle was required, Erik usually chose to take a taxi or to drive his 1939 Packard Clipper unless he was attending an official function. He rationalized, lecturing Ted on voluntary gasoline rationing as the duty of all patriotic Canadians. Furthermore, he added, an able-bodied man should walk a mile daily to stay 'fit for action'. Besides, Erik quietly assured the Commissioner, his background, as an amateur Commonwealth middleweight boxing champion would "keep the bogeymen at bay." That was that.

Reynolds capitulated, but quietly issued a short and terse directive to the Security Service that surveillance of 'Stalwart' would continue, but must be, at all times and under all circumstances, inconspicuous. It was implicit that any 'watchers' caught out would be summarily reassigned to one of the two bone yards of uniformed assignment: Customs Duty, or worse, guard service on "the Hill", Parliament Hill, in Ottawa. Both were dreaded career-stoppers for upwardly mobile staffers. Erik delighted in playing Ted's game, never divulging the occasional indiscretions of his more zealous guardians.

"Good morning. Damn glad we don't pay the taxes on this place, eh Hugh?" he remarked to his young executive assistant bringing in the usual collection of five national and international newspapers.

"I'm sure it would be..."

"Anything worth reading today?"

"Well, sir, the *Globe*, *Post* and *Times* report nothing too earth shattering, the usual London fire photos, heroics of the Home Guard and editorials to bolster the British spirit. I'm afraid, Sir, that the *Courier* is not onside. Here, look at this headline."

"Bollocks!" he exploded. "What does that blithering fool think he's doing?" The two-line banner raged in twenty-four-point type: 'CHURCHILL FIDDLES WHILE LONDON BRIDGE BURNS.' The editorial was no less vicious. Erik's 'blithering fool' was the Canadian-born press baron, Marcus Baird, Lord Oxley of Fleet. It was obvious to Hugh that the gloves were off; the gentleman's agreement between the British press and the PM had gone by the boards.

"I should have broken his nose in the ring in Regina, although fat lot of good it would have done, he's so thick-headed! Hugh, ask Mary to find 'Lord Oxhead's' private number. Also have her leave me a reminder to call London immediately after lunch. With tripe like this, he'll next be accusing the PM of being a Nazi collaborator. He owes me for that peerage. It's time to call in accounts and reign in my old friend. Hand me the New York Times, if you would, please."

"Yes, sir." Hugh complied, then waited while 'Stalwart' flipped through the pages of the first section, and paused to scan an article. He felt rattled by his normally taciturn boss's angry outburst, although the reference to 'Lord Oxhead' was as humorous as it was sarcastic.

"Now, what were we talking about?" continued Erik, calmly. "Ah yes, the castle. You were saying..."

"Sir, I was wondering how Sir Hector managed it all, financially?"

"He didn't. It nearly broke his back, and his heart. It seems that he had it built as a wedding gift for his bride, Jean, a comely Scottish lass, as a condition of her consenting to marry him. Nevertheless, it didn't suit her and soon she complained of homesickness for the family castle in Edinburgh. She took off with a gold-digging scoundrel named Daniel Lazier from Louisiana, not long after she and Sir Hector had moved in. Left Hector Osborne holding the bag, so to speak. She was independently wealthy, and soon tired of Lazier's shenanigans and philandering. She disinherited him and returned to bonny Scotland.

"Hector was well-enough off, a capitalist of the old school, a bit of a robber baron, apparently, but soon found that he couldn't afford the upkeep and had to turn over the deed to the castle to the City for use as a museum and tourist attraction. He hightailed it back to the Isle of Skye to avoid his creditors, where he died, broke, lonely, and more or less a hermit. *"Sic transit gloria mundi..."*

"Sick, sir?"

"Oh, sorry lad. It's Latin for 'Here today, gone tomorrow', roughly. I remember visiting the castle twice with my Dad when I was a young boy. I loved exploring the underground tunnels and secret rooms. Most of them were closed to the public, of course, but Father did have his ways. Fortunately, I have obtained the architect's original blueprints, so we know where the bodies are buried, so to speak. The suits of armour in the hallways scared the daylights out of me, gave me nightmares for months afterwards. I thought that Sir Hector was going to jump out and chop me to bits with his broadsword. There are stories of his ghost...

"Let's have a look out there, Hugh! It's quite magnificent." They stepped through a narrow doorway, which lead from Erik's office directly to the tower stairs. Erik often climbed to the top and gazed out over central Toronto, enjoying the forbidden pleasure of a cigar and contemplating the hardships which his friends and comrades in Britain must be experiencing.

"Poor devil, old Osborne. A pity he didn't live long enough to enjoy it. I suppose that is why they're called 'follies.'"

"Quite breathtaking, indeed. I was wondering, sir, whether you might consider me as a possible..."

The buzzer of his office intercom wafted up, then sounded again, harsh and insistently. "Did we hear that, Hugh? Unfortunately, we did and that's the end of the local history lesson for this morning. Be a good fellow. Run down to let Mary know that I'm on my way."

Erik followed Hugh downstairs to his office, where Miss Mary Ward, Erik's loyal, extraordinarily devoted and efficient private secretary waited with a cup of coffee. "Mr. Brooks is on the scrambled line. Shall I take your jacket, Mr. Williamson?"

"Thank you, Miss Ward. Rob, Erik here."

"Erik, how are you?"

Robert Brooks was Erik's flying companion from the First World War. Together, they had piloted Sopwith Camels with the Royal Flying Corps, and had briefly entertained the thought of establishing a flying school. Instead, they joined the British Secret Service, SIS, in 1919, to serve in Ireland during the first years of 'the troubles'. Robert, a proud Belfast Roman Catholic, was Erik's choice for Deputy Director of BSO.

Throughout BSO, Erik was known as Mr. Williamson, or simply, the Boss. His operational name, 'Stalwart', was Winston Churchill's less-than-inspired creation, in Erik's opinion, and was never used in his presence, being reserved solely for written communiqués. Erik thought it too pretentious, muttering out of the PM's earshot that it was a childish piece of cloak and dagger puffery. Robert Brooks was the only person in BSO who directly addressed him as Erik.

"Just taking a breath of fresh Toronto morning air. No, no cigar, I swear. Where are you?"

"Washington, D. C. You called last night? My apologies, I was engaged with our friends here until well past eleven. My report is on the wire."

"Good. I hope you're having success. I look forward to reading it. Robert, you know the situation as well as I. It's time to roll up our sleeves and get down to business. I've been talking to Winston's London Controlling Committee. A thought, which I planted there, appears to be gathering support. Do you recall a German-speaking female agent, from Beaulieu? We assigned her to England late in '39, to be on the lookout for promising 'opportunities.' She was Jewish, absolutely trustworthy, and dazzlingly bright. She topped all of her classes. The Commandant at Beaulieu pleaded to keep her as an instructor. And a bit of a looker, if I recall correctly."

"If you recall, indeed! Ah, Erik, you haven't changed from our glorious flying days, I'm glad to hear."

"Of course I have, Robert. I'm older, and it's my pleasant business to remember such details," remarked Erik, laughing.

"Yes, Erik, I do remember 'Silvia': a beauty, a charmer, and as you said, very intelligent, extremely skilled, and brimming with enthusiasm for her assignment. Has she been making some progress? I haven't seen any recent reports. Have you?"

"She was doing exceptionally well! She linked up with a young German at university. He's bright, athletic, idealistic, an Aryan superman type, and a post-doctoral medical student. He left her and a new baby in the lurch to go back home and join the Waffen SS at first crack of the guns in thirty-nine. He's already a decorated field officer. Regiment is the Wiking. I think he's a decent enough sort despite that, and he might be good material for us if we can get through to him. He has one weak spot in his SS armour, a deserter's guilt, both as a lover and a father."

"This is very good news, Erik! Nevertheless, you said 'was doing'. Is she still reporting on a regular basis?"

"No, she's gone to ground, but I do have occasional reports from their mutual friend, called the Professor. You don't know about him, yet. He's a gem, believe me, Rob. He's keenly interested in joining us. Now listen, please. I need you to put a plan together for 'Silvia'. We must get her over here at the Camp for training within the next two weeks. The mission is still being tossed about in the backrooms, as usual. It may or may not go; however, its working title is 'Tent Peg'."

"'Tent Peg'? Sounds intriguing!"

"Read your Old Testament, *Judges 4*, to be exact, old son. I'll expect you to recite it, verbatim. After all, your sainted father was man of the cloth; didn't something of that rub off? Listen, Robert, it's imperative that we meet as soon as possible. I can only tell you the nature of the subject in person. I want you to set up a meeting with Ted Reynolds and Major-General Constantine. Do not discuss anything on the telephone. Make the usual arrangements for travel to New York. The key is 'seven'."

The BSO code key was an ingeniously simple but effective cipher system worked out by Erik. A co-operative editor at the *New York Times* planted an article once a week, usually something as innocuous as a dance review or an obscure gallery opening, with the premiere and closing date. 'Seven' instructed Robert to go the day's *New York Times*, front section, page seven, the seventh story on the page, and read to the seventh paragraph. There in the seventh position of the seventh line would be the date of the meeting.

The time and location were invariably 9:00 a.m., BSO headquarters, Committee Room 3600, Rockefeller Centre, New York City. All four would travel independently: two by separate cars, another by train and the fourth by commercial airline, standard practice for senior BSO staff. In this situation, the subject was so sensitive that it could not be written down on paper much less discussed on an encoded short wave radio/telephone system, regardless of how secure that system might be.

"Now, I want you to use whatever means at your disposal to find her, Rob. Please be in touch immediately when your people locate her; however, do not approach her. I repeat, do not approach her. Locate her and then don't let her out of your sight. She's a cagey, consummate professional, so put your best people on it. We don't want her suspecting that the Abwehr's spies are on her tail, or we'll lose her for good. Admiral Cunnington agrees with this much of my plan, has given me the green light and some useful resources to help us winkle her out.

"As I said, I'll spell out the specifics when we meet and, with any luck, we will soon receive the London group's blessing. Speed and absolute discretion are essential. Be careful, Robert, we can't afford to lose her again. Goodbye."

"I promise. Goodbye, Sir."

Erik set down the hand piece of his patented invention. The device had the appearance of an ordinary telephone, but its sophisticated encoding system was unlike any other in the world, and virtually indecipherable. Only seven prototypes existed. Four were in BSO HQ's in North America. The fifth was in the Commandant's office at the Farm, Erik's usual name for Camp X, through which all of the system's communications were routed via Hydra's high frequency short wave radio. The sixth was in Will Cunnington's private suite, and the seventh in Winston Churchill's war room.

As he sipped at his coffee, Erik mulled over the implications of his plan, 'Tent Peg'. He knew that LCC, the London Controlling Committee, was divided on it for several reasons. If SOE/BSO eliminated Hitler, who might replace him? There were others waiting in the wings in Berlin who might actually prove to be far more malevolent and mentally unsound, if that were possible. Even Churchill thought it a bit risky, but not from the perspective of possible Nazi retribution against himself.

As far as ungentlemanly warfare was concerned, it certainly set a new benchmark, mused Erik. Fair play and sportsmanlike British tradition would be nullified, a hard sell with several of the members of the Committee. A mission this politically sensitive had never even been considered by a democracy in this century, much less undertaken.

"Miss Ward, please have Hugh Mason come in here at 11:30. I shall be taking him for a bite of lunch at the Club. Don't tell him. I'd like to surprise the lad, and bring in his file, please. I'm ready for the mail and dispatch bag."

"Yes, sir. Mr. Mason relayed your request for Lord Oxley's private number. I'll clip it onto the mail folder."

"Thank you, that will be all."

Hugh Mason was impressed by his superior's lack of formality. "Good afternoon, Trevor. This is my good friend, Hugh Mason. How's the brisket of beef today?" Trevor, the Concierge at the York Club's front desk responded affably then turned away to see to another member.

"Would you care for something wet before we eat, Hugh? The sun is over the yardarm," Erik added, smiling, as Hugh signed the guest register. "This way."

"As you wish, sir." They were seated comfortably with their backs to the large plate glass windows overlooking the curling pads.

"The usual, Alec, please. What would you like, Hugh?"

"The same will be fine, sir."

"Make that two, Alec, very dry. I hope you like your martinis that way, Hugh. I recall you were starting to ask me about something or other on the balcony. Please, go on."

"Yes sir. Thank you. I feel, and no offence sir, that I'm not pulling my weight. I would very much like to do...to do more."

"More. Hmm, more typing? Research? Burning the midnight oil? Thank you, Alec. Cheers, Hugh."

"Cheers, Sir. I...I mean more active, sir. I want to volunteer for service."

Erik was silent for what Hugh judged to be an eternity. "And what do you see yourself doing, Hugh?"

"Well sir, I would be honoured to be able to repay Canada for accepting Mom and me. As you know, she was a German citizen, Dad was a Scots Canadian, and I was born in Hamburg. Since Dad passed away and we came here when I was eight, we've done well enough and her origins have never hindered her promotion in the Public Service..."

"I see, Hugh. But you are doing valuable service here with me at BSO, you know. Have you no qualms about fighting against your mother's countrymen?"

"Sir, I am Canadian and a loyal British subject."

"Of course. Shall we go into the dining room? Perhaps over lunch you could tell me more about your aspirations. I understand from your file that you know something about short wave radio. Bring your drink along. It is allowed."

"Thank you sir. I really appreciate your taking time to speak with me about this. I must confess that I never thought I'd have the chance to..."

"We can always discuss possibilities, Hugh."

Erik knew exactly where and how he would use Hugh Mason's remarkable abilities. First, he had to get the young man to the Farm,

Camp X, in Whitby, as soon as the paperwork could be completed. That would take one, or at the most, two days on the fast track. Erik was convinced that Hugh was the perfect candidate for a pivotal role in operation 'Tent Peg'. But first, he had to pass the tough SOE training courses at Camp X.

Mary Ward was more than usually grim faced when Erik and Hugh returned at 1:00 p.m.

"What's wrong, Mary?"

"I'm not sure sir. It's on your Teletype. Colonel Graham called from the Camp to say that it came through there at 12:30 our time, is of the utmost urgency, and is for 'Your Eyes Only.' I'm just afraid...."

"Thank you. I'll deal with it now. Have you had lunch?"

"I'll step out for some fresh air now, sir, if you wouldn't mind."

"Of course."

Erik tore the serrated pages from the carriage. The message had been decoded in the basement radio room and sent up to his printer in plain. It read:

'YOUR EYES ONLY

TO: STALWART

FROM: WARDEN

SUBJECT: SITUATION REPORT: EXTREME STOP

DRAGONFLIES OVER ANGELS STOP

ARMADA SIGHTING EXPECTED STOP

REQUEST ALL DISPATCH WITH THE FARM STOP

LOOK FOR YOU SOONEST. STOP REGARDS STOP

-30-'

Erik was stunned. Churchill ('Warden') was saying that the German Luftwaffe ('Dragonflies') was gaining air supremacy. An invasion ('Armada') was imminent. Churchill, his Cabinet, Will Cunnington and the London Controlling Committee needed Erik over there, urgently. Now he knew why SOE had pushed so hard for a tripling of the capacity at Camp X. He opened his office door, and called, "Miss Ward!" 'Damn it, she's out.' Erik picked up the unscrambled telephone handset and dialled the BSO's Special Operator. "Williamson. Please connect me with London, England," and he recited the necessary number.

"Connecting, sir."

"Good afternoon. *London Courier*." The overseas line was clear and free of the customary distortion.

"Marcus Baird, please. Erik Williamson."

"Erik, old fellow. How are you?"

'Old fellow,' indeed! Marcus was becoming more anglicized by the day. "I'm well enough, Marcus. How are Bernice and the children holding up?"

"Surviving, thanks."

"Good. Leah and I send our best regards. Marcus, there's a favour of a rather sensitive nature that I'm going to request of you."

"I'm listening, Erik."

When Erik concluded, Marcus agreed immediately and without a red-blooded, patriotic appeal to Empire, King, and Country. He had the highest regard for Erik Williamson, his brilliant roommate at the University of Saskatchewan, who had coached him through the gruelling final year of electrical engineering. Thanks to Erik, he had graduated second from the top, *summa cum laude*. Erik, to the surprise of no one, graduated at the head of the class, earning *magna cum laude*.

"His Majesty's Government will appreciate this very much, Lord Oxley."

Perhaps the none-too-subtle use of 'Lord Oxley' had reminded Marcus of Erik's quiet, backroom manoeuvring in securing the peerage. "I'll see to it, old man, immediately. I promise. Best to all."

It wasn't quite bribery, Erik reflected. Marcus' massive ego had been bruised but not battered. There was the adroitly placed hint, just the whiff of a possible 'something', a special appointment of national importance in the offing, in return for the influential *Courier* and its string of provincial dailies burying the hatchet. Erik realised that the PM would not be easily persuaded to enlist Marcus' considerable talents and connections, but would make every effort. Marcus could prove to be useful. Erik smiled in the knowledge that despite his minor faults, Marcus was a British flag-waver, a fierce fighter in the corners, as bright as a new penny and always alert to new opportunities to advance his favourite cause: himself. 'Minister of Armaments in return for his falling in line? I'll mention it to Winston.'

"Miss Ward, could you please step in, now, with your pad?"

Mary Ward knew that was not a request; Erik Williamson was about to swing into action mode.

"Please make a note of the following.

"First: To Colonel Graham at Camp X; send a coded signal, priority 'Urgent', to inform Robert to stand down our meeting, until he receives new directions from me. He will notify the others. He is in charge of Ops while I'm out of the country. Oh, yes, you'd better tell him where I'm going.

"Second: The hunt for 'Silvia' will proceed, with all dispatch. I will meet with her in England. Include that in the first part.

"Third: Hugh Mason's dossier and other particulars to be forwarded to Recruitment and Documentation on King Street. Please type my standard recommendation and stamp it Process Without Delay. I'll read and sign it before it goes in today's courier. This is Tuesday. I want him interviewed, signed, sealed and delivered to Camp X with the next cycle of recruits going in, let me see my calendar... on Saturday, that's next Saturday.

"Fourth: Contact Air Vice-Marshall Shearer and tell him I'm requesting a seat on the next Air Transport Command flight, tonight, to Gander and then, to London, ASAP. I'd even be delighted to hitch a ride with Ferry Command's regular Lancaster runs to Bermuda and carry on from there.

"Last: When you have set my itinerary, call Winston Churchill's war office on my line and advise him of my ETA."

"Very good, sir. Will you be needing anything else, sir?"

"Yes, please tell Mrs. Williamson that a driver will be picking up my travel kit within the hour. See to those arrangements as well. A three-day supply of shirts, socks, et cetera should be about right. Please let her know that I'll call before I leave for the airport.

"Miss Ward, I know how worried you are about your sister and her family. Give me their address. I'll speak to our High Commissioner in London and see what arrangements I can make, at least for the children. I'm afraid it's bound to get a great deal darker before Britain sees the dawn. And pray God, she will."

The RCAF Transport Command DC-3 landed at Gander, Newfoundland, in freezing rain, and took off immediately after refuelling and de-icing. A journalist from Chicago, assigned to report on the deepening crisis in Great Britain, sat in a seat directly across the narrow aisle from Erik in the otherwise empty cabin. As they chatted, Erik shared the perquisites of office; a thermal container of tea and a salmon sandwich. He short-circuited her polite questions by stating that he represented a group of private Canadian business interests, who were

"...eager to pitch in to aid Britain."

"That's great. If Britain goes under the Nazi knife, who's left to defend civilisation? I wish we had some American leaders who gave a damn."

"You do, Miss Thompson. I assure you, you do."

Two hours out, over the Atlantic, Erik noticed that her attractive face had acquired a greenish tinge. Moments later, she hurried aft to the washroom. She returned, smiling wanly. "Sorry, Mr. Albertson, I think I'm in the wrong line of work. I'm a lousy traveller."

"Not at all, my dear. It's been extremely bumpy. Have some more tea. It will help."

The pilot came out of the cabin to join them, at Erik's request. "How are my passengers doing? Are you okay, Miss Thompson? Unfortunately, it's often turbulent at this time of year."

"I'm better, thank you, Captain. Do you think we'll make it, with German air patrols lurking everywhere and the awful weather?"

"Eighty-five percent sure, Ma'am. It's my tenth trip in DC-3's without any problems to speak of. Flight-Lieutenant Baker is at the controls, using evasive tactics and doing everything possible to make certain that we arrive safely, all of which likely explains why your stomach's rebelling. We've been changing altitude frequently, and darting between the clouds for cover from night fighters. I suggest that you both try to get some sleep, now."

He smiled, saluted casually, and went forward. Karen's hand reached across the aisle, gently taking Erik's. "Thanks, Erik Albertson. You are one very thoughtful gentleman. I feel much better now, really. Excuse a reporter's directness, but you are, of course, married?"

"Yes, we have two daughters."

"Of course... And I'll bet that you have lots of pictures."

"Yes, in my luggage."

The whining of the hydraulic landing gear awoke them as the twin-engine aircraft began its approach.

"That's Croydon airfield below, Miss Thompson."

"Thank the Lord!"

"And the Royal Canadian Air Force," he added quietly.

"I can't wait to start snooping about and get the real goods. You know, Erik, I'm going to join up as soon as our country gets off its aspirations to remain neutral."

He nodded, smiling. Erik was impressed and made a mental note to follow up with a thorough background investigation of Miss Thompson. She seemed the sort of woman whose politics, ready wit, attractiveness, and character might prove very useful in BSO' American theatre.

Erik directed the taxi driver to take him to the Ritz. He had barely finished unpacking when the hotel operator called his room, inquiring as to whether he wished to receive a call.

"Erik, my old Viking! I am delighted and relieved you've made it here safe and sound. How was your flight?"

"Quite good, thanks. I actually slept for the last hour or so. I was fortunate to have a charming travelling companion, a female reporter, from Citizen Hearst's *Tribune*.

"Yes, I know of her. A good reporter, if that's not too egregious a contradiction in terms, passionately anti-isolationist and a rabid Anglophile, to boot. I wonder how long she'll last at her present post. 'G' cleared her, of course. We need her sort of message over there; the cousins tell me that her columns are required reading in enlightened circles. Now, my good friend, I must let you rest. You're scheduled for meetings all day, and possibly, half the night. A driver will be waiting, at 9:15. Oh, yes, the hotel manager, Mr. Binks, has been absurdly over-compensated to look after your sundry needs. Good night, Mr. Albertson."

Erik smiled as he placed the ornate handset in its cradle. 'Albertson, indeed! Bill Donovan, you'll have some explaining to do in New York.'

The drive to No. 10 Downing Street was deeply unsettling. Despite the scores of scrupulously calculated damage estimates, intelligence briefs, and photographs that arrived daily at BSO, Erik was not prepared for the heart-wrenching scenes of desolation and destruction. London was under siege, yet, like a wounded lion, it still breathed and lived. A stream of police cars, fire vehicles, and double-deck buses swerved and zigzagged, avoiding the newest crop of potholes. Children in neat uniforms snailed to school, and other young warriors scampered valiantly to take possession of fresh hills of rubble. Factory-bound young women sporting colourful bandannas, along with bankers and government employees in black bowler hats reading their precisely folded *Times*, queued at bus stops with British forbearance. An echelon of ten Hawker Hurricanes thundered southward at low altitude. Erik felt a rising lump in his throat.

The two Bobbies framing the entrance of the Prime Minister's residence saluted and stood aside when Erik approached. "Good morning, sir. He's expecting you. Let me get the knocker."

"Thank you, Constable. How are you chaps faring?"

"Well enough, Sir, thank you," answered the sergeant. "The kids are in the country with the wives. Young Jim 'ere and me's got the life of Riley. Skittles and beer till the cows come 'ome. Adolf's going to have to do much worse than this, if he thinks he's going to set up 'ousekeepin' at Buckingham, Sir."

"That he is, indeed. Good luck."

"Welcome, Erik. Do come in. Gerald, this is, Erik, my friend from Canada. Gerald will take your coat. Would you care for something to ward off the morning chill, Erik?" He scowled. "I forget myself - not one of your vices. My goodness, but you do look well. How is Leah? I assume that the girls are off to boarding school? We're to meet LCC in the dungeon at ten. That gives us thirty minutes to catch up. Excuse me one moment, while I play master of the castle.

"Gerald, please have the car brought around straight away. I don't expect I'll be home until past eleven; therefore, if Mrs. Churchill calls, please have her ring through to Basil Hall at the office. If you venture out to the cinema, leave some of cook's delightful shepherd's pie in the warmer, please."

"That has been attended to, Mr. Churchill."

"Yes, of course. Erik, the difference between a merely good butler and a great butler is in the anticipation of one's needs. The same is true for politicians...and concubines, I'm told.

"By the way, Gerald, Mr. Hitchcock's new thriller, *Rebecca*, is receiving excellent reviews, as are Larry Olivier and that gorgeous creature, Miss Joan Fontaine. David Selznick, one of your chums, Erik, is the Producer. You do have some useful connections in that business, do you not?"

Before Erik could respond, the telephone rang in Churchill's study. "That's the secure line. Excuse me, Erik," he said, closing the French doors. Moments later, he reappeared, holding the receiver against his vest. "Robert Brooks, with an urgent message for you. I'll be waiting in the car."

"Good news, Erik?" asked the Prime Minister, when Williamson was seated.

"Sir, I have two very large favours to ask of you. Can you possibly delay the start of the meeting for forty-five minutes? And, will you accompany me to a restaurant in Shepherd's Bush?"

During the drive to Whitehall, Churchill addressed Erik's mission. "A word of caution, if I may. I take considerable pride that the individuals whom I personally selected to make up LCC represent the finest collection of creative and delightfully devious minds since Holmes and Professor Moriarty clashed at Reichenbach Fall. Nonetheless, what you are proposing, operation 'Tent Peg,' will encounter formidable opposition, from quarters that may surprise you. It's not the sort of thing we Britons do casually, at least not in recent memory, but then, the ominous threat of invasion hasn't been the currency of after-dinner table talk since the time of Sir Francis Drake. I personally believe the scheme has much to commend it, but as a politician, I'll need to be convinced that it has some reasonable probability of success and can be accomplished without squandering British or Canadian lives.

"This will do, thank you. We'll walk from here," he said, stepping out onto the sidewalk.

"Incidentally, I'm most grateful for your intervention, Erik," Churchill remarked over his shoulder, as they navigated the stairs. "Marcus and his fellow ink-stained wretches were playing fast and loose, but now seem to be back in the fold."

"He could prove to be invaluable, Sir. He's ambitious, astute, well connected, and an adroit manager but is as vain as the Queen of Sheba."

"Yes, and therefore he hates to admit defeat and he steamrollers the opposition. Sounds a kindred spirit. I could use some fresh blood to speed up heavy armaments production, a new Caesar of the Cannons. Let me think on it. Erik, you will know most of the LCC's members. Here we are. Good morning Warrant Officer, have they been waiting long?"

"They've been quite patient, Prime Minister. We received the notice of your delay and Sergeant Brower immediately arranged for refreshments to be served."

"Erik Williamson has flown from Canada, to present us with a proposition of the utmost secrecy and the greatest...delicacy. If you're ready to proceed, Erik will guide us through his proposal. That will be followed by a full and open discussion of the matter. Minutes will not be kept, thank you, Lady Jane."

As the baroness put down her pen, Erik began, "Thank you, Prime Minister. First, please let me thank you personally for your trust and your ongoing interest in and support for BSO's operations. Our relations with the 'Cousins', particularly General William Donovan's Washington office, are congenial and increasingly productive. As well, the co-operation demonstrated by Mr. Hoover, Director of the Federal Bureau of Investigation has been gratifying. These three agencies have operated jointly to effectively identify and neutralize known enemy aliens and subversive elements in North America, and, I might add, in full compliance with relevant Federal, State, Dominion, and Provincial statutes.

"An unwillingness on the part of the Bureau to permit BSO continuing and unlimited use of government land lines, without compromising our encoding system, was overcome by locating a high frequency shortwave radio installation at STS 103, Camp X. The capacity of the school is being expanded, in accordance with your directive. Before leaving Toronto, I received very good news from Commandant Graham informing me that the engineers have revised their estimates for its completion. It is now likely that construction will be finished by the first of next month, two-and-one-half weeks ahead of schedule.

"Prime Minister, the following proposal, 'Tent Peg', is a work-in-progress but is not yet a fully-articulated operational plan. Its objective is inherently distasteful: to perform a political assassination. The target is the German Chancellor, Hitler, in the brief, code named 'Sisera'. I'm sure that you all know the story told in *Judges 4* of the Canaanite general by that name. Following his army's defeat at the hands of the Israelites, he fled into the tent of a woman named Jael, who drove a tent peg into his head while he slept. Tent Peg is based upon the hypothesis that one highly trained, skilled, professional assassin, possessing the required values, attitudes, abilities and personality traits like dedication, commitment, intelligence, and so on, with accurate forms of intelligence and broad tactical support, could accomplish what regiments or fleets of bombers could not.

"There would, of course be the necessity of a small number of equally well prepared SOE associates on the ground. The logistical details are being worked out, including the range of possible locations within Germany. Several possibilities are being considered; the final selection would depend upon a number of factors, which are outlined in the brief that will be distributed now. Thank you, Lady Jane.

"The planners are keenly aware of the potentially explosive implications - morally, politically, and militarily - upon our Allies, as well as in the occupied and neutral countries. We are also acutely conscious of the consequences, should Tent Peg fail to achieve its objective, as well as the range of implications, positive and negative, of its success. Please forgive the Biblical note of explanation at the top, but my staff felt it important to provide the synopsis, complete with a rationale for the mission's name. I'll pause now for questions."

"'Jael' was a female assassin in the Old Testament. Exactly who might be yours?"

"Her operational name is Sylvia; she's a graduate of Beaulieu, and presently resides in London."

"Has she agreed...to do it?"

"Yes, less than an hour ago, in a tea room, in the presence of Prime Minister Churchill. She's presently outside, in the care of two of Sir Will's representatives. Prime Minister, would you please?"

"My pleasure indeed!" The room rose in unison as the Sergeant-at-Arms escorted in a stunningly beautiful, dark-haired young woman. With a wide smile, Churchill took her hand as he announced, "My Lady, gentlemen, I am delighted and deeply honoured to present, Sylvia, our 'Jael'."

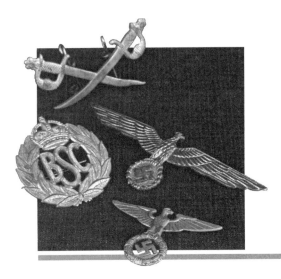

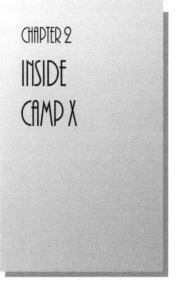

CHAPTER 2

INSIDE

CAMP X

The driver correctly gave the password of the day and the Canadian Army guard waved him through, swinging up the levered gate to admit the camouflaged olive-drab truck.

"Bags out. Everyone out. Line up, at attention!"

'He won't get any argument from me,' thought Hugh, looking up at the six foot tall, alarmingly husky armed sentry. This gate and the guardhouse, as Hugh would soon find out, were the domain of one Private 'Mac' McDonald, Royal Canadian Corps of Engineers, who took great pride in being one of the 'Camp X Originals'.

Several months earlier, without warning or explanation, Mac had been ordered by his Sergeant, 'Old Birmingham', to pack up and report directly to the Horse Palace at the Canadian National Exhibition grounds on the Toronto lakeshore. After a cursory interview in the canteen with a cheerfully witty Major Jones, Royal Canadian Regiment, he was joined by another greenhorn recruit known only as 'John.' The Major escorted Mac and John out the back door into the bitter December wind to a tarpaulin-topped army truck, parked in a restricted zone behind the building.

Leaving Toronto behind, they drove eastward for an hour along The King's Highway #2. As closely as Mac could figure by the signs that were nearly invisible in the blinding whiteout, they were now only a hairbreadth inside the eastern boundary line separating the Town of Whitby, in Ontario County, from the City of Oshawa. The truck turned south abruptly onto Thornton Road, then veered wildly on the rutted icy road in an attempt to avert a collision with an oncoming hay wagon, then finally came to rest at the edge of a ditch. The horse-drawn wagon backed up and halted alongside the truck.

"Fancy drivin' young fella! What's your hurry?" called the wagon driver.

"You know, George. Everyone's goin' pell-mell bent for hell nowadays."

"Well, let's take a look at that back axle to see if you're goin' anywhere, son!"

Both drivers stepped down to assess the truck's status, and continued to exchange more pleasantries, while the huge twin Clydesdales stamped and snorted their steamy impatience. Mac was astonished. In his experience, such a near miss would likely have led to a swearing match, or worse. But no, he reminded himself, this was out in the country where folks conducted themselves more peaceably.

Later, he would meet the wagon's owner, George Allin, a farmer whose property abutted the Camp. George and his tractor had been issued a special permit to enter the Camp to mow the two hundred and fifty acres of grass twice monthly during the growing season. Occasionally, a friendly young Scot, Hamish, who always wore a kilt, came to the Allin farmhouse to ask that George bring his wagon, half-loaded with hay, and the Clydesdales, to help out with what George considered typically harebrained army training schemes. In that he was always well paid, cash in advance, for the use of his rig and his time, he kept this opinion to himself.

Once the two drivers had determined there was no serious damage, the truck lumbered cautiously southward again, this time in second gear. Mac poked John with his elbow "Hey, did you see that sign?"

"What sign?"

"The one we just passed, on the right."

"What did it say?"

"Prohibited Area - Department of National Defence"

"Really? No, I missed it. Son of a gun!"

At dusk, nearly frostbitten, Mac and John emerged stiffly from the vehicle's deep-freeze rear coop. Looking through an eight-foot high chain-link fence, they could make out a cluster of low, ghostly-white buildings, which they assumed to be barracks. They were in an alien land, totally isolated from anything resembling civilisation. There was nothing to be seen to the east or the west beyond the perimeters except uniformly bleak, snow-covered fields. Northward, a high railway embankment cut across the property, and

The entrance to Camp X from Thornton Road, 1942.

looking southward, they decided that, wherever they were, it was within a Texas Leaguer's throw of a particularly barren stretch of windswept Lake Ontario shoreline.

"Follow me, please." An elderly, grizzled representative of the Canadian Corps of Commissionaires, whom Mac guessed to be a veteran of the Boer War, guided them haltingly under a partially raised horizontal gate. It reminded Mac of the CNR railway barrier on Eastern Avenue, in Toronto, which his father had once proudly operated by hand until replaced by an automatic switch.

"Lordy, Mac," whispered John. "Do you think it's a prison camp, like the Frenchies' Devil's Island?"

"Heads up. Here comes the Warden." A tall figure in a dark military greatcoat and riding boots approached.

"Good evening, men. I assume that you're Private McDonald and you're Lance Corporal Paine." He shook their hands warmly. "I'm Colonel Gordon Graham. As commanding officer, I'm pleased to welcome you to STS 103. Adjutant-Quartermaster Major Jones will take over now and show you about. He'll be your liaison with me. Have a pleasant stay." Mac noted that the Colonel's speech was inflected with more-than-subtle nuances of a Scots burr, as though The King's English was his second language.

Adjutant-Quartermaster Major Jones was, in fact, the same friendly, immaculately groomed young Canadian officer who had interviewed Mac at the Horse Palace. Mac reflected briefly upon the impeccable Major's probable mode of travel from Toronto, correctly concluding that the Major had been spared the bone jarring ride in the back of a freezing transport. Major Jones led Mac and John directly to a wooden storage shed and issued them each a heavy army great coat, a fox fur hat, wool scarf and fur-lined leather gloves, a rifle, and a new Sam Browne belt and holster, complete with a Canadian Army Colt .45.

In the kitchen of the non-commissioned staff quarters, balancing massive ham and cheese sandwiches with mugs of hot chocolate, Mac and John signed receipts on the Major's clipboard for the items of apparel, as well as for the weapons and ammunition.

"Now, these," Jones intoned. "They're your tickets in here. Read 'em carefully. Nothing there to worry about, boys." Mac examined the two official-looking documents headed **TOP SECRET: BRITISH SECURITY OPERATION**. His full name, rank, and serial number had been typed where required. He read the papers quickly, then shrugged, and scribbled his signature on both forms where the Major had indicated with an 'X'. John did the same.

"Jolly good, men. Mac, you'll follow me. Corporal, you'll go with Private Andy here. You're the lucky man tonight, Mac! First guard duty! Andy will see that your belongings are stowed safely under your bunk. Nippy night, though! Better dress for it!"

Adjutant/Quartermaster Jones waited as Mac donned his new issue of outerwear, then drove him in an unmarked Jeep to the small wooden guardhouse beside the gate. As they proceeded, the Major shouted Mac's standing orders.

"First, McDonald, you've just signed the Official Secrets Act. You are still enlisted in the Canadian Army and you have been accorded special status as a member of the top secret British Security Operation. I'll fill you in re: the BSO Regs tomorrow as well as other particulars re: your pay and pension. You have been assigned full time to the guard-duty roster.

"Second, re: your name. From now on, you are Mac, Private, or Private Mac. Never give out or use your last name, unless specifically directed to do so by an officer. I expect that would only be the Commandant or me. Third, re: your interaction with the camp's recruits, or 'clients' as we prefer, there will be none at all...nil.

"Fourth, re: your job as guard. It's critically important to the security of the camp's operations. You must memorize the day's password and challenge all comers, I repeat, all comers. If the response is unsatisfactory, that is incorrect in any fashion or unduly hesitant, challenge the subject again. If he is not immediately forthcoming, you will warn the subject once more. If he still fails to comply, you will shoot to kill. Do you understand? Question, Private?" With the vehicle's engine running at high idle, and the heater blowing vigorously to little effect, the last of the Major's words were all but lost in the wind.

Briefly, Mac considered asking if 're:' was simply the Major's favourite expression, or a characteristic of the officer class' speech here, but decided against it. Instead, he replied, "Yes, well three, actually Major."

"I'm listening!"

"What...what do you, that is, what do you do here, exactly, Sir?"

"Say again!" Jones kicked down hard on the accelerator pedal, but the engine refused to cease roaring.

"What do you do here, Sir?"

"I can't tell you, not yet. Next?" he shouted.

"What did the Colonel mean by S, T, 1 oh something?"

"What? Oh, yes. STS 103...Special Training School, number one-oh-three. Same as before, you'll know more when you need to know more."

"Yes, Sir. May I go to the bathroom, Sir? The long truck-ride in the cold and then the hot chocolate, which hit the spot..."

"Over there, in the bushes, Mac. Hurry.... The show starts in less than five minutes."

"Yes, Sir. Thank you." Mac returned, with a minute to spare.

"You will be relieved...replaced, that is, at 0200," said Major Jones, smiling at his own play on words. "Good night and good luck, Private." The gears clashed as the Major, cursing softly, forced the balky transmission into reverse.

"Sir?" Mac called out. He called again, louder. The Jeep stopped whining.

"Well, what now, Private?"

"Major, the password?"

"The password! Excellent work, Mac! Attention to detail."

"Thank you, Sir. And the password?"

"Attention to detail."

"Yes, Sir. Thank you very much. Good night, Major."

As he finished saluting, Mac glanced at his wristwatch, a farewell present from his son and wife. It read precisely six o'clock. He entered the little guardhouse, stood the new rifle upright against the counter, and peered through the frosted window. 'Re: *Attention to detail.* Private Mac is ready to challenge all comers. The mystery camp is open for business.'

As soon as Mac unlatched the tailgate, Hugh tossed down his canvas duffle bag and jumped onto the gravel. He scrambled to join the line-up with his nine fellow inductees. Mac and the truck had disappeared. An officer materialised, resplendent in a flawless British Army uniform with colonel's pips on the tunic collar and a swagger stick smartly tucked under his right arm. His uniform was devoid of any regimental insignia except for a conspicuous British Paratrooper's badge on the left breast pocket of his tunic. A shorter, moustachioed officer, who accompanied him, began speaking.

"Gentlemen, I'm Major Jones. I'm honoured to present our Commandant, Lieutenant-Colonel Graham. Sir, do you wish to address the clients?" The major pronounced 'Sir' with two syllables.

"Thank you, Major. At ease, gentlemen. I welcome you to Special Training School 103. It is an accomplishment for each of you to have made the grade...my sincerest congratulations. Henceforth, you will be known as 'clients', and will be referred to by your first name only. To avoid confusion, persons having the same first name will be distinguished by a number, for example, John One or John Two."

Lieutenant-Colonel Gordon Graham, Seaforth Highlanders, had recently arrived from Beaulieu, where he had served as that SOE academy's Chief Instructor. Well-educated and a graduate of Sandhurst Military College, he was already a polished career soldier and a talented organiser. Personable and politically astute, though only thirty-one years old, he was regarded in SOE circles as a promising candidate to be groomed for the prestigious position of Commandant of Beaulieu at such time as the post were to become available.

Senior staff at Beaulieu had quickly taken note of the eager young Highlander. He displayed all of the requisite characteristics for success as a field or staff officer: *esprit de corps*, a perceptive, analytical mind, unflagging courage and physical stamina, outstanding athletic prowess, and extraordinarily well-developed interpersonal skills. Marked for 'a serious second look' when he had barely begun the rigorous Commando and intelligence training course at the SOE finishing school, Graham was invited, upon graduation, to remain at Beaulieu and serve as Small Arms Instructor. At the young age of twenty-nine, he had already earned the rank of Chief Instructor.

Gordon Graham's passion for continuous improvement of the training procedures laid out in the SOE Syllabus, coupled with a sincere concern for the welfare and progress of the trainee clients, marked him for further advancement. On New Year's Day 1940, London appointed him Commandant of the as yet unfinished STS 103 in Canada. His mission was clearly stated: to have the facility fully prepared and open, meeting all SOE standards of operational readiness. He was permitted two weeks, and with his extraordinary prowess, was able to select, interview and recruit the required instructional staff from within the ranks of all SOE schools in Britain, and to make his personal family arrangements, prior to departure from Southampton.

At the same time, he was informed that Erik Williamson's British Security Operation in Canada would assume full responsibility for hiring suitable clerical and administrative support personnel as well as establishing communications with the Toronto bureau of the Commander, Military District 2, Major General C. F. Constantine. Through a co-operative arrangement with General Constantine, a Royal Canadian Regiment Major, Brian Jones, was appointed the Camp's Adjutant-Quartermaster. Jones, a district bank inspector from Sarnia, Ontario, with an interest in medieval British history, would serve as the Camp military liaison officer between the Canadian and British armies, and the Commissioner of the Royal Canadian Mounted Police, Edward 'Ted' Reynolds.

"Your time here will be quite brief, as the training syllabus is very concentrated," the Commandant continued. "You may find, indeed I expect you to find, that the courses offered are extremely tough, physically and mentally. The instructors are equally tough and demanding, although I expect most of you chaps will find yourselves looking about for opportunities to take on additional challenges. I urge you to learn and to over-learn every lesson, and to practice and hone your craft constantly. You will be expected to take all obstacles and barriers in your stride, as our sole purpose here is to prepare you to survive while conducting highly specialized guerrilla warfare, against an unethical, amoral, unforgiving, and highly intelligent enemy under exceptionally daunting conditions. Are there questions?

"No? Very well. You will find the atmosphere here quite unusual, even unconventional if you have come directly from the regular forces. Here, we are all on the same team, and resolutely dedicated to one thing and one thing only: preparing you physically and equipping you with the mental and psychological tools to be highly-trained Allied secret agents, able to carry out your missions successfully and to return. You will be governed at all times by the British Military Code of Conduct and will be expected to demonstrate the highest standards of professionalism and co-operation with your fellow clients and staff. This will apply tenfold in the civilian world if and when I decide to confer leave.

"I am here to assist each officer and instructor in ensuring your graduation from STS 103 with honours. SOE will accept nothing less from you, or from me. Should you find after a week, a fortnight, or indeed, on the final day of your stay with us, that our expectations are more rigorous than you can manage, or that the prospects of espionage, assassination, sabotage and a host of other unconventional pursuits are not your cup of tea, my door is open.

"Major Jones is the Camp Adjutant-Quartermaster. Tomorrow morning, you will be introduced to my second-in-command and meet your instructors. The Major will take you now to your assigned quarters and then familiarize you with the layout of the installation. Thank you for your attention. Good luck, gentlemen. Major!"

"Thank you, Colonel. Clients, line up. Single file. Single file, there! Pick up your bags. By the right, the other right, quick step...march!" Major Brian Jones led the ten men along a gravel pathway at a jog, stopping at the entrance to a white, asbestos siding-clad frame building, with a black-shingled roof. "Halt! Gentlemen, your home away from home. Listen while I call out your names. First name, only. The number I call after your name is posted over your bunk. Do not move until I give the order. Understood?"

"Understood, Major!" they shouted in unison.

Hugh noted that the barracks were either new or recently renovated. The interior smelled pleasantly of fresh paint, turpentine, and pinesap, and was furnished with a cot, a desk, a chair, and a small bedside chest of drawers for each occupant. With four shower stalls, sinks and toilets, and windows that actually opened, Hugh judged it would be more than adequate for a ten-week stay.

When he had finished unpacking his kit bag, stowing his few belongings in the single drawer in the small bureau, Hugh sat on the edge of his cot to take stock of his surroundings and bunkmates. They were all wearing the same fresh army fatigues and boots that had been issued at the recruitment centre in the Horse Palace.

"What time, please?" queried a heavily accented voice on his right.

Hugh glanced at his wristwatch. "Two thirty."

"I'm damn hungry. What about you?" The speaker was a dark-haired, dark-eyed youngster of Hugh's age. "What's your name?"

"Hugh."

"What?"

"Hugh!"

"What kind of name is that?"

"Scottish, Canadian. What's yours?"

"Mikhail...Michael."

"Nice to meet you, Mikhail Michael."

"That's good. Call me Mike. Did you eat that slop in the restaurant, Hugh?" he asked, pronouncing Hugh, 'U.'

The truck had stopped briefly at an establishment on Kingston Road, in West Hill, where the men were allowed to order a cardboard cheeseburger with soggy fries, and yesterday's coffee. The waitress, Sherri, all leg, and lipstick, called all of them 'Hon', and flirted with the driver, who chain-smoked and fed dimes into the jukebox while guzzling cherry cokes.

"Uh huh. Not good, was it?"

"Terrible. That girl was very nice, va-voom, a doll! What was her name? Good figure, looks like Betty Grable. I think she and that driver have a thing, don't you?"

"Sherri, I think. Ya, he probably keeps her stoked with chewing gum and nylons. She had eyes for him, for sure. Where's your hometown, Mike? I'm from Toronto."

"Born in Belgrade, Yugoslavia. Toronto's my home now. What did the Major call us?

"Clients."

"What does...uh, oh, here we go!"

"Hut A, your attention, please!" It was Major Brian Jones, again. "As you know, I am the Adjutant-Quartermaster." The room was silent. "This afternoon I'm taking you for a tour of the base. Keep up please, don't lag behind, or you may miss some of my commentary, which, I'm certain, you would not wish to do," he added, smiling. "Look, listen, and learn, gentlemen. We will return at 1630 hours. Just time to wash up; you're expected in the mess hall at 1645. There will be a short test before dinner. Line up and follow me, please.

"Gentlemen, as the C.O. has already told you, this establishment is a well-guarded secret. Only those who need to know are aware of its very existence, let alone the fact that you are here. We will begin our walk through the Camp property and buildings, beginning at Thornton Road, the entrance to STS 103. By the way, some also know it as Camp X, although others prefer 'the Farm'. Later you'll understand why.

"Chaps, this simple sign, **Prohibited Area - Department of National Defence**, is all the warning that we are required by law to give to unwanted visitors.

"Sir, just how is the Camp protected from infiltrators and potential acts of sabotage?"

"What's your name, son?"

"Tom, Sir."

"Good question, Tom. First, this entrance is the only way in. You have to pass by this guardhouse and on through the swing gate. No one may proceed even that far without the proper authorization. Second, motorized and foot patrols operate around the clock. Re: general security. I'm sure you want to know that guards have been issued standing orders, 'shoot to kill and ask questions later,' from day one. Does that answer your question?"

"Yes, sir," Tom replied.

Continuing about three hundred feet westward from Thornton Road, they passed by an old apple orchard. Directly south of that, they could see Lake Ontario and, in the fields, a massive web of extremely high rhombic antennae, which Hugh knew, were placed there to transmit and receive short-wave coded Morse traffic from the ionosphere.

As they walked farther along the gravel road, Major Jones pointed out the Commandant's Quarters, partially hidden behind the tall chestnut trees lining both sides of the roadway. Directly beside the Commandant's Quarters they stopped to look at a wooden shed, with windows starting seven feet from ground level.

"This is 'Hydra', our radio transmitter building, operated for and by members of British Security. Most of you won't get to see the workings inside, or meet the staff. The reason: Classified - Top Secret. You likely noted the antennae arrays along the waterfront. That's how it got the nickname 'Hydra'. Your W/T, sorry, the wireless radio instructor will explain all that. Take it from me: it's a very busy place.

"Directly across the road is the Communications Centre which is tied into 'Hydra' and that, too, is off limits." They continued westward. "Now, this beauty you will all come to know and love. Does anyone know what it is? A question?"

"Yes, Sir, Tom again. I was wondering: Why are 'Hydra's' windows so high off the ground?"

"I think that it's obvious. Would someone like to answer Tom's query?"

"Perhaps it's to make it impossible to see inside?" someone suggested.

"Precisely, to keep snoopers at bay. Name?"

"The Prof, Sir."

"I see. Now, what was my question? Ah, yes, can anyone tell us the purpose of this structure?"

"The world's tallest gallows?" suggested Mike. The Major did not appear to be amused, so Mike tried a different tack, "I meant to say, it's a parachute jumping tower, Sir." The Major smiled thinly.

"Right-oh, the jump tower. It's a mandatory part of your training. Anyone care to estimate the height?"

"I'd guess it's sixty-five feet, Sir."

"Good start; but higher. Name?"

"Mike."

"Another?"

"Seventy-five feet!" Hugh offered.

"Actually the drop is precisely ninety feet," attested Major Jones, "as I know only too well." The recruits stared upward in awed silence toward the tiny platform crowning the top.

"Now for the 'behind-the-scenes' part of your tour. Come with me." He led them behind 'Hydra' to a building that housed the boiler room and the shop. He explained that, like most military establishments and major institutions such as hospitals, the buildings were linked together by a network of underground tunnels providing the right-of-way for the plumbing and sewage mains, as well as for the large steam pipes supplying heat to the entire Camp.

"These tunnels are covered by a catwalk network of heavy boards so that maintenance workers can have easy access to the pipes in the event of a problem. No buried treasure here, unfortunately, lads" he chuckled. "And this half is the Repair Shop. You can have a peek inside. If these talented fellows can't fix it or patch it, it's for the junk heap. All mechanical repairs, light and heavy equipment maintenance, including care of the Camp's vehicles, with rare exceptions, are carried out right here."

"Wow, Hugh, that's quite a car!" Mike whispered.

"Yes, Mike. It is quite a car. It's a 1940 Buick Roadmaster Limited, " replied the Major. "Colonel Samuel McLaughlin, the founder and head of General Motors in Oshawa, donated it to the Camp for the Commandant's use. We must move along, men. This next building is the Lecture Hall. You'll start your training here at 0900 tomorrow. First thing you'll notice is the sign inside the front door, **KNOW YOUR WEAPONS, KNOW YOURSELF, KNOW YOUR ENEMY.** That pretty much sums up the building's purpose. This is the classroom for blackboard theory.

"We keep quite a decent library collection of military books from all ages, some of which are rare, one-of-a-kind manuscripts and such. Others, I'm told, are no longer in print. If your literary tastes run to lighter fare, there are spy books, fictional and factual. In due course, you'll be shown a special room packed to the rafters with authentic enemy uniforms, regalia, and weaponry of the Axis forces, including all ranks of the regular German army, air force and navy: Wehrmacht, Luftwaffe, and Kreigsmarine; our collection may be the most extensive outside

The Sinclair Farmhouse, 'Glenrath', 1905.

Germany of the Reich secret police, the Gestapo, the SD, the state security service, the civilian police, the SIPO and KRIPO and of course, the Waffen or fighting SS forces. We also have on the racks an assortment of Nazi Party officials' uniforms, such as the Gauleiter, or district political boss, and much more, as you're soon to discover.

"Another section of this building, which of course is off-limits to client-students, includes facilities for the planning of Special Operations. Matériel and supplies are constantly being collected from all over North America to assist us in mounting realistic simulations of proposed clandestine operations."

"How does the Camp get these uniforms and weapons, Major?"

"That too, is classified. Use your imagination, Tom! Follow me outside, gentlemen. We're going behind the Lecture Hall. Looking west now, those two identical, H-shaped buildings are the living quarters. These were built to house the Officers, NCOs, other personnel, and the client agents-in-training. Barracks are at each end of both buildings with a large mess in the middle. Each building contains a completely equipped kitchen able to feed two hundred people, each three times a day. As in your new barracks, each man has his own room approximately six feet by nine feet, appointed with a comfortable bed, a dresser, a desk, and a chair.

"When I arrived, in the midst of a brutally harsh winter, it was a pleasant relief to get up in the morning, walk down the hall to the mess for breakfast, and not have to endure the elements. Of course, the officers eat in their mess and the NCOs and other personnel eat in theirs. Eating hours are staggered so that the clients will not have contact with unauthorised persons. All of this has been duplicated in your own quarters, of course.

"The only difference between these two buildings is that the basement of the one on the south-west side has been converted into an underground firing range. The ground outside has a natural embankment and the back wall is reinforced with half-inch tungsten steel plating to protect anyone foolish enough to be lurking there.

"To save time, I'm going to read from an unofficial Camp description, then we'll finish the tour with a fast walk-past of these features. 'Approaching the east side of the Camp which runs parallel to Corbett Creek stands the old Sinclair family farmhouse, Glenrath, circa 1861, as well as a large barn, a smaller barn and an outside root cellar. An artesian well finishes off the beautiful country farm.

" 'Continuing the walk southward with the two 'H' buildings on either side of you, you now see the entire vista of Lake Ontario unobstructed by any other buildings. Only lovely, open grassy fields slope gradually toward the lake, some three hundred feet away. Training takes place on these fields; night time amphibious assault training from the shore of the lake and up the cliffs with ropes while bearing heavy back packs, explosives training under-water, and more cliff climbing. Your walking tour ends at the top of these bluffs where the road ends abruptly, dropping sharply thirty feet to the water.'

"And that, gentlemen, is the end of this travelogue. Of course, I neglected to mention some of the more daunting features, for fear you'd all be going over the hill before you get your big toe wet. It is truly a magnificent setting for our secret base, isn't it? Time and tide; we must be running back now, without a halt, so keep your eyes peeled for these last items. A question to ponder: Why is it called 'the Farm?' Forward!"

At four-thirty, Hugh, Mike, and their eight exhausted colleagues had been deposited back at Hut A. Adjutant Brian Jones had indeed taken them on a whirlwind tour. With fifteen minutes to spare to wash off the dust and get to the mess hall, they all had flopped on their cots for a five-minute breather.

"A test! Lord! What are they going to do next?" questioned a voice from down the hallway.

"Probably make us draw a picture of the farmhouse or write out our times tables, or something," shouted another.

"Be serious. I'll bet it's an IQ test. You know, to find out who's the brainiest, who's the dumbest."

"Better not unpack then, if I were you."

"Stuff it, Professor!"

"Sorry, just chitchat."

"Gentlemen, my name is Major Findlay. I am extremely pleased to be your Chief Instructor. As Major Jones has undoubtedly alerted you, there will be an exercise or scheme to test your capacity to recall details from your sightseeing jaunt. You will work in teams of two. You may choose your partner. I will distribute an outline map of the camp property and a pencil. The task is in two parts.

"On this easel, you can see a list of the buildings and training facilities. Each is numbered. Place the number of each feature where you and your colleague decide it is located. Here is Lake Ontario and here is the railway line. This then is north. Now, to Task Number 2; there were twelve distinct objects scattered over the grounds and inside the buildings, all quite visible to the eye, if you were looking and seeing. We look with our eyes. We see with our brains. These are listed on the easel to my right. They are lettered A to L. Do the same with them.

"You may confer with your partner. You will have precisely fifteen minutes. Manage your time well. There will be a summary activity and the team with the highest score will be exempted from this evening's calisthenics. Please select your partner and begin, now. Good luck, gentlemen."

"Good God," Mike whispered to Hugh after six minutes. "I'm sweating bullets! The first part was okay. This one is a bastard!" On the chart paper were listed 'Objects' which included, among other things, an upturned galvanized pail, a step ladder, a coil of hemp rope, and a two-by-four piece of lumber.

"Time, gentlemen. Now, that was easy. Here is the challenge. In unconventional warfare, one must take advantage of unconventional means. Here's the bell ringer. Select any building. Place yourselves hiding inside it, in enemy-occupied territory. You are unarmed. Choose the two nearest and most readily accessible of the 'objects' and create a scenario wherein one of you can get hold of the 'aids' and help you both escape from that building; assume that the main entranceway is being covered by one well-armed guard inside the building. You may or may not disable or kill him. Once again, you are to work with your partner. Write down your plan, in sequence of steps, point form, on the back of your map allowing no more than ten points. Both persons will sign it. I will collect them in ten minutes. The winning team will be announced after supper. Begin."

Hugh and Mike worked feverishly to complete the task and had recorded nine of the allotted ten steps when Major Hamish Findlay called "Time's up, gentlemen!" At six o'clock, ten more recruits entered and seated themselves on the opposite side of the hall. Supper was served cafeteria-style; it was delicious, hot, and plentiful.

"Beats that greasy spoon, eh, Hugh?"

"These plates are real china, Mike, and the cutlery's silver. Not too bad for roughing it in the wilderness!"

At six-forty five, as Hugh was finishing his apple pie à la mode, Major Findlay called for attention.

"Gentlemen, I have completed the scoring and have some very bad news to report. Of the five teams, one has been disqualified for using three features, one was too woefully inadequate to be counted, and two others were captured or killed." Hugh shot a glance at Mike, who appeared completely absorbed in the Major's critique.

"The winning team, I am pleased to say, has made imaginative use of the two resources at hand and, in my opinion, went one very profitable step further, by creating an outside associate." There were cries of dismay from the dining table. "If you would recall the rules, gentlemen, I did not forbid any such possibility. I simply prescribed what was immediately available; I did not mention what was not available. It is now my pleasure to call up the winning combination, who will describe their inventive scheme to us, clients Hugh, and Mike."

For the next week, Mike and Hugh were known as the 'bucket boys' by dint of employing the bucket and rope as a 'lift' in which their outside 'associate' placed a knife which they pulled up and used to overpower the guard. All the while, their accomplice created a diversion at the front of the building.

"Well done gentlemen; crude, but creative and actually, quite a sound scheme, if all of the pieces came together. Enjoy your time. We meet in the Mess at 2030. Bring money. The rest will join me, in your exercise gear, in front of the Lecture Hall at 1915." There were groans mixed with the brief applause for the winning team of Hugh and Mike. "Dismissed."

Each evening, the recruits would find all of that day's test results posted on the bulletin board in the Mess Hall, now transformed into a lounge complete with a surprisingly well-stocked bar, and run by the friendly, efficient client/bartender, Andy. SOE tradition, brief as it was, required that the day's top team or individual buy the first round of beer. Hugh and Mike were happy to oblige. 'No shows' were red-circled and were assessed double jeopardy for each evening they were absent without an acceptable excuse. Of course, an 'acceptable excuse' was either an outbreak of bubonic plague or cholera or, night training exercises. It was not uncommon for instructors and senior officers, including Commandant Graham, to buy a round, and join the client agents-in-training briefly for an enjoyably informal chat.

The morning after Hugh and Mike's initial triumph, it seemed to Hugh that Camp X was a school in motion. Rising at 0615, the inmates of Hut A assembled outside their quarters at 0645 to be met by the jovial Major Hamish Findlay who led them on a pre-breakfast dash ending back at their Mess Hall, attached to their barracks. Following a substantial meal, Findlay gathered the group and took them on a loping five-mile cross-country run, around the camp's perimeter, and across the rolling backfields. He increased the pace to a sprint for the homestretch along the sand and pebble-strewn beach. As a young, fit non-smoker, Hugh found the exercise a tonic. Instructors popped up almost literally out of the bushes, to catch any unwary recruit who had slowed down to a walk. Push-ups and sit-ups were assigned and worked off matter-of-factly, on the spot.

Hugh and Mike then ran to the Lecture Hall where classes began at 0900, precisely. From the sign posted over the entrance, in bold, large lettering: KNOW YOUR WEAPONS, KNOW YOURSELF, KNOW YOUR ENEMY, it was apparent that the staff took their jobs very seriously.

Commandant Lieutenant-Colonel Graham introduced his 2-I-C, or 'Second-in-Command,' Major Gray, and each of the Camp's instructors. He then delivered a lecture on personal disguise, entitled *Temporary Disguise*, from the SOE Manual. He outlined the basic premise: that to be successful, the individual must first study his or her characteristics, peculiarities, and mannerisms.

"Know yourself, gentlemen, and be wary of paranoia. Even the best-trained enemy agent is probably incapable of noting the significance of your every minuscule action and movement. You may think that he is setting a snare to test and thereby trap you, whereas in fact, he is doing nothing of the sort. This is the curse of undercover work. An overly cautious approach, while it may be a normal reaction, can make you behave imprudently and undo you. Whenever possible, become a bird. That is, there is safety in numbers. Join the flock; melt into the crowd, look, and act like the others and you can pretty much vanish. Finally, never use a disguise except as a last resort. Then, play it for all its worth."

Colonel Graham continued with a virtuoso performance, describing and demonstrating basic techniques for creating temporary disguises, without the use of makeup. He finished with a theatrical demonstration to show how, by re-arranging his hairstyle, discolouring his face with stove soot, and hitching up his trousers by buttoning them to his vest to acquire a slight stooping posture, then effecting a slight limp, a pursuing 'tail' might be outfoxed. The lesson ended with a volunteer client submitting to a startlingly effective 'instant makeover'. The Colonel summed up the session, "Try to be inconspicuous, and uncomplicated, gentlemen. The more complex your deception, the more likely it is that you will slip up in one or more detail. Use what falls to hand. A small pebble in the shoe heel is sufficient to make one limp." Some of the audience guffawed. "I'm delighted to know that you are still awake. There will be a ten minute recess."

Hugh was impressed with Commandant Graham's knowledge of the topic. He was not surprised when the Professor later confirmed that Colonel Gordon Graham had co-authored the *Disguise* section of the SOE Syllabus.

The most physically demanding training exercises began after lunch and continued throughout the afternoon. Rope climbing, obstacle vaulting, and running on the spot were merely warm-ups for the more intensive activities that followed. A tall and slim, almost frail elderly man, introduced in the Lecture Hall by the Commandant as Major Robert Samson, took over Hugh's group. Hugh had guessed at the time that the Major's forte was either map reading or, perhaps, forgery. His scholarly appearance, emphasised by his thick eyeglasses, reminded Hugh of the vicar of the small parish church near his grandparents' farm in Belleville. "Don't be surprised if we have to bow our heads," he whispered to Mike.

"Good afternoon. I'm Major Robert Samson." Hugh had to strain to hear over the light breeze blowing in off the lake. "Let's start with a few exercises to limber up. Please stand. We'll begin with alternate toe touching followed by deep knee bends. Counting to twenty for each, on your own time, begin." For fifteen minutes, Major Samson led the group through a fast-paced régime of sit-ups, push-ups, and strenuous stretches. By the end, Hugh was winded; Samson had not broken a sweat.

"Good, gentlemen. I'd like one of you to come forward, please."

"I will, sir."

"Very good. You're Hugh, correct?"

"Yes, Sir!" 'Pretty damn impressive,' Hugh thought.

"Excellent, Hugh. I want you to approach me silently from behind and put a wrestler's hold on me. Try to snap my neck. Do you understand what I mean, son?" Hugh nodded, affirmatively. "I don't want to hear a sound. Apply your full force."

'A piece of cake,' thought Hugh. 'This old crow will crumple like wet toast. I'd better go easy. I don't want to hurt him.' Hugh had been the Intermediate and Senior Intercollegiate Wrestling Champion at Lawrence Park Collegiate.

"Any time, Hugh," Samson remarked quietly.

Hugh approached him stealthily, prepared to apply a regulation half Nelson.

"Are you alright son?"

Hugh lay sprawled in the sand at Major Samson's feet. "I, I think so, Sir," he stammered, trying to draw his breath.

"Good. Let me help you up. There you are. Good as new. As gentlemen, let's shake hands."

Hugh reached out to comply. Suddenly, the world was upside down, again. He thudded face-first onto the sand. As he blinked to clear his eyes, he heard Samson's voice echo in the distance.

"No more tricks, Hugh. Thank you. Gentlemen, let's recognise Hugh's excellent efforts. The rule here: there are no rules. The end justifies the means, any means. Your very life may depend on your remembering that. We'll have a ten minute break; when I return, I'll demonstrate how each of you can easily carry out both manoeuvres, regardless of size or physique."

The dinner tables were abuzz with talk about the remarkable Major Samson.

"Where did he learn his profession?"

"Where's he from?"

"The far East."

"Ya, up in the Himalayas...Tibet, or something. He was a Buddhist monk."

"Don't be ridiculous! Buddhist monks are peaceful."

"I heard he was the Japanese Emperor's personal bodyguard."

"...and he was taught by a master at a secret samurai school in Tokyo."

"Have you heard anything, Professor?" queried Hugh.

"One third myth, one third bull. A true master took you down, Hugh, so no need to feel badly. The truth is, no one knows much about him, or his background, except that he's obviously English, an absolute gentleman, and the world's most-respected non-Asian master of the deadliest art: silent killing. The story is that he learned the fundamentals as a young boy on the streets of Hong Kong where he was born and raised.

"He studied and mastered the Japanese, Korean and Chinese methods of unarmed combat, then refined and wrote a book about them called *The Deadly Art.* Later, he joined the Royal Hong Kong Constabulary and put away more than one fully armed triad thug, literally with his bare hands. He was so efficient that he was appointed the force's chief instructor. He's now SOE's top man and we've got him here, which is quite a coup for the Commandant, and a bonus for us. He has a nickname, but if I tell you, don't even whisper it."

"Well, what is it?"

"Dangerous Dan McGrew."

"I can see why. Say, he must be forty, if he's a day, Prof!"

"Try fifty, Hugh!"

"Good Lord!"

That evening, as Hugh was about to leave the lounge and retire early to nurse a headache, Andy the bartender appeared, holding a tray with only a single glass. It contained a large quantity of light amber liquid. "For you, Hugh, compliments of a friend."

"Thanks, Andy, what is it?"

"Twenty-year-old pure gold...rare as hen's teeth, genuine peat-and-barley Highland Scotch whiskey, and a double at that."

"I can't drink that stuff, much less afford to pay for it. I feel like hell. I'm going to bed."

"I think you'd better drink it. It's paid for; a gesture of good will. Look over to your right...over further...at the table by the Victrola."

Across the room, Major Samson rose slightly and raised his glass, nodding at Hugh who smiled back gamely, acknowledging his benefactor. The nectar's warm, velvet smoothness was more therapeutic than anything that he could remember.

Except for the ritual pre-breakfast running warm-ups followed by the daily ten-mile cross-country run, Chief Instructor Findlay's agenda was unpredictable. His 'schemes' were sometimes offbeat and imaginative, but served a specific objective as prescribed in the SOE manual.

They were also unusually enjoyable. Early one hot afternoon, after Findlay had given a lecture called *Camouflage in the Field*, Hugh, Mike, the Professor and Joe were putting the Major's theories into action on the back acreage. The Major had instructed them to practice avoiding detection by remaining stock-still.

"Hey, Prof, where's the Major?" whispered Hugh.

"Probably impersonating that birch tree over there," Hugh quipped.

"I'm tired of this statue game," stated Joe flatly.

"Look, up there...it's a plane! What in the world is it doing?"

A bright-yellow Tiger Moth biplane flew directly toward them, no more than fifty feet above the stubbled field.

"Hit the ground! Some crazy bastard's trying to mow us down!" Joe shouted. The radial engine roared heroically as the pilot pulled the aircraft up into a steep, nearly vertical climb.

Instinctively, Hugh ducked as an object descended rapidly toward him, then landed less than a yard away with a thump, releasing a billowing white cloud. 'Mustard gas!' was Hugh's only thought. Once, as a young boy, he had coerced his Dad into telling how he had survived the first harrowing German gas attack in WWI at Ypres. As his father's words rang in his head, Hugh dropped to the ground and lay face down, his eyes shut tight and his hands clamped over his mouth and nose.

"Hey Hugh, you're as white as a sheet!' shouted Joe, over the diminishing racket.

"What?"

"It's only flour. Taste it. You're covered in it!"

"Flour! Well I'll be...." His friends ran over to help him dust off the powder.

"You've had quite a week my friend," laughed Mike. "First, Dangerous Dan and now this guy! Are you okay?"

"Yeah, fine, thanks. Who was that?"

"Sure as blazes beats me," shrugged the Professor. "He was wearing one of those flying helmets with goggles."

The answer was forthcoming at supper. Major Findlay, it seemed, was a staunch believer in simulations.

"Gentlemen, if I may have your attention for a moment, please." His Ayrshire Scots was especially thick. "My wee scheme this afternoon was an attempt to demonstrate your vulnerability to attack from the air. I do hope you're fully recovered, Hugh." Hugh waved in affirmation. "Good, then, no one is any the worse for wear. Remember to keep your heads up. Always be aware. Ach, and the first drams are on me tonight, after exercises, of course. Carry on, laddies."

The Camp expanded daily as truckloads of workers and tons of lumber and building supplies arrived in convoys each morning, and the air resounded with hammers and saws until sundown. Each day, it seemed to Hugh and his mates, a fresh foundation or a wooden framework stood where previously there had been nothing but gravel and grass. They also noted that the number of clients in their mess had doubled to fifty by the end of their second week. The inhabitants of a barracks rarely interacted with those of another, "for reasons of security" as Major Findlay explained.

It took Hugh and his classmates several days to realise that they were constantly under surveillance for psychological and emotional clues to their character. The evenings in the lounge bar were purposely relaxed to permit assessment of their interpersonal skills. Even a game of poker or bridge served as a laboratory to observe their ability to bluff or to work co-operatively. It might also be a litmus test of their capacity to manage liquor.

Each recruit's behaviour was scrutinized during every aspect of his training. His leadership potential was evaluated in terms of his initiative, perseverance, stamina and drive, as well as his ability to tolerate ambiguous orders and situations. Hugh was to find out during his 'suitability assessment' interview with Adjutant Major Jones late in the ninth week, that he had even been awarded high marks for the enthusiastic manner in which he had vaulted from the truck upon his arrival at the Camp gate!

The recruits were graded not only on individual effort but also on teamwork. There were weekly quizzes on the topics covered at lectures. Mike, whose first language was Slavic, was so frustrated in his attempts to write in English that Hugh and the Professor decided to intervene on his behalf with Chief Instructor Major Findlay. "Let's ask Hamish if it's okay for us to write down Mike's answers if he dictates them to us, Prof."

"Yes, I'm certainly game. Let's do it tonight; Thursday is test day."

Hamish's response that evening was immediate and affirmative. "I have no difficulty with your suggestion, provided that the client is not coached, that his responses are not edited, and that they are recorded accurately. On those conditions, you have my permission."

"Thank you, Sir," replied Hugh. "I know Mike will be really pleased and relieved. He's a valuable team member and tries hard, Sir, but he is afraid that he will be washed out of the course, and has been unable to sleep. The Professor and I will follow your directions to the letter."

"I must say that I admire your concern for your team-mate. Your remedy is timely, first-rate."

Hamish rose and addressed the group. "Gentlemen, I'll be off now to catch up on some long-overdue reports. Please be prepared for an all-day and night excursion starting tomorrow morning immediately following breakfast, rain, or shine. Good night."

"Night, Sir!"

"Sounds exciting, eh boys?" remarked the Professor. "Maybe this time, he'll drop water bombs on our heads from great heights. All for sport and diversion."

"You just never know what old Hamish is going to cook up," added Joe. "He's an original."

"That he is," chimed in Alec.

Hamish sat with Hugh's group at breakfast and outlined the purpose of the excursion. "It's a survival exercise. We'll meet in the Lecture Hall at 0830 sharp to look at topographical maps of the area. A truck will then drive you northeast from here and drop you off. You'll be expected to get back, on your own, by suppertime tomorrow afternoon. Two of you will be given compasses. Another two will have maps. No side arms, but you will each carry a knife. Other than that, you'll be carrying little or no special equipment."

"Will we be issued Major Samson's dagger, Sir?" asked John.

"No. It's not a toy and I don't want you running amok gutting racoons and the neighbour's chickens." Robert Samson and Joseph Price had developed and patented a lethal two-edged dagger designed specifically for silent killing.

"What about food, Major?"

"Sorry, it's not a picnic, Professor. Live off the land. There are plenty of rabbits where you're going and you've been taught how to snare and skin them. There will be absolutely no cattle rustling, begging or theft from the locals. And do not get involved with the local constabulary, unless you relish a night in the nick.

"One last item: each of you will be issued a plain business card bearing a telephone number. In the event of an emergency, you will telephone that number. It's a direct line to a special Bell operator who will then connect you promptly with the RCMP. Identify yourself by the numerals 25 dash 1 dash 1, on the card. The Canadian Government and RCMP know us only as file number 25-1-1. Anything else?"

"Yes, Sir. What about local women...girls?"

"What about them, Joe?"

"Can we recruit...that is, if we meet one who's willing, to be our guide?"

"If you think nature girl is waiting out there, good bloody luck. But this brings up a relevant point, which I will be addressing next week. Suffice to say for now that recruiting associates in the field can be a very sticky wicket. I'm not in favour of it, under most circumstances. Your objective is to be invisible - not to be seen. A good rule to follow is this: for each person you encounter in hostile or unfamiliar territory, ten more will know about that encounter PDQ. Then ten more, and so on. It goes without saying of course: loose lips sink ships...."

"You now have five minutes to get to your room and rid yourself of any personal belongings. Bring nothing of a private nature: no billfolds nor money, nor anything else that could serve as identification. No cigarettes, sorry Mike, or even a book of matches; one of you will be issued with five of the waterproof variety. Any odds and sods that you might imagine could be useful, such as string or thread or a nail from the construction site would be allowable. The barracks will be securely locked for your peace of mind and the area will be patrolled while you're gone. Meet me in the Lecture Hall where we'll have a final briefing and examine the topographical maps of your target area."

The truck bounced and swayed drunkenly along the rutted rural cow track, as aptly characterized by Alec. Hugh was certain that Sam, the driver who had delivered them from the Horse Palace, was doing his utmost to make them retch before they reached Rice Lake, just outside the town of Peterborough.

Hugh crouched beside Joe on the bare metal floor, and each firmly clutched a slat of the wooden siding to keep from being thrown out of the truck and onto the wildly curving concession roads. Mike had made a valiant attempt to organize a lusty sing-along as they left the Camp, but he gave up the effort when the Professor, his pudgy features a shade of pale green, expressed his intent to inflict lasting damage to Mike's nether parts, if he persisted.

"We're here. All out!" Sam shouted from his window.

"Good bloody thing."

"Where the hell is 'here'?"

"Looks like a lake to me."

"Would one of you guys throw down the supplies? I'm due back in Camp in an hour. Hurry!"

"Sure you are and I'll bet she's putting on a fresh pot of coffee just for the occasion, Sam," Mike chided.

Sam's non-verbal reply was the three-fingered, universally understood military salute. "Good luck, suckers. See ya!" The gearbox clashed and whined sickeningly as the rear wheels churned up clods of mud and turf.

"Thank God he's gone. What a jerk."

"Okay, let's take our bearings and set up base. Then we can divvy up the duties." Hugh continued, "I need a compass and a map. Thanks. Did that idiot Sam say it was going to rain? At least he got one thing right.

"Mike, open the supply pack, please, and see if there's enough oil-cloth to make a lean-to. There's a hatchet in there somewhere, or so Findlay said. Who's willing to cut us twelve support stakes? Five feet minimum; then we'll figure out how many more we need for the roof. Enough oilcloth? That's great, Mike! Professor, how are your Boy Scout pathfinder skills? You can take a triangular bearing between that big jack pine and the point of land, then use the map to determine where we are relative to that reference point. Show me as soon as you've got us located. Try to keep the map under your jacket so it doesn't get soaked, if you can."

In less than an hour, a sturdy shelter had been erected and a pot of tea was brewing over a substantial fire.

"Beck was right about RDX, Hugh. Sure makes a great fire starter, when your kindling is soaking wet."

"Who brought the Semtech, Joe?" asked Hugh.

"I did," admitted Mike. "The Major didn't say we couldn't bring it!"

Hugh recalled how their Explosives Instructor, Major Beck, had introduced them to Semtech, the amazing Czechoslovakian discovery.

The 'clients' training area near Peterborough, Ontario, 1943.

"Extremely intense heat is produced from a small amount, which also makes it useful for heating water quickly in the field," Beck had explained in one of the two introductory lectures.

He identified the substance in capitol letters on the blackboard: SEMTECH, RDX (British), or CYCLONITE (American), then suddenly turned and threw a clump of the white, putty-like substance against the lecture room wall. Everyone in the room ducked, but nothing happened.

Alec was 'volunteered' by the Major to hold a lump of the substance, with tongs, in the flame of an alcohol lamp. While his classmates cringed, Alec held the tongs at arm's length. Suddenly the explosive burst into all-but-invisible blue flames. Beck explained that Semtech was inert and safe to carry concealed. It required a special 'igniter cap' with an electrically fired detonator to explode. "Just don't get caught with a detonator in your trousers, or anywhere else, boys. The Jerries will draw the obvious conclusion, and you'll not be rewarded for your trouble, guaranteed."

By nightfall, a meal of freshly caught pickerel and roast rabbit slowly cooked on spits as a pot simmered over the fire, steaming the long grain wild rice harvested in abundance from the aptly named lake. Tom had 'liberated' the cooking utensils and a flashlight from a nearby farmhouse. Following after-dinner clean up, John and Hugh cut several bushy pine boughs and the others wove them into a layer of makeshift mattresses.

"Our task for this evening is to plan tomorrow morning's return to Camp. The Professor has pinpointed our location, here. Bearing in mind that we must avoid being seen at all costs, and must travel by as inconspicuous a route as possible, I suggest that we follow the natural contours of the land, parallel to the river southward. That way, we should be able to avoid the villages as well as the farms.

"We will set out at dawn. It's now 2100. I'll take the first watch until midnight. Who'll take graveyard?"

"I will, Hugh."

"Good man. Thanks, Tom. Morning shift from 0300 to 0600? It's yours, Mike. Good night, gentlemen. Sleep well." 'Tom is such a nice, quiet guy. It's good to see him coming out of his shell, although he's not shy about asking questions. Funny how he clams up the rest of the time. Anyway, maybe it's the influence of the out-of-doors. It can do that, change people,' Hugh reflected. 'He's a heck of a thief, too. In and out of that farmhouse with the goods in less than ten minutes and not even a dog barked.'

By eleven o'clock, the rain had ended, but a brisk, north wind had blown up, threatening to shred the shelter's oilcloth cover. Hugh walked around the lean-to, inspecting the tie-downs at each corner. Satisfied that the roof would last the night, he placed two maple logs on the fire and sat down to watch the cascading sparks. Apart from the swaying of the tree branches and the distant lapping of waves, all was silent.

A hand touched his shoulder. "Sleep time, Hugh. I'm taking over."

"Okay, Tom. Nothing to report. The wind was blowing earlier but seems to have died down a bit. Keep the fire going and stay warm. Wake me if there's anything comes up... anything! Good night."

"Good night, Hugh."

'What was it about him? Something was 'different'...something very subtle. He was a lone wolf. Never mixed in the fun and games and always seemed reserved, shy, formal, stiff even, in the lounge. He was a good student and a hard worker, one of the best in class. Maybe in the entire Camp, if one were to believe the mess scuttlebutt. What is it about his accent? And his persistent questioning? Oh, go to sleep,' Hugh admonished himself.

"Hugh, Hugh, wake up!" A giant's hand was shaking him by the shoulder.

"What, what is it?" Hugh struggled to focus on Mike's face.

"Tom's missing!"

"Missing! How can he be missing? I spoke with him..." he sat up and squinted at the luminous dial of his wristwatch, "...just under two hours ago!"

"Well, I got up to pee ten minutes ago and there was no sign of him at all. I figured he had slipped into the bushes at the side to do the same thing. I waited a bit, but he didn't return. I looked around and did a quick search of the surroundings. Nothing."

"Good Lord. Listen, do not wake the men. Go get the flashlight and meet me at the fire. You said you've searched the surroundings, Mike? What about down on the lakeshore?"

"Not yet, Hugh."

"OK, I'm going down to take a look. Maybe he went for a skinny dip, as unlikely as that may sound," he added doubtfully. "Stay here. Not a word to the others."

Hugh set out through the sedge along a fisherman's path, meandering downhill and onto the beach. He switched on the flashlight and scanned the shoreline, then swung the beam out over the water's sullen, dark surface. The crescent moon was nearly obscured by high clouds. "Tom!" he called. "Tom, it's Hugh!"

His voice echoed faintly for a moment, then silence. 'Damn it! If he's gone over the hill, we're all in it deep...what was that?' He shone the beam towards a stand of wild rice some thirty feet off the shore. A piece of driftwood floated in the shadows at the edge, bobbing in the gentle waves as though attempting to break through the palisade of rice stalks. 'Wait. That's no piece of driftwood.' A pale, clenched fist was visible. "Tom? Tom!"

There was no answer. Within seconds, Hugh stripped to his undershirt and shorts, and placing the flashlight horizontally on the heap of clothing as a beacon, he waded in up to shoulder depth. The lake was cold and chilled him to the bone. Taking a deep breath, he dove beneath the surface. By the time he had reached the rice stand, he was numb. He surfaced, gasping. 'If this is another of Findlay's schemes, I'll personally...Oh, My God!'

Directly in front of him, less than two feet away, Tom floated face down, his arms stretched out in silent supplication. "Tom? Tom! Can you hear me? It's Hugh!" Tom's inert form bobbed silently. Hugh tread water and reached out to take hold of Tom's body. Flipping him over onto his back as he had been taught, he cradled under the chin with one hand to keep Tom's mouth above water.

"I've got you now, Tom. Oh, no...." Tom's intestines had spilled from a bloody gash in his abdomen, trailing like obscene, bluish grey snakes. "He's been gutted!" The incision had been made with surgical precision, running directly from Tom's groin up to the sternum. Hugh fought against the urge to be violently ill. "Bastard!"

In his third year at Queen's, he had helped the Ontario Provincial Police divers retrieve the body of a fisherman downstream from a run of wild rapids on the Cataraqui River. The head and torso had been badly smashed in the corpse's passage through the rocky gauntlet. But that was an accident. This was cold-blooded butchery. 'Settle down, boy.

You've got to get him back. You've got to get him back!' He started to swim slowly, determinedly, stroking with his free arm, and heading, he hoped, shoreward, shivering, and disoriented. He paused to get his bearings. Tom's entrails glinted in the pale moonlight. The flashlight's yellow beam was visible from shore, and appeared to be blinking. Gathering his strength, he swam toward the beacon, dragging his grisly burden until his feet touched the lake bottom.

"I've got him, Hugh." Mike shone the flashlight over Tom's lifeless form. "My God, what's happened? The poor soul! That's disgusting," he whispered. "When you didn't come back right away, I came down to look for you. Here, put my sweater on. You're going to catch pneumonia."

"He's dead," Hugh gasped. "I'd say it's pretty obvious that he's been murdered, wouldn't you? Either that or he performed Hara-kiri. One of us is a murderer. God, what a mess! Help me get him up the slope.

"There. Roll up his body in the leftover oilcloth. Nothing is to be said to anyone about his condition or the circumstances. Keep him covered. If any of the men interfere, don't take any guff. Got it? At first light, I'll find a telephone. I hope that card with the emergency number is somewhere in my pockets. Ah, there it is. Now, stoke the fire and let's sit and think. We'll wake the troops at 0600."

"Men, we have just recovered Tom's body from the lake. He apparently went swimming last night, and drowned."

"Not possible, Hugh," Joe shook his head. "He told me only a few days ago that he could swim like a fish."

"Maybe he got cramps, or he had a seizure. I don't know and frankly, Joe, that's for a coroner's inquest to decide. In the meantime, here's what I've decided to do. I'm going into the nearest town, to telephone the Commandant. Everyone else stays put: no one leaves or so much as touches Tom's body. Mike, you're in charge. Prof, show me your map."

The night clerk at the 'Millbrook Arms' was reluctant to allow the unkempt and unshaven stranger in the dishevelled Army uniform to use his telephone at seven a.m. on a Sunday. "At this ungodly hour?" Hugh, politely but insistently, cited 'official government business.' The clerk relented hesitantly, and then only after he asserted his role by dialling the number on the BSO card himself. Within seconds, he handed the receiver deferentially to Hugh. "You'd better take it. It's an opera-tor."

"Thanks. Hello, 25, 1, 1? Yes, I do have an urgent message. One moment, please." Putting his hand over the mouthpiece, Hugh requested that the clerk allow him privacy.

"Yes, sir. I'll go and check in the kitchen to see how breakfast is coming along. Coffee? I'm sure you could use something hot."

Thirty-five minutes later, the Camp's Buick pulled up at the hotel entrance. Chief Instructor Hamish Findlay came to the doorway. "Come out to the car, Hugh. Get in, son."

Colonel Graham was in the rear. "Are you all right, Hugh? Quite a shock, I'm sure. Tell me everything, Hugh, from the beginning. Take your time, lad. Brian, to the overnight site. Quickly, please."

The Commandant listened intently, seldom interrupting. By the time they arrived back at the lake, Hugh had related all of the details that he could recall. The campsite was secured under the supervision of 2-I-C Major Grey, and six RCMP men in khaki carried out his orders. The Camp's physician knelt over the body on the wet grass, as two army trucks and an RCMP station wagon waited, parked in tandem. The remaining men, accompanied by two RCMP sergeants, were loaded onto the back of Sam's vehicle, and driven from the scene.

"Well, Donald, what do you think?"

Doctor Miller stood up and slowly walked over to where Commandant Graham talked with Hugh and Mike. "I can't do any more here, Gordon," the doctor remarked, drying his glasses with a white handkerchief. "I'll do a full forensic work up at the 'General' as soon as you can get him there. Speed is essential, now. Fortunately, the cold temperature of the water delayed decomposition, although the fish had started to work on...." He paused, looking apologetically at Hugh and Mike. "Sorry, fellows. I know he was a chum. Colonel, would you please have your driver take him directly to the Oshawa General? I'll go along. Can you give us a Mountie escort?"

Mike and Hugh sat silently with Adjutant Major Jones in the back of the limousine. Major Findlay drove. As the car approached the Camp guardhouse, Colonel Graham told Findlay to stop. He pulled the big Buick onto the side of the road and turned off the motor. The Colonel turned in the passenger seat and addressed Hugh and Mike. "Men, you are not suspects, but you are to consider yourselves material witnesses to these unfortunate events and, as such, you are forbidden to discuss any details of the past twenty-four hours, pending further investigations. You are both bound by the Official Secrets Act, which you swore in Toronto. I must caution you that any breach of those terms will result in the gravest of consequences. You can expect to be subpoenaed and ordered to testify at the official inquest. Until such time, you will say nothing, to any person, except under oath and in my presence.

"And by the way, Hugh, from what you told me, you acted with consummate bravery and presence of mind. Both of you conducted yourselves admirably. I want to thank you, and will see that your actions are recognised at an appropriate time. Continue into the Camp, Hamish."

The mood in the barracks was gloomy. "Welcome back. Major Grey left just a few moments ago," explained the Professor. "As nicely as he could, he read us the riot act. We're all bound by our oaths not to discuss this thing, or face courts-martial. The boys have appointed me to say this: both of you guys, Hugh and Mike, were superb. On behalf of everyone, including...him, thanks for taking charge and handling things so professionally. That's all the Major gave me permission to say."

"Thanks, Prof. Mike and I do appreciate it."

"Amen," added Ross, "sure was a shocker though, to wake up to that news!"

"That's enough, Ross! Do you want us all locked up in the clink?" asked the Prof testily.

"Sorry, sorry!"

"Just put a sock in it, do you hear me, or I will!"

"Okay, will everyone please calm down? Who wants a beer? Last man into the lounge pays!" Joe exclaimed.

It seemed to Hugh that the pace of the training picked up now. He slept fitfully and found himself nodding off during an important small arms lecture and demonstration by a burly Commando Instructor on loan from Arisaig, in northern Scotland, a Major Michael Heaviside. Fortunately, that afternoon Hugh was able to register a respectable pattern with the Sten gun on the firing range in the old farmhouse as the acrid odour and crackle of gunfire filled the basement.

The real test came next, Heaviside said, when he told the men they were to run upstairs and into a blacked-out bedroom in the old white clapboard farmhouse. Here they would find the parts of a Sten gun and clip of ammunition scattered in the four corners of the room. Heaviside's directions were explicit and clear.

"You will run upstairs to the room at the top of the landing. Go in, shut the door. I will shut it for you if you leave it open even a crack. Find the parts, sit down, and assemble the Sten. When you're ready, back down the stairs and out the front door, on the run, firing. Who's first? You have ten minutes. The clock is running, mark...now!"

Nine minutes later, a sweat-soaked Hugh emerged triumphantly from the entrance, gun blazing. "Passed" was Heaviside's laconic response as he clicked his stopwatch. In the follow-up evaluation, Heaviside commended Hugh, Joe, and the Prof for "keeping your noses level, more or less," as the Sten was notorious for snapping sharply upward when fired. Ross had stumbled and nearly tripped on the threshold, thereby liberally spraying the top branches of an aged crab apple tree. "It'll dance up on ye at the best of times, lads, and that's of no bloody use, unless you're shootin' quail, or makin' apple jelly," he grinned at an abashed Ross.

Over the next two weeks, the men watched with feelings of awe and dread as Major Samson displayed the lethal catalogue of his thirty techniques for unarmed combat and silent killing. They knew that he would expect them to be able to demonstrate each one, flawlessly, on demand, at any time. Failure to execute any 'procedure' with cold-blooded panache and exacting precision could mean a 'wash out.' Despite his bloody-minded reputation, Robert Samson was an extremely gentle and gifted teacher, whose greatness lay in his unflagging patience and quiet determination to build the men's skills through developing each one's sense of self-confidence.

His famous dictum summed up his approach; "If you believe you can do it and you know how to do it, you can do it." Hugh and his colleagues were motivated to practise for hours on the drill grounds in their spare time, to the point that they could "...do every one of them, in my sleep" as Joe correctly said.

For most recruits, the most hair-raising aspect of the entire SOE syllabus was being exposed to live 50-calibre machine gun fire, zinging and caroming only inches over head, while scrambling on their stomachs underneath barbed wire, immersed in the muddy swamp water which partially filled the obstacle course. It was the topic of after-exercise discussion in the lounge, once the officers had departed. "Did you know that an instructor was shot through the head on that obstacle course?" whispered the Prof. "Blew his head open, it did."

"Really?"

"Really, Mike," he replied categorically. "He was showing a class how to manoeuvre under enemy fire and, 'wham'! It was totally hushed up."

"Prof, how do you know that?" demanded Hugh.

"I just do, that's all I can say. He was young, a bright-as-new-paint Chief Instructor, sent over from Beaulieu. Apparently he was a first-rate bloke and one hell of a CI. He was only here for a bit more than a month when he was killed. No one ever admitted that it happened; officially, they claimed that he died of some rare, progressive kidney disease, in the Oshawa General. The rumours began and the Commandant was recalled to England not long after."

"Why would they do that?"

"Who knows, Hugh? I would imagine that SOE had its reasons, but they're all buried deep inside the Official Secrets Act."

"What was the guy's name?" queried Ross.

"Captain Burgess, Howard Burgess. He's lying in Union Cemetery, up at the other end of Thornton Road, at the Highway."

"Sounds mighty strange, in my opinion," offered Ross. "I mean, if it was a training mishap, why not admit it, bury him with honours and move on?"

"It likely was a horrible accident. But then someone on staff started a 'b.s.' story that he had dropped dead, like a stone, in his quarters. Cerebral haemorrhage. 'Oh what a tangled web we weave....' There's a lesson here: it seems you can't be too careful around this place."

"Don't we know it!" reflected Joe soberly.

All thoughts of Tom's gruesome body and any notions of dark conspiracies were dispelled quickly for Hugh at the jump tower. He found it exhilarating in the extreme to leap into space, holding onto a sisal rope no thicker than his middle finger, and sway like a pendulum. Then to let go, plummeting ninety feet onto a cushion of straw bales: Hugh was convinced that he had been born to parachute.

He listened intently as Major Blake Grey, the 2-I-C, with more than seventy-five successful drops to his credit, explained the landing procedure. "The trick is to tuck and roll as your feet touch the ground, gentlemen. Assume the position, like this. Do it. Again. No, like this. Again. Good, it's coming well, men. Again. Ross, congratulations, you would've fractured your tibia. Hugh, show him, please.

"The natural inclination is to reach out stiffly to fight the impact. That will only get you a broken leg, or worse. Assume the position, relax, and let the ground find you. Use your body's natural shock absorber...your mind; be prepared! Now, let's have another go. Who's first up the ladder?"

By the third try, all had found the knack. The next phase was to jump, or more precisely, to roll off the back of Sam's moving truck. A kinder, gentler Sam kept his vehicle steering in a straight line, at a steady twelve miles an hour.

Saturday evening, at eight, in recognition of their growing proficiency and efforts, the Hut A group was loaded onto Sam's truck and driven to the Genosha Hotel in downtown Oshawa, but not before Adjutant Major Brian Jones had given the last-minute briefing. "You're wearing Canadian Army uniforms, although technically, you're now British servicemen. To every man Jack, or Jill, tonight you're in the Canadian Army.

"Not a single word about this place, the staff, or the training. None. First names only and watch out for blockheads who'll want to pick a fight. Avoid them at all costs. If the unforeseen happens, call the number on your 25-1-1 card. Enjoy yourselves, gentlemen, and I do mean 'gentlemen.'

"One final thing, our hosts at the Genosha are fine, upstanding people. Our track record to date there is exemplary. Treat the staff and the establishment with the greatest respect. And, if any of you, by the wildest chance, should be enticed to enjoy some female companionship, look before you leap. You'll be back at Camp by 2330. That's three hours for fun and merriment. The truck leaves the hotel parking lot at 2300, sharp. Miss it and you'll walk back, if you can. Dismissed!"

Hugh and Mike found the evening pleasantly relaxing and it progressed without incident, for the first hour. The draft beer was cold, the hard-boiled eggs and French fries were fresh, and, the service was first rate. Their waitress, Maria, was, in Mike's opinion, 'heavenly'.

The calm ended when the Prof excused himself from his chums and approached an apparently unescorted, attractive woman at a side table. They were deeply engaged in conversation when, suddenly, he was tapped on the shoulder with a pool cue. Turning, he came face to face with a burly, middle-aged man, obviously capable of installing diesel locomotive engines, single-handedly.

"Oh, damn, Mike. There's going to be trouble over there. Just watch. Don't do anything, yet," Hugh cautioned. The woman looked up and spoke calmly to the intruder. He bristled, and then stalked off, muttering. Within a minute, he returned with his 'second.' The new participant raised his own cue with both hands over the Prof's head, as though he was about to bisect his skull.

The first man now clutched the woman's elbow, determined to pry her out of her chair. She protested, the man persisted, and the Prof rose in her defence. Hugh was about to get up from his chair to intervene when the 'cue man' arced in mid-air and then reeled awkwardly into the mirrored wall, and, in slow motion, slumped into a heap on the sawdust-sprinkled wooden floor. Hearing a loud crack, Hugh feared that the Prof's manoeuvre had snapped the man's spinal cord. In amazement, he watched as in one lightning movement, the Prof shattered the top of a ketchup bottle, and held the jagged neck to the other man's Adam's apple.

"I suggest that you pick up your friend and leave," the Prof stated slowly and deliberately. Despite his unimpressive physique and his lack of stature, the Prof was definitely an impressive figure under fire, thought Hugh. "This lady does not want to see you again. Ever. Trust me, I will enforce her wishes. Now get out!" The Prof's suggestion was taken to heart, immediately and without debate.

After the ketchup spatters were wiped off the tabletop and the shards of glass swept up, the Prof and his companion resumed their tryst and the evening proceeded without further incident.

"You were dazzling, Prof! Samson would've been proud!" exclaimed Ross admiringly, in the truck on the way back to the Camp.

"Just beginner's luck, my boy."

"Who was that dame, Prof?"

"The lady is named Kathryn Bell and the dreadful duo were her 'ex', name of Kostas, and his cousin, Theo, or something. A real pair of philosophers, they were. The husband's just out of the nick, the Don Jail, for attempted assault, on her."

"A really nice piece of work!"

"Careful, Joe, or it'll be ketchup bottles at twenty paces."

"I meant, a nice hand-to-hand manoeuvre."

"Just drop it, Joe," Hugh chortled, "loose lips...."

A week had passed since the incident at Rice Lake; Hugh, curious to find out whether Tom had been buried, decided to wait three more days then go to the Commandant's HQ to ask for an appointment. The young BSO secretary checked the appointment log. She had very long, delicate fingers, and smelled of gardenias, Hugh noted. Colonel Gordon came out from his office.

"Hugh, how good to see you! I was just now speaking with your old employer, Erik Williamson. He asked about you. Naturally, I told him that you're thriving. Are you here to see me?"

"Yes, Sir, if you have a moment. May we speak privately?"

"Of course. Please step inside. Betty, please hold my calls. Thank you. Tea, Hugh? Brewed just a few shakes before you arrived. Take that chair." The room was comfortably but sparsely furnished, and very cold.

Hugh thought it likely that the Colonel might be unfamiliar with central heating, something that the Camp provided through a system of underground steam pipes. A small, autographed black and white photograph of British Prime Minister Winston Churchill hung conspicuously beside the nine-by-twelve colour portrait of His Britannic Majesty in His coronation robes. A Union Jack and a red and white banner, which Hugh assumed was the SOE ensign, completed the decor on the panelled wall behind the Commandant's immaculate mahogany desk.

"Well, Hugh, I believe that I can guess why you're here."

"Likely, Sir. I'm not attempting to pry into classified matters, but I hoped you could tell me, has Tom been buried? Most of the men, myself included, want to pay our respects, Sir, even though we didn't know him well. They're still being very discrete Sir, but it feels as though there's a cloud over us all."

"Aha. I quite understand. No, you're not prying. To answer you as directly as I can, no, the client's remains are being held in cold storage, one would say, pending cutting through the usual clutter of red tape. When I receive a notice of release from my superiors and the civil authorities, he will be laid to rest, in an appropriate fashion."

"Will there be a military funeral, Sir?"

"I can't say."

"If there is, may some, or at least one of us attend, to represent the group?"

"I can't promise that, but...perhaps. Now, please give your squad my best wishes. I'm hearing excellent reports about them from the staff, and frankly, your name comes at the top of the days' lists with almost alarming frequency. It must be costing you a considerable number of shekels after hours in the lounge?"

"Yes, Sir, but it's good for our morale. Thank you for your time, Sir. I'll pass on your good wishes to the men."

'I didn't have the nerve to ask if they've told his parents or wife. No plans for a decent funeral, for a Canadian kid? That's not right,' thought Hugh as he ran to the barracks. Lying on his bunk, he reviewed the few facts, as he knew them:

'Point: Tom was obviously butchered, in cold blood, by someone, out there, under our noses. Point: none of us has really been interrogated, except for Mike and me, that one time in the back of the car. And that was pretty much a wash. Point: according to the newspapers, murder victims are buried within a reasonable length of time, even when an autopsy must be performed. Point: this has dragged on for nearly two weeks. Finally, something is definitely very screwy.'

Night training with Semtech began in the fourth week. The nine men of Hut A were assembled in the lecture hall at 1900, their blackened racoon faces smeared with special Max Factor makeup. They were eager for Major Beck to finish the briefing. "We will operate in two teams; one under the direction of Major Heaviside, the other will follow my lead.

"My group of four will proceed first to the railway line. Once there, they will be shown various methods of laying simulated charges to disable or derail a train. At the same time, Major Heaviside's squad will plant a small, shaped charge on the rock outcroppings shown in this aerial photo, on the cliff face. We will exchange locations when I blow my whistle. The Major and I will inspect your procedures thoroughly and you will follow instructions exactly as they have been care- fully and fully explained in lectures. Obviously, the exercise on the tracks is just that, a simulation. We won't actually be blowing up the CN/CP rail lines.

RDX (Semtech) explosion in fields of Camp X, 1943.

"The other exercise will be a controlled test explosion, gentlemen, employing a nominal charge: we shan't be trying to re-arrange the geography of the lakeshore. When The Major and I are satisfied that all safety precautions have been taken and the charges properly placed, the team will take cover, over here, and your Team leader will detonate the charge following a short whistle-burst sig- nal, like this. Questions?"

Hugh noticed that 'Connie' Conrad, the feisty, funny, profane Slavic gold miner from the Timmins 'Porcupine' region, and the appointed leader of the team, was almost salivating in anticipation. The most excitement Hugh's team had previously had at the CN/CP tracks was when the engineer and fireman on a Montreal-bound passenger train spotted them, lying on the side of the embankment. "I guess they'll be telling the wife or girlfriend tomorrow about how they managed to escape the Nazi saboteurs who were trying to blow them to kingdom come," laughed Connie.

Seconds later, there was an explosion at the lakefront. "Our turn now, eh Major?"

"Waiting for Heaviside's 'all clear' signal, Connie...there it is. Now, on the double." Hugh and company sprinted to the cliffs. "Right, let's get to work. Here's the plastic, the detonator, and the flashlight. You have five minutes to place the charge!"

Hugh and Mike clung to shallow footholds on the cliff face and looked on while Connie and Ross packed the RDX into several folds and crevices. "Ready, Sir."

"Very good, insert the cap. Ross, bring the coil of wire here. Everyone back up and take cover, on the ground. Farther back, men ...on your bellies. All clear, Connie?"

"Clear, Major!"

"Ready, fire!"

From his prone position, Hugh raised his head to watch as Connie depressed the firing pin. The world erupted with an ear-shattering blast, spewing a major piece of cliff material volcanically upwards, only to rain down again in a maelstrom of rock fragments, stone, and clay. Hugh felt as if his body was momentarily levitated, just like the magician's pretty lady in the Sunday School Christmas play. The effect was literally deafening. "I bet they heard that in Oshawa!"

"I'll bet they heard it across the bloody lake in Rochester!"

"You crazy bugger. You could have killed us!"

"My God, Connie. How much did you use?"

"A little bit too much, I suppose, Major."

The word at breakfast was that the Commandant's office had been fielding a constant stream of telephone inquiries through the special Bell operator from editors, politicians, and police chiefs. Beginning at 0600, the calls came from as far away as Defence Industries Limited (Ajax) on the west, to Bowmanville, on the eastern extremity of the shock wave. Adjutant Jones was finally dispatched at 0900 to meet and placate a delegation of the curious, as well as an assortment of angry Whitby and west Oshawa citizenry, including eleven outraged Whitby merchants whose plate glass storefront windows had been shattered by the force of Connie's "enthusiasm." On behalf of the Canadian military, Major Jones made restitution for damage done.

"So where's Connie now, Prof?" Mike asked at lunch.

"Where do you think? Cooling his heels, with Bomber Beck, in the Commandant's lair."

For theft and transportation of classified matériel, (inside his under shorts, as the story was often embellished) Connie was confined to barracks for two days and fined two weeks' pay. Major Beck endured a severe dressing down; to avoid a court martial, he accepted a financial penalty as well as a disciplinary citation in his record for 'questionable judgement, lacking due diligence,' or so the Camp rumour mill reported. The incident, 'Connie's last blast' quickly achieved near-mythic fame in the annals of Camp lore for creating random havoc locally, and, most improbably, several shattered windows at the General Motors works in Oshawa.

Hugh alone was invited by Adjutant Jones to represent Tom's mates at his funeral at the McIntosh Anderson Funeral Home in Oshawa. Even by wartime standards, it was embarrassingly 'by the book', brief and, Hugh thought, 'sadly uninspired, almost irreverent, more like a rehearsal than an actual burial, except there was a body. At least, I have to believe there was, inside the coffin,' as he later told the Prof. Following the conclusion of a ten-minute ceremony led by Commandant Graham, the plain, wooden, undraped casket was unceremoniously wheeled out by two Oshawa Funeral Home attendants and into a waiting Cadillac hearse.

Hugh, the only enlisted man present, rode through the rain to Union Cemetery with Adjutant Jones. The conspicuous absence of family members only added to Hugh's sense of gloom. 'What in the name of heaven had Tom done to deserve such callous treatment?'

As they stood graveside in the pouring rain, an elderly army chaplain conducted the burial service, reciting a hasty, fill-in-the-name, non-denominational eulogy. He was so frail that Hugh feared he might topple into the grave with the next gust of wind, before the final 'Our Father.' The general tone and haste throughout the proceedings only rekindled

Hugh's scepticism and deepened his personal distress with the Commandant's management of the Rice Lake affair.

He returned in silence to Hut A, thoroughly drenched and disheartened but determined to find out the truth and lay Tom's ghost to rest, even if it meant compromising his own career with SOE. A fallen comrade, particularly one who had been murdered, deserved better. He was tempted to telephone Erik to discuss his misgivings, but thought better of it. Perhaps Erik himself had ordered the now obvious cover-up. Anything was possible.

A weekend pass at the end of week six spent visiting with his mother and a few non-enlisted chums in Toronto, confirmed for Hugh what he already felt: he had never been, nor looked, so fit in his life. He returned to Camp on Sunday evening, refreshed and ready for any challenges that the instructors, and Hamish in particular, could present.

The lectures were unlike any in the past. A stream of visiting experts, most with decidedly British accents and whose expertise encompassed what would otherwise be described as questionable or illegal, if not criminal, now supplemented the regular staff. They taught the secrets of undetectable break and enter, lock picking, safe blowing, forgery, survival, advanced disguise, invisible inks, basic codes and ciphers, and interrogation techniques. Unknown to the clients, the majority of the newcomers were SOE instructors transplanted from Beaulieu.

Hamish Findlay orchestrated a series of clever simulations, which were often amusing contests or schemes, as he preferred, to test the men's newly acquired and usually illicit skills. One of the break-ins included a raid on the old farmhouse, which was well guarded, to secure a secret document 'planted' in the parlour.

On one memorable occasion, the men were outfitted in German uniforms and dropped in various locations throughout Toronto with orders to take photographs of specified munitions and heavy equipment factories. If apprehended, they were forbidden to divulge the true nature of their mission for twenty-four hours, and had to do whatever they could to work their way out of the problem.

A cheery Toronto constable, who had been watching 'Luftwaffe Pilot Officer Hugh' fiddle with the focus ring of an unwieldy Leica on Dufferin Street, inquired whether he was Danish or Dutch. "Neither, Officer, I'm Bavarian!" Hugh stated, in his best ersatz German accent. "Learning to fly, in Trenton," he beamed, pointing at the wings on his tunic. "On leave, sightseeing. May I please to take your picture?" Delightedly, the cop adjusted his uniform, and posed in front of the plant's NO ENTRY

EXCEPT TO AUTHORIZED PERSONNEL sign. He then shook Hugh's hand and, wishing him good luck, continued on his beat. Hamish treated Hugh that evening to his second 'dram' of straight malt Scotch, neat, after posting the still-damp photo prominently on the mess hall bulletin board.

In an unrelated scheme, the Prof won Hamish's heart by infiltrating a chemical research laboratory at the University and convincing the night janitor that he had been authorized to inspect the experimental logs, 'for my war work'. Tucking them inside his coat, he walked out. The following morning, Adjutant Jones drove to Toronto and handed over the journals to an embarrassed Dean with an apology and a barely credible explanation, thereby absolving the aged custodian.

Ross earned honourable mention for a daring daylight raid. In the guise of a 'government pipe inspector,' he brazened his way past a phalanx of security guards using a fake ID, and placed a 'Boom, you're dead!' sticker on the main shutoff valve of a west-Toronto petroleum pumping station during lunch break. As proof of his entrepreneurial spirit, Ross produced the supervisor's name badge and time card.

The next three weeks were exciting and so full of fresh challenges that Hugh all but forgot his vow to Tom: he took his first parachute jump and was selected for advanced short wave wireless radio (Wireless Telegraphy-W/T) training.

He had been eager to undergo parachute training since discovering the exhilaration of limited free-falls from the tower. He and his classmates, along with ten other recruits whom Hugh assumed were French-Canadian, were driven to the Oshawa airport in an army bus with blacked-out windows and headlights. Inside the hangar they inspected their parachute packs before boarding an RCAF DC-3.

The jumpmaster, a recent Beaulieu expatriate, explained the procedures that would be followed, including the somewhat obvious meaning of the red and green signal lights placed above the opening in the side of the aircraft's fuselage where once there had been a door. The men strained to catch his every word over the roar of the twin Pratt and Whitney engines as the aircraft taxied on the runway to takeoff position.

The clients sat silently in two rows facing one another on opposite sides of the otherwise empty cargo bay, waiting for the plane to reach its cruising altitude. When the jumpmaster gave the signal to stand and form a single line facing the non-existent door, each man hooked up to the static line. The jumpmaster visually checked and hand-tested each man's snap connector; Hugh felt a lump surging in his throat and his head pounded as the red light blinked out, replaced by the steady green 'Ready' signal. As third man in line from the hole in the plane's flank, Hugh felt the icy blast of the turbulence swirling outside the aircraft while it circled lazily above a toy vehicle with a just-visible Red Cross painted on its roof, nine-thousand feet below. He barely heard the jump-master shout "Go," through the pounding din of the engines and torrents of rushing air. But with the tap on his left shoulder, he launched himself through the opening.

"The first six seconds were pure magic," Hugh later wrote in a letter to his mother. It was, he said, as though he was momentarily aloft with the angels, suspended between heaven and earth, as the slipstream and prop wash locked his body in a nearly upright position and he floated effortlessly, weightless, parallel with the receding DC-3's tail section.

Too soon, the fleeting state of grace was overcome by the death grip of gravity, and he began a breathtaking earthward plunge. He fought his body's parasympathetic urge to deploy his parachute until he could hold off no longer. He pulled the D-ring as the Red Cross symbol increased in size at an alarming rate. Looking up, he saw the sky filled with white mushroom caps as his own silk canopy billowed open above his head, jerking him momentarily to a halt. He then continued in a swift but con-trolled descent.

Landing on the corn-stubbled field with what he judged to be a man-ual-perfect tuck and roll, he rose to his feet, quickly gathered the silk shroud, removed his harness, and wanted to do it all over again, right then. The stories in the lounge that evening were reassuringly pre-dictable. No one was seriously injured, discounting a sprained ankle sustained by a friendly, bilingual recruit named Armand, from Dorval, near Montréal, who hobbled around Camp on crutches for a week. After his third jump, Hugh knew that he had found his lifelong love.

W/T classes were held after supper in the radio building, Hydra. Normally Hydra was off-limits to the clients, so Hugh and the small group of students, including Armand, who favoured the name 'Frenchie,' were not disappointed to be excused from evening callisthenics workouts in order to visit this "inner sanctum."

The trio of trainer-operators, Bill, Bernie, and Hughie made them feel welcome. These three had been pre-war amateur radio 'hams,' all 'talent spotted' by BSO within Toronto's closely-knit ham radio circles.

Bill, Bernie, and Hughie, all fully qualified SOE Secret Agents, had been among the first graduates of the Camp's curriculum.

Under the direction of Chief of Wireless Operations, the brilliant electrical engineer, Colonel 'Phil' Truscott, they 'jerry built' the advanced short-wave radio equipment in what was then little more than an earthen floored temporary radio shack, using spare parts and requisitioned high frequency transmitter/receivers. Dr. Phillip Truscott, one of Erik Williamson's closest friends and business associates, was, like Williamson, an internationally recognised leader in the field of high-frequency radio communications and encryption technology. Hydra staff had recently been supplemented by four British W/T experts, sent over from Bletchley Park to assist in the expansion of Hydra's capabilities and help Colonel Truscott meet the urgent need for increased training capacity at Camp X.

Hugh, Mike, and the Prof were part of the class of twelve trainees who were crowded, elbow-to-elbow, into Hydra's cramped interior, most of which was occupied with the massive transmitter/receiver apparatus and punch tape machines. But they were too engaged in their studies to complain and were mindful of their special status after Adjutant-Quarter Master Jones informed them that they had been carefully selected for W/T training. He emphasised that only the *crème de la crème* of candidates were picked.

The Morse code classes were lengthy, intensive and required complete concentration under the tutelage of Bill, who preferred his BSO nickname 'Yorkie'. "The minimal requirement to achieve a passing grade," he said, "is the ability to 'send' and 'read' (Morse) code at a rate of twenty-five words per minute. And that's only the beginning. If you manage that, lads, then there's much more in store!" he chuckled.

"What if we flunk it, Yorkie?" asked John, anxiously.

"You won't. My students never fail. Well, hardly ever," he replied, smiling. "Only one ever did, and he ended up somewhere far away from here. Keep working; then in half an hour we'll put on our coats and step outside to take a tour of the rhombics (antenna array)."

"I bet you tell that to all the girls!"

"Just to your sister, Scottie!"

"Is it true that someone destroyed the original radio and burned down the building, Yorkie?"

"Yes, but it was a careless accident. Some person left the main 10 kW XMTTR (transmitter) on full power, without being driven, at suppertime. Of course it overheated and caught on fire; I smelled the smoke from the mess hall and ran over. The room was an inferno. I managed to douse it with three buckets of sand, which didn't do the equipment much good, although the blaze had pretty much finished it off by then, anyway. So, we built this one.

"But enough stalling now, and back to your [Morse code] keys, boys. First test is tomorrow, five words per minute. If you pass, you'll get to use a B Mark 1 radio set." Finding the requirements of the W/T course heavy, Hugh, Frenchie, the Prof, and Mike decided to combine their limited free time with their homework assignments by holding informal after-class practise sessions in a corner of the lounge. It was open to all W/T students; the price of admission was a round of beer.

Colonel Truscott and a Major Briggs from Beaulieu gave key lectures, which included an introduction to the arcane mysteries of ciphers and codes. The Colonel noted that the one-time code pads, (OTP), a nearly 'unbreakable' Russian invention that SOE readily adopted, "...are susceptible only to being compromised by human error and stupidity. Both the operator at home base and the agent in the field have identical pads, which, like this sample I am passing around, contain special groups of code. No others copies exist. Hence, theoretically, they are the only two people in the world who possess the information needed to encode and decode the wire (message).

"Once used, it is destroyed. It is a beautifully conceived one-time system. Never keep the page once the message has been sent, receipt acknowledged and a reply received, if requested. Why do I bother to burden you with something which seems so obvious, gentlemen?"

"Well, Sir, it's possible that one might be captured before the paper can be destroyed," Hugh offered.

"Yes, so you must burn or swallow the damn thing, immediately," the Major responded. It's not meant to be a souvenir. Too many fine chaps and ladies have been caught with their pants...with the incriminating evidence in their pockets. Secondly, the entire pad must be disposed of, if capture is inevitable. If not, you'll be giving Jerry *carte blanche* entry into our networks and, believe me, he's very good at doing that, even without our assistance."

"Do you mean we are to gulp down the whole...business?" queried Frenchie.

"Yes," answered Colonel Truscott. "And that was the problem. It proved to be unrealistic to expect anyone to do that, in little or no time.

The backroom boys at HQ are currently experimenting with a system that is likely to receive official blessing. It seems that they have developed OTP's printed on edible silk squares. Tests are quite favourable. The squares can be hidden easily in the hem or the lining of a uniform. They can be destroyed using a match or a cigarette lighter and they leave no telltale ash. We sincerely hope that silk will prove to be a more palatable *entrée* than paper. To answer the question which must be in your fertile minds, there is no plan that I know of to encourage you to eat your parachute, or any other article of apparel."

"But Major Briggs, Yorkie and the others have emphasised that we each have a unique signature or style when we're transmitting. Even with the code pad, how would it help the enemy, if our 'fist' can't be copied? Wouldn't the operator at the other end be able to detect an impersonator?" asked the Prof.

"Yorkie is quite right. Your 'fist' is distinct from his or mine and nearly impossible to duplicate. Our experience in the field has been that even the most courageous agents are not superhuman and as such, can sometimes be coerced by any number of persuasive methods, to co-operate.

"Now, Yorkie and the Hydra boys are going to let you in on some of the radio room's dark secrets. Yorkie?"

"Thanks, Major. Actually, men, there's not very much I can talk about as the operation is classified - Top Secret. You saw the three rhombic arrays down on the lakeshore and I described how they work like a giant short-wave trap, feeding those signals coming in off the ionosphere into our triple-diversity receiver. You've learned that much physics in the course. Of course, our traffic sources and destinations are classified. The tape machines that are clattering non-stop in the background record the incoming signals on punched tape in coded groups, which are then decoded or stored and re-transmitted. Beyond that, there's little more to say. I'll try to answer a few questions."

"When are you busiest?"

"Generally, during the day" answered Bernie.

"Why then?"

"The ionosphere becomes unstable at night. The 'skips' that the signals take from the sky down to the ocean and back up are more susceptible to interference at that time. That's all in your manual. No other questions? Then, thank you."

By the third week, the class had far exceeded the expectations of the

Commandant and Truscott. Yorkie announced the examination results: "First, none of you lads is going to Iceland, I'm pleased to say. Each has achieved the passing grade of 25 wpm. Congratulations. Wait, please. Four men, Armand, Charles, Hugh, and the Prof have exceeded the mark, with honours. Now you may applaud. Second, the award for overall achievement, which includes Morse, encryption, codes, and W/T radio proficiency, goes to a chap whose accomplishments merit our highest praise and respect. Hugh, please come forward and accept this honour, on behalf of the entire Hydra crew." The award was a large tomato soup can, painted gold and mounted on a shellacked, wooden base. A copper plate bore the inscription,

TO HUGH FOR W/T EXCELLENCE

HYDRA AWARD STS 103.

"Thank you, Yorkie. I'm truly honoured and don't know what to say. Maybe it would sound better if I could speak in Morse? I honestly don't feel that I deserve this, guys. It was a team effort. I wouldn't be here if it weren't for my three partners, and everyone else, for that matter. On behalf of all of us in the class, thank you for your support and wisdom, Colonel Truscott, Major Briggs, Yorkie, Bernie, and Hughie. You were superb teachers, all. Our sincere gratitude and appreciation."

"Wait just a minute, young fellow. That cup's not much use empty, is it? Peek inside." As directed, Hugh reached inside and pulled out a hand-lettered certificate of achievement, signed by the Hydra staff and wrapped around a crisp, ten-dollar bill. "Some small tokens of our admiration and affection, Hugh. Okay, let's dismiss to the lounge, boys, and help him spend it, as only real, honest – to - goodness W/T men know how, right? Next week, Major Briggs, I understand you will have a scheme or two to find out more practically what they've actually learned. Men, you are dismissed!"

The party was loud and long. At ten thirty, when the four hundred and thirty-third bottle of beer fell from the wall, Hugh stepped out the side door, in need of some fresh air. For no particular reason, he began to walk briskly towards the officers' quarters.

"Evening!" It was Mac, the guard, on patrol.

"Evening, Private."

"Evening," Mac smiled as he crunched past Hugh on the gravel path, his breath creating vaporous wisps as though he were a steam locomotive labouring uphill. His ample frame cast shadows that grew and receded gnome-like under each lamp standard.

'What am I doing over here? This is the CO's place. Must get back and go to bed. I've had it.' The night was serenely silent, moonless, and reminded him of that dreadful night a month, or was it a century ago? The tranquillity was shattered by a sudden crack, as loud as the report of a Colt forty-five. Hugh stopped dead in his tracks. All was silent. 'Must have been the cold splintering bark on a pine trunk...that, or a revolver?'

He was about to start back, when he saw two figures standing beside a large sedan. He could distinctly hear Commandant Gordon's crisp Gaelic cadences. Slowly, Hugh crouched down until he was squatting.

"Truth is, Ted, someone got to him before I could help... beat the hangman."

Hugh stiffened. 'Help who? Hangman?'

"What do you wish me to do, Graham?" The voice was as flat as a Canadian prairie.

"Nothing, nothing at all for now. I'll ring you when London is ready to proceed."

"Does anyone else...?"

"Of the two, Hugh Mason, likely. Michael Kristoff, possibly...." The faltering cough of an engine cold starting muffled their words momentarily. As the driver kicked the roaring motor off high idle, the only words Hugh could distinguish were "...by keeping a weather eye on them."

"I must be off. At least it's not raining, Gordon."

"Not yet. Rain or not, I can guarantee that Hamish will have the lads doing forty push-ups before breakfast. Good night. Drive with care, Ted."

"I will. Good night, Gordon." The car door slammed.

'Commissioner Reynolds?' Erik Williamson had introduced Hugh to the RCMP chief at Casa Loma. The Cadillac's partially blacked-out beams darted towards Hugh like searchlights and passed over his head. Hugh dropped face down in the grass, fighting a rising sense of dread and fear. 'Are we involved in a conspiracy to cover up Tom's murder? Are Mike and I suspects or suckers in a plot? Who beat the hangman?' Hugh coughed. 'Damn!'

"I say, who's there? Stand up, slowly. Hands up." The Colonel approached Hugh's hiding place with caution, in Samson stalking mode, the open flap of his greatcoat revealing the dull glint of a revolver's barrel, aimed directly at Hugh's head. "Stand, or I will fire!"

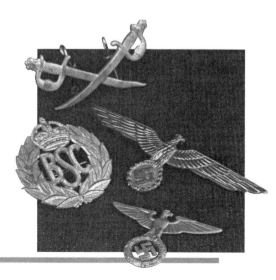

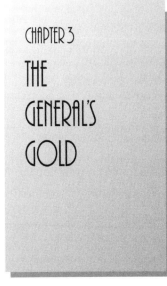

CHAPTER 3

THE GENERAL'S GOLD

"Colonel Graham, a call from General Constantine on your scrambler, Sir."

"Good morning, General Constantine."

"Good morning, Gordon. How are you enjoying our fine Canadian weather?"

"Passably, General. I suppose I should take up skiing; I remember you mentioning some excellent hills, near, is it Collingwood?"

"The Blue Mountains. Yes, we, that is, my family, have a membership at a very nice little club there. The runs are spectacular, you can rent excellent equipment very reasonably, and basic lessons are free to members and guests. In another two months, the ground will be snow-covered for the winter; then we must slip away for a day. Remind me, Gordon.

"But first, I have a favour to ask of you, and I do hope that I'm not imposing. I have tentatively invited Robert Brooks to meet with us there at the Camp, tomorrow morning. If you can manage that, I'd like to ring him back and confirm for, say, ten o'clock?"

"Yes, that will be fine, General. I'm free and clear. A hot breakfast will be waiting. It must be urgent, General."

"Quite so. Thank you for your co-operation, Gordon. Unless you hear from my office or me within the hour, you may assume we'll be there in the morning. Goodbye."

Colonel Graham replaced the receiver, stood, and turned to look out his window, gazing at the deep blue lake. 'Hello, who's that?' he wondered absently. 'McDonald, the guard...I wonder what he wants.' He watched as Mac walked past the Commandant's window, climbed the wooden steps, and then knocked at the front door.

Shortly after, Betty's voice came through the intercom. "Sir, Private Mac wishes to speak with you. He doesn't seem to have made an appointment. Shall I ask him to come back...?"

"No, I'll see him. Send him in, please." He looked up as Mac entered his office. "Good morning, Private."

"Good day, Sir. Colonel Graham, I wonder if I might have a word with you? There's something that I think you should be aware of. It's, well, a bit confidential."

Suppressing a smile of amusement at Mac's wariness, Gordon rose and shut his door. "There, what is it, Private?"

"Sir, you know the White Rose service station on the King's Highway # 2?"

"Mm, the one just west of Thornton Road?" Graham asked, distractedly.

"Yes, Sir."

"Yes, I am vaguely familiar with it, Private. Continue, please."

"Well, Colonel, yesterday, the station wagon was overheating so I pulled in to the station to have the thermostat tested and asked the fellow to check the radiator and hoses for leaks. The owner and I got talking and he asked if I was from around here. I said no, that I was on my way to Kingston, but thought that I wouldn't get very far with a 'rad' problem. He was quite the talker, and very interesting into the bargain.

"Among other things, he told me that this particular area is rich in history and that the British had once built a small fort on the shore of Lake Ontario, during the War of 1812, straight down from where his station is. Apparently there was a coach house and an inn, right on the gas station site back then. The guy said that, in fact, there's a trap door built into the concrete floor of a room at the back of the garage. Should I go on, Sir?"

The Commanding Officer's parlour, venue of top-secret meetings, 1942.

"Yes, Mac, please do. This is interesting. Were you in 'civvies' or in uniform?"

"In civvies, Colonel. Well, by now we're like old chums; it's 'Mac' this, and 'Barney' that. So then, Barney said folklore has it there was this tunnel under the floor that supposedly ran all the way down to the lake. It seems that the British started at the lake and worked back to the coach house, building a tunnel from a large underground bunker in which they stored their valuables.

"This camp had been the home base for the British troops, and the paymaster was situated here, in the bunker. Since the British were paid in gold coins, they stored fairly big quantities of them. In the event of an American invasion by way of the water, the plan was that the paymaster and his staff would enter the tunnel with the valuables and work their way up until they got to the coach house. They could then make their escape while the others stayed behind to fight the Yankee invaders."

"That's a very interesting tale, but I wonder just how true it is. Coffee, Mac?"

"Love some. Thanks, Sir, one lump, no cream."

Mac sipped his coffee, and then continued. "Well, the proprietor of the station, Barney, he said that he had been down there once and that the tunnel goes on for about fifteen feet, then stops at a large metal and concrete plate. Not being a particularly brave person, he said, he's not gone back to investigate further. I thanked him for his help with the car, and for his interesting story to help pass the time, paid him, then said good bye."

Gordon Graham sensed that Mac's informant was telling the truth. Still, he knew that this would all have to be verified, and at the earliest possible opportunity. "I want to thank you for giving me first crack at this information, Private McDonald. You did the right thing. I'm not certain how we might exploit the tunnel, but if the man's story proves to be correct, I'm sure we'll eventually do so. Of course, your information goes no further, Private."

"Of course not. Absolutely nowhere, Sir, and thanks for your time and the coffee."

Colonel Graham's curiosity was piqued, to say the least. He made a note to get in touch with Ted Reynolds. Perhaps the RCMP had some information buried in a dusty file in their archives, or knew of an historian with knowledge of the locale during that era.

At 0945, General Constantine and Robert Brooks arrived. After the welcoming formalities, Gordon Graham was about to invite them to the Officers' Mess, when the General spoke.

"It would be best if we stayed here, Colonel, although I could certainly do justice to your chef's excellent fare. And you, Robert?"

"I could manage a bite, thanks."

"Very well, gentlemen. Then I'll have breakfast sent up, immediately. Today's special is eggs Benedict with orange juice, and coffee or tea. All in favour? Very good, it's unanimous."

He paged Betty, and ordered over the intercom, "Three eggs Benedict specials, please... no, have Andy bring it on a cart and serve our guests here. Then, no further interruptions, thank you."

After the orderly had finished attending to their service, he withdrew, closing the Colonel's door soundlessly.

"Gordon, I'm pleased to see that your kitchen is maintaining its customary high standards. That meal was excellent! By the way, is that client, Quan, still here? You remember, the Chinese ex-policeman friend of Robert Samson's who used to whip up those Hong Kong dishes for us?"

"Unfortunately for us, no, General. He's been reassigned."

"Pity. Is this your first visit to the Camp, Robert?"

"Yes, it is General, not counting a quick tour with Erik when it was about three-fourths completed."

The General paused, and then continued in a sombre tone, "Are we alone, Gordon? This information is for our ears only."

Graham nodded affirmatively "Secure, General."

"Very well, gentlemen, I'm sorry to be the Cassandra this morning, bearing unpleasant news; as a matter of fact, it's damned depressing. No melodrama intended, but England is facing a tragedy of unimaginable dimensions. Robert, you may have heard through channels that it's not unlikely that the Nazis will be mounting an invasion in a matter of weeks. I'm sure you'll agree with me, Gordon, that the possibility of England being plunged back into the Dark Ages is too horrific to contemplate.

"Nonetheless, we must all get on with our assigned duties and carry out every conceivable counter measure to protect the country's vital resources, not to mention her institutions and people.

"My role is this. At this time, England's gold reserves are being loaded on a vessel that will be setting sail for Canada the very moment it's ready. As soon as the ship arrives in Halifax, the bullion will have to be secured in safe keeping for the duration of the war. This is where you and I come into play. Any questions so far?

"No? Good. To continue then, I have been assigned the task, or rather the responsibility, of finding a safe home for it in central Ontario. I have in my briefcase, documents, or more precisely, bills of lading, which account for the reserves to the last Troy ounce. The Americans were keen to take it to Fort Knox, however Erik Williamson pulled some strings, and we got the nod from Whitehall. Naturally, it all has to be carried out with the greatest care, under the utmost secrecy. There's not much time and I need your input. Any idea, no matter how farfetched, must be given serious consideration...Graham?"

"Then Eric Williamson's well aware of this, Sir?"

"Yes, he certainly is. He and the Canadian Minister of Defence are the only other two who are in the know, other than us. Not even the PM has been briefed."

"I think we'll need to bring Ted Reynolds in, General. The RCMP could be invaluable in getting us who and what we need, when we need it. And Ted can be trusted implicitly."

"I'm glad you said that, Colonel. I needed to hear you state your confidence in the Mounted Security Service."

"I was wondering. Do you think that we might stash some in the basement at Casa Loma, General?" asked Robert.

"I thought of that as well, but, the problem is, there are too many people coming and going. It might be impossible to keep it secret; don't forget; we're talking about a huge volume of gold bars. Not easy to camouflage or conceal. There is always the chance of someone accidentally stumbling upon it," replied General Constantine.

"I wonder how they're handling it over there, on the pier and on board?"

"No idea, Gordon. That's their responsibility. Once it arrives, then it becomes ours."

"Sir, this may sound crazy, but just yesterday a guard told me a yarn he'd heard from a local regarding this area during the War of 1812. It was fascinating and curiously plausible, but I don't know whether there's any truth to it or if it's merely a local legend"

"Go on, Gordon. At this stage, I'll listen to any idea no matter how preposterous it might sound," replied Constantine.

Graham recounted Mac's story in detail. When he concluded, there followed a brief silence as each of them pondered the likelihood of the tunnel's very existence.

"Well, wouldn't that be an interesting coincidence! What do you think of the prospects, Robert?"

"If it's true, and the bunker is underneath Camp X, it would be absolutely secure."

Major General C.F. Constantine, Commander, Military District 2, Canadian Army, 1943.

"Nothing's absolute, except the need now for speed and prudence. It's possibly just a good drinking story, but personally, I like it. What's your opinion, Gordon?"

"We'll never know whether it exists or it is just what you said, General, a drunkard's dream, unless we investigate."

"Colonel, I want to do just that. Today. Please enlist a half-dozen of your most capable men: a miner or two would be useful, if you have such at the Camp. Also requisition the equipment that you think they'll need for tunnelling: picks, shovels, rope, coveralls, two by fours for shoring, pulleys, and good flashlights. Our tunnel may well have caved in."

"Explosives too, General. To blow the steel plate if need be. I'll send for Hamish Findlay and John Beck."

"Good man. If you have any trouble at all coming up with the tackle, telephone Colonel Sam at GM. He'll comply and he won't ask questions, you can be sure of that. Also, Gordon, do not bring along the Private who told you the tale. We don't want the garage owner recognising him. Now, Colonel, will we be ready to move out by noon?"

"Sooner, Sir. If you'll excuse me, I'll start making the calls. Please help yourselves to the coffee." He walked to the door, spoke briefly to his receptionist, then returned to his desk. Within moments, his phone rang. "Hamish? Gordon. Listen, I want you and John Beck to round up six of your best men. Be certain they can keep their mouths shut. Do you have anyone with experience in mining? Good, bring them both. Meet me here in one hour. Bring two trucks. You and John will do the driving. Let me ask you something. Do you think that the two of you could set off a controlled charge to take out an underground concrete and steel door without caving in the tunnel walls? Fine, that's what I thought. Bring some Semtech and whatever else you and Beck think you'll need. Just tell Jones I've cleared you. Yes, I'll sign the requisition. No mention of any tunnel to anyone. Eleven-thirty. Goodbye.

"We're doing well, General. Betty, please ring Major Jones's office immediately. Hello, Brian. I have a shopping list for you. Do you have a pen and notepad?"

At precisely 11:30, two open trucks, one containing the men, and the other loaded with equipment, were waiting at the Lecture Hall entrance. Colonel Graham stepped up onto the running board of the second truck to address the men. "You are going on a top secret exercise. You have been selected because I know that you can keep this to yourselves. You are all sworn members of BSO and understand the consequences of violating your oath of secrecy. You are not to mention to anyone what you are about to see, am I clear?"

"Yes, Sir, clear!" the men replied.

"Good. Then let's move out. Major Findlay, Major Beck, follow my vehicle!"

Colonel Graham opened the driver's door of the new black Buick, dismissed his driver, and took the wheel. With General Constantine and Robert Brooks sitting in the rear seat, the limousine led the procession past the gate, up Thornton Road, and over the railway tracks, each of the three wondering whether this could be true, or if it was simply a wild goose chase. Secretly, they were as excited as schoolboys who had discovered a cave in the side of a hill and were about to explore it.

When they arrived at the top of Thornton Road and turned left onto the highway, they could see the gas station sign a half-mile ahead, on the left side of the road.

Colonel Graham touched the brake pedal, and rolled down his window to signal a left turn with his outstretched arm. At the same time, he glanced in his rear-view mirror to assure himself that the trucks were slowing. He turned in sharply, stopping between the single White Rose Ethyl gasoline pump and the station's misted plate glass window. The trucks pulled up in tandem behind the car, the convoy obscuring entirely the front of the station.

Inside, the owner stood peering out, agitatedly wiping the grimy glass with the sleeve of his blue denim coveralls. As he watched, the smart, gleaming black Buick limo and the two army trucks disgorged their contents. He came outside, scratching his head incredulously. "Jesus H.... What is this, an invasion?" He started to back up through the service station door. "I'm callin' the OPP!"

Commandant Graham approached, "Wait. We won't harm you, Sir. I will explain why we are here shortly. My name is Colonel Gordon Graham. May I ask yours?"

The owner stopped, sized up the officer warily, and then replied,

"Barnett Simms, 'Barney,' Colonel. Pleased to meet you. You Canadian?" he asked, while wiping his hands on his coveralls.

"British." Gordon turned to Small Arms Assistant Instructor Parr. "Sergeant, swear Mr. Simms under the Official Secrets Act."

"Yes, Sir."

"Hold on! I'm not swearin' nothin'! I signed up once but was turned down fair and square. The army doc in Kingston said I have a bum ticker 'cause of Scarlet Fever from when I was eight!"

"Sir, I'm sure you wanted to do your duty and tried your utmost to enlist. That's not the issue here," replied Graham. "This is a matter of national security, Mr. Simms. Please allow the Sergeant to continue."

"No tricks, now. Not so many years ago, your type roamed this very countryside lookin' for to sign up simple farm boys in the taverns by slippin' the King's coin in their beer mugs."

"Sir, I promise you, His Majesty's press gangs are not waiting to jump you. I assure you that your, shall I say, compliance, will be to your advantage, financially. Sergeant, continue."

"Mr. Simms, what you must swear is that you will never tell anyone what you are about to see or hear. You will also have to sign this document which states that if you violate this Act, you may be punished with imprisonment."

"Financial advantage, Colonel?" Barney asked, seeming not to have heard any of the Colonel's words after those two.

"That's what I said, Mr. Simms."

"You can call me 'Barney'," he replied affably. "Okay, I'll do it. What do I have to lose? Besides, business ain't so great, what with the gas rationing and no new cars being made down the road," he continued, nodding vaguely in the general direction of the distant General Motors plant. "Come on in. So, where do I have to sign?"

After a brief ceremony in the small service station's office, the C.O. addressed Mr. Barnett Simms, BSO. "Congratulations. This, by the way, is General Granite. Your name for our purposes is now Barnett or Barney, whichever you prefer.

He continued, "My friends and I understand that there could be a tunnel under this establishment. Is this true?"

"Golly, a General! Oh, yes indeed, Sir, a tunnel. That's true alright, Sir!"

"Then please take us to it now, Barnett."

"Behind the counter and through the door." He held open the swing door for the officers, and Robert followed after the soldiers had entered. To their left was a small service bay. Ahead were two closed doors. Anticipating the Colonel's next question, he explained, "The one, on the left, is my business office. The other's pretty much all garage supplies: oil drums, fresh wiping rags, some recapped tires, filters, spark plugs, spare parts, most of them stripped from junkers. I've got a '38 Essex Terraplane, rebuilt the engine and tranny myself. She's a real eye-catcher, almost mint condition. I've got her under that tarp in the service area. Nine hundred dollars, firm. Interested?"

"Perhaps some other time, thank you. Which room has the trap door, Barney?" asked the Colonel, trying to mask his impatience.

"The supply room, Sir."

"And it is accessible?"

"Oh yes, Sir. I keep it covered up with a rug. There are wooden stairs going down. Be careful though. I haven't gone down them in a few years, and the last time I did, I thought that some of the boards were about to break. The tunnel goes for about fifteen feet then it stops dead because of this here thick steel and concrete wall."

"Thank you, Barney. We'll take it from here. I must ask you to stay in your front office while we carry on. Don't be alarmed if you hear a small explosion, as we may have to remove the door forcibly. I trust your underground gasoline storage tank and lines are far enough away?"

"Over there, on the right side. The line runs across the front, from there to the pump, here," he indicated, pointing.

"That seems fine. One of the men will check it out, to locate it exactly. We'll try not to damage your building. Any losses will be put right.

"Sergeant, move the car and trucks around to the back, then come back here and make certain that no one enters the building. Take off that army overcoat and switch with Barney. Tell anyone who pulls in that Mr. Simms was called away suddenly and has left you instructions to tell his customers that he ran out of petrol and won't have another delivery until tomorrow. Keep track, and we'll pay Barney for whatever he estimates his losses to be. And stow that damn Tommy gun under the counter, for heaven's sake!

"Gentlemen, are we ready?"

The men pushed aside the rug and pried up the heavy metal plate that covered the hole. A musty odour immediately wafted from the darkness below. Hamish piped up, "Hand me a torch, Corporal. Let me go first, Sir, to see that it's safe."

As Hamish began making his way down the old stairway a board suddenly cracked under his boots. This was followed by a second report as sharp as a gunshot, and a curse.

"Findlay? Findlay, are you all right? Major Beck, take one of the men and get down there to see what's happened. Careful how you go!"

Fortunately, Hamish had kept his grip on the side railing and the men were able to pull him back up. "It's just a large sliver, Colonel. See? Nothing more than that, nothing broken. Just send someone to fetch the first aid kit and wrap it tightly. I'll be fine. Ohhh, my tailbone's a bit tender...I'm a little winded, but I'll recover. Doc Miller can look...."

"Hush, Hamish, that's no sliver, my boy, it's quite a nasty gash. Relax, and don't talk; we'll have you mended in a jiffy," the Colonel replied, quietly. "Private, help the Corporal move Major Findlay. Gently now, and see to disinfecting and bandaging his leg. Right. You three men, get some boards, ropes, and tools and get down there and repair that ladder. We are going down, aren't we General?"

After a few minutes, a sweaty-faced sergeant appeared at the top of the ladder. "All clear, Commandant! I've made certain that the rungs are safe."

"Capitol! Follow me, General. Hand me a torch, please, Robert. Hamish, don't budge unless I call for you." The tunnel was pitch black. They walked ahead a dozen feet or so, then encountered the concrete barrier just as Barney had predicted. Colonel Graham shone his light ahead, swinging the beam to reflect off both sides and from above.

"General, apparently we're encased in a concrete coffin. Lord only knows how those sappers built this, back then. Should we proceed?" asked Graham.

"Yes, by all means, but with caution, Colonel. One doesn't know what to expect after a hundred and thirty years, eh?"

"Which of your men are the Northern Ontario miners, Sergeant? Very good. You chaps, see if you can make a dent with your picks."

"It's concrete, Colonel, about four inches thick, I'd have to say," remarked one.

"And there's steel beneath the concrete face, Sir," remarked the other. "There seem to be hinges on the right side, I think. But they're pretty well buried in the wall."

"Damnation. Hamish, can you hear me?" Graham called, cupping his hands.

"Yes, loud and clear, Sir."

"Can you muster the strength to come down for a recon? Private, take your torch back to the ladder and escort Major Findlay here. John, I want you and Hamish to blow this."

"Roger, Colonel."

"How will you do it?"

"Either jelly (Gelignite) or plastic (Semtech), Sir. Hamish will have the final call. He's the far more experienced safe-cracker."

Hamish hobbled over with John to inspect the surfaces of the door and the walls, running their flashlight beams and their palms over the rippled concrete. They conferred briefly then Beck turned to the Colonel and uttered one word: "Plastic." He next addressed the pick men; "Harry, we want you and Earle to see what you can do with your pickaxes to make one inch pockets in the concrete around those indentations where the hinges are attached to the wall. Major Findlay will supervise while I run up to the supply truck. Colonel, I request that the area be cleared, if you would, please. Hamish and I will take it from here."

Graham ordered the rest of the men up the ladder and outside. Following the last man to the top, the Colonel assured himself that they were out of harm's way then yelled down, "Hamish, make certain you and John leave yourselves plenty of time to get out."

"Yes, Sir, no problem. It's a remote detonator."

Hamish pushed a putty-like piece of Semtech into the shallow depression left by Harry and Earle's pickaxes, then carefully inserted a blasting cap into the pliable explosive while John held the flashlight. "Attach the wire, John." Hamish and John slowly backed up, as John played out a trail of insulated lamp cord from a small wooden spool.

"Okay, Hamish, you go up first." John followed immediately behind him, backing up the ladder, as the wire continued to uncoil. When he reached the storage room, he lobbed the spool over the counter, and then picked it up, half-running, and continued outside, all the while trailing the wire lead.

"Further back, over here, John. All clear, Sir?"

"Clear, Major!"

With electrician's pliers, Hamish cut the cord, then peeled away the last two inches of insulation. He attached a small detonator/plunger to the bare copper wire. "Here's mud in your eye, General!" he muttered, wincing as he depressed the plunger.

Nothing happened. "Hmmm." He pressed the plunger again. "Well, Johnny my boy, I'm thinking we pulled the damned wire off the cap! Care to draw lots and...." Just then a violent explosion shook the ground. The service station front door flew open and a greyish-black cloud of smoke and dust billowed out from the interior. "I think that beggar did it! Say, are you alright, Barney?"

The owner looked on, transfixed. His entire service establishment was engulfed in a sooty haze. The plate glass window had disappeared, a casualty of the blast. "Oh, sure, Sir, just fine and dandy!"

"We'll take a ten minute rest, men, to clear the air," ordered Colonel Graham. He stubbed out his cigarette on the asphalt and turned toward the sirens approaching from the west. "Looks like we woke somebody up, General. Sergeant, have your men barricade the entrance. Weapons on safety: stay calm. Do nothing unless I give the command."

"They're 'Holsteins', General, Ontario Provincial Police. Let me do the talking."

"Holsteins, Colonel?"

"You'll see in a moment." Two black and white Dodge sedans, their roof lights flashing, screeched to a halt at the turn-in. The passenger door of the lead vehicle flew open even before the emergency siren had spun down, and a stout, red-faced officer jumped out.

"Sergeant Purvis here, Whitby Detachment, OPP. Who's in charge?" The sergeant took a large handkerchief from his pocket and blew his nose loudly. "Someone want to speak up?"

"I am in charge, Sergeant. Colonel Gordon Graham. This is General Granite, Commander of Military District 2. If you have questions, I'll try to answer them."

"Well, actually, Colonel Graham, my Detachment Commander, Staff Sergeant Shea, has received several telephone inquiries concerning a loud explosion from this location and has instructed me to bring you in to the station to investigate the cause of the disturbance."

"I'm afraid that won't be possible, Sergeant."

"Excuse me, Colonel. Did I hear you correctly?"

"Yes, Sergeant, you did."

Purvis turned to his driver. "Call the station, Constable." His face beginning to deepen in colour, he continued, "I take it that you are refusing to comply with my request, Colonel Graham."

"With all due respect to you and your Staff Sergeant Shea, yes, I am."

"I see. Please remain here." Purvis walked back to his cruiser and leaned in the driver's window. He snatched the microphone from the outstretched hand of the constable who was about to hand it to him, and carried on a rapid-fire conversation, gesturing wildly in his frustration to the person at the other end.

"Keep the men rock steady, Colonel. We don't need to have an incident reported on the CBC six o'clock news tonight," muttered Constantine.

Sergeant Purvis walked slowly back to the waiting men. "Staff Sergeant Shea wants to know whether you men have anything to do with Camp X."

"I can't say that I know what you mean, Sergeant. Do you, General?"

Constantine shook his head, a blank expression on his face.

"Then where in blazes are you and all these soldiers from?"

"Military District 2, Sergeant."

The Sergeant's words were becoming more clipped and succinct. "And just where exactly is that?"

"Toronto. Beyond that, all is classified. Including this exercise. I can assure you that..."

Purvis finally blew! "Classified, my ass! You're on my beat and I want to know who the hell gave you permission to blow up Barney's service station!"

"Sergeant, Barney here is fully cognisant of the nature of our activities, aren't you, Barney?"

Barney nodded. "It's okay, Fred. Now, for Chrissake, just go away," he implored.

"Like hell I will! I'm not leaving without you, Colonel, and Barney, too!"

"Sergeant Purvis, we are engaged in a fully sanctioned military exercise on behalf of the Department of National Defence for the Dominion of Canada. I respect the fact that you are doing your duty as you see it. However, these men are authorized to use their weapons and will do, should I so order, which I will if you persist in interfering. You and your comrades are advised to leave, now! I shall call your Commander Shea and explain when I am ready to do so."

"Bull!" roared Purvis. "For all I know, Colonel, you guys are fifth column saboteurs. Three of my men are Fergus Police Games sharpshooter medallists and are prepared to bag the bunch of you; if you want to get into a shoot out, just keep it up!"

Without averting his gaze from Purvis, Colonel Graham shouted to Sergeant Parr. "Sergeant, have the men release their safeties and prepare to fire on my command." The soldiers in front knelt, raised their weapons, and trained them on the windows of the black and white 'Holstein' vehicles. Three police marksmen who had crept from the second car were crouched in firing position on the car's far side, their carbines laid across the hood, squarely aimed at the chests of the General, Colonel Graham, and Hamish.

"I assure you, Sergeant Purvis, this is a matter of national security. As such, it is none of your concern. Order your officers to stand down: we will do likewise. Should you persist in this confrontational manner, your actions will result in the avoidable deaths of your men, and will also lead to an inquiry which, I can assure you, will not conclude to your advantage."

"Time's running out, Colonel. Tell me where you are from and what caused the explosion."

"Sergeant Parr, prepare to fire."

General Constantine indicated with his right hand. "Excuse me, Colonel. May I speak with you privately?"

Sergeant Purvis, his face now beet-red in total frustration, sputtered, "No nonsense, General, if that is in fact what you are. Remember, we have you covered."

The Colonel turned his back disdainfully on the fuming Sergeant. "Well, General?"

"Gordon, we may be able to defuse this. Ask Purvis whether his radio can be patched through to RCMP HQ in Toronto. Perhaps Ted Reynolds can work it out with the OPP head man there. It's a long shot. What do you think?"

"I think it's at least worth a try, General."

"You ask him. The more removed I am from this, the better," ordered Constantine.

"Very well, General. Just so you know, Hamish and Beck have moved three men around the back to get Tommy guns and Mills bombs from the truck in the event that Purvis won't co-operate."

He turned back to Purvis. "Sergeant, I'd like to propose a truce to allow us the time to talk this through. I have a plan that might satisfy your needs as well as ours. Can your driver ask your detachment operator to patch through a call to RCMP Commissioner Ted Reynolds?"

"Of course he can, as long as you know the Mountie's number or call sign, or whatever. Then what, Colonel?"

"Will you permit me to approach your car in order to speak to your radioman? Here is my revolver," and Colonel Graham slowly removed the Colt from its holster. He handed the gun, handle first, to the policeman, and began to walk slowly toward the cruiser. The three poised rifle barrels edged slowly across the hood's curved surface, tracking his progress. Four army Enfield .303's covered the police shooters and Sergeant Purvis's large head.

"Halt, Colonel! Constable Delaney, frisk him."

All watched as Gordon Graham raised his arms and calmly endured a clumsy body search. Delaney patted down his tunic, then nodded affirmatively, "He's clean."

"Approach. Walk ahead of me...very slowly. And keep your hands high!"

A Bell Special Operator completed the preliminary electronic cross-patching necessary to allow the negotiations to begin. While this actually took only about ten minutes, to the General, it seemed to take hours. Neither he nor Purvis could have known that such hook-ups were, in fact, routine under an agreement made with Bell Telephone by Erik Williamson.

"General, both Commissioners wish a word with you," Graham called.

After another five minutes of security clearance code verification and mutual assurances, Sergeant Purvis was finally summoned to speak with OPP Commissioner Swan. A few seconds later, Purvis handed the mouthpiece to his driver. "It's okay, men. Stow your weapons."

Colonel Graham turned, faced Sergeant Parr, and made a downward motion with his right hand. Immediately, the Sergeant commanded, "Arms down! Detail, stand at ease! Stand easy."

The Colonel then extended his hand to Sergeant Purvis who had, by now, all but returned to his natural colouring. "Good day, Sergeant."

"No hard feelings. Thank you, Colonel, and my thanks to your General Granite as well. You know, I could swear I've seen you before. Ever been in the bar at the Genosha Hotel?"

"It's indeed possible that you have, Sergeant."

"Fred. Fred Purvis, Colonel."

"Well, Fred, if we should meet again in that den of iniquity, it's 'Gordon' and a tray of draughts are on me."

"I'll look forward to it! By the way, did you really think that you had the drop on my boys?"

"Fred, have you ever seen what a well-placed Type 35 Mills bomb or two can do under a motor car? Drive carefully."

Once the cruisers had departed, the Colonel, the General and men trooped back into the disorderly storage room. The wooden staircase, splintered by the explosion, was quickly replaced with a ladder. Once it was secured, the soldiers, led by a limping Hamish with John Beck close behind, descended to the dust-filled cavern. Anxiously, John shone his flashlight toward their handiwork then tilted the beam downward to reveal a blackened, still-smoking mass of concrete and steel on the ground. Kneeling, John let out a low whistle. "Damned if you didn't peel the blighter clean off its hinges, Hamish. Jolly good show. Care to inspect the damage, gentlemen?"

Graham and Constantine nodded their approval. "Excellent work. Let's carry on and find out where it leads. Sergeant?"

"Single file, men. Step carefully. Private Andy and I'll take the point. Use your lights sparingly. We'll need them when we get further down, and for the return trip. Colonel, General, please follow me. Forward!"

As they walked, the beam of the Sergeant's flashlight, refracted by the still-settling dust, dimly illuminated the tunnel's walls. Graham noted that the wooden timbers used as shoring to reinforce the sides were in remarkably good condition, considering their age and the dampness. He drew this to the attention of the General and Robert. "Waterproofed, Gordon," the General stated authoritatively. "Royal Naval shipyards, Bristol. Likely Canadian Douglas Fir, impregnated with creosote and tar. Take a whiff, up close."

The tunnel, approximately four feet wide and barely six feet high, forced several of the taller men to bow their heads as they proceeded. The ground appeared to be solid, composed of firm, if slightly sticky, clay. As they walked on, Graham reflected that they were all walking into military history, through a tunnel of time that likely had not been entered for some one hundred and thirty years. He pondered the significance of his realisation, but chose not to comment to the General.

They walked in silence for nearly twenty minutes. Finally, Graham called, "Sergeant, halt! Majors Findlay and Beck, a conference. Hamish, I'm getting concerned about the declining air quality. Do you estimate that we are almost at the end?"

"Well, Sir, John and I were noting how much damper it's becoming. The clay is certainly much soggier now. I'm beginning to think that we are out some distance under Lake Ontario."

"Major, I certainly hope we're close," commented the General. "My asthma's beginning to kick up. What do you think, Brooks?"

"I don't know, General, but it seems that we have been hiking forever," Brooks mused. "I'm as curious and anxious as you both to find out where this will end, either inside Camp X or under the lake."

"With the Colonel's permission, Major Beck and I will recce ahead."
"Permission granted, Major Findlay. Five minutes, no longer. How's the leg?"

"The bleeding's stopped. Right as rain again, thank you, Sir."

"Remind me never to play bridge with this bluffer in the Mess, eh, Colonel?"

"Believe me, I don't need reminding, General. Hamish and John, you two take fresh torches and have a look. Sergeant, the men can fall out. Smoking for those who have 'em! Cigarette, Robert?"

Hamish and John set out with fresh determination. They were quickly swallowed up by the darkness, as the faintly yellow bobbing beams of their flashlights became barely visible points of light in the distance, and then vanished completely.

The Colonel dropped his half-finished cigarette on the ground, and watched as its glowing tip quickly sputtered and died in the watery muck. "I hope to hell we're close. This is getting..."

"Sir, come ahead!" Hamish's distinctive voice echoed back, reverberating, "*Sir, come aheadddd!*"

"That's Hamish! Move, Sergeant!" Hamish and John were waiting when Graham, Constantine, and Brook arrived at what appeared to be the entrance to a chamber. As the members of the detail excitedly shone their torches around the walls, Graham did a quick calculation. He estimated it to be sixty feet wide by eighty feet long: some forty eight hundred square feet "My God, floor to ceiling it's sixteen feet, if it's an inch! I never imagined anything like this! What do you think, Colonel! Hello, what's this?" Constantine walked toward a rumpled cloth sack on the chamber floor. He stooped, shining his torch at it.

He whistled softly, then muttered, "Poor devil! It's a skeleton, Graham! I dare say it's an English soldier. Come, see for yourself!" The skull stared up at them, grimacing, sightlessly. Lying beside the remains was a long-barrel musket, its bayonet affixed.

Colonel Graham bent down, examining the faded shreds of a once-red uniform, tarnished brass buttons and buckle, and the gnarled husks of a leather belt and boots. "Hamish, John, come here, please."

While Hamish examined the bones, John Beck inspected the musket. "Royal Fusiliers, General," stated Hamish, "judging from this scrap of right epaulet...possibly a Lance Corporal's brevet on the arm. He's small, no more than five feet five inches, about average for those days. And he's young, just a laddie, I'd estimate, roughly fourteen, sixteen tops. You can judge the age relatively accurately by comparing the ratio of bone to cartilage down here on the back of the shin bone, above the ankle."

"What do you suppose happened to him, Colonel?" queried Robert.

"I don't know, but it may be that he was somehow left behind."

"Here, Sir, on the skull's left temple. Looks like a musket ball or possibly a bayonet creased and partially pushed in the temporal bone. It's quite thin there and that would have done him in. Maybe he was mortally wounded, but managed to fend off the enemy before dying" Hamish offered.

"Good hypothesis, Hamish. Ever consider a career in forensic medicine?" asked the General. "What have you found, John?"

"The hammer's down on the musket, General, and as there's no ball in the chamber; that would suggest that he had discharged the firearm. This discolouration of the metal plate and firing mechanism is mainly surface corrosion and rust. All in all, it can be cleaned up to make a beautiful museum period piece, I'd say," concluded Beck.

"If Majors Findlay and Beck's detective work is correct, General, then this very brave young fellow was killed in what was likely a rearguard action. Imagine that the enemy was attempting a forced entry from an overhead hatch of some sort, and our corporal here managed to secure it before he died. With this in mine, the opening can't be far away and we should be able to find it. Sergeant, see that this soldier's remains and personal effects are carefully gathered and taken back for proper burial. Major Findlay, will you supervise the collection and transfer?"

"An honour, Colonel. Sergeant, send two men, at once!"

"And Sergeant, order your men to explore with the greatest care and diligence. Make certain that they understand this area was the scene of an historic battle and will be treated with the respect due to a military grave," Constantine ordered. He turned aside to his companions. "Gordon, Robert, we've found a treasure trove. I'd like nothing better than to have the military history boys from the Royal Military College in Kingston down here to survey, photograph, and catalogue every square inch, but that will have to wait till after the war. For now, we'll work around it as best we can."

The men continued to explore the cave. They came across reminders of an all-but-forgotten bitterly fought contest, between Great Britain and The United States of America, for possession of Canada. One of the junior officers found a locked, metal strong box, tantalisingly heavy. Another discovered a bayonet, its blade bent near the tip, lying beside a partially opened wooden crate of rusted and pitted musket balls. Beck found a rotted sack, examined it and deduced that it had likely contained gunpowder. There was a cache of foodstuffs and supplies: unopened, faintly labelled crates of dried fruit and tea from the Orient, boots, books, including Bibles, Brazilian coffee, and Virginia flake tobacco.

While the men continued the search for relics, Constantine, Brook, and Graham withdrew to the entrance and quietly discussed their options. They agreed that their first priority was to determine where they were, relative to the Camp's layout, and then to determine how far below the surface they were.

Colonel Graham said that they couldn't be too far below ground as there was no evidence of a ladder or stairway. "The fact that the Corporal had his bayonet fixed would point to the likelihood that he was fighting, or preparing to fight, at close quarters. So, where's that damn opening? There's no sense having anyone probe the surface; after all, the Farm covers some two hundred and seventy five acres."

"Of course not, Gordon, that's hopelessly inefficient, the old 'needle in a haystack' approach. Time and tide, gentlemen, I can feel London breathing down my neck. Any other suggestions?" asked Constantine.

"Just one, Sir! Have the men pore over every inch of the chamber's ceiling. Agreed? Fine.

"Sergeant, I need you, here and now! We need six eight-foot lengths of steel reinforcing rods to use as probes, six heavy-duty hammers, work gloves, two eight-foot stepladders, and electric lights and fans down here. These damned batteries are running out.

"We also need canisters of fresh water, thermoses of hot coffee, and sandwiches. Major Beck, go with him and take three others along. When you get up there, drive your supply truck to Camp; you'll find the metal rods, gasoline generator, fans and portable emergency lighting in the machine shop.

"Make sure you get a long, long spool of one twenty-volt wire, not thick cable. Ask the QM to find whatever else you need! Do not tell him why, got that Major? Have the Sergeant and Barney fire up the generator as far away from the hole in the floor as they can. We don't want to be asphyxiated. Then lower the wiring and everything else down the hatch with ropes. We'll all transport it from there.

"Also, have them set up an electric fan to blow full speed down the shaft. This air is getting rank. Open all the station doors wide, although I suppose that's not necessary, is it, since we blew out the window? One last item: we'll need something suitable in which to carry back the Corporal's remains. See what you can do."

"Alright men, rest easy. We have to wait for the equipment. Hot coffee and food are on the way."

Within two hours, they were up and running, powered by electricity, fresh air, tuna and ham sandwiches and caffeine.

"Well, General, it's almost 1800 hours. Let's hope for the best."

"Your team is phenomenal, Gordon. I think we'll have our breakthrough tonight. And if we don't, my guess is that Williamson's going to be euchred by a contingent of the Whitehall brass and political types who're salivating to turn it over to the Americans in return for a walloping big fee."

Moments later Hamish shouted, "Sir, we've found something. Could you come here, please?" Graham and the others walked over to investigate.

"What is it, Major Findlay?" asked Graham.

"I'm not sure, Sir; the ceiling at this spot has given way. These mounds of earth on the floor aren't at any other spot in the room. Perhaps pressure from above has caused the ground to weaken."

"You're right Hamish; you men, over here! Bring your ladders and probes," commanded Graham. Turning to Constantine he asked, "So, General, what do you think? Is this a place where you could hide Britain's gold with confidence?"

"Absolutely, Gordon! This is perfect. I'm only concerned about our fellow Barney running off at the mouth, bragging to his friends after a drink or three."

"Not to worry, Sir, I'll take care of him, I assure you." As the men hammered away at the ceiling of the room it became apparent that it would take time and care to chip away at the soil to open a passageway without causing a cave-in.

After more than an hour of painstaking labour, a voice suddenly called out excitedly, "We've broken through, Colonel!"

Graham looked up at the ceiling to where the man's probe was embedded. "I can't see anything, Private."

The soldier, standing on the top rung of a ladder, withdrew his probe. "Sorry, Sir, one moment." With a powerful upward thrust the steel rod struck something solid. "Look out below!" he shouted as wooden splinters, gravel and clumps of soil showered Colonel Graham. "Are you alright, Sir?"

"Yes, yes, I'm fine, Private" he called back, brushing the debris from his face and shoulders. "You've done it! I'll be damned!" A cool, fresh lake breeze, carrying the earthy smell of a fall evening, wafted through the small hole. "General Constantine, come here! Earle and Harry, break away the rest of that hatch cover and earth, carefully. The rest stand clear below." After fifteen minutes, the opening was large enough to allow a body to squeeze through. "Good work, men. Now keep going, we need it at least five feet wide! Sergeant, bring me that grappling hook and line," directed Graham. After another quarter hour, the Colonel halted the excavation. "Who wants the honour? I expected so, Findlay. Here, have a go, then. And if you miss, Beck is next in line."

With the group clustered about him, staring upward in silent wonder, like tourists in Rome viewing the Sistine Chapel ceiling for the first time, Hamish announced calmly, "Back, please, I'd hate to knock anyone ass over teakettle, begging your pardons, gentlemen." Holding the hook and coiled line in his right hand he threw it up as hard as he could. The anchor-like hook disappeared through the hole, and caught. "Bullseye! Bloody good show! Good shot, Major! Made it, Sir!" As was expected, it was approximately sixteen feet up to the surface. Hamish tugged on the dangling rope, then, judging it secure, began shinnying up, wondering with anticipation where he would emerge.

As his head emerged, he looked up, directly into the barrel of a Colt .45. Private Mac, feet firmly planted apart, stood incredulous, witnessing a senior officer popping out of a hole in the ground. "Halt, Sir! What's the password?"

"Password? Password be damned! You scared the daylights out of me, Mac!" exclaimed Hamish.

"Sorry, Major. Here, let me give you a hand, Sir. I've been expecting somethin' unusual this evening, what with all the commotion at the gate at noon, men and trucks moving out, special equipment being loaded, but this sure beats all. When I saw that hook come flying up, I thought, 'I'll bet Major Findlay's...'"

Private Mac McDonald welcomes Hamish emerging from the Great Room.

"Thanks, Private." Smiling, Hamish reached up for the burly guard's hand, extended to assist him. Once standing, he looked around. "So, this is the place!" He picked up a piece of rock, examined it pensively, then ordered, "Stay here until I say otherwise, Mac. If anyone approaches, order him back to his barracks, no guff, and no questions! If someone gives you lip, it is critical to arrest, cuff and blindfold him, then get him far away, at once. "

"Did you say, 'anyone', Major Findlay?"

"Anyone, Private, including officers! Now, I'm going back down. Carry on."

Before Hamish had finished his descent to the 'cave' he shouted down breathlessly, "Colonel, General, you may not believe this, but the reason for the loose soil here is that we're smack under the exact spot where I'd set off training explosions. We're almost at the lake. Wait till you see. I'll pop up and fetch an extension ladder."

When Hamish and Mac had lowered the ladder, the men climbed out into the fresh evening air. As they stood or knelt on the surface, each reflected quietly on what had just transpired. Colonel Graham broke the silence, "Gentlemen, I believe the mystery of the death of our brave Fusilier comrade can be solved. Look over there, at that large boulder." Fifteen feet away sat a massive piece of granite. "I'm willing to wager that, had we the time, and a tank to move it, we'd find that the original entranceway lies buried beneath that rock. There's a Doctorate in military history if ever I saw one, waiting for some lucky bloke.

"But, to the matters at hand. Major Findlay, look to bringing up the soldier's remains, please. Take him to the Lecture Hall for tonight and we'll deal with the burial details tomorrow.

"Beck, I want men posted twenty-four hours a day at the gas station.

It is closed to business, permanently. See to that straightaway. I'll make the usual telephone calls to the oil company's head office first thing tomorrow. I want a guard posted in the 'Great Room' and I want a two-man detail here at ground level. I also want a steel door installed at the entrance to the cavern, and concrete steps installed from here down.

"Furthermore, I want a mechanized steel door built in at this ground level entrance. I'll break the news to Quartermaster Jones and have him look into arranging a contractor to handle the engineering details. Gentlemen, as you return to your quarters, you will remember that you are ordered not to breathe a word to anyone regarding today's events." He paused. "My most sincere thanks, to all of you, for your superb efforts. There's much more to be done, but it was an excellent beginning. Dismissed."

Graham turned to Brooke and Constantine, "What did I forget, General?"

"Very thorough, Colonel. Robert and I have our work cut out," Constantine replied, "as do you. If you should happen to bring up that strongbox, Gordon, please let me know what's inside. I'm dying to find out."

"Sir, I solemnly promise I'll let you know the moment we open it," replied Graham. "I want to bury the soldier's remains tomorrow, General. May I call you in the morning for your official approval? You must be exhausted and I'm certain you want to get back to Toronto. By a coincidence, Ted Reynolds of the RCMP said he'd drop in late tonight on his way to Brockville. I'll not say anything at this time. Let me walk you to your car."

The next day, at 1100 hours, the men and women of the Camp gathered at the Union Cemetery in Oshawa for a brief, formal burial service for an unknown British corporal. They were not told of the circumstances leading to the discovery of the body, only that he was almost certainly a casualty of the 1812 War, whose remains were found during a routine excavation on the Camp grounds.

Following the ceremony, Lieutenant-Colonel Graham invited Majors Beck, Findlay, Sampson and Jones to the CO's residence, for tea. Colonel Graham briefed Samson and Jones, while the others stared at the severely corroded strongbox sitting in the middle of the living room floor. Graham instructed Brian Jones to remove the lock with the metal cutters on hand for that purpose. Once the lock was free of the box, they held their breath as the Colonel took out and unfolded his penknife and pried open the lid. There was dead silence as they all edged closer to look inside.

"Rocks. A box of stones, gentlemen! It's probably not so much a practical joke as a case of creating a little diversion from the real cash box. Well, men, I thought that it was too good to be true. At least it should serve as a valuable museum piece, somewhere. Now, if you don't mind, I have some business that needs my attention."

Barney Simms, the service station owner, was awarded a more-than-reasonable annuity in compensation for his service station, and fast-tracked into the Royal Canadian Service Corps, with the rank of Corporal. He was assigned duty as a guard and bartender in the Officers' Mess at Camp Borden. Two hours before his bus was scheduled to leave the Bay Street Bus Terminal, a Mr. Wallace called his hotel room and invited him to lunch at Simpson's Arcadian Court Restaurant.

The affable Mr. Wallace reminded him quietly over their Waldorf salads, that as a member of BSO, British Security Organisation, he, Barney, was forever bound by his oath of secrecy, which, if breached, would render him subject to 'the full horror of His Majesty's laws'. Afterwards, Robert Brooks wired Erik Williamson to report that he was fully confident that 'the subject' would never divulge what had taken place.

Earlier that same morning, General Constantine sent an encoded message through Camp X to Warden, (Churchill's code name):
'WARDEN MUST COME VISIT YOUR FAMILY IMMEDIATELY STOP
WILL MAKE ARRANGEMENTS FORTHWITH STOP
PLEASE ADVISE EARLIEST POSSIBLE STOP
GRANITE STOP
-30-'

What Constantine had to tell Churchill could not be entrusted even to highly secure BSO coding. There was absolutely no allowance for the possibility that this memorandum would be intercepted. Constantine would personally carry the plan for the disposition of Great Britain's gold to Warden.

Mid-afternoon, the Camp X Hydra radio room received an 'OU' Top Priority signal through Bletchley Park. Chief Wireless Operator, Yorkie Hardcastle, realising the importance of an OU heading, tore off his headphones and fed the one-inch wide punched paper tape directly into the Rockex decoding machine. Across the room a Bell teleprinter responded, spewing out characters onto a continuous roll of eight-and-a-half by eleven-inch sheets. When the printer stopped chattering, Bill tore off the message, and in his shirtsleeves, dashed out of Hydra and across the road to the CO's residence. Betty, the CO's Personal Assistant, reacted with characteristic charm and efficiency. "Coffee, Yorkie?" Then, "Colonel, Yorkie is here with an OU level signal in clear. Shall I send him in?"

"Yes, please do."

"Thank you for your prompt action, Yorkie. Carry on. Dismissed."

'Now then, what's all this about?' Graham mused. As he began to read, he quickly realised that the concise note he now held in his hand possibly ranked first among the very short list of top priority wires that Hydra had processed:

"'GRANITE' FAMILY LOOKS FORWARD TO SEEING YOU ASAP STOP

WILL ARRANGE DINNER IMMEDIATELY YOU ARRIVE STOP

WARDEN STOP."

As he read the memo he walked directly to the secure telephone and dialled General Constantine. "General, Gordon here. I have a package for you, from Warden."

"Thank you. Would you please be kind enough to have your driver deliver it to me directly?" asked Constantine.

"Of course, Sir. Good day."

Graham hung up the telephone and buzzed Betty, asking her to locate Private Mac and have him report to his office. When he arrived, the Colonel ordered, "Mac, you are to courier this message to General Constantine, downtown. Spring another guard for company and be on your way directly. No allowance for balls-ups or dawdling, Private! Get it there, or never mind coming back. There is no other option. Take my automobile. I'll ring the motor pool. Treat it well, mind, and do make every effort to avoid another speeding ticket, as per your last...adventure. Here's a blank chit to cover you both for supper. Not the Royal York!"

He smiled slightly, inserting the folded paper into a plain white envelope and then sealing it. Mac saluted, took the package, and slipped it inside his tunic.

"My word of honour, Sir. Like a newborn baby. No summonses, scratches or dings, and the package will arrive in record time. Supper at Fran's on St. Clair, Sir!" As he hurried toward the garage, he recognised his pal, Andy, jogging past. "Hey, Andy, are you on duty? Good enough, come here! Listen, the CO says you're to help me take an important message to the brass in Toronto. Go get the Colonel's limo from the motor pool, make sure it's gassed up, and meet me at the gate. And hurry. After, we can grab a decent bite and put it on the cuff, courtesy of Colonel Graham." Minutes later, Mac and Andy were off to Toronto to complete their mission.

"So, what's the big bloody rush, Mac?"

"How the hell would I know? What the Colonel wants, the Colonel gets. And in this case, my friend, it's a do or die delivery downtown to the District Commander. Now just sit back and watch for OPP!"

"Hey, Mac, you know what? Montreal's playing an exhibition at the Gardens tonight!"

" 'Lead us not into temptation,' Andy, my boy. Deliver, dinner, and 'do no evil.' Colonel's orders! Too bad, but I'll bet there aren't any tickets between here and East Borneo, anyway!"

The loud drone of a Mosquito's twin Rolls Royce Merlin engines as it flew over the Oshawa Airport tower nearly drowned out Foster Hewitt's play-by-play CBC radio broadcast of the Leafs vs. Canadiens hockey game being piped into the cramped waiting area. 'A one-one tie, starting the third period; wouldn't you know it!' Even if it was only an exhibition game, it was the Leafs against their old archrivals, the Montreal 'Habs.' Constantine seldom missed listening to a Toronto Maple Leafs match, but this one time, it would have to go by the boards.

The airport manager looked up from his *Toronto Telegram's* sports pages and noticed the General, his fingers drumming nervously on the chipped counter top. "Any signs of improvement in the weather?" the General asked. An unusually dense bank of fog had rolled in from the lake, rendering visibility, at least at ground level, virtually nil. Constantine, a cavalry man from the get-go, and an unenthusiastic flyer at the best of times, disliked the idea of taking off unless conditions were CAVU (ceiling and visibility unlimited). The manager assured the frowning General that the crew always flew by instruments at night, and wouldn't take off if conditions were the least bit hazardous. Between them, he emphasized, this pilot and navigator had logged thousands of hours on Mosquitoes. 'How very reassuring,' thought the General.

Once on board, the General nervously tightened the buckle of the canvas lap strap. Turning to him, the pilot said, "Welcome aboard the wooden wonder, General!" Constantine flinched. "I'm Flight Lieutenant Harris and this is First Officer Norrie. I hope you don't mind the full load, Sir, but I have to deliver these four ninety-day-wonder flyboys to Gander. From there, they will be travelling on to London with you."

"No, not at all, Flight Lieutenant. I'm happy to have the company."

The flight proved to be uneventful, as promised, until the approach to Gander. Just as the Mosquito touched down, a crosswind suddenly caught the underside of the starboard wing, lifting the right wheel clear of the runway. The aircraft careened lopsidedly toward the edge of the asphalt, its engines whining in protest as the pilot reversed the pitch of the propellers. After what seemed an eternity, the plane shuddered violently as its right wheel regained contact with the ground and it taxied to a stop close to a row of hangars. When the General's feet touched the tarmac, an ashen-faced Harris was waiting for him. "My apologies, General, but the wind shear around here can be dicey! Lucky for us, First Officer Norrie had it under control, all the way."

"I'm glad of that! I'm quite alright now, thank you, Flight. By the way, , where is Norrie?"

"Oh, he's in the washroom, Sir. Throwing up!"

The base CO was waiting for him in a Jeep on the edge of the runway. "Sir, I trust that you had a good flight, the landing excepted? I hope that our flyboys in the back weren't too rowdy. They're full of piss and vinegar and just itching to jump into the fight."

"Yes, thanks, Commandant, the flight was pleasant enough and the boys behaved themselves commendably. I heard a lot of Polish and Dutch and God knows what else; quite a mix we're sending over these days" replied the General.

"We have a new DC-3 all fuelled and waiting to go. But, guessing that you might be too tired to get right back on board and head straight out again, I thought I'd best check with you first, Sir. Would you like to rest overnight, then head out first thing in the morning?" asked the CO.

"I rather think that I would like that. I'm sure that I would feel better about flying over water if at least it were daylight" replied Constantine.

"Perfectly sensible, Sir. We'll set you up at a local tourist home just down the street. Very comfy, quiet and you won't be bothered a tick. I'll have someone call on you at 0630 hours. There will be a warm bath ready for you, a large breakfast, then we'll have you on your way. Oh yes, I should mention that you will be flying into a new base in Northern

Scotland, just routine, Sir, to avoid the Jerries. From there I understand that you will travel south via British Rail. Completely safe they tell me," added the CO.

'That makes me nervous,' thought Constantine.

The General alternately studied the papers in front of him and gazed out of the porthole window of the DC-3. He was morbidly fascinated by the occasional glimpses of the vast and seemingly boundless body of water. Two of the young aviators were chatting quietly; the others were asleep. As he stared out the window, he thought about his impending meeting with Churchill. 'Have I covered everything? Have I missed anything? Is the plan good enough? Yes, it is an excellent plan, and I'll see to it that it works'.

"The much anticipated General Constantine, from Canada, my Lords, my Lady, ladies and gentlemen. General, I won't bore you with the usual interrogations about your flight or the state of your equilibrium. Pray tell us the solution you have brought for us."

"Thank you, Prime Minister. If I may make use of your chalkboard, it may save us time. It will also give you a clearer picture not only of the setting, but of our transportation and security plans."

"Proceed, General. We are your captives."

Forty-five minutes later, Sir Willson Cunnington rose to his feet. "Brilliant, General. Beautifully crafted! And to think it all began from a yarn told to one of your men by a petrol station attendant! How long will it be before the Great Room is ready to receive the goods?"

"Our most optimistic estimate of the time it will actually take to cross the Atlantic, offload from the ship directly onto the CN/CP special rail cars, and transport from the Port of Halifax to the Camp, is two weeks. The room will be fully readied, well before that, Sir."

"General, I can tell you that Sir Will's enthusiasm speaks on behalf of each of us, am I correct? Need we take a vote? No? Champion!

"General, I must say that rarely have we reached complete accord so quickly. It speaks volumes for your superb preparation, and sterling presentation, I might add. Excellent, indeed! I'm afraid that our endorsement of your scheme, however, means that you are going to be a very busy man over the next day or two. You must meet some key people, straightaway. In truth, for the past hour I've had them waiting to pounce and take you to task in an anteroom if your plan seemed flawed or worse. I shall assure them that this will not be necessary and that you can get down to talking turkey immediately. Let me introduce you to the British half of Operation, shall we say, 'Balthazar'?"

"Balthazar, Sir?"

"Yes, you know, he was one of the Wise Men, the King, who brought the gift of gold."

"Yes, certainly, Prime Minister."

In Toronto, a woman approached a ticket booth at Union Station.

"Good afternoon, what can I do for you?"

"I would like one return ticket to Montreal, please. I have to travel to my grandson's tenth birthday party. I wouldn't miss it for the world."

"Yes, Madam, and when would you like to leave?"

"Tomorrow, in the afternoon, please."

"Oh, I'm sorry, Madam, we've been informed that there has been an emergency declared due to a derailment involving dangerous goods in the Oshawa area. The CN/CP lines are closed, possibly for up to ninety-six hours."

"Ninety-six hours! But I need to be there tomorrow night."

"I understand, Madam, but there's absolutely nothing I or anyone can do. You might want to check the Toronto to Montreal bus schedule with Grey Coach at the Bay Street Terminal. I believe they may be adding extra busses. It's just a few minutes from here. Thank you."

The great vessel edged towards its slip, gently kissing the massive timbers of the wharf in the Shearwater Naval Base, Dartmouth, Nova Scotia. The twin propellers reversed thrust, thrashing up a spray of oil-slicked foam until the ship was snuggled alongside, then stopped. The deckhands, with practised precision, flung rope hawsers down to the waiting naval shipyard hands, who quickly secured them to four, stout, salt and rust-crusted capstans. Twelve Naval Shore Patrolmen stood at attention on the dock, the barrels of their rifles glinting in the setting sun. As soon as the ship began flushing its bilges, a flock of mewing seagulls appeared over its stern, which bore the name, *The Royal Anthem*.

"Secure, Mr. Jones?" the Captain shouted down to the First Officer.

"Aye, aye, Sir. All secure!"

"Lower the gang plank, Mr. Jones!" He turned to his VIP passenger. "I hope you've found everything satisfactory, General."

"Captain Shaw, my compliments on a smooth and remarkably uneventful voyage. They told me that I was sailing with the very best, and you have certainly confirmed it" replied General Constantine.

"Thank you, very much, General. It has been a pleasure. I can't take all of the credit, however. My ship is blessed with an exceptional crew. I'm not sure what the freight in the hold comprises, but I realise that it must be of the utmost importance. My men and I are proud to have brought you, and your goods, here safely. May I accompany you down the gangplank, Sir?"

"Yes, thank you. Tell me, Captain, now that we're almost on terra firma, were you worried at any time about enemy attacks: submarines, aircraft, destroyers...?"

"Honestly? Every minute," he chuckled. "But, if it's any consolation, General Constantine, our friends in the British Admiralty and Royal Canadian Navy Maritime Command were never far away, and we steered far North of the usual submarine lairs. We were recently outfitted with some fairly advanced electronic gizmos, which certainly helped us stay out of harm's way."

"Ah, land, at last! Captain Shaw, we will wait until 0100 hours, then we will begin. Naval Command at the Base should have made all necessary arrangements to unload the cargo and transport it to the rail siding. I ordered night lighting and cranes to move those crates. I think I'd better pop over to Naval HQ to make certain we have..."

Just then a jeep pulled onto the quay in front of them. A Royal Canadian Navy Captain and an Army Colonel jumped out and saluted smartly.

"Captain Smith, Sir, bringing you greetings from Base Commander Rear-Admiral Thompson. He will be joining you shortly," stated the Captain. "Colonel Patterson and I have arranged for the equipment you require, along with fifty guards and one hundred Able Seaman and soldiers at the ready to take care of the offloading and transfer of your cargo to the siding, Sir!"

"Excellent. Thank you, Captain, Colonel. I'm impressed that our two senior services mesh so well together! I do look forward to meeting the Admiral. Except for the guard detail, you can have the men stand down; we have to wait several hours before beginning at 0100. Please post your sentries dockside and onboard *The Royal Anthem* now,

Gentlemen. Captain Shaw will escort you aboard. You will advise the guards that this operation is of the greatest importance and that security must be absolutely airtight.

"Furthermore, I am authorizing you both to issue 'shoot to kill' orders until I signify otherwise. No one, except your people, I repeat, no one else, gets within a mile of here. Carry on, Gentlemen."

"Okay Colonel, let's begin. Have your men start unloading the cargo onto the trucks and then move them over to the siding." At 0100, as scheduled, the operation commenced. Ten high-wattage spotlights mounted on two immense naval dock cranes provided near-daylight illumination. General Constantine and Admiral Thompson watched as the long boxes were swung up and out of the ship's hold and then neatly deposited in precise rows on the backs of a convoy of twenty transports.

Each truck, when loaded to capacity, drove slowly to the nearby rail siding where an endless line of boxcars equipped with winches lifted the crates from the flatbeds into the containers. "Fifty per car, Colonel," Constantine instructed. "No more, no less. It's going nicely, Admiral. Let's get the remainder on board and then we'll be off." Privately, he wondered if there were enough rail cars to hold the entire consignment of freight.

An hour and forty-five minutes later, the cargo was completely loaded and the train was ready to pull out. "Admiral, Captain, my sincerest thanks. I will be in touch. Colonel Patterson and I must make tracks," the General said, smiling. "Colonel, please post your guards throughout the cars in whatever manner you see fit. Just make sure that we have plenty of protection. You may ride with me in the caboose, if you'd like."

"Thank you, General, I would!" Colonel Patterson replied, enthusiastically. "I haven't had a train ride since I was shipped out to summer cadet camp in Alberta!"

"Good. Then if you're ready, you can drive us first to the front of the train to meet the Engineer, then back to our post at the rear."

The train, already under steam, pulled very slowly away as the two men clambered up and into the caboose. Once they had introduced themselves to the Conductor, they settled in for the sixteen-hour journey.

The long freight train rolled along the tracks in the darkness while in the caboose, an exhausted General Constantine and Colonel Patterson slept in their seats, huddled under blankets the porter had provided. When the first rays of the rising sun came through his window, General Constantine awoke with a start. He had been dreaming about German-speaking masked desperadoes ambushing his train.

There was a knock on the door.

"Come in!" he muttered.

"Good morning, General. Sir, may I get you tea or coffee before breakfast?" asked the porter, mildly.

"Tea would be fine, thank you. The Colonel is likely awake by now, too."

"Yes, I am, thanks. Good morning. Hot coffee would be great, thank you."

"Do you have any idea where we are?" the General asked.

"Yes, we're in Quebec," replied the porter. "Another eight hours and we should have reached your destination. I'll be back directly with your beverages. Then, you can order your meals. I must tell you that our Chef Paul is a world class Canadian chef."

"That certainly sounds promising, as long as 'Chef Paul' can rustle up old-fashioned bacon, extra crisp, with scrambled eggs and toast," General Constantine remarked, smiling at the effusive porter. "Let's freshen up, Colonel, then we'll see what Maestro Chef Paul has to offer."

"We're within the yard limit of Whitby, Gentlemen; less than five minutes."

Gradually the train began to slow as the engineer backed off the throttle, applied the brakes, and brought the rolling stock to a halt. It lurched backward, stopped, then lurched forward, and came to its final rest. A last great blast of steam, then all was suddenly and eerily silent.

"Feels like we're still moving, eh Colonel?" the General remarked opening the back door of the caboose. He stepped out onto the small landing and looked about. He saw a familiar face in a jeep, fast approaching and now parallel with the rear of the train.

"General Constantine, welcome!"

"Gordon, how good to see you again!"

"Did you have a pleasant trip, Sir?"

"Couldn't have been better. I slept like the dead. No attacks by vigilantes, either."

"And our cargo, Sir?" asked Colonel Graham, missing the General's drift.

"Safe as Fort Knox," he smiled, "and ready for your boys to start offloading. Come aboard and we'll discuss how we're going to go about this. Gordon, I would like you to meet Colonel Patterson who helped me immensely. Now, to get down to business; what does your plan entail?"

"General, I have a convoy of twelve trucks which we've obtained from your Quartermaster John Ferguson at MD2. We're going to back each truck up to the siding doors and load the cargo onto the trucks, each to the weight limit minus twenty percent for good measure. Each truck will be manned with a signalman beside the driver, as well as with two armed guards, one on either running board.

"The cargo will be driven to the mouth of the tunnel, where Camp personnel will unload the boxes and take them into the Great Room. We are extremely well protected. In addition to your soldiers, twenty of our men will be carrying out foot and mobile patrols of the entire Camp perimeter. Furthermore, we have arranged with Ted Reynolds for two RCMP motor launches to be on water front patrol. Hamish will be in the air with an observer during the entire operation. They will be in constant radio contact. I can assure you, General, no one is getting anywhere close to the booty."

"Then let's get underway. Pray that the plan is foolproof, Colonel Graham."

The Colonel opened the door and stepped down from the caboose. "Major, tell the men to start the trucks and move them into their positions."

As the doors of the boxcars rattled open, the convoy flashed on their headlights and advanced toward the first twelve. When each truck was in position, two men offloaded the small crates, one at a time, passing them to two handlers on the truck whose job it was to stack them carefully.

The loaded truck then proceeded down Thornton Road to the entrance of Camp X where it turned in through the gate, drove several hundred feet to the perimeter roads, and turned south toward Lake Ontario. As the first truck pulled up to the entrance of the Great Room, Colonel Graham was waiting to supervise the storage of the cargo.

"Very well done, men! Major Findlay has designed this pulley system. All you need do is place each crate in the carrier platform and someone below will lower it. Major Heaviside is underground to supervise the storage. Right then, begin."

Painstakingly, each crate was removed from the truck by two men and placed on the lift platform. Inside the Great Room, Major Heaviside instructed his men to place the crates neatly against the far wall and to stack them four crates high. It took eight hours to remove every crate from the train, transfer and transport them, and then store them in the Great Room.

"Colonel, please have your radio room chaps send an OU message to BSO HQ. To:

"WARDEN AND STALWART STOP

OPERATION BALTHAZAR COMPLETED AT 0245 STOP

GRANITE"

"Impressive job, Colonel Graham! Well done. Not a hitch, eh Patterson?"

"A textbook exercise, General."

"Shall we nip up to the mess and see if the liquor cabinet key is still under the potted palm? Did we forget something, General?"

"Almost. Gordon, will you first look after sending the 'all clear' to the railways' regional dispatch office? Then, I think a little celebration would certainly be in order."

Shortly after, the train proceeded to the marshalling yards at General Motors in Oshawa where it was loaded with a shipment of armoured personnel vehicles. The CN/CP rail lines were re-opened, and a very happy grandmother enjoyed an uninterrupted return journey from Montreal to Toronto Union Station.

CHAPTER 4

CODENAME: TENT PEG

Colonel Graham's expression abruptly shifted from apprehension to curiosity, then, finally, to indignation. "Mason, I say, is that you? Stand up, man. What in the blazes do you think you're doing out here, spying on me? Keep your hands in plain view!"

Shivering almost uncontrollably from exposure, Hugh cautiously stood up, his hands held high, palms outward. He realised that his dream of making the grade as an SOE secret agent was presently and precariously balanced with the prospect of his being hanged as a spy. The next fifteen seconds could well determine his fate: his dream of a graduation could instead turn to the nightmare of a disciplinary hearing, or worse, a career-ending court martial. It all depended on the outcome of this awkward, almost grotesquely embarrassing encounter with the Commandant.

The possibility of a dishonourable discharge followed by a long prison sentence was nothing less than daunting. Were he unable to muster the clarity of mind he desperately needed to give a believable account of himself, his future as he imagined it would be shattered completely. He would disappoint every person he cared for and admired; his mother, his father's memory, Erik Williamson, his Camp X classmates, his BSO colleagues at the Castle, and, most of all, Hugh Fredric Mason. "Yes, Sir. It is Mason. I know I'm pretty far off base Colonel, but may I please have a moment to explain myself, Sir?"

The Commandant imperceptibly lowered his revolver. "Approach, very slowly, hands on your head. I don't relish the thought of shooting you in cold blood, at least until I've heard your explanation for this behaviour. Are you armed, Mason?"

"No, Sir."

"Permit me to verify that. Stand here. Back towards me. Don't move a hair." The pat down, though quick, was thorough. Hugh heard the snick of the Colonel's revolver holster fastener. "Very well. Come inside quickly. It's a cool night to be standing out here. This had better be good, Mason, and brief. The only reason I'm bothering to listen to you and not have you thrown into a cell, is your exemplary conduct and training record."

Seated in front of an electric space heater in the Colonel's sitting room, Hugh gradually warmed up as he recounted the steps that had led to his situation. The Colonel nodded from time to time, saying nothing.

"That's all, Sir...just wandering, without any thought to where I was."

"Anything to add, Mason?"

"No, Colonel."

"I see. Hot cocoa?"

"Yes. Yes, Sir, please..."

Hugh waited while the Colonel went to the kitchenette. Moments later, he heard the whistle of a boiling kettle and, "I'll be there in a jiffy."

Colonel Graham returned with two seaming mugs. "I must say, it's too farfetched and too strange a tale to be make-believe. Either that, or the chaps downtown recruited the world's greatest pathological liar." He sat down, levelled his gaze, and with a new and ominous tone to his voice, added, "Or perhaps you are a double agent."

A split second passed, as his words made their impact. Then he resumed, more affably, "Here's your drink. Be careful, it's hot. Fortunately, Mason, I know your history with this whole regrettable affair."

"Yes, Sir. No, Sir, I mean.... Truthfully, no, Sir, I'm not a spy and I'm not a liar."

"I know that. I apologise if my words just now were offensive. However, I must tell you a few things.

"First and foremost, I cannot discuss the incident at Rice Lake, not now, not ever. That is final, Mason. Categorically. I warn you as your Commanding Officer, do not pursue that subject any further. If you do, it will come a cropper and I'll see to it that you're appropriately dealt with.

"Secondly, you have almost completed your ten week training stint here, Hugh. Your suitability reports have been consistently excellent. If Beaulieu were operating, I would have no hesitation in recommending your appointment there. Even here, at STS 103, for that matter, although you're still 'green' and completely inexperienced as a field officer, I can spot remarkable talent. There are most urgent issues at hand requiring a consummate professional: a person of high intelligence, and of unquestionable character, who shows initiative, and who has demonstrated the highest level of leadership. He must also be capable of being, and willing to be, a team player.

"One of the top priorities is an overseas assignment...quite risky, actually, and wholly voluntary. Please be in my office tomorrow morning, at 1130 hours. Now, back to your quarters. You may count your lucky stars that I found you skulking about and not a less understanding Officer. Good night, Mason. Eleven-thirty sharp. Go with care, lad!"

"Thank you. I intend to, Colonel. My sincerest apologies, again, for this incident. Good night."

"Are you fully recovered from your flight, Sylvia?"

"Almost, thank you, Colonel. It was chilly, noisy, and rather bumpy, although a sight better than seven days of seasickness. I must say that my travelling companion, Mr. Williamson, was very pleasant and most considerate."

"I won't waste your time with unnecessary prattle. 'Desperate times call for desperate measures'. Trite, but true, isn't it Sylvia? I must be frank; the odds of your safe return from Tent Peg are less than even. What we're asking of you, essentially, is to single-handedly eliminate the world's most closely tended head of state. 'Assassinate' is such an unpleasant word; it conjures memories of Sarajevo, the Archduke Ferdinand, and the chaos of the Great War. Nevertheless, that is what you are being asked to do.

"You will have the support of some quarters of the anti-government German Resistance, as well as our own operatives, but I feel it is my moral responsibility and professional duty to reiterate that this is a one-person show.

"Whether you succeed or fail, Sylvia, I needn't remind you that will be tracked, trailed, and hounded in a massive dragnet consisting of tens of thousands of the most fanatical, dedicated and efficient professionals in the world. This doesn't even take into account the legions of secret police snitches, informers and a civilian population of millions, all slavering after the king's ransom that will be on your head. We are preparing contingency plans..."

"I beg you pardon, Colonel Graham, but I have gone over, around and through this quite thoroughly, both with Mr. Williamson and with the Prime Minister," she said, softly.

"Then you are quite certain that you wish to commit? You understand that you may back out at any time, Sylvia, right up to the very last second before the drop; no questions, no recriminations, no apologies, and no dishonour."

"There's no question in my mind, at all. Colonel Graham, I am not suicidal; I fully intend to complete the assignment, evade the hounds, and return to live to a disgustingly ripe old age in Canada. I will do it, provided that my Joanna is looked after, in Canada, now, during and afterwards, and that my parents will be relocated here as well."

"You know that you have our solemn word on both those points, Sylvia. The Toronto office has taken care of their transportation and residence. You'll be seeing them all shortly."

"Very well, Colonel Graham. When do I begin my training?"

"This morning. I have arranged for you to be listed on the Camp staff roster; you are extremely well qualified, an honours graduate of Beaulieu. In addition, you have been awarded the rank and allowance of Captain, in the British Army. Congratulations! Adjutant Major Jones will see to the paper work and the required details with the District Military Office. Of course, you'll be paid according to your rank. Jones will see to it that your pay is deposited in Whitby, Oshawa, Toronto, or any other branch account at a bank of your choosing.

"Expect to be the object of considerable interest and attention, here at 103, at least for the first while. Your official duties will be limited. You will attend an occasional lecture on whichever section of the Syllabus is being studied at the time, and no more than once, or at the most, twice a week, in order to keep up appearances. Moreover, speaking of appearances, you must be fitted for a British Army uniform, straight away. I've arranged that a military tailor from an established and very respectable Toronto company will meet you in a lady's wear shop in Oshawa tomorrow morning. You'll be driven into town for the fitting. Would nine o'clock be convenient?"

"Perfectly fine. And my training, Sir?"

"I'm about to come to that," he smiled. "We really have no precedent for this venture, so in a sense, we're exploring, uncharted territory."

"That's quite alright, Colonel! I can promise you that I shan't wilt away. I only appear fragile."

"Well then, I suggest that I accompany you to your private room in the Officers' Quarters. We will drop off your things, then have a quick tour so you can get down to work with Major Samson..."

"Excuse me, Colonel...Major Robert Samson? THE Major Robert Samson?"

"The same. So you know Dangerous Dan?"

"I worship that man! He was my Unarmed Combat instructor while I was at Stokes House, Beaulieu. What an amazingly talented and civilised gentleman! How exciting to think that I'll be working with him again!"

"Major Samson assured me that he remembers you very fondly as well, Sylvia. He expressed the most positive reaction when I told him that you were due in today."

"Does he know why I'm here, Colonel?"

"Frankly? No, he doesn't. Not entirely. It will be clarified, as needed, when needed. I'd like you to think about taking someone along who can be trusted to handle the radio duties and to watch your back. Interested? Please let me take your suitcase, and I'll accompany you to your lodgings. If we walk briskly, we will be there in less than five minutes."

"Well Mason, what do you think? You were hand picked from a very select pool of well-qualified candidates. You speak conversational German fluently. You have achieved outstanding results as a W/T operator by SOE standards, and you have intimate knowledge of the area being considered for the drop.

"Sylvia, the Captain, has been appointed Mission Commander. She requires a reliable W/T man for radio liaison with HQ and superior logistical support. Shall we continue? Any questions?"

"I'm in, Sir."

"Good. Are you in agreement, Sylvia...that is, Captain?"

"I am, Colonel."

"Excellent, then HQ will so be informed. Welcome, officially, to SOE, Mason. Preparations for Mission Tent Peg will commence today. First thing, you must go next door to see Adjutant Jones who's waiting to make you a First Lieutenant, British Army, and explain the usual details, et cetera, et cetera. He'll assign you each your operational code names. When you're finished, we'll meet up in the Officers' Mess, for a wee celebration of your new venture. I'll leave word at the door to expect you. At one-thirty, we'll drop in on Major Samson for a get-acquainted session."

Major Robert Samson's small office was furnished exactly as Hugh had imagined: spare, sparse, and almost Spartan. He welcomed them all warmly as they entered, particularly Sylvia, whom he wrapped in a great hug. The two of them chatted briefly while Commandant Graham and Hugh stood silent, waiting. The Major then turned to the Colonel. "Congratulations, you've done a superb job of recruitment...the brightest and the very best, I dare say."

"Thank you, Robert. I had the benefit of something much like divine guidance, as you might surmise. Now, as time is very short, we'll get on with business, starting with the basics." He looked directly at Hugh and Sylvia, seated side by side on Sampson's mock-leather sofa. "Your code names, 'Hugh Miller', and 'Sylvia Smith' will be used exclusively henceforth.

"You and Major Samson will be spending most of your waking hours together over the next three weeks. He'll be briefed by me daily in order to co-ordinate and update all aspects and components of your training. He will also serve as your counsellor, master instructor, and wet nurse. Nominally, I'll serve as CO for Tent Peg, however my role more precisely is Executive Liaison Officer, principally responsible for keeping Robert informed of current intelligence assessments and procedural developments, which, you can be assured, will flow in from our stations.

"Now, if you would both be good enough to toddle over to Hydra, you'll find Yorkie and his crew champing at the bit, anxious to begin Hugh's advanced W/T training. HQ has requested that you be in on the initial sessions, Sylvia. Thank you."

Together 'Miller' and 'Smith' walked quickly to the radio shack. "I'm awfully pleased to have you as my partner, Hugh. Tell me, does it concern you that I'm a woman?"

"No, not at all, Ma'am. I'm certainly not ready to lead a mission, or take on such huge responsibilities. You are SOE's choice, which is just fine and dandy with me. Anyway, I came awfully close to being cashiered, so I'm on parole."

"So I heard. 'Best foot forward' for the next while?"

"I'm forbidden to discuss it, Ma'am."

"Yes, I know. By the by, Ma'am isn't necessary. I prefer Sylvia and either Captain or Captain Smith only when absolutely necessary."

"Thanks, Sylvia. Anything I can do to help see this through, I will. What's more, I know that I'll learn from you in the process."

"Thank you, Hugh. I'm confident that we'll be a wizard team. Just so you know, I'm opinionated, quick-tempered, and pig-headed. And those are my best qualities! But I'm nearly always open to sensible suggestions, if you can convince me of a better way to do business."

'And you are incredibly gorgeous,' thought Hugh. Out loud he said, "I'll remember that and try not to take things personally. There's Yorkie, at the side of the building, watering his precious tomato plants. If you're nice to him, he might be persuaded to give you a couple of plump, juicy ones."

"Sounds worth a go. Would you please introduce us?"

As a comfortable working relationship developed between them, Hugh often found himself reflecting and wondering about Sylvia's background. He tried to imagine what influences or circumstances might have driven her to volunteer for so dangerous and demanding an assignment as Tent Peg. Was it political or religious beliefs, or perhaps grief over a personal loss or a tragic affair? 'Likely, none of these.' He wasn't quite certain himself why he had signed on, except to demonstrate to the Colonel that he was worthy of his leniency and faith.

That she was exceptionally bright and almost supernaturally capable was undeniable. Nevertheless, despite her light-hearted banter, she was a consummate professional and possessed the steely will of a born assassin: her personal wall was impenetrable. Hugh knew better than to even attempt to violate the sanctity of the growing sense of trust, central to the plan's success and to their very survival. It was a cardinal rule in the SOE canon that a fellow agent who knew you too well was a liability if captured and tortured. 'The less I know about Her Ladyship, the better, and vice-versa.'

They spent two hours together each morning pouring over topographical maps and high altitude photographs of Germany. Twice weekly, at 1100 hours, they huddled together over mugs of strong coffee, and spent the time until lunch honing their conversational German under the tutelage of Paul, who, Hugh suspected, was an ex-Luftwaffe pilot PoW.

For the first half of every afternoon Hugh spent immersed in advanced wireless telegraph training with the powerful new Mark 11B suitcase radio. He drilled on its set up, tuning, receiving, and transmitting, and worked daily with Yorkie, his base operator, to maintain his Morse at the minimum twenty-five words per minute.

Other field craft essentials included learning and memorising secret codes, the methods of concealing code-imprinted silks and one time code pads (OTP's), and Hamish's elaborate field simulations. In addition, Sylvia had requested that Hugh take responsibility for managing the

Mission's finances, which, she explained, would be crucial to their survival behind enemy lines.

"Okay, Sylvia, but I can't even balance my own chequebook. How much money are we talking about?"

"At least three, possibly four thousand pounds in gold coins for unforeseen events. Of course, we'll need a ready store of Reich paper currency and coins, to avoid arousing suspicion."

"God, I'll sink like a rock if I hit the water by mistake. How am I supposed to carry it all, and what are you planning to do with it?"

"The currency is to be sewn inside the lining of your army jacket, with your radio crystals, silk codes, OTP's, and whatever else you think you might need. I'll carry a small amount of German money as well, but you're our banker. Pack the sacks of gold napoleons in your jump kit. When we land, we'll take out some *gelt* for emergencies and bury the remainder. Understood?"

"Yes, Captain." '*Gelt*? Where did that come from?'

They met mid-afternoons in the underground training bunker for small arms practice with Instructor Michael Heaviside. Hugh was rated an excellent shot with his revolver of choice, the superb German-made Walther **PPK**, and only slightly less proficient with the bulkier standard British-American-issue Colt 45.

Sylvia, he noted approvingly, was simply a splendid, all-round shooter. Heaviside quickly conceded there was nothing left to teach her. Her accuracy when sighting in and test firing the small arsenal of specially-commissioned, lightweight, collapsible sniper rifle prototypes never failed to astonish them both.

Following an outdoor practice session, in which she consistently outscored Hugh and Heaviside, they turned in their weapons. As they walked away, now beyond Michael's earshot; Hugh ventured to ask, "How did you get to be so damn good, Captain?"

"I'm not really sure, you know. I never fired so much as a pellet gun before Beaulieu. I grew up in a small rural village and the opportunity never presented itself. It wasn't something that proper young ladies did, certainly not in my family.

"But from my very first experience, it seemed there was an almost mystical, magical connection, as though each firearm somehow became an extension of my being and my senses. I was ecstatic; I had discovered that I was better at something than any of my classmates. I became a fanatic, a touch obsessed, I suppose; I spent hours and hours with the instructors until I surpassed them all. Yet I have absolutely no desire to go into the forest and shoot wild animals. I abhor hunting."

"How will you reconcile your personal ethics with the mission's objective?"

"I detest him and his totalitarianism more. I have my own private reasons. Now, if you'll excuse me, I've a lecture to prepare for tomorrow morning."

"May I ask the topic?"

"Aren't you attending, Hugh?"

"I'm to meet with Major Findlay in the new lecture hall at 0900 for review, and to be briefed on the latest intelligence re: German military service ranks, insignia, and so on. I find the civilian police authorities, the SIPO and the KRIPO confusing."

"So do I. Hope you sort it out, for both our sakes. Good luck. Oh, incidentally, I disliked Morse code with a passion, Hugh; I squeaked through with scarcely enough command of the material and speed to qualify. And that, my friend, you can be certain, is one of several compelling reasons why we're together. I'll join you and Hamish when I'm finished. It's rather important that we're both totally up to date over there."

Hamish's face betrayed no trace of emotion. "The Commandant wishes that you remain, please. He's on his way." Hugh glanced sideways at Sylvia. She shrugged, almost imperceptibly.

Colonel Graham entered with a guest who reminded Hugh of a linotype of General George Custer: over six feet tall, wavy blonde hair, moustached, split-rail lanky, and devilishly handsome. "Thank you for waiting. May I present Major Carson. The Major has been following your progress with great interest from Military District Headquarters in Toronto via daily Teletype digests. He and his group are scheduled to take charge of the final phase of planning. Am I correct Major Carson?"

"Yes Sir, Colonel Graham."

"Lunch will be served here so we can talk and not lose valuable time. Major Samson will also be joining us. Please, do carry on, Major."

"Please call me 'Kit' from now on, at least in close quarters, folks. As you might have guessed, I'm American, from the west...Montana, to be exact. I'm officially enlisted in a Reserve Ranger battalion. Beyond that, I'm not at liberty to say much more, except to mention that I had my intelligence grounding here and at a number of spots in Britain. I've just returned from a quick tour of the "Fatherland," uninvited. That's about it for me. Now, let's dig into these rations and get down to this Tent Peg business a bit."

Hugh and Sylvia were unprepared for the volume and depth of information about Germany, and the intimate knowledge of the Führer's routines and daily habits, which Kit related to them. It was soon apparent that he had been designing the framework of a secret project similar to Tent Peg, code-named Operation 'Magic Apple', with the co-operation of the American Bureau of Security and Information Services, or ABSIS. Unfortunately, it had been unmasked then and quickly terminated by the Pentagon's Chiefs of Staff, citing 'political and ethical concerns.'

"Begging your pardon, Miss Sylvia, in simple language, it was judged kinda 'premature elimination', you might say, since officially we don't have a bone to pick with the Reich leader, at least not yet. Now, if you'll kindly follow me downstairs, my folks have set up some displays that should help us all get a clearer picture of what we know today. 'Course, that's liable to change by tomorrow."

Despite Kit's homey, almost offhand, personal style, Sylvia and Hugh were immediately absorbed in the programs that followed. Each of four Lieutenants, two Canadians, one British and one American, proceeded to describe and explain in exhaustive detail, an illustrated presentation of an operational scheme as prepared by international intelligence teams working closely with SOE and BSO's New York and Toronto offices. With the working titles 'Sleepy', 'Bashful', 'Grumpy', and 'Happy', each was a fully articulated and meticulously crafted scenario for the parachuting of two Allied secret agents into Germany to: 1 - Carry out the assassination of Hitler/'Sisera'; 2 - Go to ground; 3 - Avoid capture; and 4 - Ultimately, return. By suppertime, the four presentations had been completed.

"I don't think my particular Bible mentions those four characters. Who are Sleepy, Bashful, Grumpy, and Happy, the missing Wise Men?"

"Sssh. They're four of the Seven Dwarfs in *Snow White*."

"How quaint!"

"Are you with me, Sylvia, Hugh? Next, the hard part. Each of the plans is grounded in a particular set of assumptions. These are merely conditions and circumstances through which our intelligence sources have tried to predict where he'll be the most vulnerable. In some instances, they are little more than educated guesses. None is perfect or guaranteed to be failure proof, but neither is any one so far out of the ballpark as to be completely improbable. You might have been amazed at the ingenuity of the two or three which didn't quite get off the ground: poisoned darts, an exploding rat; why, someone even had the brainchild that it would be a nifty idea to introduce a diamondback sidewinder into the airshaft of Der Führer's bunker!"

Sylvia looked at Hugh, perplexed. "A rattlesnake, a poisonous North American viper," he whispered.

"Ugh. I hate snakes. I'll take my chances with the Führer and a silver bullet."

"Nevertheless," continued Kit, "we must now choose the one plan that is the least likely to fail. Please note that I said 'the least likely to fail'. Our second choice will be the fallback, or the alternate. That means that two jokers will be discarded from the deck right off. Sounds like a strange way to play poker, eh? I suggest that we take a short pause to refresh and then continue our discussion over a scotch or two before supper. Is that agreeable to you, Colonel?"

By eleven o'clock, they had argued, debated, and finally narrowed the options to two. Sleepy and Happy were rejected. By midnight, Bashful was endorsed as the primary, Grumpy the secondary.

On their way back to quarters, Sylvia remarked to Hugh, "I like the Bashful approach of stalking our man in the Bavarian mountains at his Berchtesgaden Eagle's Lair. Unfortunately, the intelligence reports said that he doesn't go out onto the balcony often, unless he's showing visitors the view, playing with his dog, Blondie, or relaxing with Eva Braun, his lady friend. Our landing could be devilishly difficult, if we're dropped even half a mile off course."

"Yes and to top it off, we'll be at the mercy of alpine updrafts. I suppose we can overcome that, if we're very careful and lucky. The maps and charts are impressive - very high quality. We can only hope that they're also accurate."

"If I can squeeze off at most two, or, ideally one, clear shot from a reasonably close range, say a thousand yards, and all other factors such as wind speed and direction, and sunlight are favourable, the plan has a better than fifty-fifty chance of succeeding. We'll have a good chance of vanishing before the mountain troops realise what has happened. I can see us getting away with it. What's your opinion, Hugh?"

"I agree generally, Captain. It's the getting in that presents some obstacles. Bavaria's far down in the south. I suppose it's up to SAS, the Special Air Service to work it out so that we can skirt enemy territory for as long as possible, before the drop.

"Grumpy appeals to me less because it requires tight co-ordination with the Resistance, which I think is iffy. Who knows whether they'll comply? Who are they? Where are they? A bomb is great, if it's in the right place, powerful enough to do the job thoroughly, and the time delay fuse actually works. Hitler's SS lifeguards watch him like a hawk, constantly. His schedules are always changed at the last moment, as Kit said. There are far too many details left to chance."

"Major Samson needs you both in his office," Adjutant Brian Jones stated flatly.

"Very well. Can it hold until after breakfast?"

"Yes, Captain. But he did emphasise that it's urgent, extremely."

It was Monday morning, their second week of training. This week was set aside for in-depth intelligence briefings and rehearsals for Bashful.

Samson greeted them upon their arrival. "Thank you both for being prompt. HQ has instructed me to tell you that your preparation will, of necessity, include some rather last-minute mountaineering experience. You have been ordered to be ready at 1000 hours; a car will be waiting here to take you to the Oshawa airfield. Wear your uniforms, bring a week's worth of underwear, woollen socks etc. And a toothbrush. Everything else will be supplied."

"May I inquire where we're going, Major?"

"Yes, you may inquire, but I can't tell you yet. That's all. Good luck!"

Sylvia looked past Hugh's shoulder, through the Hudson's porthole. "It's so incredibly beautiful. Are those the Canadian Rockies?"

"Those are called old-fold mountains, just the foothills," replied Hamish, from behind. "We're passing over western Alberta. We'll start to see our first of the newer, more rugged and spectacular pre-Cambrian ranges in less than five minutes, I'd estimate."

"It sounds that you've been out here before, Hamish."

"Yes, Hugh. I came with some chums for a glorious summer of mountain climbing and rock hounding when I finished my final year at

Edinburgh. I've been keen to come back to British Columbia ever since."

"I confess, I'm a dyed-in-the-wool lowlander," Samson chuckled. "What about you, Hugh?"

"I climbed a bit, bare knuckle, in Bavaria, and the Swiss Tyrol, with Dad, as a youngster, that's about all."

"I am impressed, Hugh. I had absolutely no idea that you are so accomplished. I mean that sincerely!" Sylvia remarked.

"Everyone listening, please," Robert announced. "Pilot Officer Johns indicates that he'll be landing on an airstrip approximately 5, 000 feet above sea level. It's quite narrow, plumb in the middle of dense pine forest, and there's water on both sides, so 'best be prepared for some fancy low-altitude manoeuvring,' were his exact words."

"Sounds jolly exciting. Has he...done it before, or did he say?" asked Sylvia.

"He didn't say."

"Just as well. If he hasn't, I'd rather not know," Hugh added, quietly.

"How did anyone ever manage to build this Shangri-La, way up here?" Sylvia wondered. "It's breathtaking, amazing! You're certain that we won't topple over the edge?"

"Quite certain. A Vancouver engineering company specialising in high-alpine construction built it for a business associate of Mr. Williamson in '36. Most of the firm's contracts are with extremely wealthy patrons, all of whom require luxurious ski chalets and summer resorts with all 'mod cons' located in some of the most remote areas of the Rockies. Each must be inaccessible to the great 'unwashed' and complete with a private landing strip. Mr. Williamson bought it in '39 with plans to make it into a fully-operational, scaled-down advanced training station," Robert explained.

"At present, there's a complement of four staff, including a remarkable Chinese-born SOE Major, Gerry Quan. Gerry's a fellow dabbler in my field and a cordon bleu chef, to boot. He was a rising young Lieutenant on the Hong Kong force when I convinced him to accompany me to Camp X, I'm proud to say. He later volunteered to come here, once he had qualified, because he's burning to get into action in the Asian theatre."

"So, you've been here before, Robert?"

"Yes, Gerry and I stopped off en route to Toronto when Mr. Williamson brought us over. Now, let's take a quick tour while they finish unloading the plane. Then we can stow our gear, meet Gerry before suppertime, after which, if you don't mind, I'll be toddling off to bed.

"Please follow me and step carefully. We're one hundred miles by air from a hospital. The facility is still not finished completely according to Mr. Williamson's plans: it's a bit rough-hewn in places. You'll notice there is neither electricity nor heat, except for wood stoves and the fireplace in the main hall, but I think we'll find that it suits our needs. I'll show you where the outbuildings are to be built as we go."

Sylvia pulled back the window drapes before getting into bed. She placed her pillow against the pine headboard, and leaned back in the darkness to watch the sky's spectacle as it slowly rotated its bejewelled display of constellations. 'God, please forgive me: am I completely insane? What am I doing, pretending to be Your chosen one, Your avenging angel? Just because I'm Jewish, why do I suppose that's it's up to me, little Rebeccah Weiss, to right the world's wrongs, practically single-handedly. I'm capable, competent, committed, yes, and probably crazy, too. 'But then, if not me, who? And if not now, when?' the wise man asked.'

Each day's exercises were more rigorous and challenging, physically and mentally, than anything Hugh and Sylvia had undergone in their previous training. The first day began with a morning-long intelligence briefing complete with aerial photos, maps, and a lecture by Major Quan on alpine meteorology. Then Hamish Findlay took them for what he quaintly called "a skirmish with the 'noble Laird of the Granite' ", which comprised a half-day's instruction followed by ground-level demonstrations and practice on the fundamentals of rock climbing.

The second day began at 0700, with two back-to-back parachute drops from an Anson. After their first landing, they gathered their silks and jogged the mile back to the airstrip. A smiling Robert Samson was waiting to congratulate them. "Well done, team! Spot on the money. A good warm-up, nothing broken or twisted, I see!

"Now comes the real test. Hamish will accompany you. We've selected a landing site with a slope and terrain identical to your target area. You'll go in with your full kit: radio, shovels, rifle, a canister with five days rations, ammunition, and all other essentials. Hamish will pass along the rest of your instructions in the aircraft. Have your chutes repacked and be on board in twenty minutes, if you please!"

"Beaulieu was a killer, but compared to this, it was a piece of cake. When I looked out through the bomb bay opening I could see those pine things zipping by on the treetops," Sylvia commented.

"Cones. It wasn't those that concerned me so much; it was the rocks!"

After landing and burying their chutes, they concealed the small metal canister in a deep crevasse, then scrambled, and clawed their way partway up a sheer rock face. Suddenly, and without warning, the gently swirling dusting of snow turned into a howling, blinding blizzard. The wind and the white engulfed them, leaving them exhausted and disoriented. "I can see it now," said Hugh. " 'Agents Miller and Smith, missing in a training exercise, were reportedly camped on a minuscule mountain ledge seven hundred feet above a rock-hard valley floor, in the blizzard of the century!' "

"A thousand thanks for pulling me up, old chap. I owe you several hot toddies. I really thought I was a goner when that piton came loose and I began to swing and sway in the gale. I wonder where Hamish is? It's damn good thing for my sake he was the anchorman. Do you think that he's alright?"

"Probably. He's a sight more experienced than the two of us put together. I'd say he's perched safely somewhere below, waiting out the storm." Hugh glanced at the luminous dial of his watch. "It's almost time to send a confirmation signal to Base. Can you please help me get this radio pack off my back?"

"Sure, hold onto my gun case and don't drop it over the edge, or someone will have to be dispatched to retrieve it, Lieutenant: Property of His Majesty's Government, and all that, don't you know!" She laughed and her coal-black eyes radiated sparks from beneath the white fur trim of her parka hood.

He knew that she spoke the truth, even if in jest. Hugh had watched with fascination at the Camp X pistol range as she had methodically sighted in, evaluated, then eliminated all contenders in a field of six or seven distinguished English, American and German rifles. She had systematically rejected all but one: a superbly balanced, collapsible, ultra-lightweight handcrafted representation of a Czechoslovakian gunsmith's art. She was not about to part with it now.

Just a few yards back from the edge of the gaping drop-off, Hugh could vaguely make out through the whiteout the mouth of a shallow cave, protected by a rocky overhang. They half carried, half dragged themselves and their gear into its shelter, and then lit a small fire for warmth and light. Sylvia watched closely as Hugh set up his B Mark 11 radio and attached the antenna and battery pack wires to the radio's terminals. "Power, Captain!" he exclaimed, smiling, as he put on the metal earphones. "Gees, they're cold! That's a strong signal, seven by seven. Okay, Hugh," he addressed himself by name, "what's the code for the day? Here it is. Come in Berlin!"

He began to key in his identity, and then waited for a response. Seconds later, a rapid burst of Morse filled his earphones. He lifted one earpiece and turned to Sylvia, "Message received. Samson says to sit tight and wait for Hamish..."

"...Weather is expected to clear. Continue the exercise tomorrow, at first light, or when Hamish shows up, whichever comes first; if Hamish doesn't appear, they'll send out a rescue team," she murmured.

"So, you could hear and understand it all? I thought you said that you barely scraped through Morse?"

"Affirmative. I guess I dragged my heels a bit on the final tests.

"Let's share some of those rations in your knapsack, Lieutenant, and then try to get some shuteye, as Kit would put it."

After what seemed only moments, Hugh awoke with a start. Someone was shaking him by the shoulder. He slipped his hand under the headpiece of his bedroll, groping for his revolver. "It's me. Sylvia. Were you asleep?"

"Yes and no. It's actually a bit too warm in this grotto. Is everything okay, Captain? What time is it?" he yawned.

"Twelve-ten. No, it's not at all okay. I'm very concerned for Hamish. What if he has fallen? He could be lying injured somewhere down there, freezing, unable to move. I have to find him before I can rest. Will you help?"

"Yes, of course. Maybe he's been calling us. With this gale blowing, we wouldn't have heard him."

"Well, it's much quieter now. Do you have any suggestions?"

"We could try the whistle. I assume that he has one, too."

"Yes, he does"

"Where's the torch?"

"In my knapsack. Hold on, I'll get it...hey, what do you know, it works! God bless the Canadian Army!"

"What was that sound?"

"What sound?"

"Hush, listen...there it is again!"

An eerie, strangled snarl was coming from somewhere near the entrance of the cave. It repeated, more loudly now. "That's a big cat, a lynx or maybe a mountain lion. I'm going to scout it out. Stay back here, Sylvia."

"Be careful, please!"

With his revolver cocked, and the flashlight in his left hand, Hugh crept out of the cave's entrance.

"Son of a ...!" he shouted.

"Hugh, what is it? Are you alright?"

"We're just fine, lass!"

"Hamish, what...?" Hamish and Hugh stood in the cave's entrance, both grinning widely.

"Captain Smith, meet my friend, Delilah. Delilah, this is the illustrious Captain Smith. Delilah is an abandoned mountain lion cub; apparently her mother went for a Burton and got lost in the blizzard."

"Oh, Hamish, she's adorable! Why 'Delilah'?" she inquired, peering into the opening in his knapsack.

"I thought the name was fitting since I'm giving her to Robert."

"Samson; now that's very clever! Hello, baby, are you hungry? Listen, Hugh, she's purring!"

"Famished enough to chew your leg off, if she could, aren't you, my wee bairn."

"I'll find her something else in the supplies, if you don't mind. Tent Peg, Jael, Sisera, Delilah, Samson...perhaps we should re-name this Mission Biblical. Tell us all about meeting Delilah...from the beginning."

"Not much to tell, actually, Captain. I found a niche not too distant from here and was holed up quite comfortably for the night. But it seems that Delilah found it first. We formed an instant bond when she discovered a taste for the Swiss chocolate that I had tucked away, for emergencies, of course, in my breast pocket. I thought it wise to vacate the premises, in case mother returned. Delilah wouldn't stay behind, so we made the trek together, following the smoke from your fire, which, I hope you both realise, is forbidden."

"Just as forbidden as adopting a menagerie?"

"A menagerie is a collection of wild animals, Captain. This is one animal. Besides, you two blokes are the mission operatives. I'm simply here as an observer," he laughed.

"Would you please feed the little moocher, so we can get at least a few hours' sleep!" Sylvia pleaded.

"HQ is very relieved that you are safe, Major Findlay, and no, I didn't mention your companion. I've been told to stand by for further instructions," Hugh related.

"I expect that this is the day for the big show, chaps" said Hamish, finishing his tea. "The sky looks promising. CAVU. Anything from the mets (meteorologists)?"

"Base is waiting anxiously for the 'probabilities' from RCAF, Vancouver. Hold on please, it's coming in now." Hugh bent over the set, transcribing the incoming stream of code on a one-time pad. After five minutes, he looked up. "We're on! Here's the signal, Captain."

"Thank you. 'Jael proceed co-ordinates Alpha, Tango, arrive 1100 hours. Confirm,'" Sylvia read. " 'Recce. Report situation. Out.' That's what we've been waiting for," she smiled, tossing the crumpled code page into the fire. "Come, see." She took a folded map from inside her parka and knelt on the rock floor, examining the chart closely while positioning a small protractor compass. After a brief silence she announced, "There's the location, Hamish, Hugh, seventeen degrees, thirty-two minutes, five seconds north-north east, two miles, five hundred yards. It's almost all easy going, up through this narrow pass. Secure your rig, Lieutenant. We're moving out," she asserted, folding and stowing the map. "Hamish, here's the compass; douse the fire. What about Delilah?"

"I'll bundle her up snug in my backpack. She was no trouble at all, coming here."

"Very well, but keep her quiet, or she's a goner."

"Roger, wilco. Here, kitty! Chocolate!"

They set off, single-file. Sylvia broke the trail through the snow, followed closely by Hamish, and Hugh. By ten-fifteen, they reached a ridge shown on Sylvia's map as the sun broke through the clouds, just as Base had predicted it would. Sylvia gestured, "Halt! Major Findlay and I will check our position. Lieutenant, the glasses please, quickly!"

"Here, Captain. What's up?"

"I'm not sure. Have a look." She handed the binoculars to Hugh. "There, six hundred yards, at one o'clock."

"Holy smokes! There are at least ten guys, all in German uniforms! Major Findlay, look!"

"Correction, mate. Those are German soldiers," Hamish whispered. "Take the glasses, raise them about ten degrees to the right. Tell me what you can see, Captain Smith."

"I'll be damned," exclaimed Sylvia. "Am I dreaming or is that the Berghof, Hitler's Eagle's Lair? Would you care to fill us in, Hamish?"

"Get into the woods, now! Follow me!" Hamish ordered under his breath. Lying prone in the snow, in a dense thicket, Hamish commanded, "Keep your heads down!"

"What's going on, Major? Is this some kind of game?" demanded, Sylvia, in a loud whisper.

"Hush, lass! Keep your eyes fixed up there, fifty yards to the east. Do you see the knoll?"

"Yes."

"Keep watching it and don't move!"

A helmeted sentry wearing a Wehrmacht soldier's greatcoat appeared at the top of the rise. Raising a pair of field glasses, he began a methodical scan of the sloped terrain leading up to the hillock where he stood silhouetted. Suddenly, he lowered the massive binoculars and reached back with his right hand to clutch his shoulder strap. Kneeling cautiously, he aimed the rifle in their direction.

"Damn, he's seen us!" As Hugh watched in helpless anticipation, the soldier slowly swung his gun horizontally toward his right, and paused, fixated on a target. A single shot rang out, echoing off the rock walls. The shooter rose, then turned, and called out. Two more soldiers materialised at his side. Without hesitation, the three figures half-ran, half-slid, each ricocheting off the other two down the slope, out of sight.

"What or who do you think he shot at?"

"Cursed if I know! I think if we stay hidden here we'll find out in a moment, though."

"How's Delilah?"

"She's asleep, Sylvia; see for yourself."

"Soundly, the little darling. Well, will you look at that, lads?"

"Fresh venison, me hearties!" Hamish declared. They watched as the three soldiers struggled, dragging a bloody deer carcass up the slope.

"Hamish what is going on? Is this what I think it is?"

"What's your guess? Sylvia? Hugh?"

"Enough guessing games, Major Findlay. Given your reputation at Beaulieu for masterminding training pranks and outrageous amusements, I'd venture to say it's all an elaborate sham."

"I see. And you, Lieutenant?"

"I thought it was phoney, but that deer and the blood sure seemed real."

"You're both correct. The shot was genuine and so is the dead stag. It's a show that we've been perfecting for six months or more."

"But, surely, you didn't actually build the Berghof?" The last time I checked, we're in Central British Columbia, not Berchtesgaden, Bavaria."

"No, of course not, but as Mr. Williamson is such a stickler for detail, he first enlisted a master illusionist, an Englishman by the name of Jasper Maskelyne. Maskelyne comes by his talents naturally. He has a magician's pedigree going back two generations, and is, as they say, wondrously gifted.

"The British Army was damned reluctant at first to believe that magic had a place in this or any war. But eventually, he wore them down and they let him have some space. He collected a team of illusion wizards and oddballs, calling them the 'Magic Gang.' Mr. Williamson had powerful friends. So he hired Maskelyne and the top special effects man from the biggest London film studio. Together they designed and oversaw the construction of the blessed thing. It's an extremely realistic work of fakery, movie-magic illusion, if you will, make-believe, stagecraft wizardry. Smoke, mirrors, wood, cardboard, lights...some day, they should make a film about Jasper's exploits, but no one would believe it."

"And the soldiers; they're actors?"

"No, Sylvia, they 're very real...Germans, PoW's. Several, perhaps half, are ex-SS. They've all been told they will earn special privileges and generous perks for nabbing you or anyone else. Subsequently, they'd like nothing better than to 'interrogate' you for twenty-four hours at a stretch. I was put through a dress rehearsal at the German Officers' Prison, Camp 30, at Bowmanville, near Camp X. Believe me, it was a very impressive performance. Afterwards, my nerves were a mite unsteady for a day or so."

"Why don't they scarper, just take off? I mean, what's to prevent them from escaping?"

"The terrain and the fact that the place is under extremely tight surveillance, Captain. There's a rigid 'shoot to kill' rule and they've accepted it as a condition of their extra perks and 'services.' "

"I suppose there's a Führer, too, Hamish?" asked Hugh.

"Oh, most definitely; he's a professional stage actor, from Toronto."

"Hugh," Sylvia interrupted, "you'll remember to send Base the confirmation signal at 1100 hours. I make it 1057, in five seconds."

"Roger, Captain, right away." Sylvia watched expectantly while Hugh prepared to send his identification code group. Within seconds he looked up at her, smiling. "Contact!"

"Jolly good. Anything to report, Lieutenant?"

"Aye, aye. Just give me another minute and I'll have it written for you in plain, Captain Smith. Here it is." He handed her the code pad paper.

" 'Proceed with all dispatch. Return'," she read aloud. "Is that all?"

"That's all, I'm afraid."

"Can you ask for clarification?"

"I'm afraid not, Captain. The coded group at the bottom orders me to shut down. Maintain radio silence. No queries, no response. It's for our own security. You know the routine."

"Well, gentlemen, this is a puzzler. Does HQ mean 'Execute the mission immediately, then proceed back directly,' or the opposite, 'Mission nullified; return immediately'? What's your interpretation, Hamish? Hamish? Hugh, where's the Major?"

"Isn't he here? Maybe he popped into the woods to answer a call of nature."

"He might have been picked up by a guard."

"Not possible. He was standing here, right beside us."

"You're right."

"May I suggest something, Captain?"

"Go ahead."

"I think we should continue, follow through with the original plan, and assume that the Major is off doing whatever he's been ordered to do. It's a sure bet that he was directed to carry out an assessment of our performance."

"Yes, of course, you're correct. Standing around here isn't going to earn us citations and, heaven forbid, a desk at HQ. Lieutenant, I expect that you've kept the final instruction packet dry inside your jacket. Take it out, break the seal, and decipher it."

"Excuse me Captain, but you're the only person who's explicitly authorised to open it!"

"Very well. Hand it to me. There, it's open. Now do your duty and write it out, if you wouldn't mind...please."

"This'll take about ten minutes, Captain. It's a bit more complicated because of the manner in which the groups are transposed and..."

"I know you will do your best, for Yorkie."

"I need you to cover me, Captain. Don't pull a Hamish on me and vanish!"

After a few minutes, Hugh declared, "Done; look in Quadrant B-4 on your map. See for yourself, Captain; it's like the script for a play. We're to scout out the high ground, locate ourselves at this point and blast our target the first moment he shows himself. Then we get our butts out of there, by this route, hell-bent-for-leather. If all goes well, a Lysander will be dispatched to meet us, once I send the confirmation."

"Fine. So let's put a nickel in, as you colonials say, shall we? We will have lost daylight by four-thirty up here and I don't have a night scope."

"Okay. One question though; if Sisera's a stooge, an actor, are you really going to shoot the blighter?"

"Those are my orders, so, yes, I am going up there fully intending to do just that. It may be a game to Robert and Hamish, but I'm deadly serious. Are you still with me, Hugh?"

"Onward and upward, Captain!"

"Good, then lead on. Keep quiet, stay low to the ground, and wait for me, up there. We're taking this route to avoid patrols. It's presumed to be impassable. Go!"

Hugh advanced to the appointed site, all but confirming the futility of their chosen course. Silvia joined him in short order.

"So far, so good. At this rate, we'll be there in fifteen minutes. I'll take the lead. Count to five, then follow me.

"No, wait," he whispered, grabbing her arm. "Freeze!"

Nearby, two male voices were arguing in crude Low German. It sounded to Hugh as though they were disputing the rights to an American wristwatch. Hugh pointed to his timepiece, inclining his head in the direction of the two speakers. Sylvia nodded in affirmation. As they crouched together behind a slab of granite, the voices grew louder and the raging debate threatened to develop into a full-blown altercation.

Luckily, the disagreement resolved and the two men began leaning metallic objects against the rock. Hugh and Sylvia were able to piece together parts of their conversation

"Cigarette, corporal? 'Lucky Strike'?"

"Yes, thanks. I wish I had some brandy."

"I have some, but it's Canadian crap. Have a sip." There was silence. "This country is colder than it ever was in my hometown in Austria."

"Mine, too, in Thuringia. But it beats breaking rocks into little pieces in the middle of nowhere, no? That brandy wasn't so bad. Thanks."

"You're welcome. This is the middle of nowhere, or haven't you noticed? All right, you can keep the watch. I'll settle for the twenty dollars, Canadian."

"It's a deal. I'll give it to you Wednesday. It's pay-day, isn't it?"

"Yes. Imagine what our comrades would say if they knew we get paid for running around in this god-forsaken forest, playing soldier. I hope it lasts. Better still, I'd love to get back home. I'd try to make a break, but where would we go from here? We'd die of exposure in this wilderness, if the Canadians didn't shoot us first. They're everywhere, watching us, all the time. Some are native Indian trackers. We wouldn't stand a chance against them."

"I know. They'd hunt us down and.... Remember the Panzer lieutenant who used to brag that he could slip clean away. He tried, and the guards brought him back half an hour later on a stretcher, a crossbow bolt clean through his skull. That got my attention. Let's go back to the guard house and see if Father Willi will part with a nip of his five-year-old cherry kirschwasser."

"Don't forget your gun, Karl, or you'll be on report for a week. That or sent to a labour camp."

"Don't worry! A lot of good it is, loaded with blanks. That Indian sharpshooter bagged a fine deer. I'd hate to miss some nice, fresh meat dinners!"

"You can't eat it yet...too tough, gamy! Maybe in two weeks, after it's been hung." Their voices trailed off.

"So, the Germans are only scarecrows. Good to know" Hugh whispered, when the men had gone.

"What are 'scarecrows'?"

"These guys are dummy's, armed with blank ammo. By the way, you do understand German?"

Sylvia nodded. "Very well thank you. I'm ready, are you, Lieutenant?"

The final leg of the traverse was made treacherous by a fresh coating of glassy ice on the horizontal face of the steep incline.

"Whew, I'm knackered, but we made it! Nice bit of belaying work back there, Lieutenant! I'll mention it in my report. Now let's get busy and set up for the kill. What time do you have?"

"Two-thirty-one, Captain. Two hours of good light left.

"That should be more than enough, assuming that our man shows up. While I'm putting this rifle together, take the glasses and keep an eye for any activity on the terrace. Have you noticed how warm it is now? I'm perspiring like a canal horse under this goose down, aren't you? Perhaps he'll come out for a stroll in the sunshine."

"Do you want something to eat?"

"Yes, please. It appears that those crows do as well." She motioned upward with the unattached gun barrel to a raucous flock in the middle to top-most branches of a lofty jack pine.

"That's not good, not good at all. A dead give-away. Sorry fellows, no free lunch today. We'll just have to wait them out, Sylvia, or they'll be dive-bombing us for tidbits."

"Okay. Here, hold my glove." She fastened the short stock to the barrel with a snap and then lay prone, sighting in the scope. "Damn, it's fogging up, Hugh."

"Give it a few minutes to adjust to the ambient temperature. The case is obviously well-insulated."

Shortly, the lens cleared. " Ah ha, Lieutenant, some action. Do you see what I see?"

"I see a largish man in an SS officer's dress uniform standing at the railing, lighting a cigarette, if you please. His beady little eyes are looking in our direction. Our ersatz Führer mustn't be nearby, or else they're not playing their roles to the hilt."

"Good intelligence observation, Hugh. Kit would be right proud of you," she laughed quietly. There was a sudden commotion overhead as the flock of crows took off, noisily. "The birds must have given up waiting for lunch. Which reminds me, I'm famished. How about it?"

"Coming right up, Captain. You nibble and I'll keep watch."

She handed the high-powered rifle to Hugh. "Use this. The lens has cleared now."

"The SS fellow just flicked his butt. He's...well, well, lookee there! It's Himself! Action stations!"

"Give that to me. Perfect target! He's taking off his hat. My God, Hugh, the resemblance is startling. Set-up the radio and have it ready the instant I tell you to send the pickup request."

He heard the smooth click of polished metal as Sylvia latched the rifle's bolt. "Two rounds in the chamber. One for King, one for Country." She smiled grimly, looking into the sight. "Quiet on the set, please. Okay, Adolf, turn a smidgen more, stage left. That's the boy..."

Hugh stopped breathing, as he stared through the binoculars. The actor/Führer was raising a china teacup. The gas silencer muffled the shot.

"Got you! What the hell? Lord, it hit him, didn't you see it? Who's that waving the semaphore? Hamish? Oh, you bastards! I give up."

"It says, 'Well done. Target achieved. Please report to base, without delay.' "

"Well, bloody well do it! Sorry, Hugh."

"Hang on. Okay, message reads, 'Friendly, repeat, friendly patrol is coming to bring you in now. All is well. Congratulations. Robert Samson.'"

Inside an operations shack, an exuberant Hamish, Robert, and Kit greeted them. Hamish immediately drew an angry Sylvia aside, as a large tumbler of brandy-laced hot chocolate was thrust into Hugh's hand.

After five-minutes of heated discussion, Hamish announced, "Ah, there you are, Jim! Captain Smith, Lieutenant Miller, allow me to introduce our star, Der Führer, Mr. James Watson."

"How do you do, Mr. Watson. I see that you're none the worse for wear," commented Sylvia, curtly.

"No, fortunately, Captain."

"So, this was all just a ruse, Robert?"

"Yes, actually."

"And my rifle, that was a blank load?"

"No, it was a live round. And dead on."

"So, how do you explain...James? I mean, nothing personal, James, but..."

"The conjurer's art, my dear Captain," remarked James, smiling.

"Precisely," added Hamish. "You'll recall that I mentioned the motion picture effects man? It was all his doing, simply smoke and mirrors, employing cinema studio lighting, plywood mock-ups, background paintings on canvases...devilishly clever illusions, and arcane hocus-pocus. He created an entirely phantom tank regiment out of cardboard, canvas and inflatable rubber in another setting that had the enemy absolutely hoodwinked. I'll take you and Hugh for a look at the set-up outdoors when you've warmed up."

"So, that's it, Robert? Smoke and mirrors?"

"Pretty much. You and the Lieutenant have won the assignment."

"What do you mean, 'won', Sir? There were other competitors?" queried Hugh.

"Actually, two other teams, Captain Miller. One chap, an American friend of Kit's broke his leg quite seriously, and the other team, well, let's just say they were never really in the game."

"We are going to get you back first thing. A Lysander is truly coming to pick you up. Its ETA is in half an hour. Please help yourselves to the refreshments and relax a bit."

"Very well, Major Carson."

"Excuse me, silence please," Robert announced. "I have just received a Most Urgent Bulletin from HQ Toronto.

'BRITAIN SURRENDERED STOP

CONGRATULATIONS ALL ON GRUMPY STOP

ALL DWARFS TERMINATED STOP

TENT PEG RE-ACTIVATED STOP

RETURN JAEL EXTREME URGENCY STOP

GOD SAVE THE KING STOP

STALWART STOP.' "

With tears in his eyes, Robert Samson added, "And may God help Great Britain. That is all." The room was hushed in stunned silence.

Hamish, obviously shaken, took Hugh and Sylvia aside. "Sylvia, you, and Captain Miller will go to base and then fly directly to meet

Stalwart. And this time, I swear to you, it won't be a game. Colonel Graham has asked me to thank you for what you've been through and for your outstanding accomplishments. They have not been in vain. He also added, for you Lieutenant, 'All is forgiven.' Good luck and God bless you both."

"Thank you, Sir. With Hugh, I know we stand a better than even chance of pulling off whatever is asked. Take care of Delilah...or did you already give her to Robert?"

"Oh no, the dear wee bairn's grown on me like wild thistle down. I'll not part wi' the beastie."

"So, that means you're keeping her then, in plain English?"

"Aye lass. Moreover, if I can get assigned a mission, I'll take her with me to chew off the Führer's... Now, get you to the airstrip before I get weepy and launch into 'Auld Lang Syne'...in Gaelic!"

Hugh and Sylvia spoke little during the long return flight to Toronto, preferring instead to sleep on the floor in the chilly cargo bay, using their parachute packs as head rests. Barely waking for the refuelling stop in Winnipeg, they slept fitfully until the DC3 landed at RCAF Base Toronto and taxied to the entrance of a hangar. A Cadillac limousine was parked inside, waiting for them. With one glance at his two groggy charges, the driver relieved them of their meagre luggage, and held open the car's rear door. In less than an hour, Sylvia and Hugh were comfortably settled into their respective luxury suites at the King Edward Hotel in downtown Toronto, examining their room service menus.

As previously arranged, their driver awaited them in the hotel's Taxis' Only area at 9:00 a.m., ready to transport them to their next briefing. When the car pulled into the circular driveway of the majestic Casa Loma and a red-coated Mountie approached to open her door, Sylvia was the first to speak.

"Well, this is a bit of a shocker." She looked around her, taking in the opulence. "Who lives here, pray tell?"

"BSO, Stalwart and company."

"How do you know?"

"I used to work here... with him."

"Impressive. Hugh, do I look presentable to meet the great man?"

"Barely. Actually, smashingly radiant, if you really want to know, Captain."

"That's enough, but thanks. Just so the red eyes aren't showing.

Are you as worn out as I am from the flight?"

As her heels clicked across the lobby's marble tiles, the admiring looks cast by the RCMP guards, resplendent in their scarlet tunics, confirmed Hugh's judgement. Sylvia was not only competent, but also was a striking woman.

The warmth of Miss Brown's greeting took Hugh aback. The typically reserved, austere, perfectionist receptionist was now hugging him with obvious affection. She detached herself long enough to knock on her boss' door. "Excuse me, Sir, our Hugh is back!"

Erik Williamson's office was darkened, its blackout drapes pulled tightly across every window. Hugh had to squint to see his chief in the dim light of a brass desk lamp. Erik shrugged as he approached them, "Just the usual air raid precautions.

"I am truly overjoyed to see you both! Welcome to Toronto, Sylvia! Are you tired? Neither of you looks any the worse for wear. Have you met our good friend General Constantine?" The general rose and greeted them cordially.

"Please, come in" Erik continued. "Someone else has been waiting patiently to see you." As Hugh and Sylvia followed Erik and General Constantine to the farthest corner of the study, an eerily familiar voice spoke.

"I expect that you are both in fine fettle! Come into the light and let me see!" Hugh's heart skipped a beat. Under the shadowy glow of a fifty-watt floor lamp, he could see a mature male figure seated in a dark leather armchair, legs outstretched casually on a hassock. As the man put down the newspaper he had been reading, a wreath of pungent white smoke formed a halo around his balding head, which as it turned, revealed the unmistakable features of Winston Churchill.

"Home are the hunters, home from the hills.' Forgive my misquoting a fine old poem," he remarked, rising from his chair. "Sylvia my dear, how delightful to see you," he exclaimed, beaming. "It seems aeons ago since our conversation in the teashop."

Erik then introduced Hugh. "I feel as though I know you, young man, from the reports I've been reading. I want you both to know how deeply grateful I am and how impressed with your exceptional endeavours. But please, do sit down. No need to stand on ceremony. Erik, have you some decent tea for our friends?"

"Is Earl Grey to your liking, Sir? I hope you're up for a guided expedition, Sylvia. The Prime Minister is fast becoming an expert on the secrets of these halls and hidden passageways; he informs me that he's keen to show you about. Correct, Sir?"

"I am and have no need for a trail of breadcrumbs, Erik. I do know my way through this maze. Why, when the General and I visited Niagara Falls weekend last, I was pleased to be able to serve as his tour guide. Having first visited that wonderful spectacle forty years previously, did I not do well, Charles?"

"Indeed so, Prime Minister. Your commentary was most informative, and entertaining!"

Turning to Erik, Churchill added earnestly, "Perhaps you would be good enough in the interim to inform Lieutenant Mason of the situation, as I will Sylvia. Would tea and scones be in order when we return, Erik?"

"Of course, Prime Minister. Lunch will be served at 1230 in my dining room, followed by the strategy meeting at 1400 hours. Enjoy your tour, my dear; a trail

Winston Churchill confers with General C. F. Constantine at Niagara Falls, Ontario, 1943.

of breadcrumbs is optional, but not to be discounted."

As the two departed, he turned. "Hugh, let me recount to you the events which have brought Colonel Warden, as the PM is now known, to Canada, and to offer a proposition. General, please stay."

Hugh listened intently. When Erik had finished, he sat silent for a moment, reflecting on his superior's startling, but somehow, not entirely unexpected proposal. "I must advise you, Hugh, that the back room planners rate the chances of your success in carrying out this assignment and the probability of your return at thirty and twenty percent, respectively...not exactly favourable odds. Because of the obvious risks and dangers, and due to other factors, this is a Class A voluntary mission," he added gently. "No dishonour or disgrace should you refuse, rather, choose not to go. I guarantee you won't be shuffled off to a desk job or cashiered from the Service."

"Thank you, Sir. Can I wait to hear the Captain's opinion?"

"Of course, Hugh, of course. I expect them back presently."

"The establishment in the Rockies is really quite remarkable, Sir. I'd love to serve there sometime."

"Yes, I'm pleased with the progress we've made. Did you find the deceptions believable or were they amateur? Ah, here they are and just in time for your elevenses, Sir."

It was apparent to Hugh that Sylvia and Prime Minister Churchill greatly enjoyed one another's company. Over lunch, Churchill was openly amused by Sylvia's humorous impressions of Casa Loma, and countered with witty rejoinders when she alluded to his occasional directional lapses.

Erik described the castle's history to her as he had to Hugh, five months previously. Then, after broaching the mission proposal, he stated, "In half an hour, we'll be joined by members of a select group of the PM's advisors. Sir, is there anything you wish to add?"

"Yes. I cannot urge you in strong enough terms to weigh every word, consider every implication, before making your decision. Now is the time to interrogate us and express your reservations, whether personal or tactical. By the time we are finished today, Erik and I shall need to know your answer, 'yea' or 'nay'. Even then, there is still some time for reconsideration, but not a great deal, as you'll learn.

"Erik, if you would be good enough to have the table cleared, I'm most eager to get this meeting underway. Perhaps our Committee would enjoy coffee and some dessert. It's going to take every morsel of our energies to convince the doubters of this plan's merits. I leave it to history whether to praise the foresight and wisdom of our actions, or to condemn us as opportunistic merchants of murder."

An hour and forty-five minutes later, despite the grave reservations of some members of Churchill's LCC, Mission Tent Peg was re-instated, with modifications. Together, Sylvia and Hugh would mount an attempt to assassinate the Nazi Führer, Adolf Hitler. Admiral Will Cunnington had sent a wire from Washington expressing his opinion that April 23 was the most likely date that Hitler would arrive in London claiming sovereignty over his new regime.

"That means you must be infiltrated into Britain, travel to London undetected, contact the Resistance and proceed to finalise your preparations under their direction," declared Williamson. "My people and Admiral Cunnington's will co-ordinate all necessary arrangements on the ground, Prime Minister."

"See to it, please Erik. By tomorrow I shall expect a detailed situation report from your London operatives, in order that we might proceed to grapple with hard logistical realities, and not wishes, dreams or wild theories. Are there any further questions before we adjourn proceedings until ten o'clock sharp in the morning?" queried Churchill.

"One, Sir. Will I see my little Sarah and my parents before we leave?"

"Erik, I believe you are best qualified to answer that," Churchill stated, smiling. "Meeting adjourned."

"Yes, indeed Sir," Erik concluded. "They're due to arrive at five p.m. at Union Station. Their train is running ten minutes ahead of schedule, so I think it would be wise if we were to leave here no later than 4:15."

CHAPTER 5

DER ADLER TAG: THE DAY OF THE EAGLE

It would be the crowning humiliation of Imperial Great Britain: on April 23, 1941, St. George's Day, the German Führer was to proclaim Adler tag, Eagle Day, in the heart of the stubborn nation. Due to arrive in London at noon, Adolf Hitler would take formal possession of the island kingdom and announce his choice of Deputy Reich Protector. Thereafter, the so-called 'cradle of democracy' would be known as THE BRITISH TERRITORIAL REICH PROTECTORATE. The Nazi Chancellor had accomplished what the Emperor of France, Napoleon Bonaparte, had only dreamt.

Two dates had been under consideration for the event: St. George's Day on the twenty-third, and Hitler's birthday on the twentieth. After weeks of bitter backroom wrangling by Party officials and general staff, the Führer approved the Reich Air Marshall's disclosure within minutes, giving his enthusiastic endorsement to their choice. "Brilliantly ironic, Hermann, really quite brilliant! See to the arrangements, today!" Delighted when his Air Marshall had announced that the victory celebration would have the greatest impact on British morale if it were to take place on the national holiday, Hitler rose from his armchair part way through Hermann Göring's presentation. Smiling, he grasped Göring's hand warmly. "I congratulate you, Hermann! Truly!"

Much to the relief of everyone in the Chancellery's crowded reception salon, their jubilant leader walked out on the arms of Air Marshall Göring and Secretary Bormann. In his agitated state, he either chose to forgo or forgot to deliver a prepared, tedious, and lengthy anti-British harangue.

Adolf Hitler's delight was short-lived. An hour later, his private secretary, Martin Bormann, informed him that British Prime Minister, Winston Churchill, and the entire War Cabinet had fled the country.

Hitler was enraged. "I want him back here, now! I can't believe that the bastard has managed to slip through our naval blockade so easily and evade his punishment! I want answers! Where the hell is Admiral Raeder? Where were his U-boats? This is outrageous, unforgivable!

"Churchill has made a career of humiliating me personally,

Bormann, and I will not endure one moment longer with him at large, spewing his lies and venom! Get that bastard here and I'll be done with him, once and for all!"

"My sources in North America report that they sailed on the liner *Queen Elizabeth* by a far northern route to evade our U-boats, my Führer. These criminals are holed up, like rats, in a castle in Canada," Bormann quickly explained.

"A castle? Nonsense! What preposterous twaddle! You must recall and execute all your V-men (agents), if you actually have any! Either they or you are raving mad! There are no castles in Canada, Bormann. I suppose you'd believe it if 'your agents' told you they're living in igloos with the Eskimos up in the Arctic?

"I want professionals handling this, not your shoddy collection of half-baked, incompetent Party bunglers and cut-throats! Get me Heydrich and Canaris. Now!" Hitler picked up his telephone and spat out orders maniacally to his Chiefs of the two counterintelligence branches of the State Security Service, (Sicherheitsdienst, SD) and the Abwehr (Military Intelligence) to employ all measures necessary to locate the fugitives immediately and bring them back alive. A small flotilla of U-boats operating from bases in Argentina would be required to bring them to justice in Protectorate courts.

"Heydrich says that he already has a very good man, in Canada, Martin," the Führer remarked, more calmly now. "He's courageous, devoted and extremely clever. Reinhard expects that he is about to infiltrate Canadian intelligence operations and will prove to be invaluable in tracking down these fugitives. Once they are captured, we'll have to whisk them out of Canada, into South America. However that's for the SD to work out. Reinhard assures me that it shouldn't pose a problem for his Service."

Hitler had planned to publicly exhibit Churchill and his cronies in cages, manacled and naked, first in Berlin, then in London's Hyde Park. Finally, he would imprison them in the Tower of London to await prosecution as war criminals. All would have legal counsel, receive 'fair' trials and be convicted of capital crimes against the Reich. Ministers of the Crown found guilty would be sentenced to death by public garrotting suspended from meat hooks. Depending upon the Führer's interpretation of the transcripts, convicted lesser functionaries would be accorded leniency: either execution by firing squad or by hanging, or transportation to one of the Protectorate's new concentration camps. Prime Minister Churchill's execution by beheading would be carried out on

Tower Hill. Hitler relished the image, dismissing Bormann's reservations.

"It's not known as 'the bloody Tower' for nothing. You should know, Bormann my old friend, that The Protectorate's history provides untold numbers of bloody precedents, if you would only trouble yourself to become acquainted with its past. Oliver Cromwell, the first Protector of the Realm, beheaded his King, Charles the First. That, my friend, is regicide. We'd never stoop so low. Churchill's only a loud-mouthed braggart, just another cheap politician. Not a drop of royal blood to be spilled there, so don't be concerned.

"I suggest that you begin your research with the Tudor King, Henry the Eighth, and his troubles with his trusted friend, Sir Thomas Moore. King Henry was a fellow who truly knew how to wield power, and the broadaxe. Seven of his wives were decapitated, either for failure to provide him with a living male heir, or for their treacherous infidelities."

He paused, reflecting on Churchill's public rants, brimming with vitriol, intended to degrade and humiliate him, Adolf Hitler, the democratically-elected German Chancellor. Churchill taunted and ridiculed him with vile, unfounded invectives: "The criminal perpetrator of heinous crimes against humanity"; "That little corporal, a pathetic nonentity"; and the most telling, "An uncommonly common Nazi street thug."

"And the Royal Family, my Führer? What are your intentions, if I may inquire?"

" 'What are your intentions, if I may inquire?' Stop being so patronising, Bormann! You'd think I was considering sending you to Dachau, tomorrow. You're no traitor, like Thomas More, are you, Martin?"

Not waiting for an answer, he continued, "For your information, I've already made a decision. They are of more use to me, to us, alive, than dead. They'll be well taken care of, isolated somewhere in the backwaters. A detachment of SS guards and household staff has been trained and is waiting to be assigned by Himmler, on my order. Naturally, all arrangements for their security and upkeep will be financed directly from the royal coffers," he chuckled.

Upon his return to his Bavarian retreat, Valhalla, Hermann Göring related the details of the meeting to Marianne, his wife. As she had anticipated, the Führer had accepted her husband's recommendation. Elated, Hermann told her that when the Air Ministry's Chief of Protocol had advised the Air Marshall that St. George's Day was not only a significant English national holiday, but was also the generally accepted birth date of William Shakespeare, "I felt that it was my master stroke. Do you think I am being overly dramatic, my dear?"

He had shrewdly and correctly predicted that the dual symbolism of the date would appeal to Chancellor Hitler's 'unusual' sense of humour, a heaven-sent opportunity to mock and humiliate the stubbornly arrogant, British people. Perhaps, at last, his appointment to the office of Deputy Protectorship was within his grasp.

"My dear," added Marianne, "this will only improve your standing as one of Hitler's closest and most trustworthy confidants. Coincidentally, I had already planned to celebrate your air victory with a small party, an intimate reception for him, and a hundred of the Party faithful, along with your usual Luftwaffe comrades and political associates. Hermann, I think that this can be our opportunity to win the Führer's nod to your installation as Deputy Reich Protector, don't you? The occasion calls for something more regal and dignified, on a grander scale. It must be splendid and glittering, but not vulgar. And it must be in Berlin, your Ministry, of course. But we must not appear over confident, mustn't we? Tomorrow morning, Franz and I will draw up the guest list, subject to your approval, as always.

"Meanwhile, do be a darling; trot out to the pantry and ask Franz to bring a chilled magnum of champagne upstairs straightaway. Tell him I want our sterling wedding chalices. Have him leave the tray on the night table and draw the curtains, my love. Let me take that heavy tunic, Mutti. You must be dying in this heat."

"Yes, I am, and totally exhausted. The planning is overwhelmingly complicated. I feel a migraine coming on. However, I think a cup of the French nectar and a dark room will revive me sufficiently, Mari, darling."

The bomb and fire-ravaged city of London prepared to receive its conqueror. Eagle Day would mark Germany's greatest victory since the blitzkrieg juggernaut had first sliced eastward across Poland. The Wehrmacht's High Command, OKW, had flown in the army's crack engineering and construction battalions to clear up the mounds of shattered brickwork and wood, and the tonnes of splintered glass at and around the site of the upcoming ceremony. It had been decreed that all reminders of the devastation must be swept away for the particular benefit of the American press. Millions would see The New German Reich, not as the plundering Hun of the past, but as the enlightened, civilising torchbearer of a New World Order.

All of the preparations on the ground in London were under the command of SS Gruppenführer (Lieutenant General) Walther Lange. The bilingual thirty-two-year-old lawyer's credentials for the appointment were immaculate. His SS dossier listed a pre-war Master's degree in Linguistics, and a Doctor of Laws, Berlin. His service record reflected extraordinary organisational abilities including his particular talent for achieving seemingly impossible objectives in unrealistically short time frames. He demonstrated this repeatedly at the frontlines, leading his Waffen-SS Panzer tank corps throughout the Polish campaign.

It also helped to have been the first choice of his Chief, Reinhard Heydrich, head of the Sicherheitsdienst, the Reich Security Service. Heydrich, an amateur but accomplished violinist, had noted that Lange's dossier hinted at the possibility of a remote genetic link with the Führer's favourite composer, Richard Wagner, although Himmler's SS birth records experts were unable to confirm this. Nonetheless, with other factors taken into consideration, Lange's candidacy had passed muster with the Führer and the General Staff under Heydrich's deft sponsorship.

Heydrich admired men who could quickly make a decision, act upon it and deal with the consequences without procrastination or pangs of conscience. He also had accumulated ample eyewitness evidence of Lange's ruthlessness in dealing with some uncooperative city officials in Lodz, a principal factor in his unusually rapid promotion from First Lieutenant to the rank of Lieutenant-General.

Walther Richard Lange was also noted, if not feared, among his SS colleagues for possessing a very short fuse combined with a notoriously low level of tolerance for any subordinate whose performance failed to meet his expectations. Impatiently, he switched on the intercom to listen to his receptionist, and then picked up the secure telephone. "Lange, here. Heil Hitler. Good morning. Thank you. It is raining, quite miserable. It's springtime in England. When is my specialist arriving? Who! You know exactly who I mean!"

Hans von Tresköw, a noted ornithologist and civil engineer in the non-combatant or administrative branch, the Allgemeine-SS, had become Himmler's top authority on 'preventive security'. Whether because of his international pre-war reputation as an unusually gifted amateur zoologist, or his 'eagle-eyed' ability to detect subtle vulnerabilities in the most thoroughly planned security protocols, he was known in SS circles simply as, 'The Birdman'. For detecting and correcting several potentially lethal flaws in Hitler's élite Liebstandarte-SS (Lifeguards Division) security measures, and, for his engineering accomplishments, the Führer had promoted the modest autobahn designer to the honorary rank of Sturmbannführer-SS (Major). Heads had rolled because of his security analysis, earning The Birdman several powerful enemies including the Führer's influential Private Secretary, Martin Bormann. Nevertheless, Lange could not rest until von Tresköw had signed off on the Eagle Day security file.

"What? Well get The Birdman here. I don't care how. If there are no transports available tonight, he can fly across the Channel, on his own, for all I care. I want the package here, in my office, tomorrow morning at eight hundred hours. I needed him here a week ago, damn it! I don't care why the Gestapo needs him. What did you say? My line's full of static. It's this damned British telephone system, the bloody incompetents! No wonder they lost the war! He's an engineer, for God's sake, not a policeman! Tomorrow, 0800; Heil Hitler!" he barked as he replaced the handset and then swung around in his chair to view the activity on Fleet Street, six storeys below his office window. He was thoroughly annoyed by the Gestapo's uncooperative and persistent foot-dragging. Chief Heydrich would be informed, in due course. For now, time was of the essence. Von Tresköw would have only a couple of hours to carry out his inspection, approving the elaborate plans to safeguard the Führer. Berlin confirmed that the ceremony would commence as announced, at one o'clock, exactly.

Walther Lange now felt confident that he had everything in order. All of the armed forces at his disposal had been strategically positioned throughout London, ready for immediate activation. The remainder of England and Great Britain was Berlin's headache. Massive SS troop deployments, with the necessary supporting armoured detachments, combined with SD security service regiments to seal off and take complete control of all access routes into and out of the city. Martial law had been imposed to prevent any incidents of civil revolt or armed resistance. Retaliation would be immediate and without remorse against any members of the civilian populace who dared to defy the Supreme Command's orders of the day as broadcast nationally at half-hour intervals and posted prominently throughout the country.

Under the newly enacted Emergency Measures for Protectorate Security, Lange had decreed that designated grocery stores would remain open around the clock until valid ration card holders had depleted their stocks, or until forty-eight hours prior to the event. At this time, a general curfew would be imposed. The city would be locked down. All Londoners would confine themselves to their homes unless explicitly ordered otherwise. After that, 'shoot to kill' directives would be the troops' orders until instructed to stand down.

Mobile SS military police patrols roamed the city, as a deterrent to civil disorder. Any suspicious activity would be met with summary reprisals. Mindful of his experience with the Polish Resistance, Lange had ordered corps of SS engineers to walk through and inspect the miles of sewers and then seal off surface access by welding the gratings shut.

Lange had selected some city officials and accredited National Socialist sympathisers and granted them restricted access to the ceremony and limited privileges during the two-day state visit. The Propaganda Ministry would ensure that they appeared more numerous and prominent, of course. The Reich Security Service and Gestapo Secret Police had already arrested any Londoners who had been overheard by plainclothes agents or informers objecting or even complained mildly.

Lange had also rounded up others suspected of resistance to the order; these dragnets were co-ordinated in consultation with SD Chief Reinhard Heydrich and 'Gestapo' Heinrich Müller, from their Berlin HQ's. All of these subjects were subsequently 'interviewed.' A few had been strongly cautioned, then released under surveillance. Many hundreds of others had been detained indefinitely in local jails, schools and courthouse lockups, pending construction of two large concentration camps being rushed to completion; one on the bleak Yorkshire moor and the other close to the Welsh border.

Reich Minister of Propaganda, Dr. Joseph Goebbels, had ordered the BRPBS (British Reich-Protectorate Broadcasting Service), 'The Burp' or, the 'BS', as it was instantly ridiculed by the citizenry, to provide coverage of the Führer's inauguration. Newsreel footage, complete with Minister Goebbels' personal commentary, would be processed and delivered, ready for screening, at every cinema in the Protectorate, the Greater German Reich, and throughout occupied Europe, within forty-eight hours of the event. Prints designated for North and South America and Asia would take up to a week to reach their destinations, depending upon distance, method of transportation and ease of entry.

Hans von Tresköw arrived punctually at eight o'clock. Lange thought the little engineer looked rumpled and appeared to be either poorly rested, nervous, or both. Von Tresköw, noticing the General's look of disdain, apologised for the state of his uniform, explaining that he had slept all the way over from Berlin. He requested an undisturbed location where he could examine the thick dossier, marked 'Most Secret.' Lange escorted him to a back room and shut the door. There was nothing to do now except wait and watch the time slip away.

"Gruppenführer Lange! Your guest is ready to meet with you."

Lange glanced up at the clock. 'Nine forty-five. He can't have finished...' "Yes, yes, please send him in, Frau Bernt. Bring us coffee, please. Strong!"

"So Sturmbannführer, what do you think of our plans? Will our beloved Führer's celebration be as secure as I hope and pray?"

Von Tresköw removed his eyeglasses, polishing them with deliberate care on his black tie while he spoke. "Herr Lange, on paper, your planning is exemplary and superbly professional. My congratulations. However, I must inspect the site, as you would expect, to satisfy myself that all necessary safeguards and precautions are fully factored into the equation. Only then I can endorse it. That will take, say...an hour, an hour and a half at most. Dignitaries will begin to arrive, when?"

"Twelve fifteen."

He looked up, blinking myopically, carefully fitting the wire-frame of his spectacles over his ears.

'He looks like a miniature version of SS Himmler, without the silly little moustache!' Lange thought.

"I see. That is cutting it close, but there's nothing to be accomplished by complaining. I would have been here yesterday, but business in Berlin kept me tied up. We have precious little time, and none to spare. May I take this with me? I have made some notes and sketches in the margins and have some questions, particularly regarding the reviewing stand. Nothing major, however; perhaps we can talk in your car."

"Of course, one moment, please. Frau Bernt, send for my car and please see that fresh coffee and sandwiches are provided in the back. Immediately." The eight-cylinder Horch limousine was Lange's sole indulgence, an extravagant gift from his pretty and inordinately wealthy young mistress in Cologne.

"Gruppenführer Lange, as an experienced field officer, please don't be offended by an amateur's observations. Your plan seems very thorough and I'm quite satisfied with your explanations. But in spite of all that, a crafty, skilled, and dedicated killer, with nothing to lose, would be virtually impossible to stop.

"An assassin's strength lies in thorough planning, subterfuge and surprise to execute his scheme. He would need all three to penetrate your defences. My task is to seal off every possible option and avenue maximising your opportunities for prevention by detection, and reduce his chances of success, to almost zero."

"Almost zero, Sturmbannführer? I think that is not good enough, frankly."

"I am not particularly thrilled that this circus is taking place out of doors, Gruppenführer Lange. My engineer's instincts warn me that it leaves too much to chance with numerous, far too numerous, possibilities for breaches of your security."

"Nor am I happy. However, it cannot be changed, von Treskow. Our Führer has ordered it so."

"I realise your task has not been easy. Now, if you don't mind, Gruppenführer, I need to walk and think. May I borrow these binoculars? I'll take along that coffee and sandwich you offered. First, I must speak to the security squad commanders. Perhaps you could escort me over to their bivouac and vouch for my credentials. Otherwise, I should expect to be shot," he remarked, smiling thinly.

When he returned to the Horch, Lange rolled down the car window, lit a cigarette, and watched The Birdman trudge toward the reviewing stand accompanied by a Field Police Captain. From time to time, they stopped and von Treskow raised the field glasses, scanning the roofs of Whitehall and the Houses of Parliament.

'Horned larks he's looking for, no doubt,' Lange mused. 'At least, the weather is finally co-operating.' He glanced at his wristwatch as he flicked the third butt out the window. 'Eleven thirty. Come on, Birdman, it's my tail if we're not out of here by noon!'

Light armoured cavalry now charged across his field of view, manoeuvring into position, followed by thundering diesel demons on half-tracks spraying rooster tails of wet turf into the air. In the midst of it all, von Treskow knelt on the grass, examining a map. He rose and, after an ineffective attempt to brush the debris from his trousers, carefully refolded the map and enclosed it in the report. Lange opened the door and stepped out, squinting up at the now-brilliant sun. "Sturmbannführer, you're just in time. I have to get back and change into my dress kit. What's your verdict?"

"It passes muster, Gruppenführer. I've made a note here, and another there, inside the cover. My reservations, which I have stated, stand. Essentially, the wide range of exposure presented by the government buildings' rooftops is cause for considerable concern. May I show you on the map?"

"That's all dealt with in Section II, parts I to XXIV," Lange replied impatiently. "Snipers, roof patrols, sealed buildings, alpine troops, aerial surveillance, all of it."

"Yes, I know, Gruppenführer, but I must say that it does make me very uncomfortable."

The last few words were drowned out as two Focke-Wulf FW 190A fighter aircraft, in wingtip-to-wingtip formation, buzzed Big Ben. Lange looked up, shielding his eyes from the brilliant sun. A single-engine Fiesler Storch was making lazy-eight circuits over the Thames.

"What do you recommend, at this late hour then, Sturmbannführer? Cancellation? That's him, you know, up above us, in the Storch." He pointed skyward, for emphasis. "This location was selected by the Führer himself. It was not my choice: I think his reasons are obvious enough."

"Not a criticism, Gruppenführer Lange. Not of you," von Tresköw shouted above the drone. "You have accomplished wonders."

"Will you sign it then?"

"Say again?"

"Will you approve it, Sturmbannführer?"

"Yes, with the proviso that the problem areas are diligently attended to, with the highest priority and without delay."

"Yes, of course. It will all be done. Thank you. Here, use my pen. Driver, let's get going!"

Barely a hundred meters below the Führer's small, single engine Fieseler-Storch, the Houses of Parliament and Whitehall lay nestled in the sinuous bends of the River Thames' calm surface. "Look down, there, Albert. It's quite remarkable, actually!"

"Truly marvellous, my Führer. I am honoured to be here, on your Eagle Day."

Adolf Hitler was supremely confident that this event would surpass the anticlimactic French surrender on the rusty railway siding in the Compiègne Forest, that sweltering afternoon of June 21, 1940. He opted to use the same luxury Pullman coach that had served as the setting of Germany's humiliating surrender in November 1918. He related to Speer how he had abruptly exited the stifling car on that summer day, after only fifteen minutes. He, Adolf Hitler, followed by Air Reich Marshall Göring and Deputy Führer Rudolph Hess, had left as General of the Ober Kommando Der Wermacht, OKW, the German High Command, Wilhelm Keitel, had begun to read the terms of capitulation to the sombre French delegation.

"It was not only the heat, believe me, Speer, but it was a well-planned blow to Gallic pride and insolence. That Corsican, Napoleon Bonaparte, must have had Aryan blood in his veins. How else could he have accomplished so much? Himmler's experts will be directed to look further into this matter to confirm my theory. It is simply impossible, Albert, that a weakling nation of Communists, Marxist philosophers, second-rate sidewalk artists, sexual degenerates, and wine-swilling braggarts could have produced such a great military mind. I will find the underlying truth of it. Perhaps, in a few more years, I will have the luxury of leisure time to write another book..."

"Certainly, that would be an excellent project for you, my Führer." Albert Speer squinted into the sun, absorbing the magnificence of the great city, soon to be at the centre of his fiefdom. He was an architect by training and an engineer by inclination, not a student of history, but thought it prudent to acknowledge his Führer's admiration for the other little Corporal.

Hitler continued, "Now, as for the English, my dear Speer, they are quite a breed apart from the French, quite different, indeed. Bonaparte called them a nation of shopkeepers. But he badly underestimated their fortitude. Relatively civilised, are our fellow Aryans, though distantly related. I must admit that I find them cunning, stubborn, and resourceful.

"They do drink far too much, though, Albert. Mind you don't fall into that bad habit. A national flaw. Avoid their 'public houses', or 'pubs.' They are foul smelling, smoke-clogged establishments. Have Müller's Gestapo keep a weather eye on the goings-on inside them, though. They've been hotbeds of dissension for centuries. Control them through intelligence gathering. Use prostitutes, barmaids, local gossips, to inform on the leaders, but be careful not to...are you listening Albert?"

Albert Speer nodded while diplomatically suppressing a comment about Hitler's own clumsily abortive Munich beer hall revolt in November 1923. Arrested, tried, and sentenced to five years for conspiracy to commit high treason, Hitler was jailed in Landesburg Prison. Indulged by the Bavarian authorities, he was well fed and coddled; close friends and associates dropped by without restrictions, bringing him treats along with encouraging news of the increasingly fragile condition of the post-war Weimar Republic.

Imprisoned, he dictated the first volume of his best-selling work, *Mein Kampf* (*My Struggle*), a startlingly prophetic blueprint for his Nazi Party's meteoric rise to power, and its plans for world domination. It was a racist masterpiece, filled with virulent anti-Semitic, anti-Catholic, anti-French, and anti-Marxist sermonising, and seasoned with national-socialist (Nazi) political and economic theories and Aryan cultural philosophy.

His adoring disciple, Rudolf Hess, faithfully transcribed every syllable. After serving a mere nine months, Citizen Hitler was released to continue his quest, unabated. Translated into several languages, the two volumes of *Mein Kampf* sold more than five million copies worldwide and its author became a millionaire celebrity.

"I have been here, to London, before, did you know?" Hitler reflected. "As a veteran recovering from my battlefield wounds, and also an aspiring artist, I had the youthful desire to travel, to get away from the mess that Germany was in. I also knocked around Liverpool for a week. They couldn't understand me, nor could I make out more than a word or two of their dreadful 'Limey' accents and thoroughly corrupt slang. I have kept my sketches of the harbour. Quite good, if I may say so. Have I shown them to you, Speer?"

"Yes, very fine work, Sir. You have remarkable mastery of the subtle nuances of watercolours."

"Coming from you, my dear Albert, that is a high compliment."

He paused for a moment, and then continued, "I expect that you will quickly start a compulsory national program of re-education, preparing the natives to become model citizens of our new, Greater Germany. They must be taught to speak, read, and write in German, beginning early in grade school. It shouldn't be an impossible task for adults generally, at least the educated and bourgeois classes. English is, after all, merely a corruption of German. The grammar and many words are similar. The riffraff may not be worth the effort, at least for now. Just give them enough to make productive workers of them.

"The discrete application of whatever other reform measures you deem necessary are your responsibility. I have given you a very difficult assignment. There are still many centres of strong resistance, which need to be tamed or eliminated. Be harsh, ruthless even, and thorough, but be also mindful that I plan to build a pan-Germanic Europe based on co-operation and a willingness of spirit to participate freely.

"I will achieve my goals. I will not accept failure, not from you or from anyone, Albert. I know I can count on you to keep me fully and personally informed of your progress. I do expect to be pre-occupied with the eastern campaign, as you know, but don't think I won't have the time for you. I will expect detailed, weekly reports in my personal, highest security code, sent directly to my whereabouts. We'll meet again in three months to look over your progress and plan the next stage. My congratulations, again, Herr Deputy Reich Protector."

Albert Speer was losing the point of Hitler's meandering monologue, but had the presence of mind to accord his leader a Nazi salute. "Upon my honour, I will serve you faithfully until death, my Führer."

The morning sunlight flared briefly off the lightly-misted glass of the Fieseler-Storch's high 'greenhouse' canopy as the pilot dipped the right wing and gently banked to starboard, affording her passengers a breathtaking view of the face of Big Ben and the Clock Tower. As she began the short, steep downward approach toward the span of Westminster Bridge, Luftwaffe test pilot Hana Greiff was confident that her nimble, high wing aircraft would bring her VIP passengers safely down, barring an unlikely attack by resistance ground fire or a suicidal Spitfire pilot.

"There is, after all, still a chance of that," Hana reflected. "No occupied country can ever be fully protected from marauding patriots seeking vengeance."

Politics were of little interest to Hana personally. She had been in love with flying ever since sneaking into a cinema as a ten-year-old. A few brief minutes of newsreel footage showing daredevil World War I aces, including the present Air Marshall of the Luftwaffe, Hermann Göring, performing impossible barrel loops and rolls in the cloudless Bavarian skies, and she was smitten. As a realist, Hana had eagerly embraced the new Luftwaffe, formed under the noses of the Allies, contrary to the terms of disarmament of the hated 1918 Treaty of Versailles.

She had used her family's connections to ensure her acceptance as a glider pilot cadet at the age of seventeen, immediately gaining the attention of her instructors with her perseverance, intelligence, and intuitive sensitivity at the crafts' 'touchy' controls. She studied hard, attended student activities sponsored by the new Nazi Party and, although she enjoyed the attention of her male classmates, she remained friendly, but reserved. Upon receiving her glider license, she was asked to sign on as a Luftwaffe glider school instructor by the 'father' of glider transport, General Ernst Udet. When she declined, citing that it had been her childhood obsession to qualify for powered flight, he reluctantly agreed to endorse her application.

Barely eighteen years old, Hana mastered single and twin engines, tri-motor transports and light bombers, and then graduated to four-engine heavy bombers, many still in early prototype stages. Flight-Lieutenant Greiff's recollection of each aircraft's characteristics, her encyclopaedic knowledge of aeronautical theory, combined with an engineer's ability to push any aircraft's performance far beyond design limits, and to relate the results in clear language, made her the designers' test pilot of choice.

She was deeply honoured when her Führer, Adolf Hitler himself, announced that he had selected her personally for his historic flight. She silently wished the handsome and charming Herr Speer success in his new position.

Exactly as she had planned, she landed the high-winged plane gently and precisely on its long, stork-like undercarriage. She taxied to a halt at the centre of the arch of Westminster Bridge on the smooth, worn cobblestones, and then killed the high-revving engine. The Air Ministry photos and local intelligence had been accurate this time. A Storch required only eighty-eight feet of landing strip and *The Eagle* fit quite comfortably at the centre of the bridge span. The wings jutted safely, drooping ever so slightly over the low sides. When the three-bladed propeller stopped, two attendants in Luftwaffe grey materialised to swiftly chock the wheels while a third trundled portable steps to the fuselage door.

Five hundred meters above, twelve twin-engine Focke-Wulf FW 190A fighters of Major Adolph Galland's much-decorated Normandy–based Jagdgschwader Squadron executed precision, sequential snap-rolls in trios; then reformed in echelon. Major Galland pulled his own craft up, out of formation and, at full throttle, climbed vertically to 2,500 meters. He paused at the peak of his ascent, then, a split second before stalling, executed an aerobatically perfect hammerhead turn, transformed it into a falling leaf pattern, and ended in a victory roll before pulling up and rejoining his squadron.

This was Galland, offering the fighter pilot's ultimate salute to his Leader's glorious day of victory and a gallant gesture of admiration to the intrepid and beautiful woman aviator. The German Ace, Max Immelman had perfected the hammerhead manoeuvre, in WWI dogfights over France. Pilots had named their country's highest medal for air combat, the coveted 'Blue Max', in tribute to his legendary feats.

Adolf Hitler followed the stunning aerobatics display with evident pleasure, shading his eyes to see through the cockpit glass, then rose and walked with Speer the short distance aft for a final briefing.

As she completed the shutdown procedures, Major Galland's voice crackled in Hana's helmet headset, resting in her lap. *"Kurwenal to Eagle.* Wonderful! Heil Hitler! If you had missed the bridge *Eagle,* you might have been able to land that crate near the shore and walk it in on those long legs. I still remember when you and Udet showed us the prototypes in the mountains at the Führer's retreat at Berchtesgaden, back in '37, wasn't it? You both had your Storchs hovering like dragonflies in the wind. Our Russian friends may have the first real helicopters, but your amazing little plane was doing the impossible: flying backward into a headwind blowing at twenty-five knots. That called for a few drinks that night, as I recall. Over."

"Eagle to Kerwenal. Those are only a few of the tricks I've learned in this little wonder. Thank you for your company over here and that tail-burner of a display. I do appreciate your gallant fighter pilot spirit! I'll wager that gets the young girls' hearts pumping in Rouen! Pardon. I hear my call letters in the background. Have a safe trip back and please remember to save me a place at your mess table tomorrow night. *Eagle,* over."

"The champagne is already on ice; my treat! Don't be late or I'll have to go out searching for you and we both might end up in the drink sooner rather than later. Ha! I'll guard the caviar 'til you arrive, but in return I want all the details about today. Photos, too, please! How did your passengers fare? Over."

"Affirmative, *Kurwenal.* I think The Eagle was quite pleased with the approach we took. He asked me to pass along his appreciation for all that you've done. Ah, he's coming forward. Must go, now! Someone's trying to call in and there's a very young, tall and quite wonderful-looking SS lieutenant pacing outside my window. *Eagle,* Out."

"My best to all for a gala celebration. Wish I could stay, but duty calls. One thing, though, *Eagle,* about your approach. You were so low coming in over the coast that you vanished from the screens of our radar. They thought you might have dropped into the Channel. Was

your radio on? They were calling you frantically on the emergency frequency. Couldn't locate you at all until I gave them your vectors. There
could be hell to pay for both of us from the Air Ministry for breaching
procedures. Best to stick to the plan on the return leg. Okay? Seig
Heil! Heil Hitler...over and out."

Major Galland's reprimand though gentle was unfair, she thought,
as she removed her leather helmet and fluffed her short blonde hair with
her red-lacquered fingertips. She had maintained radio silence in transit, as instructed by Berlin. The Fieseler-Storch's high frequency emergency band had been set to intermittent scan only, to prevent hostile
intercepts from locking onto her plane, though she had to admit that her
altitude was substantially below the approved level. Wasn't that one of
the benefits of the Storch's aeronautics? The Führer had commented
enthusiastically that he enjoyed her picturesque route over the sweeping,
hilly, green English countryside, even if a few score sheep farmers would
have disagreed.

Hana, ever the professional, accepted full responsibility for her
exploit, apologised, and got her friend Galland off the hook, too, when the
time came for her flight log to be signed, submitted and the official mission report filed. Procedure forbade her inquiring on air about the two
Storch decoy flights that had been sent over as diversions. No doubt
those pilots had followed the flight plan

She had proven once again a point that had long since become evident to Luftwaffe combat pilots: by flying very low and following the contours of the terrain, even the most advanced British radar that German
Intelligence had captured, analysed and replicated, could be fooled.

The SS major stepped up to unlatch and swing open the aircraft's
cabin door. Hana greeted him with a captivating smile and Heil Hitler,
which he quickly returned as he stepped back down to the ground. At
his command, a twelve man SS honour guard, resplendent in black and
silver dress uniforms, came to attention and saluted as the Führer and
his escort party descended the short ramp to the bridge's roadway. A
gleaming black Rolls Royce Corniche landau waited, idling silently.
Hitler paused, acknowledged the guardsmen's' salute with a perfunctory
snap of the glove in his right hand, and then entered the limousine.

A forty-eight man SS Security Police Guard mounted escort
appeared. They swiftly manoeuvred their two-dozen motorcycles, each
with a sidecar bearing an SS combat-veteran marksman of the Führer's
personal Lifeguard Regiment, automatic weapon at the ready, and
formed a precisely co-ordinated mobile shield around the limousine.

Four personal security specialists riding in the car intently scanned the curbside throngs and the buildings along the police and troop-lined route, watching for the slightest sign of anything remotely unusual.

During the flight from Paris, Adolf Hitler had railed against the two security specialists who had to tactfully remind him of the pre-approved procedures. He had so much wanted to enter the city standing erect in the rear of the Royal Family's Rolls Royce Corniche. Hitler intended to convey to the world, especially to Russia and the United States, which he, the godlike conqueror, was supreme in his victory over the English, and would be so over any other nation that he might select in the future. This was to be the celebration of an historic event, equal in glory to the defeat of the army of the Czar, Ivan, by the vastly outnumbered Teutonic knights in the Prussian swamps of Tannenberg, two hundred years before.

He had finally relented, only because Propaganda Minister Josef Goebbels, though ever mindful of his newsreel camera's usefulness in portraying the Nazi leader as a popular hero, had himself expressed deep concern from Berlin for the Leader's security in a country so recently occupied. The general wisdom of his public entry into England at this time had been hotly debated. But Hitler had insisted on his rights as the conqueror of the country; his uncertain chiefs had no choice but to acquiesce and make all security preparations as thorough as possible. The Führer's motorcade and escort riders proceeded from the bridge towards the reception area, at the regulation eight kilometres per hour.

Lange had carried out every precautionary measure imaginable with efficient, Teutonic thoroughness. SS, Gestapo, SD and SIPO intelligence countermeasures specialists, as well as Intelligence staff from the regular armed services, had secured and sealed off all residences and government offices within a two-kilometre radius of the parade route and Whitehall. Offering no explanations, but courteously 'encouraging' compliance, all buildings were evacuated, forcibly only when necessary.

Electronic eavesdropping specialists of the military's Intelligence branch, the Abwehr, were assigned to continuously sweep, intercept, and evaluate all civilian communications, using trucks commandeered from the locals and refitted as mobile radio laboratories. Six cumbersome television cameras, the new British invention, had been taken from BRPBS Broadcasting House and set up to relay ghostly images of rooftops, doorways, spires and gargoyles, to supplement the teams of SS snipers in saturation coverage of the targeted potential killing zones.

Surveillance and swift measures by the SD and Gestapo had resulted in the round up of thousands of potential troublemakers throughout the English Protectorate. Hitler had ordered caution in these initial stages, so as not to set off the entire population and create mass insurrection.

Nonetheless, the Army and SS had been inserted into all aspects of civic life from the Scottish Border to Lands End. Rail travel was tightly controlled by the Protectorate Rail Authority and fuel rationing made driving more than twenty miles a luxury for all but a few that could obtain Essential Industry Worker Passes and petrol ration cards. Air defence, artillery, and mobile panzer units were positioned, as unobtrusively as possible, at every key strategic location, to intimidate and suppress civil disobedience, and to discourage resistance activity.

At the appearance of the familiar, diminutive figure in Party uniform brown, the one hundred members of the Kaiser Wilhelm Naval Academy Band began the Overture to Wagner's *Tannhaüser* as Hitler stepped from the royal family's car at St. James' Park. The reception had been hastily orchestrated in the wake of the surprise acceptance, by the British Interim Cabinet, of the manifesto of unconditional surrender as presented at 10 Downing Street by Nazi Foreign Minister Joachim von Ribbentrop, less than three weeks previously.

Albert Speer, Hitler's newly appointed Reich-Protector of the English Territorial Protectorate, stood stiffly at attention beside his Führer; like modern Caesars, they waited to receive their tributes, from the conquering legions. The subjugation of the vanquished tribe had begun. As the band began *Deutchesland Über Alles*, the German National Anthem, Adolf Hitler glanced upward at the twenty-four massive red and black swastika flags, snapping smartly in the river's breeze.

He recalled briefly how he had suspended the German onslaught at Dunkirk in order to consider his options. He waited while his incredulous officers fumed in frustration. At first, he had been inclined to let the British forces go "in a sporting spirit," he later wrote. But the force of the arguments by his General Staff overcame his respect for the British and their plight. After a brief respite, the new Imperial legions were unleashed in an all-out offensive against the retreating British Expeditionary Force at the channel port. The result was the most thorough rout of British arms in modern history.

At Dunkirk, Air Marshall Hermann Göring's arsenal of Messerschmitt 109's, Stuka dive-bombers, Focke-Wulf 110's, Junker 88's, Dorniers, and Heinkel bombers had barely managed to overcome the RAF's nimble, speedier Hurricanes and the much faster, heavily armoured Spitfires. Though fewer in number, the RAF fought valiantly with clever feints, radio games and the new Oboe airborne location scanners.

In the end, the sheer numerical superiority of the Luftwaffe had prevailed, throttling shipping in the Channel, and wearing the enemy down by attrition through relentless 'sitting-duck' round-the-clock bombing attacks on airfields, heavy industries, and aircraft factories. This, along with the strafing of munitions works and fuel depots rendered the RAF unable to replenish its diminishing petrol reserves needed to keep their aircraft aloft. It was slow death by strangulation and starvation of supply lines.

The submarine wolf-pack hunting methods had taken a severe toll and had all but crippled allied shipping. The unrestricted bombing of cities, particularly London, was Hitler's signature piece, intended to convince the British Government of the futility of continued resistance. After eight months, it succeeded. An underground cadre of politicians and wealthy industrialists, sympathetic to the Nazi cause, conspired to throw Prime Minister Winston Churchill out of office for defying and ridiculing the Führer's offers of peace. The Wartime Cabinet vanished. As had Churchill. Herr Hitler was not amused. Churchill had to be captured or killed; he was too potent a force, a rallying point for bruised British pride, to be left at large.

As a psychological propaganda display, the Führer had chosen to make the final leg of the flight from Paris with limited fighter aircraft support. Air Marshall Göring offered his personal assurance of safety, boasting that he would fly a captured Spitfire from his palatial country mansion, Valhalla, to the ceremonial acceptance of surrender, later in the morning. The Luftwaffe's defeat of the vastly-outnumbered but excellent RAF, and the resulting loss of the Royal Navy's capital ships and destroyers, combined with the debacle of Dunkirk, all led to a chain of events that forced the collapse of England, the Lion, the bastion of democracy. The 'green and pleasant land' now lay prostrate at Hitler's feet, betrayed from within and without. Soon, very soon, Russia, and then the Americas, would follow.

As the last note of the anthem faded into the breeze, Adolf Hitler approached the microphones on the dais, and waited for silence. After a minute passed, he raised his right arm, as an impatient schoolmaster might gesture to quiet an unruly class of children. He glared unblinkingly at the mass of his SS Praetorian Guard; its vast, silent ranks seemed to stretch like an endless black sea. All faces turned upward in silent anticipation. Still, he waited.

Upon his arrival at the dais, he had been informed that the two trains carrying General Rommel and Grand Admiral Doenitz, as well as several other commanders and junior officers of his own personal staff, had been delayed en-route by simultaneous acts of resistance sabotage. All Germans on board were reportedly unharmed, but the English Secret Intelligence Service thugs had cleanly evaded justice, for now. Gestapo Chief Müller vowed that they would be hunted down and summarily executed for sullying the dignity of this day. The image of the SIS perpetrators being led in shackles from Gestapo 'special treatment' cells in the Tower to join the seven wives of King Henry at the same chopping block, pleased him.

Hitler's initial alarm turned quickly to fury! As he waited, he composed himself, and then began to speak, slowly and with restraint.

"Citizens of the new British Protectorate and Fellow Aryans. I welcome you to the comradeship of our glorious Reich. You have made the wise decision: Capitulation or destruction to the very last village. Your government and its armed forces have been turned over to German authority. I congratulate you on your wisdom and proclaim this land as the English Territorial Protectorate and all of its inhabitants as subjects of the Greater German Reich. Your security and well being, as well as that of your families and relatives, will be ensured by your total co-operation with and unswerving loyalty to my Deputy, the Reich Protector Albert Speer and thus to me, your Führer, Adolf Hitler. Seig Heil!"

The magic was working. For hours, in his Paris hotel suite, he had practised his delivery in the dressing-room mirror. Only Bormann, his Secretary, and Ländler, his speech coach, were privy to the Leader's preparation, which now preceded every public appearance. Using eyes, hands and voice, the actor's arsenal, he made his own compelling stagecraft to charm, bully, seduce and cajole his audiences.

He knew how Josef Goebbels' Ministry of Propaganda newsreel cameras and technical wizards could enhance and enrich his performances into Wagnerian drama. This was to be his finest hour. Nothing, not a syllable or gesture could be left to chance. He, Adolf, the corporal from Linz, Austria, had accomplished what neither Napoleon Bonaparte nor Frederick the Great could manage. Only a few invaders in history had managed to invade and subdue this proud island nation. The glorious Roman Dictator Julius, the Danish Vikings and later William the

Bastard, were his only recorded forerunners. The Treaty of Versailles was dead. In addition, with its demise, the humiliating, ignominious terms of surrender suffered by his adopted homeland had been paid back in full, to France in June 1940.

Now it was England's turn. They had been warned, but Winston Churchill had spurned Germany's generous peace offers and continued on his destructive path to national ruin.

England, Western Europe's jewel and industrial dynamo, with her bountiful mineral and technical resources, industrial might, skilled labour force and fabulous wealth and treasures were his for the taking. Himmler's SS Office of Economic Development had located and tabulated every troy ounce of the Bank of England's vast gold reserves. The crown jewels and the accumulated wealth of centuries of Imperial rule and foreign plunder had been appropriated and were being evaluated and catalogued. Göring had requested the Führer's special permission to inspect the country's art collections, for possible future 'selective relocation' to Germany.

The Royal Family had been placed under lenient house arrest at Windsor Castle; all, that is, but the two young Princesses. They had been removed to Canada, on the liner *Queen Elizabeth*, near the war's outbreak. The King and Queen had refused to leave their country with the royal children. Hitler had no immediate plans for the couple and their close relatives, only to keep them in relative comfort in the countryside, as invaluable trading markers for future consideration with the rest of the Empire. That and whatever propaganda uses Goebbels could orchestrate. He sensed the Royals to be typically reserved, quietly resistant aristocrats who might ultimately prove to be untrustworthy. The King's half-brother, Thomas, could serve as a figurehead Regent, if Hitler lost patience with the royal couple.

England was secure. Ireland would follow. Scotland, situated on the northernmost border of the Protectorate, was not. Its geography and the lessons learned from history made the enormous cost of forays by German troops and armour into that country too great. With Case 'Barbarossa' against Russia ready to proceed, Hitler and the generals agreed that, while Scotland posed a threat, enforced containment was the best they could hope for. Until Russia was taken down, Scotland would be kept at bay.

Hitler appointed Albert Speer, the energetic, dashing and gifted Reich-Minister of Munitions, to the position of Reich-Protector. His brilliance in masterminding the slave labour programs in the factories of occupied Europe, his early party membership and unswerving loyalty, and his organisational genius, all combined with an engineer's grasp of the need for structure, order and strict accountability, making him the perfect choice. Hitler also needed his architectural vision to fulfil his bold plan for the construction of a magnificent new centre of Germanic culture in London.

Speer's fluent knowledge of English would also be an advantage in communicating the Führer's 'master plan' to the notoriously lazy, monolingual British lower and middle classes. As for the nobility, they could be moulded to his ideals through the example of compliance to be set by the King and Queen. Many, like the Windsor Family itself, were intimately related to the German Hanoverian royal house and were likely, by genetic disposition, at least in Himmler's opinion, to be amenable to the Party's will. Those who resisted would be imprisoned and held without trial, as would their heirs and servants, and their possessions would be confiscated for transport to the Reich.

Reichsführer-SS Heinrich Himmler had managed to disguise his loathing for and envy of the brilliant young Speer; he politely applauded the Führer's announcement in the Reich Chancellery politely but unenthusiastically. A bitterly-disappointed Reich Air Marshall Hermann Göring, whose Luftwaffe was largely responsible for the German victory over England, petulantly excused himself from the meeting, complaining of a sudden, splitting migraine.

But Himmler, ever the strategist, conceded that Speer, Hitler's 'wonder child,' might well prove to be a useful and manageable tool for overseeing and implementing his sacred SS/Nazi doctrines in the occupied territory. After all, the youthful, ambitious, and attractive but indiscreet Speer had inadvertently supplied Himmler with prima facie photographic evidence of his predilection for serial sexual indiscretions with numerous women of questionable character and racial attributes.

Himmler's SS Planning and Race Departments were proceeding with a controlled reign of terror, a 'carrot and stick' policy under the zealous guardianship of Gestapo Heinrich Müller. They would ensure rapid pacification of the troublesome elements of the population to in order to eliminate residual resistance, all the while promoting racial purification, and 'cultural harmonisation' with Nazi ideals and Aryan spiritual values.

Sturmbannführer Johannes Bosch, of the Waffen-SS Wiking Division, had been personally selected by Himmler to present the ceremonial red battle flag to the Führer, which would be used in administering Reich Protector Speer's oath of office. Bosch, a double specialist medical graduate in Internal Medicine and Surgery of the University of Tubingen, had been pursuing post-doctoral studies at Cambridge when war was declared in 1939. Returning home, he was quickly scouted as a likely recruit and courted tirelessly by SS talent-hunters.

The SS was desperate for highly qualified medical staff to serve in the field with the élite Waffen armed forces, as well as for other, undisclosed purposes. Bosch politely refused the Admissions Board's offer of non-combatant honorary membership in the SS and volunteered instead for Waffen training at the Leipzig Academy. There, his leadership abilities, discipline, Aryan idealism and preparedness to undertake and master the most rigorous training assignments with ease, quickly marked him for future leadership.

Bosch's credentials were impeccable. Athletic, handsomely dashing, fiercely loyal, and well educated, he was the embodiment of the Nazi world order. His racial purity had been meticulously traced back six generations by the SS Office of Racial Purity, and was not found to be wanting. His pedigree extended back to solid Silesian land-owning gentry in the sixteenth century.

Several distinguished public servants, as well as a continuous source of decorated, volunteer soldiers and sailors for the major German wars of survival were to be found among his ancestors. Johannes' father, Alfred, had served the Kaiser with distinction at the First Battle of the Somme. He survived a badly botched German gas attack when the wind changed direction, as the meteorological officer had correctly predicted, blowing the lethal fog of mustard gas back over the hapless German trenches. He was hospitalised briefly and discharged honourably.

When sufficiently recovered, he purchased a fabric factory, with the assistance of a local Jewish dry goods merchant. The enterprising pair soon secured a major and exclusive contract with the Kaiser's Imperial Government to provide the highly specialised fabric covering the fuselage and wings of German military aircraft. Other lucrative contracts were to follow, as they expanded their research in the new field of synthetic materials.

Johannes was an eager student of his father's teachings and, by early boyhood, had amassed an encyclopaedic knowledge of organic chemistry and the arcane mysteries of synthetic dyes, as well as the related field of explosives. However, his first love was biology and with his father's blessing, applied for and won a scholarship for pre-medical studies at Tubingen.

Himmler's researchers had been ordered to re-examine Bosch's meticulous Academy entrance records but could uncover no evidence of Jewish or Slavic genetic degeneration of the pure Germanic breeding stock. Nor was there any reason to suspect Bolshevik political contamination lurking under the family bedsheets. He was the perfect cupbearer to the god, Adolf Hitler, for this momentous occasion.

The Wiking SS-Division had been formed to recruit suitable "Germanic/Nordic types" from such locales as Scandinavia. Many of its senior officers however, like Bosch, were German. The Wiking SS had been in the vanguard of the final amphibious assault from the south up towards London. Bosch had distinguished himself, winning an Iron Cross, with oak leaves, for valour.

He had spearheaded the capture of an entire Hurricane fighter airbase and secured almost all personnel and the twenty-five aircraft intact, before the English sappers could set off the explosive charges. His battle group suffered severe losses but persevered, advancing into the capital. Hitler chose the regiment for the day's ceremonies for the historic irony of their name: a reminder of the Viking invaders of yore, as well as their respectable combat record. His judgement, once again, seemed infallible.

Johannes was ecstatic to have been selected from so many candidates for the day's event, but his personal demeanour reflected nothing except the SS-man's pride of membership in this most vaunted of the Nazi fighting arsenal. As he awaited the signal from the podium to begin his procession with the furled battle flag, he thought of his father, long dead and the pride the old soldier would have felt in his son's achievement today. The Führer was nearing the conclusion of his oration. Johannes eyes flickered briefly to the fire-blackened stone walls of the remains of Westminster Palace, the British House of Parliament.

Then, it came flooding back: the Cambridge autumn of 1938 and the long walks riverside with his English lover, Julienne. She had been his laboratory assistant in the Department of Cardiology, and was so reserved that it was more than a month before she would accept his invitation for an after-lecture celebratory beer and snack at the off-campus pub, 'The Ox and Firkin'. It took less time and little persuasion for them to become "known, in the Biblical sense," as Barnes, his post-doctoral advisor, delicately phrased it.

Juli, which he pronounced 'Yuli', had done her homework and had taken the time to check up on this handsome and accomplished medical student through the underground singles network on campus. As their attachment deepened, 'Johnny' grew impatient with Juli's absences from

Friday afternoon to Sunday morning, every week, to visit her family. He could not understand such unremitting devotion, good family member that he was, too.

His patience turned to brooding, moodiness, and wild supposition. She obviously was playing him for the fool and he was determined to confront her upon her return to their shared flat. It was Barnes who had first noticed the deterioration in his student's attitude and, when he asked why, he was informed that, "It is none of your damn business, anyway. Stick to your pickled hearts and I'll keep out of your way. If I need your advice, I'll ask for it!"

Fortunately, Barnes did not give up so easily. A few pints later, an apology accepted, and the truth was out. Johannes had a broken heart. His Juli was two-timing him, he sputtered, with some goon in town.

"I really think you're a bit off-base, old man. The girl goes straight home, and comes directly back. She's with her family every blessed moment when she's not here with you."

"No, I don't know. Why in hell would she want to see them that often? Is she that attached to them that she can't bear more than a few days out of their sight? She's not a child."

"You're correct, Johnny my lad. No, she's not a child, she's Jewish. Is that a problem for you?"

"She's what?"

"Jewish."

"But why does that compel her to leave me every weekend?

"My thick-headed friend, she loves and adores you beyond reason, but she goes home to be with her aged parents and her sister for the Sabbath, as any good Orthodox Jewish girl would. Did your sainted Lutheran pastor never talk about the roots of Christianity? Good Lord man, her parents would be so humiliated just to know that their beautiful daughter was consorting with the likes of you, a German, and a Christian. She's risking a lot, to be with you, in these times."

"So. And what makes you the expert, Doctor Barnes?"

"My father was a Jew, a doctor, with a modest family practice in Winnipeg, Canada. Father used to remark that he was unsure whether we were the chosen people or the frozen people. But my mother's not of the faith, so I'm not a full member of the tribe; I do know the traditions and history. I can read the Word in Hebrew, and can speak it well enough to curse and say my prayers. I try to attend synagogue at least three times a year, to observe the high holy festivals.

"Before they bury me, I dream of going to Palestine as a Zionist pioneer. Make love to a gorgeous raven-haired beauty, dance the *Hora* naked, and drink myself stupid on the shores of the Red Sea."

"I'm really sorry to have been such a damn fool, Andrew. I love her very much. I didn't know. Thank you for putting up with me. One more thing..."

"Anything."

"If you're Canadian, why do you speak like a real Limey?"

"It's a bit of a gift, actually, Johnny. I pick up accents and languages very easily. I could have survived nicely in most of Europe, including the Fatherland. I was actually doing linguistics at Leeds when the thunderbolt hit. I can learn the structure of a language and become fluent with very little effort. Better to do something more practical, so here I rest, a medical hack."

The rift healed slowly and passionately upon Juli's return, with warm, teary love and good German hot chocolate. After her shower, she returned to the bedroom wearing only one of his dress shirts, unbuttoned. She knelt at the end of the bed, lit a cigarette, and lazily blew out the match as she exhaled a long cloud of smoke in his direction.

"Well, my love, it seems that it's your day for surprises," she smiled mysteriously.

"Don't tell me. Oh, no. I've forgotten your birthday. Forgive..."

"No, no. Nothing like that. Guess again, my fine young doctor. Look!" Watching his eyes, Juli rose from the bed and turned sideways, pulling the shirt open and holding it against her hips with her fists.

She watched his expression change from confusion to recognition to wide-eyed wonder and pure joy. "Oh, my God. Ja, yes, yes! You're expecting. I'm going to be a father!" He bounced on the bed in childlike delight. "My Juli! My darling! I love you! How did I miss it? Put out that cigarette! Come here, I want to kiss you!"

"Now you and Barnes will really have something to talk about other than heart surgery on pigs. Your child will be Jewish, because, you see, I'm the Mommy and I'm certified kosher. One hundred percent. And that's how it works. The child belongs to the mother's tribe." She paused, noting a subtle change in his face. Or was it in his posture? "Are you alright?"

The command from the podium, ordering him to proceed forward and join the honour guard, jolted Johannes back. He shook his head imperceptibly, trying to remember. Trying to forget. It must have been

IP X - (1968)
ore close down.

Camp X looking north from Lake Ontario, 1968.

just a dream. It truly couldn't have happened. As he knelt to offer the ceremonial red flag to the Führer, the realisation flooded over him. It was not fantasy. He could hardly breathe.

His ears rang loudly and he was only vaguely aware of taking the Führer's left hand. He stood, head bowed, his hand still gripping the flagstaff, while the oath was administered. Dazed, he released his grasp only when Speer tugged it sharply from him. The sergeant-at-arms gave him a peculiar glance, as he solemnly marched, at funeral cadence, backwards, to his place in formation.

The deed was done. Great Britain no longer existed, annexed, another fiefdom in The Greater German Reich. He was a small part of that history. But he was also a disgrace to the Holy Order of the SS and a coward, as well. Some day he would pay for his sins to the Fatherland, to the service, and to his beloved, lost Juli and his unknown child.

The officers and staff had by now arrived and were quickly led to assemble with Hitler and Speer on the reviewing stand. It was the time in the ceremony for a display of German physical excellence with a gymnastics exhibition by scores of lithe, teen-aged girls.

All eyes in the reviewing stand were turned to the cordoned area where the athletes began an intricate display of callisthenics, creating a kaleidoscope of languorous multi-hued ribbons, and coloured hoops swirling gracefully over the heads of the young performers. Their artistry and obvious collective physical beauty were a welcome contrast to the solemnity of the swearing-in ceremony.

Hitler looked on with subdued amusement, and then turned aside to speak with an aide. The continuing absence of Hermann Göring, the

Luftwaffe Air Marshall, was upsetting and most annoying. Why had he allowed him to fly solo, in an enemy aircraft? It was just like him, the barnstorming, harebrained daredevil of the heady post-war Weimar Republic days.

The rasping drone of a single engine plane approaching overhead drew the spectators' attention from the choreographed grace of the golden-haired athletes. Hitler looked up, shading his eyes against the direct glare of the mid-day sun. "It's Hermann, finally! Thank the gods." He made a mental note to address this breach of protocol and common sense.

A single shot shattered the left breast pocket button of his uniform and he fell backward with a low moan. A fusillade of 50 mm cannon shells flayed a deadly hail of wood splinters and chips from the granite walls, as an RCAF Mosquito fighter-bomber dove directly out of the sun at the reviewing stand. A red, third eye appeared on the forehead of the massive Sergeant-at-arms; he careened backwards, arms splayed like a drunken saloon-fighter, and took the Deputy Reich Protector with him over the shattered wooden railing.

Pandemonium reigned. The assembled troops and athletes scrambled for cover on the ground, or raced for the river. The small flotilla of armed motor launches that were moored offshore, attempted to return fire while evading the Mosquito's guns, colliding and capsizing, while their frantic crews jumped overboard. A few soldiers managed to fire their rifles impotently in the general direction of the speeding aircraft, while strafing rounds chunked through the river's surface like the needle of a monstrous sewing machine, churning it into a crimson-flecked mass grave. Abruptly, the Mosquito banked and pulled up, climbing into the sun, and vanished. Triple A fire from anti-aircraft batteries made the ground tremble, then it, too, sporadically died out and ceased altogether. The fuel tank of a launch exploded with a thunderous flash, just as the vessel was sinking. Then, an eerie, shocked stillness fell, but for the cries of the Mosquito's wounded quarry.

The Morse signal flashed off the ionosphere down to radio Hydra, at Camp X, on Lake Ontario, punching Braille-like coded groups on the machines' paper tape. Rapidly decoded by chief radio operator Bill Hardcastle, the information was taken immediately to Camp X Commandant, Colonel Gordon Graham:

'TALON TO STALWART:

RE: TENT PEG STOP

JAEL HAS SPIKED SISERA STOP.'

The signal was instantly retransmitted to British Security Operation HQs in Toronto, New York City and to POTUS, The White House.

SOE and BSO had set England on fire, exactly as Prime Minister Winston Churchill had ordered.

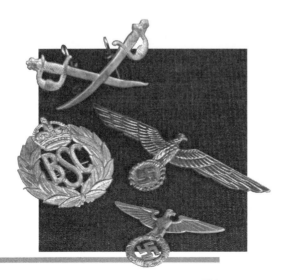

CHAPTER 6

IN THE BEGINNING

In the twenty-odd years since Gord MacKenna had been demobilised from His Majesty's artillery regiment, he and his wife, Gloria, had rarely missed a Wednesday evening at Watsmede's only public house, 'The Ploughman and Scythe'. He had returned home safe, and reasonably sound, on New Year's Day, 1919. As far as his general health was concerned, he did admit to having "lost a bit of his edge, 'over there' ".

Fondly, Gloria explained to anyone who would listen, "What he says he lost, he never really had in the first place. What's more, he's nearly stone deaf from the shelling, and growing worse by the day. Either that, or he's been ignoring me ever since, haven't you, Dearie?"

The heavy incendiary bombings had shut down power and water in the cities, making all early attempts at organised or effective response to the fire alarms nearly futile. The blazes created a trail of destruction, vaporising everything in their paths: brick, steel, concrete, or wood. Only through the heroic labours of volunteer bucket brigades, and the toil of local fire companies, were they all eventually quenched. The valiant efforts of those who braved the hellish conflagrations and falling chunks of crumbling structures were made all the more difficult by the necessity to dodge the deadly strafing of low-flying Messerschmidts, Focke-Wulffs, and the rest of Germany's air forces. "God save England? More bloody like *Gott strafe England!*" was the local headmaster's pronouncement.

Watsmede, a coastal village in Kent, numbered little more than a thousand souls. It straddled the intersection of two major Luftwaffe radar-guidance beams, becoming effectively a 'blind spot.' This stroke of good fortune spared the little village from heavy damage. The occasional bombardment that it did receive was more the result of unintentional afterthought than malicious intent, and usually occurred when near-mortally damaged German bombers were forced to discard their remaining payloads before limping homeward across the Channel.

The greatest threat that this posed for Watsmede's inhabitants was not the fiery infernos that ignited the more populous cities, but the inconvenience created when a half-dozen duds fell like the hammers of the gods in a single week. Most of the impotent bombs landed harmlessly in the River Wat, playing havoc only with its indigenous trout, catfish, and frog populations.

One monster, however, a two-ton blockbuster, plummeted through the roof of the Hepple family home, and plunged three storeys into the basement, where it lodged, unexploded, narrowly missing the aged housecat, and terrifying the sleeping lodger. After both had been administered brandy and then evacuated, the Chief Air Raid Warden posted 'Gunner' Gord MacKenna and two of his Home Guard mates as sentries to prevent entry by any morbidly curious neighbours. He then drove his venerable Austin 7 to nearby Hopespur, dodging bomb craters, to summon an Army explosives disposal unit to see to defusing the intruder.

Gord had encountered no difficulty in persuading the Home Guard recruiting officer at the Town Hall that he was fit enough to serve King and Country once again. He, along with many of his drinking companions, known collectively as the 'Old Contemptibles', had answered "Yes!" to Field Marshall Haig's "I Need You" posters and had joined up in 1914 to defend hearth, home and empire from Kaiser Bill's rampaging Hunnish hordes.

"History repeats itself," Gord had remarked dryly, after telling Gloria that he had been accepted for duty once again. "Deaf as a stone, and a bit stiff in the joints, but fit enough to give old Adolf the royal welcome, if the bugger dares show his plug-ugly, my dear!"

"That's if you hear him first, Love."

During the temporary lull following Dunkirk, Winston Churchill had correctly predicted the Nazi leader's intentions. Churchill made urgent nation-wide radio appeals to all able-bodied men, women and youth of the newly-created Citizen's Defence Force to 'make all necessary preparations to drive back the Nazi invader into the sea, resolutely, even mercilessly; at the point of pitchforks, if need be.'

For many of the Home Guard, the 'pitchfork' was not too far from reality. Gord's detachment was issued 1914-vintage Lee-Enfield rifles, which, even in their heyday had the unpleasant and frequently fatal habit of jamming if the firing mechanism overheated. Even these unreliable weapons were far better than those of other unfortunates whose 'call to arms' yielded rusted, antique fowling pieces, better employed by gentlefolk of another era for taking sporting pot shots at small, low-flying game birds.

The Prime Minister had ordered that church bells be silenced, to be rung only in the event of imminent invasion. Miles of barbed wire lay in wait on the shorelines. Floating mines by the thousands bobbed offshore. Tens of thousands of 'beaters', or derelict automobiles and assorted obsolete pieces of farm machinery, were enthusiastically collected, carted to, and dumped randomly in open fields to deter landings by troop-carrying glider transports. Signposts were uprooted or turned helter-skelter to mislead and confuse prospective pathfinders of an invading force.

Britain's people's army was armed and ready. They would repel the vanguard and crush any survivors on the beaches. In the text of his address, the Prime Minister had only briefly alluded to the extensive military defensive preparations being carried out jointly by the unified Chiefs of Staff. He judged that there would be a greater psychological effect were he to appeal to the pride of ordinary Britons as the sole defenders of their native shores.

Overall, it was a valiant strategy. And it succeeded. Almost.

The German High Command's (OKW) plan for the invasion of England, 'Case Sea Lion', was readied in detail by early 1940, as was the corollary post-invasion plan, designed to consolidate, exploit, and expand the German beachhead in order to take control of London.

Führer Adolf Hitler's puzzling and frustrating hesitation in pursuing and annihilating the retreating British Expeditionary Force on the beaches of Dunkirk in June finally turned to talk of invasion. Relieved and ready, the OKW immediately proposed that Case Sea Lion be mounted under the supreme command of General Field Marshall of the Armed Forces, Gerd von Runstedt. Von Runstedt's loyalty to Hitler had come under a cloud of suspicion in 1938 and he was subsequently retired from service during the ferocity of the pre-war army purges, but was not tried for treason. In August 1939, one month before the outbreak of hostilities, von Runstedt was recalled to active duty and promoted to Commander of Army Group South. Hitler's shrewd choice was rewarded by the rapid collapse of France, under von Runstedt's extraordinary leadership.

As per OKW's recommendation, Hitler accepted von Runstedt as Supreme Commander, Case Sea Lion. He issued a Führer War Directive to Reich Air Marshal Hermann Göring that a successful cross-Channel landing would be contingent upon the Luftwaffe's pursuit and destruction of the British Royal Air Force, as well as the neutralisation of the

Royal Navy. Marshall Göring eagerly accepted the challenge; his Luftwaffe would carry the standard as the chosen instrument of the Führer's will.

Von Runstedt, with no option but to bow to Göring's superior political shrewdness accepted Hitler's decision, knowing that others, more favoured than he, would continue to be the 'invisible hands' influencing his leader's decision-making. He also fully realised as an article of faith that supremacy in the air must precede a landing and a modified 'blitzkrieg', or lightening warfare, was the only chance for success on land. It would require an all-out assault to swiftly neutralise or obliterate Britain's still-potent defences. For that, he needed Heinz Guderian.

Blitzkreig was a highly mechanised offensive battle strategy, secretly perfected in the 1930's by German General Heinz Guderian, on Russian soil, in co-operation with the Russian military. Thus, the terms of the 1918 Versailles Treaty forbidding German re-armament, were cleverly skirted. During the March 1938 forced union of Austria with the Fatherland, the Anschluss, Guderian's armoured columns, were on hand, to emphasise and lend dramatic effect to the advisability of caving in to German pressure.

Most recently, it was the linchpin of the battle triumphs of General Guderian's panzer divisions' tanks, mobile panzer troops, artillery, and Stuka dive-bombers against Poland, Belgium, and France. Although some historians argue that it was a British innovation, a young French Colonel, Charles De Gaulle, had detailed lightning warfare's highly original theories, in 1934, in his book, *The Army of the Future*

France's general staff commanders had belittled or ignored the junior officer. De Gaulle's radical ideas called for the rapid deployment of first strike, highly mobile mechanised units, and followed by waves of light infantry with artillery support. The French military paid dearly for their hide-bound complacency in their surrender to Germany on June 21, 1940, in the Compiègne Forest.

Many of Britain's leading military strategists were old enough to have personally witnessed, if not experienced, the Great War's appalling toll in human lives and the horrific slaughter created by years of static trench warfare snaking across France and Belgium. Of these, a few were sufficiently aware of the stunning potential of integrated mobile assault units. Those who dared speak out were hard-pressed to convince more than a handful of politicians of the urgent necessity for an immediate, enormously costly, and politically unpopular national program to refit, rearm, and retrain the British Army during the pacifist and prosperous 1930's.

Case Sea Lion called for a mass landing on a two-hundred mile front from Ramsgate to Lyme Regis, throwing into action 1,722 barges with 470 tugs, 1,161 motorised dinghies, and 155 troop transports. A horrified Grand Admiral Erich Raeder objected directly to Hitler, citing that the exposure of so vast and so widely dispersed an armada to enemy shore artillery, and to British craft, no matter how feeble, was complete folly. Raeder proposed a narrower front, from Folkestone to Eastbourne. Chief of the General Staff, General Franz Halder, took great exception to Raeder's 'tinkering'. He exploded, "Complete suicide, Admiral! I might just as well feed my men through a sausage grinder."

Von Runstedt knew that Case Sea Lion was fatally flawed and that Raeder was posturing to avoid admitting the shortsightedness of his Admiralty's plan. Halder was correct in that Germany was not prepared for a cross-Channel amphibious assault of the magnitude prescribed by Sea Lion. In addition to the need for complete prior mastery of the air over England and The Channel, the German navy lacked the numbers of transports, barges, and landing craft required by Sea Lion. It had no aircraft carriers and half of its destroyer fleet was in dry-dock for repairs, or worse, had been sent to the bottom of the sea by the Royal Navy in the recent battle for Norway.

Von Runstedt needed to find a better approach, and quickly; he knew that Göring's mission, if successful, would be a costly victory unless the means to take and hold the island were immediately at hand. The plan must be multi-pronged, precisely timed, and tightly co-ordinated.

It must also come as a complete surprise to the island's defenders. The need for total secrecy was, obviously, paramount to its success. It could not be a wholesale marine invasion; it would be impossible to prepare and mount a massive assault on the coast of France without Allied agents gaining knowledge of it. The Channel weather, unpredictable at the best of times, could blow up a gale without warning and sink an entire fleet of overloaded and unwieldy troop vessels.

There was only one feasible option open to Von Runstedt: the first wave of opportunity must come from the sky. Crack paratroops with airborne 'shock troop' regiments would drop in waves from bombers, and more would land simultaneously in gliders, at strategic locations across the country. They would spike defensive positions, intimidate and subdue the civilian population, seize key communications posts, and capture and neutralize command centres.

All but the most senior armed forces officers and politically important captives would be immediately eliminated. Of those spared, most would first be 'interrogated' by Reinhard Heydrich's counter-intelligence branch of the SD for information critical to the military. Then they, too, would be summarily executed. A very select few would be culled for transport to Berlin, for further 'counter-intelligence interviews'.

"The head of the snake having been cut off, the body will die," Heydrich concluded coldly.

Reinforcements, comprised of light infantry accompanied by panzer heavy armoured and artillery units, would make up the second assault wave. Equipment would have to be transported by vessels seized from, or manufactured in, the occupied territories; while air transport would be required to ferry the troops, yet another key role for Göring's air command. Co-ordination was essential or the entire assault would fall apart, before it could even begin, von Runstedt realised.

Despite OKW's assurances, Hitler remained sceptical. The planned invasion of Russia, Case Barbarossa, was straining resources even though Reich Minister of Armaments, Albert Speer, had coerced the Ruhr's factories to double their output of weaponry and matériel.

The Luftwaffe's tactics, however, were paying dividends. Britain was under round-the-clock siege from the air. Her Fighter Command's ability to maintain a constant, potent defensive cover for the entire country was being daily eroded. True, German losses were mounting, but the RAF's were even greater. The Luftwaffe had the capability to harass and bottle-up the Home Fleet in the Channel. This, coupled with the U-boat campaign to strike at every possible opportunity, kept the Fleet on the defensive.

Britain was like a prizefighter who had been knocked off balance; the country was still swinging dangerously and defiantly, and connecting effectively, but it was winded and losing its offensive edge. Germany had only to continue to circle warily, looking for and exploiting every weakness, to land telling body blows before administering the *coup de grâce*.

Gerd von Runstedt had no choices left if he was to have men and equipment ready before the English could re-group and restore their severely mauled ordnance and resources. He carefully prepared his final presentation for Hitler and the Supreme Commanders at the Führer's eastern headquarters, the Wolf's Lair.

The air outside the East Prussian stronghold was filled with annoying swarms of gnats; inside, the atmosphere was equally buzzing, electric with a mixture of tension and anticipation. The leader of the Third Reich, who personally poured the Field Marshall's tea, welcomed Gerd von Runstedt warmly. Following pleasantries concerning the well being of von Runstedt's only son, currently serving with the Wehrmacht in Poland, Hitler took him by the arm and led the Field Marshall to the head of a massive oaken map table.

Putting on his wire-rimmed reading glasses, the Führer called the meeting to order. "I need you to convince me that this invasion is not just possible, Field Marshall, but that its success is highly probable. You have my full attention for as much time as you require. I have set aside the morning.

"Gentlemen, you will bring your chairs and gather up here with the Field Marshall. Please, no questions and no interruptions. General Pfaff will be forced to forgo his nicotine habit for the duration. You thought I didn't know? Your uniform reeks of it. Your fingers are the colour of a coolie's. Take my advice and drop it. Herbal tea is the antidote and fresh spring water: at least a litre an hour. Flush the poisons from your system! Then you'll wonder why you ever gave in to the weed in the first place. You'll feel like a new man. See me after for some reading material on the subjects of abstention and Zen, from a monk in Tibet. Himmler's library is an excellent source. He has studied the likelihood that there exists a racial wellspring that unites us with Aryans of the East. I commend a visit to his Studies of Racial Origins Archives to you."

The room was deadly quiet. Embarrassed, Pfaff could only wonder if the Führer had ever considered the logistics of clambering in and out of a tank turret in a battle to relieve oneself at a frequency dictated by the 'cure'. Perhaps not, and best not to raise the question, he thought.

"Yes, thank you, my Führer. I have been..."

"Discussion will follow the presentation," Hitler snapped, dismissively. "Kindly proceed, Field Marshall."

"Thank you, my Führer," von Runstedt began. "Gentlemen, I can save everyone a great deal of time if you would allow me to assume that you are all quite familiar with Case Sea Lion. This new approach which I am about to present to you, requires your concession that, although brilliantly conceived as an exercise in marine military planning, Sea Lion was quite hopelessly out of alignment with the reality of the enemy's disposition, and with our naval capabilities at this time.

"I certainly do not discount the value of our navy's contribution, but it must be in a significantly ancillary role; to ferry troops, equipment, support personnel and matériel once we have gained a foothold by air-drops and gliders. Let me explain how this would proceed, in three major stages..."

Von Runstedt expected an angry outburst from his colleagues. There was not a murmur. Either the commanders had been intimidated by their Leader's admonition, or were waiting to see him fall flat on his face. Four members of Sea Lion's original planning group were stolidly studying the intricate patterns of the Persian carpet overlaying the dark oak floors.

"Colleagues," he continued, "may I draw to your attention this chart showing the disposition of airborne troops and glider crews. We will need every available means of aerial transport...." His monologue, illustrated with topographical maps, charts, aerial photographs and projected images of war weaponry continued for two hours. When he finished, the room sat in hushed silence.

Hitler rose from his chair, extending his hand to the distinguished Prussian warhorse. "Wonderful! Congratulations, von Runstedt, to you and your staff. Gentlemen, if we all do our jobs as Heinz has described them, England shall be ours. I give you my unqualified approval and expect all officers here to co-operate and follow this plan to the letter. Without deviation! Seig Heil!"

The room burst into applause. Hitler declared a recess and the briefing room emptied quickly into the blistering Prussian noontime. Von Runstedt, momentarily left alone, was taken aback by the Führer's enthusiastic approval.

Hitler was secretly relieved that the plan did not depend on a first strike invasion by ships, over water. As a confirmed dry-lander and a one-time prison inmate, he unwittingly shared with the English sage, Dr. Johnson, the belief that 'being in a ship was like being in jail, with the added chance of being drowned.'

Von Runstedt had convinced Hitler that he could deliver the decisive opening blows, but he was counting on General Erwin Rommel, another brilliant panzer strategist, to continue his command of the Seventh Panzer Division. Nevertheless, anything could happen. Rommel was obviously marked for higher command and could be whisked off without notice to another theatre by the Führer, a distinct possibility now, what with the events developing in North Africa.

The invasion timeline, as explained by von Runstedt in precise detail, allowed less than a year for preparation. It would depend on the

full co-operation of all branches of the Supreme Command, the
Intelligence Services, and Reich heavy industry.

The operation was still code-named Sea Lion, although Air Marshall
Göring, with his usual dark humour, had argued at lunch for the name
'Case King Harold,' to reflect the hapless Saxon monarch, who, during
the Battle of Hastings in 1066, was shot in the eye with a Norman arrow.

The Abwehr's Admiral Wilhelm Canaris and SD Chief Reinhard
Heydrich were both closely informed of England's formidable military and
secret intelligence services, even more so than was Göring, the founder of
the Prussian state secret police, the Gestapo. They advised that the original name, Sea Lion, be retained to mislead M-5 and M-6. Britain's intelligence 'eyes and ears' at home and abroad, though severely hampered
by the lack of an organized resistance network in the occupied countries,
was not without 'friends', "eyeless in Gaza", as Heydrich, ever the scholarly dilettante, had remarked, darkly.

Gloria and Gord were unhappy. It was bad enough that the country
was occupied, crawling with troops and tanks, and that the
Protectorate's puppet government toadied up to the Nazis. But then the
'bloody Jerry's' started carting people away, like their neighbours Kate
and Phil, who ran the local pub. Gloria had heard that the two publi-
cans were accused of subverting the civil order, whatever the devil that
meant. Maybe the 'Ploughman and Scythe's bangers and mash had
done in the District Gauleiter (Nazi governor-administrator) and good rid-
dance to the officious little bugger. He'd been missing for a week and the
Boche military police were looking everywhere for clues to his disappear-
ance, 'detaining' and questioning anyone they chose.

The Jerry officers seemed to have taken a liking to the 'How's Your
Wife', the locals' rhyming slang name for their 'establishment', and were
threatening to become regular patrons. Local gossip told it that Kate and
Phil's daughter, Jenny, the starry-eyed barmaid, had been seen three
times going into the Gestapo HQ in the old Harmony Arms Hotel, 'in the
company of one of the top dog officers, a Colonel, and 'one-armed to
boot,' after closing time. But that rumour had started after her parents'
arrest.

"Police business, lads," said Fred Cobb, with a wicked grin.

"That's not the kind of business I'd like to give her," said another.

"Dream on, old darlin'. Never mind. She's an informer and that's plain as the nose on your face. Her day of reckoning will come. In France, the Resistance has no truck with turncoats when they capture one of 'em. The Germans found one, just a child of sixteen, with skull and crossbones painted on a sign around her neck. She was crucified, alive, upside down at the town crossroads."

"Too good for her, I'd say."

"Hold on, lads. Has anyone here any proof about our Jenny? Anyone seen her mooning around this goon?" asked Gord, defiantly. "No? I thought not. You're all daft. She's a good lass and that's that. Show me proof and I'll be the first to...."

"Quiet down!" Gloria snapped. "Do you want to get us all arrested? You'll be doin' nothing of the sort. Shame on you all. Her Mom and Dad's in the Scrubs, or worse, and she's doin' what she thinks is the best thing for them, poor dear. Let's just mind our P's and Q's and let the others take whatever steps needed. We will rid the country of these weasels, but not while we're fighting among ourselves." She swept some non-existent crumbs off the oilcloth table cover with a dismissive gesture of finality. "Hush now. Here she is. Not one word from any of you!"

As she stepped into the pub, Jenny's pale, striking features were less than radiant. She walked quickly to the back office without speaking a word to anyone, and closed the door.

The German military behaved with considerable restraint after taking control of the town that morning. The first wave of invaders had dropped from the sky swiftly and silently just before dawn like a plague of lethal locusts. The few townsfolk who were outdoors at the time were either unaware of, or unable to immediately comprehend, what was happening in their town.

One young woman, walking home alone after finishing night shift at the local textile factory, was seized and hauled into an alleyway, confronted by a ten-man unit of glider paratroopers. A colonel, seemingly familiar with the town's layout and local government, had questioned her politely in near-flawless English regarding any knowledge that she or her family and friends might have had of an impending German raid.

When he was satisfied that she'd had no prior information, he ordered her gagged and bound, and held in an abandoned cellar. At noon, she was released, shaken and hungry but unharmed, and escorted to the Town Hall. There the town's entire population was assembled on the lawn, under the scrutiny of German paratroopers armed with sub-machine guns. Most, who had been rousted at gunpoint from their beds, sat in dazed silence, in their nightshirts, including the Mayor his council-lors and the Town Clerk. Wailing babies and crying children, the old and infirm, were given sips of water ladled from buckets provided for that purpose.

Off-duty police and senior officers were arrested in their homes and thrown into their own nick. The lone night Watch Commander and his sergeant had been killed while attempting to telephone the district super-intendent, and the invaders quickly disabled the telegraph and telephone lines, making it impossible to find out what was happening elsewhere.

When the sporadic fighting ended, confined to skirmishes on out-skirts of the town, the parachute Colonel addressed the townspeople. His message was simple, clear, and direct, "Go home and stay indoors for the next forty-eight hours. Abandon all thoughts of resistance. Troublemakers will be shot, on the spot, regardless of age or gender. Handguns and rifles, regardless of their vintage must be unloaded and ready to be confiscated. To avoid the unpleasantness and more serious consequences of discovery in your home following the amnesty period, have all firearms and ammunition ready when we come to your door. Meanwhile, your Mayor and Town officials will be held as 'security deposits' to guarantee your good behaviour and full co-operation. That is all. Heil Hitler!"

In the following weeks, despite curfews, patrols, checkpoints and the eternal presence of the Germans, the town's people were allowed to resume most of their pre-invasion activities. In lieu of the local newspa-per, and to counter German propaganda 'The Ploughman and Scythe' served as the community bulletin board and public opinion forum.

"One minute we were listening to the announcer tell about all the lit-tle boats from Dover picking up our boys on the French shore, and where's the bloody Jerry? I remember him talking about the 'miracle of Dunkirk,' don't you Glor, and next thing you know, boom! The Germans are blasting the daylights out of 'em. Poor sods, they didn't stand a bloody chance."

"But we put up a pretty good fight, just like Mr. Churchill said we ought to. And surely some got away."

"Fat lot of good, Fred. Churchill's giving his orders from God-knows-where, the government's gone over the hill with him, and we're left hold-ing the bag. We're joining the Thousand-Year Reich as soon as Adolf decides to drop over for a cuppa. They say he'll run the country into the ground, make us all his slaves to work the factories and mines, steal our gold and haul away our kids for the army."

"Just put a cork in it, will you?" Gloria responded shortly. "It's bad enough without your harping on the gory details. The Prime Minister's done the right thing. You can bet that he's not sitting there, twiddling his thumbs"

"Like I said, wherever 'there' is!"

"Alright, alright" Gord interrupted. "She said enough and that goes double for me, mate! You're forgetting who's the enemy here. Glor, let's head home. It'll be half an hour or more to get through the Jerry checkpoints. Best we get started or we'll miss curfew. Roy, time to go. Keep us company on the way, lad?"

Under cover of the moonless night sky, the Special Operations Bristol Blenheim bomber circled the drop zone for the third time, as the pilot evaluated the beacons laid out on the ground 1500 feet below the aircraft's belly.

"What's the hold-up, Flight?" queried Sylvia, leaning into the cockpit.

"Just checking thoroughly, Captain Smith. The flares are not placed precisely where I expected, but the pattern's arranged accurately. Here, have a look for yourself at my briefing sketch," he offered, while inclining the aircraft's port wing for a clearer view.

"It looks fine to me. What do you think, Lieutenant?"

"Close enough; I'm happy with it," Hugh affirmed.

"Nav, try to get a confirmation."

Using a miniature Morse key strapped to his upper leg, affectionately known as a 'bug', the Flight Navigator tapped out a rapid string of code. He removed his headset, holding the earphones so that Sylvia could listen. "Hugh's my W/T man. Here, you take it."

"Nothing but noise," Hugh remarked, pressing an earpiece against his helmet. "Resend, Flight?" he asked.

"No can do, too bloody risky. We either take you 'Joes' in now, or cut and run. This sector's usually safe from 'bandits', or night fighter patrols, but no guarantee. Hello, here's something, Nav."

As Hugh and the navigator concentrated, listening intently, they heard a faint Morse signal. After ten seconds of tense silence, the navigator broke in. "Those are the magic words, Flight. These blighters must be powered by a ruddy dry cell. Man battle stations," the navigator shouted, grinning. "We'll be over the jump point in...fifty-five seconds, Flight."

"Roger, Nav. The updrafts in these mountains are bloody treacherous, as you've likely been told. Wind speed, thirty knots: holding steady out of the north, northeast. Altitude, 1200 feet. Tail gunner has opened the hatch door. Have an eye for Nav's green light when we're over target, then tally ho; and good luck, chaps. Sorry, Captain."

"I prefer Chaps, better than 'Joes' anyway. Thanks, Flight, we'll need all the luck we can get. You too, Nav," Sylvia smiled.

Hugh and Sylvia scrambled aft to the Bristol's bomb bay as the pilot levelled off the four-engine aircraft, commencing his run. They attached their parachute static lines, then crouched on opposite sides of the opening, looking down into the darkness. The chorus of *Bonnie Charlie's Now Awa'* passed through Hugh's mind: 'Will ye no come back again?' He had often thought of returning to his father's ancestral hometown, close by Aberdeen, to purchase a small parcel of land for his retirement. His reverie was interrupted when Sylvia reached over and tapped his right shoulder.

"Heads up, mate!" The jump signal light had flashed green. "I'm going first," she shouted over the air turbulence. She was seated on the floor, her legs outstretched, and her feet over the edge of the opening, when she signalled 'thumbs up'.

Just as she was about to launch, the aircraft suddenly shuddered violently, like a wounded leviathan. 'Jesus, what's that?" A projectile whined ominously close to Hugh's ear, embedding itself in an overhead bulkhead. Another, narrowly missing Sylvia's shoulder, thudded into the fuselage and burst into flames. A dozen more followed it.

The interior of the plane began to fill with acrid, choking black smoke. From the rear, they could hear the chatter of the Bristol's tail gun. The plane lurched drunkenly to the right and began to climb steeply, its engines roaring as their propellers clawed for purchase in the thin air.

Fighting to keep himself from being thrown headfirst against the wall, Hugh struggled to lie face down, tightly grasping the edge of the 'Joe hole' hatch. For a split second, he recalled the helplessness he had once experienced during a terrifyingly exciting, wild ride on a one-man sled, careening uncontrollably sideways on the metal runners down an icy, tree-covered hill in High Park. That time, he had required six stitches over his left eye.

Both sides of the compartment's metal skin were being riddled with ragged punctures, the size of silver dollars. Fiery fragments of metal flew about, caroming wildly or piercing the structural magnesium plates. "Incendiaries, cannon tracers! Get the hell out, Sylvia...now!" Hugh shouted. But she was already gone. Leaning over in an attempt to catch sight of her receding parachute, he was thrown out of the plane as it staggered, and seemed to stop, under the force of an invisible fist. He hit the slipstream, headfirst, suspended upside down. 'Steady, boy...steady! Free fall...count to five.' The buffeting forces of the oncoming air stream and the aircraft's prop wash made breathing impossible. '...four, five.'

He looked upward, attempting to orient himself. Above and behind, he could make out the dark silhouette of the Bristol, its tail gun Perspex bubble and the entire rudder section streaming dense, black smoke and orange flames. 'That poor bastard! Pull the cord! Now! Deploy, you son of a bitch!' He fell, plummeting vertically like a curling rock, for a heart-stopping second. Then, the canopy opened, billowing gracefully, catching air. Hugh could breathe again. 'Thank God! Where the hell is she?' Sylvia's parachute was not visible.

Suddenly and without warning, a twin-engine aircraft appeared, bearing down directly at him from out of the dense cloud cover. 'Christ! An Me110 (Messerschmitt twin engine fighter/bomber)! He's got me!' Hugh shut his eyes, bracing for the inevitable hail of cannon shells. The engines' roaring intensified.

'He's going to ram me!' Hugh remembered hearing that some hot-shot Luftwaffe pilots enjoyed the sadistic thrill of shearing a paratrooper's control cords with the leading edge of a wing tip, severing jumper from canopy. The resulting free fall was an unimaginably horrifying death plunge. 'Even if he misses, I'm mush anyway when the props hit.' He dangled helplessly, unable to evade the oncoming disaster.

'What is that bastard doing?' The aircraft's two machine guns were spitting their lead: thankfully, not at him. He turned in his harness to look for their target. Above and to his right, the glass canopy of a single engine Me109 flamed and burst open. A figure, perhaps that of the pilot, struggled to jump clear, then vanished in a second explosion. The Messerschmitt cartwheeled dizzily downward, in a lazy, spiralling death dive. Five seconds later, it disintegrated with a sickening 'whump', and a final, thunderous, orange, and white flash.

A stunned and partially deafened Hugh looked around for his white knight. 'No time!' His beacons on the ground were quickly being extinguished. Five or six figures scurried about, now less than a hundred feet below, and growing rapidly closer. Within seconds, he had impacted the ground, rolled perfectly, and stood up, somewhat shakily, to fetch in the control lines and silk canopy.

"Top hole, Lieutenant! What took you so long?" exclaimed Sylvia. "There's your hero!" A Mosquito with RCAF roundels on its wings over flew them, its twin Rolls Royce Merlin engines screaming like banshees as it waggled its wings in salute, and then climbed into the thick clouds.

"Thank God for him!" exclaimed Hugh, shaking his head in disbelief. "I thought I was a goner. I'm still in shock. What happened to the Blenheim? Last I saw, it was in pretty serious trouble."

"Nav radioed that Flight's going to be able to make it back to base, just barely, somewhere up in God's country, thank heavens."

"And that Mosk jockey's probably playing nursemaid. I damn well hope he gets the DFC," Hugh replied.

"I'm more worried now about the attacker. Let's say he was a loner; then it's the fortunes of war. If he had the time to radio in before he went for a Burton, on which I'd stake my life, we're in for some very rough weather, Hugh. And if their Fighter Command knew..."

"Exactly, suppose Luftwaffe Intelligence knew we were coming? It's only a matter of time before rescue patrols come looking for their missing plane."

"That's a Pandora's box full of nastiness with implications going all the way back to Canada, isn't it? If they knew, then why not send a whole squadron of the blighters? But come and meet our new friends, Hugh. They're all wild Highlanders, MacDonalds at that, so I hope there's no' a speck of Campbell blood in ye, Miller," she laughed. She would use his code name, no?

"Where do I stow this?" he asked, removing his harness.

"They'll look to your chute and take us from here."

Sylvia introduced four Scots: three men and a woman, all in their twenties. They all wore woollen fisherman caps and had the legs of their coveralls tucked into thigh-high brown leather boots. Andrew, their stocky, bearded leader, wasted no time with banter. "Stay here while we douse the signal flares."

Within minutes, he and his comrades had retrieved and stowed the flare pots, recovered and folded the parachutes and, upon Peter's low whistle, started out on a daunting hour-long up mount, down dale trek, single-file, the Scots toting the cargo on their shoulders. Peter signalled a halt, on a rugged outcropping of land overlooking a channel. Not far beyond the water, through the mist, Hugh saw the ghostly outline of a coastline. "Where are we, Peter?" asked Sylvia.

"That's the Winged Isle, 'Skye' to the English, Captain. We're nearly home. Less than one half-mile further up to the height of the crag and then you can rest. Come!"

'Home' was, by all appearances, little more than a remote, roughly hewn crofter's cottage, but it was unexpectedly spacious and warm, sparsely but comfortably furnished, and well equipped for its purpose. As he poured them each a tumbler of deep amber malt whiskey, Peter explained that this was an RAF/Special Operations short-wave radio station and resistance command base.

They relaxed with their drinks, discussing the events of the day. Andrew's female companion, Annie, stood up and removed her wool cap, shaking out a fiery red shoulder-length mane. She walked to the wood-fired kitchen stove. "Who's hungry?" she asked softly, stirring the contents of a large cast iron pot. "Mmm, it's ready," she announced, after tasting. "Come to the table now, before it's cooked to death."

The meal was a delicious venison stew, with carrots and dumplings, and steaming hot scones. After the dishes had been cleared and tea served, the conversation turned to Scotland's role since the invasion of England. "Many people have scattered, simply disappeared from sight," Annie commented.

"They're lying low in the hills, biding their time, much like we are. The Germans can go on bombing our cities to kingdom come, but all they'll reap will be empty shells," Ross stated.

"How long can you hold out up here?" asked Sylvia. "Surely the Germans don't intend to leave you free to do as you like against them?"

"They have tried to find and stop us, but they haven't penetrated beyond Dumfries Town. We are stronger and wilier, and are growing ever more so. Our geography is our best ally, a natural barrier, and we know it far better than they do," Andrew declared. "Plus, we are determined to never give up. Call it Gaels' pride or whatever you like. It's as if the historic wounds and jealousies have been set aside and the old federated clan system has been reborn.

"Oh, they'll keep making their forays, all right, and we'll keep on slaughtering them. We're harassing them and giving them trouble at every turn; Commando raids out of Arisaig and Morar, and the English are rebuilding their forces in secret throughout the Highlands..."

"And in parts of Ireland, too, thank God for that," Annie added, her green eyes blazing. "Heaven help the Huns when we unite and swoop down across the border, seeking His vengeance, as we will."

Andrew agreed. "Amen and spoken like a true daughter of Erin. A dram anyone? You look like you could handle at least one more, Lieutenant."

Hugh declined politely, glancing slyly at Sylvia for tacit approval and then asked about the next phase of their journey into England.

Andrew answered, "You'll set out tomorrow morning at daybreak. We've arranged safe houses for you with contacts along your route as far south as Newcastle. There, you'll be handed over to another group for the final leg to your destination. Your contact is a person called 'Claymore'."

"Who makes up these fanciful names?" Sylvia asked with a smile. "At least we're no longer dealing with the seven dwarfs!" More seriously now, she added, "There is one more thing, Andrew: the attack on the Bristol Blenheim may have just been an unlucky break: Johnny on the spot. But if it wasn't, or if the Jerry crew reported its location, our assignment is in danger. Either way, I must know. Hugh has been authorized to contact HQ directly in emergencies. May he use your radio?"

"Of course, Captain. Sergeant Ross, take Lieutenant Miller out to the wireless hut. You'll want to put on this jacket, Hugh. That one over there is yours, Sylvia. As are the boots. Try them on. I think you'll find the fleece lining's warm enough to brave even this weather. Now, the woolly cap. God, if ever any Brit looked like a Scot sheep farmer, it's you."

"I do hope you meant that as a compliment, Andrew!"

Fifteen minutes later, Hugh returned. "Captain Smith, I need to speak with you, now, in private, please."

"Use my bedroom, on the right," Andrew offered.

"Close the door, Hugh. Well, how bad is it?"

"Hard to say. HQ's been trying to raise us since we landed. An unnamed officer at Camp X caught a client red-handed, passing information to a very suspicious individual. What the information was, they're not certain. The client's gone missing, disappeared, whereabouts unknown. BSO's investigating, with no results reported. Warden and

Stalwart are beside themselves with concern for us, as well as for Tent Peg, as you might expect."

"Are we to proceed or not?"

"Affirmative, for the time being. I'm scheduled to call in at 1600 tomorrow. That was the extent of the message."

"Disturbing, to say the least, but not desperate, so far. Maybe a problem in the offing, but perhaps it can be averted," she added, thoughtfully.

"Captain, we're going to be okay."

"I know, Hugh. We'll just simply have to make it work, because we won't have another opportunity to take him down."

"Captain, Sylvia, I've wanted to say..." he paused.

"Sssh. I've known, Hugh, for some time," she smiled. "Not now; let's put on a brave front, and not a word about this to Andrew or the others. You do know he's a Lieutenant Colonel, SOE; they're all Beaulieu graduates, but still it's unwise to mention anything."

"Agreed. How do you know about the Beaulieu connection?"

"Andrew and I were in the same House and in many of the same classes. He never said as much, but he's from a branch of the Skye MacDonald clan: bags of old money, brains, and real influence. He's also a World Cup class footballer. And I clearly remember that all of the men, instructors included, were gaga over Annie's gorgeous red hair. Peter and Ross were among the new recruits coming in as I was leaving."

"Your rifle. How are we going to take it into England without being caught?"

"We'll have to carry the sections separately. I'll show you what I have in mind in the morning."

As Sylvia and Hugh returned to the kitchen, Annie turned to them. "Breakfast will be ready at 0530. Come, let me show you to your cots."

The hearty Highland breakfast was complete with an 'eye-opener' nip of straight malt. Sylvia sipped politely out of consideration for their hosts, but Hugh again declined, causing Andrew to break into gales of laughter. "Hugh, you're certain that name of yours is Scots are ye, man? Now Sylvia's the kind of bonny English lass that can win over a Scotsman's heart. Eat up and we'll have a look at the signal from HQ. Is it decoded yet, Ross? Excellent, bring it here, will you?"

Sylvia looked intently at Hugh.

"Annie, the maps too, if you would, please. Time's getting on."

The W/T message was a routine confirmation of travel arrangements, including routes with alternates, radio schedules, and addresses of safe houses.

At six thirty, they bid warm farewells to their three SOE agent comrades then set out in a misty fog and penetratingly cold, fine drizzle, described eloquently by their guide Peter as, "Highland 'mizzle', standard fare for a Caledonian spring."

Andrew had reckoned that they would need four days to hike cross-country the one hundred-twenty miles to Newcastle. They bettered his estimate by one and one half days, walking twelve hours during the daytime, four hours at night, and resting two hours for tea and meals. The remaining six hours of the day, they slept wherever they found shelter: in barns or deserted outbuildings. Where no shelter could be found, they camped outdoors, huddled together under any makeshift cover if it rained, as it frequently did, and occasionally, under the stars, when it didn't.

They supplemented Annie's generous provisions by taking advantage of nature's abundant larder; trapping rabbits, and harvesting the wild berries and native grains, as they had been trained to do at Beaulieu and Camp X. Peter's intuitive knowledge of the rugged highland terrain, combined with his almost supernatural ability to predict the habits of his fellow inhabitants of the glens, were essential factors in their ability to move rapidly and stealthily, avoiding human contact.

"Sure, I feel like Flora Macdonald, so I do, waiting for my Bonnie Prince Charlie to meet me, comin' through the rye," Sylvia declared, as they rested sipping tea and admiring a magnificent highland vista.

"Sounds suspiciously like an Irish Flora to me," responded Peter.

"Irish, Scots: what's the difference, Peter?

"One pint of whisky a day, more or less," he answered, grinning slyly.

"No offence meant, Peter, but I really know very little of either people," Sylvia responded. "Hugh, you're part Scots, am I correct?"

"Yes, on my Dad's side. His mother was descended from Lachlan MacLean, one of the MacLean clan founders and Chiefs. The MacLeans later divided into four distinct clan houses, several of whose members were notable warriors."

"What was a Clan Chief, Peter?"

"To answer that, Sylvia, you first need to know more about the clan system. It reaches well back in Scottish history, to the eleventh century.

Long before that, even before the Roman era, Celtic peoples, some likely from Ireland, settled Scotland.

"After Julius Caesar's Roman legions packed up and left, there remained five of these Celtic groups. They didn't get along at all well with one another, particularly the Picts and the Scots. The competition and rivalry for power and control between these two warring groups was fierce. Then, during the eighth century, the Norsemen, or Vikings, and the Danes invaded and conquered much of the far north and the western isles.

"By 1264, the Danes had largely been driven out, except in the Orkneys and Shetland Islands. You remember Shakespeare's bloody king Macbeth? Well, King Malcolm succeeded him around or about 1056. It was as a result of the influence of Malcolm's English-born Queen that the clan system became the Highlanders' form of government. Prior to that it had been a loose confederation of blood-related tribes, located in tribal districts,

"Clans were identified by their plaids or tartans and some held extensive lands and great wealth. Each normally had Chieftains and Chiefs, who were the clan heads, and Captains as well. All served the clan as lawgivers and protectors, and in times of war, as generals. Sometimes, a Captain was also a Chief, and the Chieftain was a kind of chief-of-chiefs. Appointment followed a hereditary line of succession, although blood feuds and other factors often disrupted what we might call the smooth transfer of power."

"Well, what happened to the clans, Peter?"

"Politics; Culloden, April 16, 1746. It's all very thorny and it's hard to separate the gold from the dross. The Protestant English King, George II, feared that Charles Edward Stuart, the young Scottish Catholic 'pretender' to the throne..."

"Wait," interrupted Sylvia. "Pretender? He was Bonnie Prince Charlie?"

"Right you are. He was living in exile in Europe, half-heartedly talking of staging a comeback for the Royal House of Stuart. His family, you see, had been booted out of England. To cut it short, Charles Stuart's followers in France and Scotland, and in England as well, were determined to restore the Stuarts to a united throne of England and Scotland. Naturally, the Protestant English ruling class thought that was a bad idea especially when Charlie's army was only a menacing 127 miles north of London..."

"I had no idea any force had ever marched that far south," exclaimed Sylvia.

"Yes," Peter continued. "In fact, we're following much the same route the Prince's forces took from Dalkeith, south of Edinburgh, to Newcastle. Then, one of the most astonishing reversals in military history occurred."

"They turned around and went back to Scotland," Hugh exclaimed. "Why, no one seems exactly certain. Theories abound concerning an English spy infiltrating his camp with false intelligence and the like. The Highlanders were certainly outnumbered, 30,000 to their 5,000, and England was in a holy panic at the thought of hordes of Highland barbarian cutthroats at the gates of the capital, and a French army poised to come in on their flank across the Channel."

"It has a familiar ring."

"More tea, anyone? We must move on shortly.

"Anyway, the whole episode ended very badly, months later, at a final battle, actually a bloody rout, called Culloden, on the fields of Drumossie Moor, on a drizzly and cold April 16, 1746. The 4,000 remaining brave, mostly starved and ailing Highlanders, faced a redcoat army of English, German mercenaries and even rival Scots. Their foe was some 9,000 strong, complete with cavalry. The Highlanders were out-gunned and out-generalled. They were cut to ribbons by grapeshot and General Cumberland's four-pounder cannon fire. The Prince's cannons were three-pounders, but they had been supplied with four-pound balls."

"A true military 'Fubar': Fouled Up Beyond All Recognition," Hugh commented.

"A right royal cock-up, any way you care to describe it" Peter added.

"The Highlanders had broadswords and dreaded two-handed claymores, but the few Jacobites, or Stuart men, who had muskets and pistols had little or no ammunition left. The famous Highlanders' charge of yore, which Charles held back far too long, was heroic but futile, blunted by the Duke's withering fire as much as His Highness's hopeless strategy and the clannish bickering over the order of battle. The clansmen's battle cry was 'Claymore.' I trust that will have more significance once I get you to Newcastle.

"Within forty-five minutes, the heather was crimsoned with ghastly piles of heads, limbs and torsos. More than two thousand of the Prince's men lay dead, disembowelled, or beheaded by flying cannonballs and shrapnel. Many of the mortally wounded and the dying were hacked, bayoneted, or pistoled for sport. Some of the surviving wounded rebels were imprisoned, without the least medical attention, eventually to be transported in irons as common criminals to the colonies, such as Barbados. Cumberland's losses were fifty dead and two hundred-fifty wounded."

"So, I can see how Charlie's cause was defeated there. What happened after?"

"He took off, went into hiding and was protected by the northern people, with a £30,000 price on his head. He got out of the country, disguised as an Irish maid, thanks to Flora MacDonald."

"Were they lovers?" asked Sylvia.

"She was a well-to-do Jacobite, a Stuart sympathiser, married to a redcoat officer. Whether she did what she did out of love, marital treachery or a higher allegiance, is unclear. Her daring deed is shrouded in the mists of legend.

"The aftermath was horrendous, absolute butchery. William, the Duke of Cumberland's, cavalry pursued and massacred the fleeing Scots. The order of the day was, 'Not one left standing.' As if that wasn't enough, anyone suspected of Stuart sympathies, even the relatives of such sympathisers were hunted down, put to the sword, and oft times burnt alive in their homes and kirks. The pillage and rape of the Highlands went on with barbaric ferocity for five months. Neither women nor wee children were spared. The clan system was destroyed, utterly. Parliament decreed it a hanging offence just to wear the tartan or to speak the Gaelic tongue. Highlanders by the thousands emigrated to Australia, North America, or just about anywhere.

"The memory of William, Duke of Cumberland is cursed to this day. The common wildflower, Sweet William, is forever tarnished as 'Stinking Billy'."

"The infamous Highland clearances," intoned Hugh. "My Granddad used to tell the story about his grandfather arriving in the middle of a Montreal winter, with only his prized, illegal Gaelic bible. He had no shoes on his feet."

"But despite this history of horrors, Highlanders such as yourself are still dedicated to helping us, the English, defeat Hitler?" Sylvia asked, quietly.

"Of course, Captain. You'd have to agree that some of the finest British regiments of the line are Scottish. We Scots are loyal and proud, but not stupid. We have long memories. We might have forgiven somewhat, but we haven't forgotten.

"For nearly two hundred years, Culloden was the last military battle fought on British soil. We intend to ensure that there will be one more, the final battle, a bloody Armageddon if necessary, to rid us once and for all of the Nazi vermin, after which, we'll be in no mind to take a back seat to London or anyone.

Peter stood and stretched. "Now, I suggest we get a move on while there's still daylight, Captain," he continued. "Those hills up ahead are the Cheviots. Once we cross them, we're in your jolly old 'Blighty'. We can expect to see scads of German border patrols, so I ken we'd be wisest to travel to Newcastle only under cover of darkness. Do you agree, Captain?"

"You've been bang-on the money so far, Lieutenant." She glanced at Hugh. "Yes, we agree. Let's push on."

"One last thing and I hope you won't find it presumptuous..."

"That depends..."

"I have no idea why you're bound for Newcastle, but if I may, don't make the same mistake as the Pretender, if London is your objective."

"Thank you, Peter. I can assure you we won't be turning back. Lead on, MacDuff."

Through the night they travelled south, parallel to the Great North Road, the A1, to Haymarket Street. Bypassing a German checkpoint at the intersection of Gallowgate and Percy Street, they briefly marvelled at the remnants of Hadrian's Wall on Stowell, then continued south on Newgate to St. Nicholas Street.

Arriving Tyneside at daybreak, Peter pointed out the nondescript safe house on St. Nicholas, overlooking a floating train of coal barges on the river. Sylvia and Hugh crouched in the shadows under the High Level Bridge, directly beneath a German sentry box, while Peter went on ahead.

"I don't want to hear it," Sylvia whispered.

"Hear what, trolls on the bridge, or coals to Newcastle?"

She poked him with her elbow. Peter walked nonchalantly around to the side of a house and disappeared. Seconds later, he emerged at the front door, and with a low whistle, signalled 'all clear.' Hugh and Sylvia loped across the street.

"Come inside, quickly. I'll fetch your host." As he spoke, a familiar face appeared at the sitting room door, halfway along the dark hallway. "Captain, Lieutenant, meet 'Claymore'," Peter announced.

"Andrew, is that you?" Sylvia exclaimed.

"At your service, my lady," he boomed, kissing her cheek lightly. "Hugh, how are you, lad?"

"Better for seeing you, Sir," he replied softly, his hand locked in the Colonel's bear grip.

"Relax, lad. We're alone and safe here from Jerry's eyes and ears. You'll join me in a libation and a chinwag to celebrate your safe arrival, and then we'll have a bite of breakfast. No shirkin' a Highlander's duty this time, Hughie; you can both bathe to your hearts' content and then sleep like judges…separately, of course," he chuckled.

Sylvia's pale, olive complexion reddened slightly at Andrew's outrageous remark. Hugh, for first time in his life, was silently thankful for the malted spirits as Peter topped up his glass, seemingly the size of a jam jar.

After breakfast, Andrew led them up the narrow staircase to show them two snug bedrooms and the WC. The white and black tiled bathroom was complete with what Sylvia thought to be a luxuriously large, white enamelled tub sitting on flared metal legs, and sporting two chromed arches for the water faucets. She couldn't resist the urge to test the hot water. Andrew, for Hugh's benefit, meticulously demonstrated the chain action flush toilet, which complied enthusiastically in the production of a trickle of water and resultant sucking sounds. With a promise to awake them in time for supper, Andrew clomped back downstairs. The last thing Hugh heard as he fell asleep after bathing and shaving were the plaintive wailing and shrilling of the riverboats.

He awoke with a start and sat up. The room was in total darkness. 'Damn, someone knocked?' There was more, insistent tapping. "Who is it?" he half-whispered.

"It's me, Sylvia. I have tea."

"Hold on, okay! I'll be right there," he mumbled, leaning over to grope for his trousers, lying in a heap on the floor. As he stumbled to the door, he struggled to fasten his belt buckle. "Hi, come in. What time is it?"

"Seven o'clock. You've been asleep nearly ten hours. How do you feel? Mind if I sit? Drink your tea. It's quite sweet; that's real sugar. Luscious!"

"Okay, sure, sit here. Thank you. Sorry, I was out like the proverbial light; I'm still a bit fogged in, " he yawned, hastily sweeping up socks and briefs from the seat of a creaky rattan bedside chair. "Here, have a seat. How long have you been up?"

"About two hours; so, where's my rifle barrel, Lieutenant?" she inquired.

"Over there, behind the radiator. It took ten minutes to scrub the last of that damn adhesive tape off my legs and chest in the bathtub. Where's Andrew?"

"You don't have to tell me about sticking plaster. Andrew and Peter went out about an hour ago. Didn't say where or what time they'll be back. Hugh?"

"Yes, Sylvia?"

"I hate to put you on the spot and I swear I won't ask again, but I must know for the sake of the mission, if for no other..."

"Shoot. What is it?"

"Are you still thoroughly committed to this operation?"

"Yes, I am. Why? Do you suddenly doubt my nerve?" he asked, testily.

"No, not at all. But ever since we were told of the possible security leak, I can't assume anything. You can still back out."

"And miss the fun? Not a chance."

"Good. Next, are you...that is, do you think that you are, that you might be, in love with me? Please, answer 'yes', or 'no'."

"Yes," he considered for a moment, then continued. "Sylvia, I Hugh, being of sound mind, admit that am in love with you." He looked away, meticulously fastening his watchband, then continued softly, "I also know that this constitutes reasonable grounds to have me declared *persona non grata* and to send me packing to explain myself to Stalwart at HQ, that is, if I could get there from here."

She didn't respond immediately. "As I suspected," she murmured. After another deliberate pause, she continued, "Then we, that is, you and I, have a problem."

"Which is...?" he inquired, setting his teacup on the bureau. "What are you driving at, Sylvia?".

"Don't do that. It will leave a horrid white stain on the wood. Set it here. I'm afraid that it's very complicated. Case one: Hugh, you have seen my baby daughter, in Toronto, and 'being of sound mind', as you professed only seconds ago, you assumed that there must be a father for the child, somewhere."

"Well, yes, of course."

"Of course. However, where he is or what he is doing is of little consequence to me. No, that is almost, but not entirely true. I can't go into it, now, but that is a problem. Case two: as you may have inferred, when I introduced you to my aged parents at Casa Loma, I am Jewish..."

"I tumbled to that. So?"

"So, please, let me finish, Hugh. Nothing is as important to me as our operation Tent Peg, nothing.

"Long ago, during my carefree school days, then at Beaulieu and university, I earned the quaint nickname, the Iron Maiden. I took excessive pride in it, preserving my pristine reputation, honouring my father's old-world values, and sharing his unquestioning acceptance of a Biblical code of morality and righteousness. I still do, in spirit, if not always in practice, or I wouldn't have accepted the assignment. The First Commandment...believe me, it wasn't easy for this daughter of a cantor...and, at this moment, I want to make love to you...very much." She sighed heavily, then continued, "I'm also afraid..."

"...That God will strike you dead for consorting with a gentile?" he asked gently.

"No, that Andrew and Peter will be back soon. May I come over to your bed?

"Oh, yes, consort away."

"Well, no sound of Andrew yet. What shall we do?" she murmured, playfully.

"Hmm...are you hungry?"

"You wild, romantic fool! All right, call me crazy, but I might just be persuaded to cook up a little something for us. First though, give me one more ... damn! They're home. Button, button, Juli!"

"Who?"

Just then Andrew called up, "Halloo! I have hot victuals! Get 'em before they're a soggy mess!"

When Sylvia and Hugh came to the table, they found him standing, alone, with a large newspaper-clad bundle under his right arm. "No man or woman alive can swallow this English pap without a draught or two of fine McEwan Ale." With that pronouncement, he produced three brown bottles from the pockets of his dockworker's jacket, setting them with a flourish on the kitchen table. He opened the newspaper package to a mound of fish and chips. "Vinegar, salt, knife, fork...first we dine, then we plot. Now, tell me about your Scottish expedition..."

Sylvia briefly recounted their journey, lavishly praising Peter's professional skills. Hugh added a few details while Andrew listened silently, occasionally voicing his approval. Afterwards, Andrew stood up to clear the table, and spoke, now without a trace of the *faux* Highland accent or country mannerisms. "It's time to talk seriously, my friends."

His clipped speech reminded Hugh of Colonel Graham, the evening he had caught Hugh snooping at Camp X. "You've been prudent enough not to question why I'm here, in Newcastle. It's not that mysterious," he smiled, lighting a cigarette. "Help yourselves" he offered, sliding the open package of John Player's Navy Cut across the table toward them. "You should know that I'm your SIS/BSO principal. I am known as 'Claymore', but in reality, that's more of a generic name for the whole support operation, of which I'm in charge. I arrived here the day before you, thanks to an associate, a small-time crook in Edinburgh who nicked a Hillman. A fraudulent work permit, and a minor deception or two thrown in for luck, and here I am."

"Is it a breach of protocol to ask about Annie?" asked Sylvia.

"Yes, it is. But she's well, doing God's good work, as always. Now, there are some critical intelligence up-dates: background, schedules, details, and one or two significant operational changes that HQ has forwarded for your immediate attention. Let me begin with your itinerary and then your cover.

"You will travel to London by coach via the London and North Eastern Railway, which stops at Central Station nearby on its run south from Edinburgh's Waverley Station. I'll get to departure times shortly. The trip should take no more than three hours, four tops, depending upon the number of unscheduled stops to allow the railway police to vet the passenger list and to generally make their presence known.

"You must be in place, fully ready, one week before, which gives you two days. Otherwise, you'll be left out, vulnerable, in the cold. My sources report that massive security measures and countermeasures, both within and surrounding the city, are nearly impenetrable, even now."

"How will we do that, Andrew? Pierce the walls?"

"Yes, you'll be walking right through. However, I'm afraid that brings to mind some unpleasant developments. BSO HQ has confirmed that the client at STS 103 has definitely compromised Tent Peg. They cannot determine with certainty to what extent you are personally at risk, but it's judged grave, in fact serious enough to consider pulling you out. Stalwart's expected to give Special Ops his final decision tonight. Which means that he's depending upon the three of us for a risk appraisal. Now, here are the facts. So far as I am aware, your identities are not..."

And so Andrew continued, outlining the intricate details of the mission ahead. He answered their few questions, then concluded, "...may I safely assume from what you have said, both of you, that you understand the dangers and personal risks and are prepared to proceed?"

"Yes, and yes, I understand. Hugh?" she asked, turning to face him.

"In for a penny, in for a...yes."

"Very well. I thank you both. I will inform HQ overseas. You will travel as German nationals, newlyweds, honeymooning, and you are both electrical engineers. These documents, which you can see are superb forgeries, include party membership cards attesting that you are Drs. Franz and Ilse Kortner, with the internationally-known firm, *Sieglinde* AG, Berlin. You are presently stationed in Manchester...is something wrong, Sylvia?"

"Ilse? Damn it, Andrew, what kind of name is that?" she demanded.

"It's German, very common and not hard to remember."

"I know it's German, but it's so...cold, so bloody unpleasant. Can't you switch the vowels to make it Elise, you know, that tinkly piano piece by Beethoven, *Für Elise?*"

"The decision was made in Canada and the papers can't be changed holus-bolus overnight. It could be days before they're ready and we don't have time to spare as it is."

"When are we going?"

"Tomorrow morning, eight thirty-five. May I continue?

"You may; my apologies to you and 'Franz' for the digression."

"Not at all. You met here when you were transferred separately from Germany: 'Ilse' from *Sieglinde* in Berlin, and 'Franz' from the Hamburg office. You are both card-carrying Nazi party members, dated 1937. You were bright-eyed, eighteen-year-old Hitler Youth and Maedel recruits respectively, making you relatively early joiners. You are visiting London in the fervent hope of partaking in Hitler's victory bash.

"A room has been reserved at the Ascot Arms in the names of the doctors Kortner. You have clearance to enter London, thanks to some astute finagling by my colleagues there. Movement, once you arrive there, is another matter, not entirely resolved, as yet."

"Sounds alright so far. What about transporting Sylvia's rifle and a portable radio for me? I don't see how..." Hugh inquired.

"Those will be taken care of and delivered to your destination."

"Which is...?" Sylvia asked.

"Let's just say it's a well-known, timely landmark. My agent, Alfred, the day desk clerk at the Ascot in London will supply that information when Sylvia approaches him to inquire about sending a telegram to Bristol. Now, I suggest we should pop down to the cellar where your clothes, tickets, passports, hotel reservations, and personal items are waiting to be packed up prior to your departure tomorrow. The geniuses who doctored your passport photographs added some features that we should be able to duplicate, without much trouble.

"My God, when was that taken? I do look like an 'Ilse'!"

"Case dismissed," Hugh added.

"Sylvia, could you fetch your rifle from upstairs, please? Hugh, come with me, I need your jiggery-pokery to sort out the bloody W/T. At best it works intermittently, and seems prone to interference. It could be the antenna or the damp may have corroded the tuning condenser."

At seven forty-five the next morning, the 'Kortners' set out at a deliberate pace. Toting one suitcase apiece, they walked for less than ten minutes to the vast Victorian era Central Station. They located the London-bound platform and were searching for the LNER; a conductor directed them to the ticket master's wicket.

The agent's contempt for the vacationing German couple was obvious in the petty bureaucratic pantomime with which he inspected their tickets. He treated them as though they were day passes for dangerous offenders, about to be let loose on an unsuspecting population. Finally, and reluctantly, he applied his official stamp. Hugh, inwardly applauding this quixotic show of British defiance, nodded in mute acceptance when the vouchers were brusquely thrust back, "Track Three."

Sylvia stopped at a news kiosk to buy a day-old copy of the Party newspaper, *Die Völkischer Beobachter*, before they boarded the train. Once they were seated, a pleasant English conductor accompanied by a youthful Reich railroad policeman, welcomed Dr. and Dr. Kortner in passable German. After examining and punching their tickets, he continued down the aisle of the swaying coach, the policeman following in his wake. Perhaps impressed with Sylvia's selection of reading material, or maybe her charming, attractive blonde appearance, the Reich constable turned slightly as he passed and winked knowingly at 'Dr. Ilse.' She smiled slightly and continued to read.

The journey was leisurely, making all eight scheduled stops, and without further interruption, the train arrived exactly on time at London's Kings Cross Station, St. Pancras. The 'Kortners' produced their passports at the request of the flirtatious police officer, who, with a perfunctory glance and "Heil Hitler," gallantly waved them to the exit.

Outside, in a downpour, they hired a cab to take them to the Ascot Hotel, Westminster. They entered the sumptuous lobby and a politely insistent Bell Captain carried their suitcases the twenty feet to the imposing registration desk. He waited patiently as Hugh fumbled for some coins, while Sylvia scanned the names on the burgundy and gold-trimmed tunics of the three clerks, looking for 'Alfred'. She spotted him and nudged Hugh. They queued in front of his position, which had a gold sign on the counter proclaiming, *German spoken here.*

Without a flicker of recognition, 'Alfred' processed their reservation, and then mutely directed them to the lift, where the vigilant Bell Captain, 'John', was now attending. Over Hugh's mild protestations, John took possession of their bags, and then ordered the operator to take them to Level Nine, Private Suites. At the door of Suite 909, he set down their suitcases and held out his hand as though expecting a gratuity.

"The key, please," he whispered. "Follow me, it's safer to talk inside." Once they were in the room, he shut the door, then bolted and latched it with the chain. Seconds later the bedside telephone rang softly. "I'll take it." He listened for a few seconds then set down the receiver. "SD and Gestapo blockheads are crawling all over the lobby and lower levels. That's why you're up here, where they won't bother to check, lazy bastards that they are.

"Alfred must be very careful. You will not approach him as planned. The reception clerk on his immediate left is a suspected informant. Therefore, you will dial room service at 5:30 this evening and order dinner for two, the house speciality, poached Aberdeen salmon *amondine*, with a decent bottle of Chardonnay and a magnum of champagne, *Pouilly Fousse* of course, iced. A complimentary copy of *The Times* will be included. The key is 'seven'.

"Now, I must go before the manager gets his knickers in a twist. The old dear suspects that I'm having it off with Sizzling Suzanne, a chambermaid. Ah, if only..." he smiled. "Jolly good luck, you two, stiff upper-lip. Do take a peek in the closet. You'll find some comfortable, warm, English-style sightseeing clothes, sensible shoes, and so forth, to wear on your jaunt tomorrow. Also, two inconspicuous travel bags for your essentials. Leave those dreadful European rags here. I swear I'll personally burn them. Do take full advantage of our facilities. Enjoy your evening, darlings!"

"Thank you, John, I'm sure everything will be fine." Hugh replied. When he shut the door, he turned to Sylvia, "Stiff upper-lip old darling. Ah, the English. Now, what's your pleasure?"

"You, old darling. But first, a half hour soak, with mountains of bubbles, a nap between those clean sheets, champagne, and dinner, in that order. Then, you can do with me as you will. Unless you'd like to join me now in the tub?"

"How hot do you take your bath water?"

"So, what do you think of your new natural blonde, my husband?"

"Magnificent, ravishing...." Hugh was interrupted by a discreet knock at the door. "That'll be room service...cover yourself, madam!" No sooner had the waiter left the room, then they both lunged for the neatly folded newspaper wedged between the sweating silver champagne bucket and a crystal rose vase on the serving cart. "You get the flower, I get the *Times*," Hugh exclaimed, triumphantly. "Page seven. Look, here it is, seventh paragraph. 'Notice of Closures.'"

He spread out the paper on the bedcovers in front of Sylvia, and together they read excitedly, "Until further notice...to celebrate the Führer's birthday and St. George's Day...Beginning noon April 17...Big Ben... St. James' Park...."

"The clock tower...Big Ben! Have you seen Hitchcock's, *The 39 Steps*? We'll be Robert Donat and Madeleine Carroll. We have to be in the place tomorrow, April 17, by noon. Nineteen thirty-four, wasn't it, Sylvia?"

"What was? Oh, no, 1935. So, it seems that the lord of the realm is coming either on the twentieth, which is the blighter's birthday, or on our national holiday, St. George's Day, the twenty-third. Either one make perfect sense, I suppose, if you think like your enemy, as they taught us to do."

"Uh huh, but what do you suppose 'St. James' means, Sylvia?"

"I'm not certain, but perhaps that's where his coronation is taking place, in St. James' Park? Or, The Horse Guards' Parade grounds? Whichever, we're almost there. Look out the window, over there, to the north, just north west of Big Ben."

"How does anyone expect we're going to get past security and stay out of sight?"

"Go to the closet and bring me the silk scarf under the collar of that blue jacket. Yes, that's it. Over here, please darling. Now open it up."

"Well, I'll be.... When you did find this?"

"While you were snoring. I couldn't sleep, my dear, so I went exploring to see what I had to wear. I was going to show it to you later. Come, dinner is getting cold!"

"This is amazing. John gave us the clue and I missed it. Here's a diagram of the interior, our entry point, contacts, times, our cache...your rifle, ammo, my radio, food, supplies. Even an escape route, an alternate, and contacts...we memorize it and then, what did he say, 'take advantage of the facilities'? Meaning, burn and flush it."

"I've already memorized it. We'll make a Secret Agent of you yet. Now, would you please crack that bubbly?"

"Yes, let's eat this gourmet meal before it's completely spoiled. Sylvia, do you still believe we can do it?" he inquired, filling her glass.

"You, Hugh, a doubter? Of course we can. If we're half as good a team as I think we are, it will be a cakewalk. To us!"

"To us! You still haven't told me why you volunteered for this, Captain."

"All in good time, my Franz, all in good time. More champagne, please?"

They checked out of the hotel, without seeing Alfred, at 9:30 the next morning. After a light continental breakfast, they decided, as proper sightseers would, to walk the short distance to their destination.

Movement throughout the city was restricted and closely monitored by frequent security checks under the stringent clampdown imposed by Gruppenführer Walther Lange. Their documents, although examined three times, were never challenged. "It helps, I suppose," Sylvia observed quietly, "that our safe conduct is assured by the signature of the big man of London himself, SS Walther Lange."

Lange had done his work well. He had posted army blockades, guard posts, mobile and static SS security stations; all bolstered with roving detachments of SD and SIPO security forces. The streets and storefronts along the parade route in Westminster were awash with seemingly limitless bundles of coloured bunting and red swastika flags, all framing massive portraits of the soon-to-be-anointed conquering hero, Adolf Hitler, and his Governor Designate of the Reich Protectorate, Albert Speer.

Sylvia and Hugh arrived at St. Stephen's Tower at 9:55. A band of six Liebstandarte- SS Lifeguards were eying them closely. As she gazed upward into the face of Big Ben, Sylvia felt a sudden and overwhelming rush of emotion. Standing close beside her, Hugh felt her draw a deep but broken breath and he gently placed his hand on her arm, fearing that she would break down when the clock chimed the hour and would give them away to the other two onlookers close by, both very obviously German. She cursed under her breath, regaining her composure. The moment had passed. Relieved, Hugh remarked loudly, pointing to a small sign that stated in English, 'Not Open to the Public.'

Sylvia smiled thinly when the sonorous chiming began. Despite the incendiary bombing that had engulfed and all but destroyed the Houses of Parliament prior to the surrender, the tower and clock, Big Ben itself, had miraculously emerged, unharmed, from the flames.

The sole male attendant, just as foretold on the SOE silk scarf, was reassuringly English and, as it appeared, on to their game. Their two German fellow tourists were both gentlemen sporting the green felt hats, complete with bands and feathers, typical of Bavaria. One of them stepped forward to ask a question to which the guide replied, "Sorry, guvs, but no visitors are permitted inside the structure, at any time. Do you not understand English?" He pointed to the sign and read it aloud deliberately. He paused, then shouted for emphasis, "No visitors, that's all!" and he waved his hands as though shooing them away like so many annoying flies.

Sylvia smiled inwardly at the attendant's thinly veiled contempt, and nodded her understanding. She put on the appearance of disappoint-ment and turned to translate the exchange to 'Herr Doktor Kortner'. When the clock had chimed for the tenth time, the attendant began his spiel as the two Bavarians earnestly focussed their Leicas on him, step-ping back and panning upward to include the clock in typical tourist fashion.

In a broken mix of German and English, Sylvia asked to be directed to the washrooms.

"The washroom, did you say, madam? Well, it's highly irregular, but, if it's an emergency. Well I know, at my age...." He lowered his voice, "Go! Now! You know the door!" In a whisper he continued, "Hans and

Fritz, your two Jerry mates there, are serious trouble: secret police, likely Gestapo. God be with you!" he added, smiling broadly at the now distant cameras.

"Thank you, and with you," she murmured as they slipped around the corner of the tower to the entrance.

"Gestapo? Looked like fancy boys to me!" Hugh remarked when they had stepped inside onto a flagstone floor.

"Oh, shut the door. Lord, look what's ahead!" she whispered. "Good thing we had all of that rock climbing in the Rockies to prepare us."

Wedged between rough brick and masonry walls was an imposingly steep and narrow stone stairway, which seemed unending.

"Last one to the top is a rotten egg!"

"Fine. I'll walk and you scamper along. Then we'll see who finishes first, mister! "

Some fifteen minutes later they reached the top; both winded in spite of their vigorous training. Hugh whistled. "We're above the clock! Now that's what I call a million-dollar view. Well worth the climb, eh? I lost count, but there must have been four hundred steps; what do you think, love?"

"I think I'm going to keel over unless I sit down." After a pause, she continued, "Actually there are precisely three hundred ninety-three; it only feels like four hundred. Did you know...?"

"Did I know what?"

"That I love you. And that we passed a Prison Room about one-third of the way up? It was built as a jail cell to house unruly members of parliament."

"Ditto. Has it ever actually been used for that?"

"Mmm, hardly ever, according to this guidebook...twice, and both times in the nineteenth century. On the first occasion, the cheeky beggars actually threw a suffragette in here! The other was a freethinker, name of Bradlaugh, who refused to swear allegiance to Queen Victoria. She was not amused, one might imagine. Here, you can read the whole story."

"I'd rather you tell me bedtime stories. Let's look for the radio and gun. I must be on air with Camp X promptly as directed."

"You meant my rifle, of course, Lieutenant. My God, here we go!" she exclaimed, covering her ears, as the great clockwork mechanism began its ponderous wind-up to tolling the half-hour. After the six tones had finished reverberating, she declared authoritatively, "And that wasn't even Big Ben. He only sounds the hours."

The final chime echoed into silence. Their mood quieted, reflecting the gravity of their situation, as the tension became almost palpable.

"He'd better come sooner, rather than later. Have you found anything, yet?"

"It's all there in these two tool cases: your scope, rifle, ammo, cleaning kit, and a brand new Mark 11 B W/T complete with dry cells." The kit also included every other necessity; rations, canteens of water, flashlights, blankets, waterproof matches, warm clothing and boots, as well as first aid supplies, small hand-held weapons and RDX with detonators. "Good work, Andrew, old man!" Hugh exclaimed. "We are definitely ready for you, Adolf, you bastard!"

"Keep it low, Hugh. There could be workers about. This place runs like clockwork, but..."

"What's next, Captain?"

"First thing, I want to inspect, clean and carry out some calculations to sight-in my rifle. Tune up your wireless, in the meantime. Let's put in the ear protectors and get on with it."

Hugh switched on the radio and immediately received a high-speed burst of coded groups. Within seconds, it was complete. He acknowledged the transmission, and then shut down. "Wow, that hit like the proverbial ton of bricks. Yorkie must have that damn thing supercharged. Nearly blew off my headset! They must be doubling it from Andrew's rig up north. I'll have this in clear for you in a jiffy.

"Okay, done. Which do you want to hear first, Captain, the bad news or the worse news?"

"You decide" she stated flatly. "Is there a Phillips screw driver in one of the boxes? I need to adjust my scope."

"Here. It says that the event will be held on the twenty-third, not the twentieth, outdoors, thank God. It will take place at either The Horse Guards' Parade grounds, which can accommodate at least 2,000, or more likely, at St. James' Park. It seems that the suspected double agent in Canada did, in fact, spill the beans before he met with an 'accident'...yeah, I'll bet!

"We arrived here just in time. Lange has been tipped off that there's going to be an attempt made on the Führer. Luckily for us, he's convinced that it will be an SOE or Special Air Service ambush on the motorcade. Still, every precaution to avoid discovery must be observed.

Apparently the Nazis are using some kind of new, highly sophisticated radio jamming and detection equipment. I cannot transmit again until the deed is done. Finally, we're going to receive some assistance. The sender didn't say when or what kind. Best regards, from Warden and Stalwart."

"You got that all in a three second message?"

"Yes, and this too: your family's fine." In the momentary lull, Hugh asked, "Now, would you care to tell me about your reason for doing this?"

"Alright. Have you ever heard of *Kristallnacht?*"

"Yes, of course, I remember Crystal Night. It was in November 1938, when the Nazis went on a rampage. Jewish businesses and synagogues were pillaged and burned."

"November the ninth, to be precise. It was well planned. Only a few days later, Göring and Heydrich assessed the Jews in Germany and Austria one billion marks for the damage that they, the Nazis, had caused. That's chutzpah!"

"Neat trick. Blame the victim and make him pay for your dirty work. How did it get you personally involved?" he asked. "Here's a revolver. It's clean and loaded."

"Thanks. My older sister, Rachel, was studying economics on exchange in Nuremberg. She was attacked, beaten, raped, and murdered, right on the university grounds by brown shirts, Nazi storm troopers. She was a beautiful, bright, talented kid, partially paralysed by polio when she was just ten."

"Jesus... Now, I understand, Sylvia. I'm so sorry."

"Thank you, darling. 'Vengeance is mine, saith the Lord', it says in Torah. But I took a sacred vow that I would make them pay. Maybe I'll burn in hell fire for eternity...so now, you know; I'm no dewy-eyed patriot. But do you think it will make a difference in the big picture?"

"Yes, it will. Definitely."

"There's more to it, but that's enough for now; we should try to get some sleep, if that's possible. Join me?"

"In a...wait! Did you hear voices?"

"No."

"Ssssh. Someone's coming up the stairs! Quick, get over there by the equipment and cover me!"

CHAPTER 7

GENOSHA
ROOM 301

Bait the hook well:
this fish will bite

William Shakespeare

Lieutenant Colonel Gordon Graham sat in his office at the rear of the Lecture Hall, staring dejectedly at the newly fallen snow outside his window. 'Will it never stop? This is March, for Heaven's sake.' His intercom buzzed, startling him.

"Yes, Betty?"

"Sir, Mr. Robert Brooks on your secured line."

"Betty, please be a dear and warm up my tea while I take this call. Thank you.

"Robert, old man, good to hear from you. How are you?"

"Fine, thank you, Gordon. Lovely weather, eh? It was a freak storm. It shouldn't last out the day." He paused, and then continued, " Colonel, Stalwart is getting somewhat anxious about the status of Jael and company."

"I agree. I've received nothing at all, however, not a whisper, Robert. Please assure Stalwart that as soon as I do hear anything, I'll forward immediately. Is there something that I can actually do for you this morning?"

"Yes, there is. I've been asked to find three Italian-speaking clients for some special operation, the details of which will be coming to you by wireless. I wasn't allowed much time, but I did manage to come up with six local candidates who may fit the bill."

"Send them here. I'll assign them directly to Robert Samson. Don't worry about a thing, Robert, we'll take care of it from here. When should I expect them?"

"They'll be ready a week Monday. Is that satisfactory?"

"Yes, that's fine. Let me make a notation in my desk diary." After a pause, he continued, "The usual arrangements?"

"Yes. Have your driver pick them up, unmarked car, at Camp Borden. They'll be ready at 1000 hours. Thank you, as always, for your co-operation, Gordon."

"No trouble, Robert. Good speaking with you. Please drop by soon. Goodbye for now."

As he hung up the receiver he called "Betty, have you forgotten my tea?"

"No, Sir, I didn't want to bother you. I assumed that call must have been important."

"No bother at all. You may interrupt me any time when it comes to tea," he stated, smiling. "We must keep our priorities in order."

She blushed. Betty Robertson thought him the most handsome male ever, with the possible exception of Errol Flynn, to whom he bore more than a passing resemblance.

"Betty, it's March, is it not? Now, I ask you, how much longer will we be seeing this type of weather?" He put on his warm boots and winter greatcoat, recently requisitioned from Charles Constantine's Quartermaster at Military District 2. The standard issue was just not up to Canada's winter. On the other hand, perhaps he was not yet up to Canada's climate.

"This is not that unusual for this time of year, Sir. I've seen more than a few white Easters."

"Easters? Oh, well. Then I suppose I had best get used to it. When does spring arrive in these climes?"

"On the twenty-first or the twenty-second of this month, Sir. I always confuse the official starting date."

"I'll believe it when I hear the first cuckoo."

"That'll be quite a long wait, Colonel. We don't have cuckoos in this part of Ontario, as far as I'm aware. Plenty of robins, though."

"I'm off to find Major Samson, Miss Robertson. He's likely in the barn with some of the lads. That's where I'm headed if you need me."

"Very good, Sir. Do fasten your coat."

Lieutenant Colonel Graham smiled, snug in the warm greatcoat, his collar turned up against the chill wind. He walked along the old Sinclair farm road until he came to the Hydra building where he spotted Bill

The barn at Camp X, where the silent killing training took place.

Hardcastle in the doorway. "Good morning, Yorkie! How's that transmitter working? Humming along, I hope?"

"Morning, Sir. Yes, she's tip top."

"Does this weather affect it in any way, Yorkie?"

"It doesn't at all, Colonel. It's quite stable and I must add, it can generate quite a bit of heat on its own. The steam plant puts out enough heat to keep the building at a constant seventy degrees. Floor gets a little cold though, with no basement, just the cement pad. Pop in anytime, Colonel. Off to breakfast?"

"No, I had mine earlier, thanks. Yes, I will drop in. Carry on, Yorkie."

"Good seeing you, Sir."

As the Colonel continued westward toward Corbett Creek, the chilled wind off the lake blew straight into his face. He increased his pace until he reached the barn door, then

Camp X looking east from Corbett Creek, 1943.

opened it slightly. Looking in he could see Major Robert Samson demonstrating a hold on one of the young Hungarian recruits. He thought, 'I can't believe that this man, in his late fifties, is still tossing around young men almost forty years his junior. Bloody well remarkable!'

"Major, may I have a moment?"

"Aye, Sir!" The Hungarian, 'Joe G.,' seemed relieved when Samson announced, "Men, take a five minute recess; I suggest you keep the blood circulating by moving around the gym or by running on the spot. I'll be back shortly.

"Greetings, Colonel! Care to go a round? I'll spot you one fall."

"Do you think me insane? With you blindfolded and both arms tied behind your back, I might be persuaded! Rob, I have three new clients coming in a week Monday. I'd like you to stay with them as the brass has some concerns. Are you free to do so?"

"Yes indeed, Gordon. This lot finishes up Friday. They'll be shipped out the following week."

"Thanks for the reminder. Are we having a send-off?"

"Friday night, at eight, Sir. Officers' Mess, as usual. We're expecting you, Colonel. There are the usual trophies to be awarded."

"I can never say no to your festivities, Robert. Right, then. They're yours, a week Monday. Thank you. And do take care not to incapacitate any of these lads before graduation. HQ has rather grand plans for them."

"I'll try my best. Thank you, Sir." The Major saluted then turned back to his class. "All right lads, form up, into a circle, please. I'm not finished with you yet. Now, who wants to demonstrate that last manoeuvre...on me?"

The unmarked truck pulled into the old lane, lumbered past the guardhouse, turned down the road, and came to a full stop in front of the Lecture Hall.

"Right, men, off the truck and into the building. Please be seated and wait until someone arrives."

Six men jumped down, picked up their gear, and proceeded silently, in single file, up the wooden steps and into the lecture room. There, they seated themselves, spaced well apart in the first two rows, and waited. Five minutes later, Adjutant Jones entered. To a man, they stood up at attention.

"Good day, gentlemen. Please be seated. Thank you. Welcome to STS 103. If you're unfamiliar with that name, Camp X will suffice. I am Adjutant-Quartermaster Major Brian Jones. It's my job to make sure that your stay here goes smoothly. I will be your eyes and ears. Any concerns that you might have should be brought directly to me, and I will do my best to help you. You have been assigned to Major Robert Samson who will be your personal instructor for the duration of the twelve-week course.

"Shortly, I will take you to your living quarters where the Major will join us. For your welfare, as well for greater concerns, you will associate only among yourselves, and with no one else other than the Major, the Commandant, or me, for the duration of your stay. Failure to comply will result in either your immediate dismissal or worse, in further sanctions. You will also take all of your meals with Major Samson or with me. Do I make myself clear, gentlemen?"

"Yes, Sir."

"Clear, Sir!"

"Questions...No? Good then. Gentlemen, stand and follow me."

One week later, over lunch, Hamish Findley asked Colonel Graham, "Sir, would you happen to know the new client, Marco?"

"I've read his dossier. We've already got him lined up for some important business. How is he coming along? When can I tell Robert Brooks that he'll be ready?"

"Colonel, that's the problem. He's seems more interested in asking questions than in learning the Syllabus. For example, yesterday, he was questioning the others in his class whether they knew anything about my background. Did anyone know what was going on in Hydra, and so forth. Seems a bit too curious, for my liking. If I may ask, Sir, what's his story?"

"Let me try to recollect. Marco Palermo. Age: twenty-three. Toronto-born, speaks two languages, fluently. Has spent time in Italy. He's bright, Senior Matriculation from Riverdale Collegiate, with Honours in Maths, Physics, and Chemistry. Parents are both old country, Abruzzi. They own a small speciality bakery, in the west end of town. He fits Brooks' profile to a 't'. Why? Are you concerned about him, Hamish?"

As were all of the officers, Hamish was in awe of Gordon Graham's prodigious memory. "Yes. I am Sir. There's something that just doesn't add up, that I can't put my finger on...."

"I'll speak with Robert in the morning and advise him of your reservations. In the meantime, keep a close watch and report to me promptly anything that's not to the letter. Anything at all, Hamish! Perhaps he's simply a brighter light than most."

"Yes, Sir, I expect that you're right. Thank you."

A few weeks later, Robert Samson and Michael Heaviside were having a drink in the Mess, enjoying a break from routine. They were quietly arguing the merits of the most recent revisions to 'The Bible', the name by which SOE staff officers unofficially referred to the Service's training handbook, the Syllabus.

"Speaking of clandestine entry, Michael, I have a promising client, the lad Marco, whom I would like to test. I wish to send him on a 'scheme'. I've decided to see if he's up to snap, if I should bring him forward for further assessment for leadership training.

"I'd like you to send him into Oshawa to the Genosha Hotel. His assignment: to find out in which room one Terence Browning is staying. Browning's not involved in any way - simply a name I picked up from a source in Oshawa.

Once Marco has made his way past the desk clerk, he is to slip into the room, while Browning is out, obviously, and remove some personal papers that Browning has supposedly hidden away. They will actually have been planted by my source. Our client, Marco, must not be armed but may carry a burglary pry and a torch. Once he has the papers, he is to return here directly and check in with you. No one else is to be informed of this. Do you agree?"

"Rob, if you don't mind my curiosity, why are you asking me to do this? It seems the sort of thing you like to manage...your forte, no?"

"True enough, Michael. Normally I would organise this sort of escapade, but in this case I don't want him to know or even suspect that I'm involved. I'd like to turn him over to you. Then, if you would, after an interval of a day or two, send him on this assignment. Kindly let me know the evening before so that I can make the necessary arrangements."

" 'Ours is not to reason why....' Robert, it will be my pleasure, so long as the Colonel has no objection."

"Thanks, old chap. Leave that to me, Michael." He nodded, indicating the empty glass on the table. "Time to recharge the chalice?"

"Plying a colleague with drink now, are you Robert? Yes, I'll do it and yes, you can fetch me two fingers, neat, one ice. Ta."

Colonel Gordon Graham was not amused. It was one thing to send young men and women out on training schemes, as he had routinely done previously as Chief Instructor at Beaulieu, and now, as Commandant of STS 103, but it was quite a different kettle of fish this time. He had received no information as to their whereabouts, nor was he apprised whether they were even alive or dead. These two brave youngsters, as he perceived them, had volunteered for a mission so daunting and with implications so enormous, that he couldn't get them out of his mind.

It mattered not to him whether the mission was a success or a complete washout; he liked and admired them both. Despite his recent run-in with Hugh, and contrary to his better judgement, he found himself personally caught up in their undertaking. He felt responsible for them in spite of everything he had been taught and had insisted upon from his own officers. The rules of intelligence were often callous by necessity and they dictated otherwise, but he couldn't shake his concern.

'Did I do everything to prepare them sufficiently? Can our people in Britain be completely trusted to help see them through? What if the British circuits have been compromised and I, Gordon MacKay Graham, am handing over Tent Peg's operatives to the Gestapo on a silver platter?'

He picked up the Camp telephone and dialled Hydra's operations room. "Bernie, Colonel Graham. Listen, old chap, I need you or Yorkie to send this to Claymore:

'FRAGILE GOODS SHIPPED STOP

REPORT CONDITION AND ANY BREAKAGE IMMEDIATELY STOP'.

Sign it with my code name, 'Red Ticket', 103. Got that? Read it back, please.... Very good. That is all, thank you. And do let me know immediately you get something back."

He set down the receiver. Somehow, it made him feel better. 'Red Ticket'; he could still chuckle at his *nom de guerre*. It had been conferred by the SOE brass in England to reflect his dubious personal achievement as the second-most penalised right striker in Sandhurst Military College's football team history. He glanced at his wall clock. 'Time for a bite.' "Betty, I'm slipping out to the Mess." 'I

Dundas Street and Highway #2, looking southward, 1939.

wonder if Samson wants to join me?' "Hullo, Rob, Gordon, care to go for a nosh? Oh, I see. Well, perhaps an early dinner then? Yes, I'll ring to remind you. Cheerio."

Robert Samson was unable to join the Colonel at that particular moment as he was counselling the client, Marco.

"Sir, may I please have a pass to go into town tomorrow?" Marco asked. "I feel that I need to get away for a few hours and clear the cobwebs."

Dundas Street and Highway #2, looking north, 1940.

"Is there anything wrong, lad...something not right on the home front, girl problems...?"

"No, Sir. None of those, I assure you," he smiled. "I just feel that I need a little bit of private time, a break to get away from the books and the other clients, that's all, Sir."

"I understand. Don't see why not, Marco. I've worked you and your mates hard; by and large, I'd say you're progressing quite nicely. Mind you, I'll be deluged with requests when the other chaps find out, but I can cope, since you were all due for eight-hour leave mid week anyway.

"I can meet you at the guardhouse at 0900, waiting with a day pass. Please be on time, as I have a lecture at ten. You do realise that I have to take you into town? Camp Regs. You'll call the number on this card when you're ready to come back, no later than 1600 hours, mind. Leave a message and I'll pick you up at the drop-off spot. Agreed?"

"Yes, Sir! Thanks a million, Sir."

The next morning at 0855, Marco picked up his day pass at the guardhouse, and then trotted over to where Samson waited for him in the station wagon. As they drove westward into Whitby, Samson reminded Marco of his responsibilities as a member of BSO; "Stay out of trouble, lad. I don't want any 25-1-1 calls from the RCMP." He concluded by asking Marco if he had enough money for the day. "Here's an extra ten. Take it...have a beer and lunch on me, but watch out for talkative strangers. Where shall I drop you off?"

Marco thanked him and replied that the corner of Brock Street, Highway 12, and Dundas, Highway 2 would be ideal.

"Four Corners, they call it locally. So, what do you have planned Marco?" inquired Robert affably, pulling up to the curb.

"Well, first thing is breakfast at the restaurant around the corner and then a visit to the barber shop; I'm not sure after that, Sir. Maybe a little window-shopping, or a stroll down at the lakeshore before lunch. After that, I might take in a matinee of *Citizen Kane,* that new movie that's creating all the fuss. The paper said it's playing at The Strand.

Thank you for the lift, Major. I'll call you this afternoon."

As Robert Sampson drove away, Marco watched until the station wagon was out of sight, and then slipped quickly into the restaurant. Instead of sitting at the counter, he went straight to the cash register. Using Robert's ten spot, Marco purchased a $1.25 Grey Coach ticket to Highland Creek, Return, about fifteen miles west of Whitby. The cashier assured him that the bus was due at Four Corners in ten minutes, "...more or less."

Marco thanked her and went outside to wait on the wrought iron bench in front of The Canadian Bank of Commerce. Although the sun was shining directly in his face, he didn't mind as a cool breeze from the lake countered its heat.

Ten minutes later, right on schedule, the Grey Coach bus pulled up at the stop, its air brakes shattering the morning stillness with a high-pitched screech. Marco waited while the bus driver punched his ticket, and then took the window seat mid-coach, in an empty row. The driver threw the big diesel into gear and wheeled west, making several brief stops along Highway 2, and taking aboard a dozen or so Toronto-bound passenger.

Marco stared out at the passing farmland, avoiding any eye contact or conversation with his fellow travellers. After twenty minutes, the driver announced, "Highland Creek, Highland Creek." Marco yanked the overhead cord to signal his intention to get off at that stop.

The bus pulled over onto the gravel roadside, slowed, and stopped. Its front door opened and Marco stepped down. He waved to the driver and, when the bus pulled away, Marco could see his destination directly across the highway.

The large, old barn looked completely out of place so close to the road. Marco had often wondered who had chosen this location. A car sped past and it was then clear to cross. A husky man, apparently the shop foreman, greeted Marco as he walked into the barn, long since converted into a machine shop.

"Hello, I'm here to see Günther, please."

"Who?"

Marco raised his voice, in an attempt to be heard above the incessant whining and roaring of the machinery. "Günther...Günther, please!"

"Günther? Ya, that's him, over there at the lathe, but you'll have to wait five minutes. He'll be on break then."

"Oh sure, I have all day. Thanks a lot."

A few minutes later Günther walked up to Marco and greeted him, extending a huge and filthy ham of a hand. "Sorry," he apologized, "I'm a bit greasy." He wiped the offending hand on his coveralls. "Come over here, Marco. Perfect timing, I'm just starting my break. I get fifteen minutes, so we can talk a little." They walked over to the work area where Günther had set up a wooden table and a chair next to his metal lathe.

"Sit down, I'll get another chair. Would you like coffee?"

"That would be great, thank you, Günther."

Günther opened his lunch box and pulled out his thermos and a wax paper-wrapped sandwich. "We'll share."

"No, you eat the sandwich and I'll just have a sip of your coffee. Günther, I've always wondered, what is it you make here, tanks, or something? It's certainly loud enough!"

"We make parts for General Motors. Right now, I'm making brake plates for a new personnel vehicle. They really don't tell us very much. Everything is Classified, Top Secret, nowadays. I practically have to sign in blood for new metal stock every time I run low. But there's no end to the overtime, so the money's good. Sometimes I wish we weren't so busy, though; I could use a rest."

"Soon you'll be so rich that you can build that cottage up in the woods, eh? Where did you say it was?"

"Haliburton. Another time. Land's too expensive and there's no building material at all for civilian use right now.

"So, Marco, how've you been? What are you up to lately?"

"Oh, I'm working in a Department of Defence lab right now. But I'm looking for a transfer to something a little more daring."

"Sounds pretty important and exciting to me, no?"

"It has its days, but generally, not as much as you'd think."

The two men chatted idly for another ten minutes. As Marco finally stood up to leave, he dropped a folded piece of paper into Günther's lunch pail.

"Well, Günther, it sure has been nice seeing you again. I'll be in touch."

"Yes, good to see you again, Marco. Take care!"

Marco stepped off the bus at Four Corners in Whitby, and walked directly to the Strand Cinema. The grey haired woman in the box office stopped filing her nails long enough to remark that the matinee of *Citizen Kane* was already underway. He thanked her, and then proceeded into the foyer, noticing a pay telephone beside the washroom doors. Taking note of the time on the large electric wall clock, he slipped into the Men's Room and entered a stall, closing the door behind him, then quickly crumpled and flushed away the incriminating bus receipt.

When he emerged, the usher took his theatre ticket, tore it in half, and absently handed him the stub, gesturing with his flashlight toward an aisle seat. Marco settled down in the darkness, smiling as he careful-ly placed the paper scrap in his billfold, secure in his alibi should Major Samson decide to check his story.

Günther knew that he would have to be off the airwaves quickly in order to avoid detection by the government's listening posts. Amateur, or 'ham', radio operators were expressly forbidden on air during wartime. With the message in the exercise book and a one-time-code pad, which he kept in his travel kit, he converted Helmut's note onto the code pad in five-letter groups. With less than a minute to go, he was ready. At eight fifty-nine forty-five, he switched on the power. Exactly at nine, Günther began to tap out his Abwehr W/T ID.

At Camp X, Bernie Sandbrook was manning Hydra, twiddling the powerful receiver's tuning dials, listening for traffic from BSO agents in South America, when he detected an unusual transmission on a rarely used, high frequency band. The groups were coming in at a rapid rate.

"Hey, Yorkie, come here! Have a listen to this guy! He must be practising for the ruddy Morse Olympics!"

Smiling at the usually unflappable Bernie's excitement, Yorkie put on his headphones and start-ed to jot down what he could catch of the rapid transmission. In a matter of seconds, his smile turned to a look of pure consternation. "Bernie, something strange is going on. It's not Allied code and it's not any ham, at least not one in his right mind. You'd better get the Commandant, PDQ! I'll stay with it."

Bill Hardcastle (Yorkie) in the Hydra building at Camp X, 1945.

Bernie raced out of the building and ran across the road the short distance to the CO's residence. Without knocking, he opened the front door and went directly to the Commandant's closed parlour door. There, he knocked once and called through the door, "Colonel Graham, it's Bernie from the radio room. We need you over there, urgently, please, Sir!"

Graham and Robert Samson were having a scotch while drafting the junior staff officers' performance reports that were due in less than a week. "Come in!"

"Commandant, Major Samson, I really apologise for barging in, but you must come. Now! We've intercepted a signal that I think you need to hear."

The three sprinted to the Communications Building. Graham, who excelled at Morse, immediately put on a spare headset and listened intently. "Paper, Yorkie!" he barked, then commenced scribbling down the coded groups. After the transmission was finished, he took off the earphones and looked at Bernie and Yorkie. "You were certainly on your toes, boys. Jolly smart work."

"Major Samson, I'll be damned if that wasn't an Abwehr high level code!"

"Meaning what, Colonel?"

"Meaning we have, somewhere in this fair land, a loose cannon, an active Axis agent."

"Colonel, it's not possible to pin him down now that he's off the air, but judging by the signal strength, I'd guess that the transmitter's probably not far away," Yorkie asserted.

"Thanks for the information. Put the blighter's message through the encoder, then off to Bletchley, with an OU priority, chop-chop, there's a good man. You two have certainly earned your keep tonight. Many thanks. Well-played chaps. Enjoy the evening, or what's left of it, and keep me informed as always. Good night."

The signal, bearing an OU prefix was sent directly to Bletchley Park General Code and Cipher School, where, after decoding and encoding, was assigned Most Secret, Your Eyes Only status, and routed to SIS HQ, London, Attn. 'G', and BSO HQ, Toronto, Attn. Stalwart.

"Sir, our U-99 off Halifax has just forwarded a signal from Helmut."

"Let me have it, please, Corporal." He picked it from the radio operator's hand and read it, twice, then strode into the office of the Abwehr Director General of Foreign Counterintelligence Communications.

"Pardon the interruption, Sir; I have finally received something which may be quite useful from Helmut, my Canadian agent at Camp X. He says he strongly believes that the British are training two agents for an assassination attempt on a high ranking German individual, but he doesn't know specifically who the target is meant to be."

"Those Brit bastards are always cooking up something. I think that SIS plants these nuggets of misinformation, just to test the integrity of our system, or to mislead us and divert our attention from something more significant. Do you think there's anything to this one?"

"Yes, Sir. Yes, I do. Helmut's not the sort of fellow who's inclined to let his imagination run amok."

"Sit down and close the door. Let's think about this. The immediate question is, should I inform the SD and the Gestapo? If your Helmut proves to be mistaken, or we find he's a double agent, they'll eat us for lunch. Perhaps the Boss should go over their heads, directly to the Führer?"

"Well, Sir, I strongly suggest that you leave that decision to the Admiral; perhaps you could have a glass of wine at an outdoor café? I don't trust our newly crowned Obergruppenführer Heydrich. He's probably listening in, right here and now. Remember how he wired the bedrooms in that bordello, 'Salon Kitty', and caught those officers giving away the game to the girls? He could have made mincemeat of the lot of them."

"Oh, he did. More than a few careers were torpedoed, just by innuendo. Luckily, I never frequented the place."

"Of course not, Sir, luckily."

"Very well then, I'll make an appointment for an after-hours drink with Rear Admiral Canaris without delay. I can't risk being held accountable for knowingly suppressing a Commando plot to assassinate our friend Heydrich, Marshall Göring, or, heaven help us, the Führer himself.

Marco opened the door of the Genosha Hotel and walked up to the front desk. The young female clerk looked up from a dog-eared crossword puzzle book. "May I help you?" she asked, smiling sourly, reluctantly turning the paperback face down.

"Yes, please. I understand that an old friend of mine is in town and I wonder if you would be good enough to tell me what room he is staying in? His name is Ralph Breen, Mr. Breen, R."

"I'm really not allowed to give out room numbers." She had already sized him up in one glance: the handsome but harmless type you could actually bring home to mother. He stood motionless, waiting, not breaking eye contact. Flustered, she reconsidered. "Well, I guess if he's an old friend of yours, then it's okay," she murmured nervously and she began scanning the register. "Let's see now, B...B...Breen. Hmm, you say he's a guest here?"

"That's what the telegram said. This is the Genosha Hotel, isn't it, dear?"

"Uh huh, sure it is, but I don't see that name listed. When did he check in?"

"Listen, sweetheart, I'm not supposed to say this, but he may be staying under an alias. He uses two, sometimes three. Secret war work, hush-hush, cloak and dagger, you know the drill."

"No kiddin'! Just like the movies?" She was now definitely very interested in this intriguing turn of events.

"Uh, huh, just like the movies. If I could take a look at your register, I'd recognise him, right off the bat."

"Gees, I dunno. I could get fired. What if he's a spy and they..."

"No, no, nothing like that. He's definitely on our side. Besides, who's going to tell? Not me, you can count on that. Your name's Dianne?" he read from her nametag. Leaning closer, he whispered, "I'm Sergio. Confidentially, Dianne, you'd be making a small but very important contribution to the war effort, I swear."

She looked at him and decided he was not only above board but cute, too, in a dark, Latin sort of way. "Okay, Sergio, but just one quick look," she responded anxiously, glancing furtively over her shoulder, then turning around the book so that he could read it. "Please, hurry. Okay?"

"Thanks, Dianne. You're a real doll." He scanned the entries, thumbing the pages until he located 'Terence Browning, Room 301'. "Okay, so how do I get upstairs, babe?"

"You can take the elevator, but it's kind of rickety. I'd use the stairs, there, at the other end of the lobby."

"Thank you very much, Dianne. I really appreciate it. This could be a big help to our boys at the front. Oh, here's something for your co-operation, with thanks from the Government of Canada. But you can't tell anyone about this. 'Loose lips...' you know? Good luck with that crossword!" he added, placing a crisp, new five dollar bill on the counter in front of her.

She seemed taken aback by this act of official generosity. "Gee, thanks a lot! Any time. Hope you and your friend have a nice reunion, Sergio! Drop by again!"

"For sure. *Ciao*, kid!"

'*Ciao*! Goddamm, how'd I let that slip out? So much for blending into the background.' Five bucks...cheap at twice the price. As he walked across the lobby toward the stairs, he felt her eyes boring into his back. He stopped at the fireplace to warm his hands. Now to determine where Browning was and how he was going to get into and out of Browning's room without being discovered.

When he reached the door at the far end of the hall, Marco turned quickly and looked back, but the desk clerk had apparently forgotten about him already and was absorbed once again in her puzzle. Cautiously, he turned the knob, pushed open the door, and tested the handle on the other side. He looked around for something to shove in the latch so that he wouldn't be locked out. He found a burnt match-stick lying on the floor, and breaking it in half, he jammed it into the mechanism so that the door would close, but remain unlocked. 'Just like they teach us!'

Satisfied, he went out the nearest exit and, shielding his eyes, he looked up, squinting into the bright sun. Directly overhead was a steel ladder that could be pulled down almost to street level. The ladder led to the second floor where it met the steps of the fire escape that ran up one floor, then turned, and continued on to the next. 'Perfect, I'll wait 'til dark, and then make my move. Now, to fill in some time. Too bad that dame is working!'

He sat at the counter drinking coffee until a booth near the rear of the Rose Bowl Restaurant emptied, then he sauntered back, sat down, and leaned against the backrest. Casually reading the greasy pages of the Sports Section of a two-day-old *Toronto Star*, he drank more java and chain-smoked. At seven-fifteen, he asked the waitress for a double order of the local favourite, the Oceans O' Fish and Chips Special, which he ate slowly, all the while keeping an eye on the street.

When he finished, he checked his watch again: eight o'clock. He ducked into the Men's' Room; when he returned, he lit his tenth cigarette just as a Toronto/Hamilton-bound Grey Coach rumbled out from the Bus Terminal. Its interior lights were still switched on, illuminating the faces of the passengers: soldiers, sailors, flyboys, WREN's, and assorted civilians. His face flushed as he reflected how much he hated them all for their English-Canadian-Protestant arrogance and their air of superiority towards 'foreigners' like his own Momma and Poppa, and even him, Marco, a Canadian, born and bred.

Major Heaviside had told him that Browning was employed at the Genosha Hotel as a bartender and that he followed a precise routine. His shift began at 8:00 p.m. and lasted until closing time at 1:00 a.m. He took two fifteen-minute breaks, at 9:30 and 11:30 p.m. Heaviside said that Marco should be inside the room before 9:00. No later.

Marco's eyes darted towards the black cat wall clock, its wide eyes panning the room, back and forth, in perfect cadence with its swishing tail: 8:27. He butted his cigarette, gulped the dregs of his sixth coffee, and dropped fifty cents on the table for the bored waitress.

Genosha Hotel, Oshawa, Ontario, 1940.

From the Rose Bowl, it was a short, brisk walk back to the Genosha. As he rounded the southeast corner of the hotel, he walked directly into a middle-aged man in a bus driver's uniform kissing a young woman, pressing her hips against the building just beside the ladder.

Marco began one of several well-rehearsed scenarios. "You got a light? Hey, you two love birds, can you knock it off long enough to give me a light?"

The woman was momentarily flustered, but recovered and snapped back indignantly, "Drop dead, you bum! Let's get out of here, honey!" Reluctantly disentangling themselves, they hurried away as she delivered her parting shot, "Why don't you try doing somethin' useful, like sobering up and joining the army, you little creep!"

'Little creep. That's a good one! Hey, the light routine works every time. Can't say I blame her,' he sighed, as he glanced around the corner and watched the woman indignantly walk away from him on her high heels. 'All clear, now get the ladder.' It pulled down easily. He climbed to the first landing, then tugged the ladder up behind him and secured the rungs. Looking in the window, he could see a deserted hallway. 'So far, so good; two to go!' Climbing up the fire escape to the third level, he tried the hall window. It was locked. '301, there it is. First on the right. Coming right in!' The metal landing extended as far as Browning's window; the open drapes showed that the room was empty and in darkness.

Marco tried to pry the window. 'No luck. Bring out the heavy artillery.' He took a short metal object from inside his jacket, an SOE Break and Enter 'slim jim', lent to him by Heaviside, and pushed it gently between the top of the window and its sash. This lock was doubly unyielding. He glanced impatiently at his wristwatch. The luminous glow of the hands indicated 8:57. 'Give, you bastard!' he muttered. Suddenly, the catch gave, ever so slightly. He pressed harder, too hard, and forced the tip to slip off the heavily painted brass.

'Damn!' He repositioned it. 'Easy now.' This time, the catch gave way. 9:02. But the window still refused to budge. He inserted the thin end of the pry underneath the frame and pressed down, very hard, on his end. 9:03. 'I might as well break the bloody window!' He pushed down once again with all of his strength. The paint seal broke under his fourth try and the window creaked open an inch. Marco pushed and coaxed the window with considerable effort until it finally and totally jammed halfway up, then, crouching, he clambered over the wooden ledge into the room. 9: 05.

'Christ, I'm sweatin' buckets!'

He wrinkled his nose. The room had the stale aroma of a bachelor: cigar smoke, forgotten, half-empty beer bottles, and unwashed socks. 'What a slob!' As he moved in the near darkness, his elbow bumped something that clattered onto the floor. He pulled out a miniature flashlight, courtesy of Heaviside, and shone the beam around. A glass ashtray was lying upside down, its contents scattered on the scuffed parquet floor.

'Where the hell would someone hide documents in a room this size?' He looked under the bed. 'Nothing. I'm not looking in those bed sheets!'

He pulled open the three drawers of the unpainted dresser and dumped the contents of each onto the bed. He picked the items apart using the tip of the metal pry bar. 'All crap. Still nothing. Last chance!' he muttered, as he sucked air through his teeth, walking toward the closet.

He opened the door. In the flashlight beam, he saw a single wooden support rod bowed under the weight of a jumble of coloured shirts, gaudy sports jackets and an assortment of dress trousers and work pants, and a tangle of belts and ties on one wooden hanger. 'This guy's wardrobe definitely needs help. Jesus, it's 9:16. I need to take a leak. What kind of shoes are those? Army boots? What the...?

A white-hot ring of fire closed around his throat. His shallow scream of surprise, terror, and agony abruptly ended as his hands clawed frantically at the piano wire tightening its death grip. Gagging and gasping for air, his body arched and twisted grotesquely backward. Trying desperately to relieve the terrible pain and pressure, he dug his fingernails into his own flesh underneath the steel loop. He tried frantically to kick his unseen assailant with his right heel, earning him only a brutal and immediate tightening of the snare.

His feet lifted from the floor. As Marco lost consciousness, his bladder emptied in a spreading dark pool on the worn carpet. He ceased struggling. Completely limp now, his rag doll body dangled for another eternity then was lowered, almost gently, onto the floor. 'Nine seconds.' The man in the combat boots looked down at the corpse as he calmly coiled and pocketed the garrotte, then walked to the half-opened window, climbed over the sill and was swallowed up by the night.

Terence Browning looked at his watch. It was 12:50 a.m. It had been an unusually slow night for a Saturday. He called over to Joe, the night manager, who was sitting across the bar, counting out the evening's take. "I've cleaned the tables and washed up the glasses. I'm heading home now, Joe; you mind locking up?"

"Nope, I'll do it. See you Monday, Terry. How 'bout those Leafs!"

"Killer dillers! We're square... till next week. Okay, Joe, see you."

Terence walked toward the stairs past Dianne's desk. 'What a cutie-pie' "Hi, Di. How's it goin'?"

She smiled and shrugged, "So, so. Slow night, dull as dishwater, but I'm finished soon. G' night Terry." The elevator, slow as molasses at the best of times, wasn't worth the five-minute wait. Besides, a three-floor walk up wouldn't kill him.

He unlocked his door, entered his room, and then turned, double locking, and chaining the door by touch. He flung his bow tie in the direction of his armchair, and went into the bathroom to run some warm water to rinse his face. In the light of the single bulb, he looked into the mirror as he dried off. 'Man, you look like you could use a brew!' He switched off the bathroom light, and, as usual, walked back down the short hallway in the dark, toward the kitchenette.

He stumbled over something beside the closet. "What the hell?" He reached for the light switch. "Oh, dear God!" It was a pair of legs; worse, looking up at him was a grotesque caricature of a human face, frozen in a state of perpetual terror, eyes bulging like obscenely overripe grapes, and the swollen black tongue lolling absurdly from purple lips. An angry red welt ran across the throat from ear to ear. "Christ, he's, he's been strangled. I'm getting the hell out of here!"

He struggled with the locks and chain. Finally, in spite of his trembling hands, he managed to fling open the door and ran, stumbling along the hallway to the stairs shouting, "Help, help, please somebody!"

Dianne heard his cries, and as he ran down the final few steps, she had already started around the counter. "Terry, what is it? What's wrong?"

"In my room...I don't know...a body, he's dead!"

"Who's dead, Terry?"

"A man...on the floor...I don't know...how he got there!" He was shaking and sobbing now, uncontrollably.

"Terry, come, sit down; I'll get Joe." Dianne led him gently behind the counter and helped him sit in a chair. After a reassuring pat on his shoulder, she went to the entrance of the Time Out Lounge. Seconds later, she called back, "Terry, it's okay. Joe's calling the Oshawa police right now. They'll be here in a jiffy. I'm getting you coffee."

Detective Sergeant Paul Cummins was a twenty-two-year veteran of the Ontario Provincial Police. He was looking forward to his well-earned retirement in three more years. As he pulled up to the hotel, he swore silently and hoped that this call was not what the dispatcher had reported, but just some kind of Saturday night drunken prank. It was a classic handoff. The Oshawa boys had a full-blown arson investigation going on at a lumberyard in the south end, and begged off on the Genosha call. It landed squarely on Cummins' lap, along with a hot coffee when he hit the roof light and peeled out of the vacant lot.

After a brief and garbled attempt at conversation with "the poor sap who had allegedly found the stiff," Joe, the night manager accompanied Cummins to the third floor. Cummins motioned him to stay back and removed his gun from its holster, pointing it toward the door, which Terry, in his flight, had left ajar. He slowly pushed the door open with his free hand and entered the room. In the dim light, the lifeless eyes stared up at him.

"I don't think you want to see this, Joe."

"What is it, Sarge?"

"Well, it's not a joke, that's for sure," he sighed. "No pulse. Looks like we have an old-fashioned homicide on our hands. Gimme your passkey. Sorry, you can't go in, even if you are an Auxiliary. I'm sealing this room. Is there a phone in there? Good.

"Listen, Joe, go down stairs, and keep a close eye on the guy in the lobby. Don't let him out of your sight. Take him by the hand to the can, if he needs to go. I'll need to question him later. And get him to calm down."

"Gees, Paul, he's Terry Browning, an employee. He was working with me in the bar, all night."

"Did he take any breaks, Joe?"

"Yeah, only two, fifteen minutes each."

"That's more than enough time. I'm calling for backup, the coroner, and crime scene boys. I want this place dusted, photographed, and then taken apart, if necessary. Till another copper arrives, Mr. Browning's your baby. Lock him in your office and call this number fast if he tries to bolt. Keep your clerk here until I can get to talk with her, too. I want to look around some more."

Dr. Donald Miller, the Coroner, arrived within twenty minutes.

"Hi, Paul, what have you got for me? Another 'john' with a bum ticker?"

"Nope, Doc, it's a murder. See for yourself. Strangled. And whoever did it meant business. That poor bastard's half-decapitated."

"Huh. We haven't had a homicide in Oshawa in years. Let me take a closer look, Paul. By the way, the window's partly open. Your killer might have flown the coop..." he remarked, opening his bag.

"Donald, you look after the medical mumbo-jumbo, I'll handle the detective work. Tell me when I can search him for his ID." He dialled the telephone, holding the receiver in a white handkerchief. "What's the time of death?"

"Turn on the lights, please. Thanks. I'd roughly estimate, based on preliminary observations, between three and six hours ago. I'm taking the body temperature now." Dr. Miller continued his methodical examination. Judging by the marks around the neck, it was likely that he had indeed been brutally asphyxiated, strangled by something very fine and very efficient. 'No fibre burns,' he thought, 'so it was probably metal, a wire, or possibly a lamp cord.'

The examination continued down the body, from the neck to the torso. The Coroner inspected the hands and fingernails for signs of abrasions and for tissue fragments, which could be harvested for analysis at the Provincial Lab. He froze. On the cadaver's left wrist there was a metal chain-link ID bracelet, bearing the lettering, ST25-103. Hastily, he unfastened the clasp and slipped the bracelet into his vest pocket. Dr. Miller rose. "Paul, I'll be right back. I have to get something. Don't touch him, yet."

He exited the elevator at the lobby and walked into a sea of blue uniforms. "Detective Cummins is waiting for you boys, Room 301." Dr. Miller walked immediately to the lobby pay phone and called Commandant Graham's private residence line.

"Hello, Gordon?"

"Yes?"

"Donald Miller here."

"Hello, Donald, is there a problem?"

"I'm afraid so, Gordon. Can you come to the Genosha Hotel right away? I'll fill you in when you get here."

The Commandant's black Buick pulled up in front of the hotel. He got out of the car and looked across the street at the flashing marquee lights of the Regent Theatre: 'Now Playing - *Murder In The Air* - starring Ronald Reagan'.

When he stepped into the foyer, Dr. Donald Miller met him. "Over here, Gordon." The two men walked toward the fireplace. "I..."

"Donald, what in blazes are the police doing here?" Graham interrupted, impatiently.

"That's why I called you. There is a dead man upstairs. He was wearing a Camp bracelet."

"Was? You've removed it? You're sure that it's one of ours?" Graham asked, incredulously.

"No question," he stated, palming the bracelet to Graham.

"Yes, it's one of ours, alright. Do you know who he is, Donald? Have you ever seen him before?"

"He's not one of your staff officers, so I assume that he must be a client."

"Oh, Lord! A client? I don't know what to say." Graham thought for a minute. "Your contact at the funeral home, what's his name?"

"John?"

"Yes. Call him. Have him come over straight away to pick up the body. I'll get hold of Ted Reynolds at the RCMP and tell him to come with some plainclothesmen. This could be messy. The OPP are going to claim privilege...first to the scene. I'll have to use the desk phone, if you don't mind."

Dr. Miller went back to the pay phone. He inserted a nickel and dialled the number. After two rings, a voice answered, "McIntosh Anderson Funeral Home; this is the Director speaking. How may I help you?"

"John? It's Donald Miller."

"Hello Donald. It must be urgent business!"

"Very. John, I need a hearse at the Genosha Hotel, as soon as you can be here. Back entrance. The fewer people you bring, the better."

"I understand. I'll be there in a flash."

After rousing a sleepy Commissioner Reynolds, Colonel Graham called his own private nightline. "Betty? Colonel Graham."

"Yes, Colonel?"

"Sorry to bother you at this ungodly hour, but I need you to contact Michael Heaviside. Please have him meet me ASAP at the Genosha Hotel in Oshawa. Tell him to bring the station wagon and come alone. That's all. Thank you, Betty."

"Yes, Sir. Of course, right away."

"Well, Donald, success?"

"John should be here momentarily. You?"

"Ted sounded as if he was already getting dressed while as we spoke. I expect him shortly. Let's slip into the lounge and lie low until they arrive. Above all, I do not want an incident. Do you see the man in the brown fedora? He's the local police reporter. I pray he doesn't recognise me."

"Thank you, Ted. Your driver must have flown at low altitude! You remember our Physician, Donald Miller?"

"Yes, hello again, Donald. So, Gordon, what's all the commotion?"

"It appears that one of our clients has met with foul play upstairs in Room 301. It hasn't been confirmed yet, though. Fortunately, Donald retrieved this bracelet from the body before the detective noticed it. Beyond that, I don't know what has happened. Donald has called the funeral home to come get him."

"I see. What do you want me to do, Gordon?"

"Run interference, essentially. Go upstairs and smooth things over for us with the local constabulary. The policeman's name is Detective Sergeant Cummins. I need him out of here as soon as possible. Then, I need your forensic chaps to investigate the situation, along with Donald, of course. And as soon as you're finished, I want the body taken away."

"I brought along my top man, Dr. Phil Douglas, and an assistant, from Toronto. Of course, neither you nor I can authorize the release of the remains. That's up to Donald as the Coroner and attending physician of record."

"I know. And time is of the essence. Send them out as soon as you can then, Ted. Donald, I'll leave it to you to deal with the undertaker. Please explain that he may have a considerable wait. "

"I will. There he is now, Gordon." Dr. Miller approached the undertaker and his two assistants entering through the rear door as Ted Reynolds walked toward the staircase.

When the Commissioner reached Room 301, he found the door locked. He knocked. "Sergeant Cummins? Commissioner Ted Reynolds here, of the RCMP. May I have a word with you?" he asked, holding open his billfold to display his identification.

Cummins stood at the doorway and scrutinized the newcomer's credentials. "RCMP, Sir? May I ask who sent you?"

"If I may step inside, Detective, I'll gladly tell you."

"This is highly irregular...very well, come in. May I ask what brings you here, Commissioner?"

"Detective Cummins, this fellow's apparent murder has created some, shall I say, unusual circumstances. I'm not at liberty to tell you precisely what is going on, or even how I know the details, but suffice to say there's much more to this than meets your very professional eye."

"Commissioner, I mean no disrespect, Sir, but, as I said, this is all very unusual. I'm sure you will agree. I'll have to call my duty Captain, Billy Bell. I can't hand this over to you on my own."

"Absolutely, Detective. Of course you can't. I strongly recommend that you do call; I'll be more than pleased to discuss the situation with him."

From the tone of Detective Cummins' directives, and by the frequent and furtive glances cast at him, it became clear to Ted that the Captain was less than favourably inclined to show the spirit of inter-service co-operation. When Cummins hung up the receiver, he wiped his forehead with his white handkerchief. "He's coming here. Captain Bell's orders to me are that you must stay put, Commissioner."

Captain Bell arrived at 2:00 a.m. Joe, the weary night manager, met him in the lobby and showed him to a table in the darkened bar, around which sat a British Army Lieutenant Colonel, two RCMP types, the Coroner, Donald Miller, and John, the funeral home director. Terry the bartender sat forlornly apart form the others, looking pale and shaken. The Colonel stood and introduced himself, then led Captain Bell upstairs, where Ted and Detective Cummins were waiting.

"Captain Bell, I am Commissioner Ted Reynolds of the RCMP. You've met Lieutenant Colonel Gordon Graham, of course."

"Yes, pleased to meet you, Commissioner Reynolds. I'm a great admirer of your force's work. I confess that I didn't know where to start, as I had never run into this situation before. I will say though, I have just concluded a discussion with the Mayor, who, as you know of course, is also the Chief Magistrate for the City. His Worship said that, provided you are prepared to give your assurances that a full report of your findings relative to your criminal investigation will be made available to him, then we can turn the matter over to you."

Ted looked over to Colonel Graham, who nodded his assent, then answered, "That would be satisfactory, Captain Bell. The Colonel and I must get our people down to business now, if you have no objection. Whoever did this must be half way to Timbuktu by now."

"Very well then. It was a pleasure meeting you. Sergeant Cummins, follow me. By the way, does our 'John Doe' have a name, Detective?"

"No ID that I could find, Captain. Good luck, Commissioner, Colonel."

As the two OPP men walked down the stairs, Captain Bell turned to Cummins and remarked, "Paul, this matter has now been turned over officially to the RCMP and is closed as far as the OPP record will show. Your logbook should indicate this. Can you handle a coffee and a sandwich? The Rose Bowl's not far. Follow me over and I'm buyin'."

"Sure, Captain, but I'm curious about one thing. Where does that Scotty Colonel fit in the picture?"

"I wouldn't waste your time trying to figure out any of tonight's events, Paul."

"Whatever you say, Sir."

Colonel Graham turned to Commissioner Reynolds, "Thank you again, Ted for bailing me out. That was too damned close for comfort. I'll let your men and Doctor Miller get on with the investigation. Call me when the body is ready for release. I'd like to get it secured over at the funeral home as soon as possible so we can begin to piece this thing together.

"Doc, your friend John deserves a medal for patience. I'll go back downstairs and keep him company."

"Phil says he'll need about half an hour to take pictures and finish examining the scene before you take away the body, Gordon. I'll be calling in some more staff to inspect the room, when it's time. Of course, there'll be an official autopsy."

"That's fine, Commissioner, you're in charge. We'll be waiting downstairs."

A concerned Major Heaviside arrived at the front desk. "I'm looking for Colonel Graham, please."

"One moment, Sir. I'll call the room.... Oh, here he is now, Sir."

"Michael! Glad you made it. Where in blazes were you?" Gordon whispered.

"Colonel, I came as quickly as I could. What is it, Sir?"

"Come upstairs, please...it's been quite a night. Major, I want you to go into this room and tell me if you recognise the body lying on the floor."

"You did say, 'body', Colonel?"

"I did. Go ahead."

When Major Heaviside walked into the room, he could see Dr. Miller, Commissioner Reynolds and two other men talking in the tiny kitchen area with Colonel Graham. A moment later, Graham joined him.

"Where is it? He? Oh, there." He saw the man's body, naked from the waist up, lying face down on the floor. He knelt down on one knee beside the corpse, and then looked up at Colonel Graham. "Is it okay if I move his head for a better look, Colonel?"

"Yes, the medical examiners say they're finished with the body, for the time being. Do you need some assistance?"

"No, it's okay." When Michael Heaviside turned the head gently towards him, he was stunned.

"God, it's Marco!"

"You knew him then, Major?"

"Yes, Sir, he is, was, a client name of Marco Palermo, one of the boys in the special Italian ethnic group. This is a shock!"

"Would you have any idea why Marco is dead, Major?"

"Sir, he was sent into town on a routine field training assignment. How he ended up like this, I have no idea."

"Thank you, Major. I expect you have a ready explanation for your delay in arriving here? You may go now and await my call when I return to the Camp. Of course, do not breathe a word of this to anyone. I will expect a full report, ASAP, on this man including all of his structured activities at the base. And see what you can find out regarding his off time pursuits, who his chums were, problems with other clients... I'll address this situation with the other instructors in the morning briefing."

"Yes, Sir. Understood, Sir."

"Michael, I want you to wake up Brian Jones and tell him I need a guard sent over to the McIntosh Anderson Funeral Home. Now. Use the back entrance, no uniform or sidearm. I'll be there to meet him, in an hour."

"Very good, Sir. I'll see to it immediately I get there."

"Did I hear that he was one of your clients, Colonel?" asked Commissioner Reynolds.

"Yes, Ted, an Italian-Canadian lad. Now we have to find out who killed him and for what reason. You're through with the body, Doctor?"

"As much as can be done here, Gordon. We've packed up all the tissue and fluid samples, ready to go directly to the Pathology Lab downtown. Phil will take them: he's going that way. I'll get the Funeral Director."

"Thanks, Donald."

"John, you and your assistants are to take the body to the mortuary. I'll follow you there and will remind them they've been sworn to secrecy under the Official Secrets Act and are not at liberty to discuss any particulars with anyone. I will be assigning an armed sentry, plain clothes, full-time, to guard the body twenty-four hours a day, for as long as I deem necessary. They'll be out of sight in your basement: however, should they cause any problem with your customers or interfere with your staff in any fashion, ring Doc Miller straight away."

The McIntosh-Anderson Funeral Home, Oshawa, Ontario, 1940.

"I understand, Colonel Graham."

The hearse travelled along King Street for approximately a quarter mile, turning into the narrow lane of the elegant redbrick McIntosh Anderson Funeral Home, and proceeding slowly to the rear parking lot. Colonel Graham followed the Cadillac limousine in his Buick, and parked while the hearse backed up to the service entrance. The body was removed and carried directly down a short concrete stairway to the basement. Just inside, the staff placed the stretcher on a gurney then awaited further directions from Colonel Gordon and John.

"Take him straight into the prep room, boys, and then you may leave," John said. "Thanks very much for coming over on such short notice. I'll finish up."

"And thanks to each of you for your patience," Colonel Graham added. "Sometimes these events take on a life of their own, well, that's not exactly.... I think we're all a bit tired. Just remember your oath of secrecy. I trust that you will bear that uppermost in mind."

"Colonel Graham?"

Gordon turned toward the voice. Sergeant Jack Wright, reporting for guard duty, in civvies as ordered, stood at the basement entrance.

"Come on down, Sergeant and I'll introduce you to your hosts."

When he had finished explaining the guard's duties, Colonel Graham shook John's hand and went up the stairway. When he had gone, John turned to the guard, "How long will you be here, Sergeant?"

"Until 0800 hours when my replacement will show up. I get the shortest graveyard shift, this time only, I suppose."

"Then let me show you where things are. That's the Preparation Room. The door will be locked and you are not expected to enter it, as the Colonel just said. Doctor Miller will be here at eight in the morning to perform an autopsy. The telephone is there, if you need it: the private washroom is just around the corner. Across from it you'll see a comfortable chair and a table with a hot plate, and the makings for coffee and tea. And homemade cookies! Our receptionist bakes them fresh! Please help yourself and we'll see you around 7:30 in the morning. I'll be locking up on my way out. Oh, I almost forgot. There's a small radio in my office. You might be able to find some music to listen to. Let me get it for you."

"I'd better not, Sir, but thanks for mentioning it."

"No? Very well, then. Good night Sergeant."

"Good night, Sir."

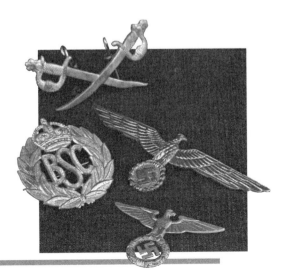

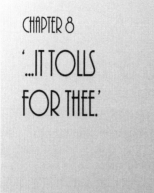

CHAPTER 8

'...IT TOLLS FOR THEE.'

"Thank goodness. It was only our friendly guide, that time. It was very risky but lovely of Cliff and the missus to think of us and send us real food. Such a relief after these dog biscuits and distilled water. I'm thankful Cliff will be our man on the ground. Aren't you puzzled, though, why the SIPO haven't ventured up here, for a look about? Very lax, not at all typical of their methods," she murmured.

"If you or I were in charge of protecting our leader, would it not be the obvious starting point to search for a sniper post? Besides, I'd probably want to sneak up here, if only to have a look at the spectacular view and take some photographs for the family album.

"There must be well over a thousand SS with scads of others and at least that many flags on the park grounds."

"I can see them. Sure, but that may just be why it hasn't been checked. They assume it's too 'plain as the nose on your face' or a 'hide in plain sight' spot, so they didn't even bother putting it on the list," Hugh suggested.

"That scene below makes me think. Did you study nineteenth century German philosophy, Hugh? I adored Kant's *The Critique of Pure Reason*; Hegel bored me silly. But to get to my point: Friedrich Nietzsche, the Nazis' golden boy, was not a 'Nazi-before-his-time'. He was fiercely anti-German actually. 'Wherever Germany extends her sway, she ruins culture.' "

"Poor Nietzsche has been hijack by the Hitler gang of dolts with their 'master race' superiority drivel; Nietzsche never for a moment believed Germans or Germany capable of or worthy of achieving his supreme state of being, the 'Superman'. As for another Nietzschean view, he was dead wrong: God is not 'a blunder of man', although He does seem rather inattentive these days. Friedrich, mad old duffer, ended up debating with his horse."

"Who won? The closest I ever got to Philosophy was one forgettable date with a wacky French Canadian Philosophy Major in Montreal."

"Beer, brotherhood, non-stop 'snogging', and that pathetic North

American excuse for real rugby that they call 'football'? I know your type.

"Seriously, though it could be that we're not out of the woods yet. The last message at 0700 confirmed that his aircraft is due at noon, weather permitting. Correct? There's still a whole hour left for some bright light down there to clue in."

"True enough, but not everyone is as brilliantly intuitive as you, my dear Captain. There were no fraternities and yes, I played football, Canadian rules... far superior. 'Snogging', you call it? That's descriptive. I still don't see where an aircraft could land in this area. What's your guess?"

"There," she gestured, "on Westminster Bridge. Take the glasses. See the blue uniforms clustered on the roadway?"

"Luftwaffe. Looks like ground crew. If you're right, the pilot must be the superman!"

"More than likely a ruddy superwoman, dear boy. You might be surprised to know that the Luftwaffe has more than its share of non-combatant female aces, Hugh. So do the Soviets, unlike the boys-only flying club, the jolly-old RAF. I actually thought I'd try out for a place in flight ground school, but the hoops were ridiculous. I had all the academics and whizzed through the physicals, but it dead-ended there. SOE is far more welcoming to women."

"What kind of airplane could land there without shearing off its wings? They obviously don't have Lysanders. There's no way a light bomber could possibly do it. I vaguely recall they've something similar to the Lysander, high winged, slow, meant for pinpoint landings and take-offs, but I can't remember what they're called. Is it Fiedeler?"

"Fieseler...Stork...Storch," she replied, "definitely. Listen, I'm not sure that I completely understand two particulars in last night's signal. One, the nature of the diversionary tactic to be staged was not clear; and two, the details of our escape route and destination seemed vague to nebulous at best. Perhaps I missed the point of both. Hand me the message pad, please. Thanks awfully," she grinned. "Lord, I could use an hour in Andrew's lovely tub just about now. If we come out of this alive..."

"A week in the most elegant honeymoon suite at the Ottawa *Chateau Laurier*. What is it that you don't understand?"

"Hold onto that thought. Now, here's what I don't get. Who's responsible for...? Oh, wait. Very well. Now I understand: the RAF is providing some tactical cover and we're to change back into civilian clothes. We then head south at the first opportunity, with help along the way."

Sylvia picked up the field glasses. "I must admit that I admire this Teutonic talent for, or rather, obsession with organisation. Just look at the masses of troops, all lining up tightly in formation, by company, battalion, regiment, division... just like so many ants. It's as if each knows what the whole is doing and where they're going. Sort of a collective consciousness." She stopped.

"What's wrong, Sylvia?"

"Pardon? Oh, nothing, nothing. I must be coming unhinged, going spare; besides hearing bells, I'm seeing things! Good Lord! Look! There are scores of great army lorries, huge personnel carriers brimming with black helmets, panzers, and God knows what else, darting, lumbering and churning up great chunks of sod on the field. And no one's been knocked down.

"I count fifty pieces of field artillery, plus a queue of impressive, black salons for the bigwigs, sorry, I meant limousines, forming up at the far end. It's like a huge cinema stage. In a way, it looks genuine, but the sheer magnitude of it, and the distance, makes it all a bit stagy. It's all so contrived and surreal, like so many toy soldiers.

"Careful, Hugh. Two very real Nazi officers at the reviewing stand; one of them, a Sturmbannführer, I believe, is gawking directly up here. Keep your head down or we're done for!" she whispered. "You said there's a mirror with a handle in Andrew's kit? Get it for me, but stay out of sight," she gestured, huddling below the edge of the parapet. "It seems the short one, the Major, is arguing with the General; I'd say that's he's either fairly nervy, or he's demented. Hand me my rifle."

"Speaking of demented, you're not going to try to nail the two of them, are you?"

"No! Here, hold the damn mirror. I'm just getting a trifle edgy. I feel more secure with the rifle close by, that's all. What's the time?" she asked quietly, her dark eyes burning with emotion.

"Eleven-forty two." The sudden, ear-splitting thunder of two single-engine fighter aircraft, silver wings flashing in the emerging sun, drowned out the end of his response. They flew in tight wingtip formation directly over the clock tower, so close that Sylvia and Hugh could see the robin's egg blue of their bellies, landing gear hatches, and the undersides of their wings. "Focke-Wulf 190's," he shouted above the din. "Ten feet lower and they would have seen us!"

When the planes had roared past, she shook her head, trying to quiet the echo still ringing in her ears. "Have a look below. Are those two still eyeing us? It's time."

"I don't see...no, wait a minute, they're getting into a limo. Nice one, black and silver! Okay, it's driving off the field. You're clear to set up, unless the bloody Luftwaffe makes another flyby."

"Pass me the clip. This wall is just the perfect height for a bench rest. Quiet, please, while I check the range and sight in." After a pause, she turned to him with a smile. "Excellent. I've worked this trajectory out in my head a hundred times and it seems to hold up.

"From the information we have, our elevation is between two hundred ninety-five and three hundred feet. Horizontal range from the tower base to the podium centre field: 16,540 feet. Wind velocity at ground level, no more than five miles an hour, to judge by the flags' motion. Wind direction, south by southwest. Subject stands five feet six inches. I'm aiming for his...what in heaven's name is that?" She had turned slightly and was staring at a white figure chalked on the grey stone wall behind him.

Kilroy was here!

"That's obscene!"

"No, no, it's not like that at all, Syl! It's a signature, a signal that the Yanks plaster everywhere. Now, you see it on railway boxcars, walls, army tanks, trucks, even on bombs. Factory workers and little kids put it on their lunch pails."

"Who is, 'Kilroy', pray tell?"

"No one knows... like Santa Claus...he just appeared."

"So, this is our final sneer at Adolf?"

"You betcha!"

"Just wondered. Pity we can't stamp it on his forehead, like gangsters dropping a Queen of Spades on their victim's chest," she responded, peering through her riflescope.

"Syl, look at that pilot put his FW through its paces! He's making quite the show!"

"That's a good sign. If I'm correct, it indicates that the target's approaching. Come, have a look at the reviewing stand through my sight. See all the Nazi four-flushers in their fancy dress kits? One good burst of machine gun fire and the Third Reich is ancient history."

"There's the Storch! Look, Sylvia, due east, into the sun. It's circling the Thames," Hugh shouted.

"I see it! This is it, Hugh." Softly Sylvia began to recite, in Hebrew, words foreign and haunting to Hugh.

He listened silently, until she had finished. "Was that a prayer, Sylvia?"

She turned with tears in her eyes, "*Kaddish*, the Hebrew Prayer for the Dead. Papa taught me. I said it for us, you, me, not him."

"It gave me goosebumps," he said softly, putting his arm around her shoulder, and pulling her head down against his chest. "Time to get changed, Frau Kortner." He kissed her forehead. "I love you, Sylvia."

"And I love you, Hugh. *L'chaim.*"

"*L'chaim.*"

"To life, ours... and a steady hand."

SD Signalman Private First Class Wolf Kurtz was certain that he had intercepted some very suspicious short wave radio activity, and immediately reported so to his sergeant. The sergeant's response was a pained look of impatience and dismissal. When Kurtz detected portions of a second transmission, he had the presence of mind to switch on the wire recorder.

"Sergeant, I ask you please to listen to this recording."

"Kurtz, you are driving me to distraction with your ghost signals. There are no spies anywhere except in prison, or coffins!" he laughed. "Well, what is it now?"

"Sergeant, I don't know...it's not identifiable. It could be an amateur playing around, but by the keying speed and unusual groups, I believe that it's a British Intelligence operator."

"You have my attention, go ahead, Private." The sergeant listened intently to the three-second W/T burst. "Play it again, Kurtz. Can you filter out the static?" The sergeant picked up a field telephone handset, "Lieutenant, Sergeant Stein here. I think you should hear this...a possible illegal, Sir. Yes, Sir, Private Kurtz recorded it on my orders."

Gruppenführer Walther Lange received the call on the portable radio/telephone in the rear of his automobile. "What the hell do you mean you can't locate it, Lieutenant?" Lange shouted into the handset.

"Find it. Don't give me that technical crap about triangulation. I want that bastard's address, eye colour, and shoe size, now, Lieutenant! The ceremony is starting!"

He slammed down the receiver, knowing full well that it was impossible to locate a radio electronically that wasn't turned on and transmitting its telltale carrier wave fingerprint. Seconds later, he picked up the instrument again. "Excuse me for a moment, Sturmbannführer von Tresköw. Perhaps you were right.

"Give me Site Security!" he demanded. "Lange, here. Listen carefully." Signals have found what is likely an enemy radio. No, they do not know where it is. Obviously! Yes, I strongly urge you to do that, Standartenführer. If it is in your bailiwick, and you find it in time, I'll personally see to it that the Führer himself confers your decoration. If not... You do get the idea, Standartenführer?

"Less than fifteen minutes! I don't care if you have to blow up half the city including the Tower and London Bridge, if that's what it takes! Heil Hitler! What? Big Ben, you mean the bloody clock? You must be having me on. No one could stay in there for five minutes without going insane! Impossible! Besides, it was thoroughly inspected four days ago and is now sealed tighter than a can of sardines. There are six Liebstandarte guardsmen on duty, 'round the clock. Don't waste your manpower. Just find him! Heil Hitler!"

He hung up the phone and turned to von Tresköw. "Hans, it appears that Canaris' Abwehr incompetents have it right, for once. There's an English rat holed up somewhere in this city; there can be one reason and one reason only for its presence. How in God's name could it have slipped in unnoticed? That Standartenführer, what's his name, the horse-faced one, believes it's either a bomber or a sniper, maybe both. Either way, we must take another look at the situation. I don't even want to think of the repercussions if we fail and I'm forced to recommend cancellation at the last minute. Or the alternative... Hans, I'm begging you for your help. Please!"

"You know you have it, Walther. I don't think grenades or bombs are likely: security on and surrounding the grounds is supremely tight. Unless perhaps the attackers were planning to way-lay the motorcade between the bridge and the field, in which case they might try.

"It's most vulnerable here," he indicated, jabbing at a street map with his finger, "where the procession must slow to seven kilometres an hour for the left turn coming off the bridge. I would make very certain that the motorcycle escort commanders are made well aware of the necessity for extreme vigilance before, during, and after rounding that corner. All lookouts must be prepared to fire instantly at the first sign of any trouble."

"I will see to it immediately. One moment please, Hans." He made one more phone call, barking his orders urgently into the receiver.

"Done. We have seven minutes before the Führer's aircraft lands. That will leave me two minutes to make the decision whether to radio Hana that I'm calling off the show. Any more thoughts before Herr Müller himself comes to collect me? I'd put my revolver into my mouth first rather than face his gang of butchers."

"There's nothing more to be done, Walther, if everyone else is doing his job."

"Our lives and the future of the Reich are in your hands, Hans. Come now, we must not be late for the arrival of the Führer. We will know soon enough if we are to be the first heroes of the new Reich Protectorate or suspended side by side on meat hooks like so many sides of beef at Dachau."

"It's coming in!" Hugh exclaimed. "I can see the pilot's head, but can't make out if it's a male or female. My God, he's touched down right...exactly on the centre of the bridge span. That's just astounding...! It's so pretty; looks like a dragonfly."

"Yes, it is. I have the pilot in my scope. Here, take the rifle; do you notice anything?"

Hugh could clearly see a cascade of short blond hair framing a delicately featured, feminine face in the crosshairs. "Not bad...for a Nazi."

"Herr Focke-Wulf is apparently in complete agreement with you. Look at that cock-sure exhibitionist doing his mating dance!"

"He's paying tribute to her flying skills!"

"Of course he is. Hold on, an SS man is approaching her hatch window...the steps are being wheeled up...the door is opening...here come the security moguls. Where's His Nibs?"

Hugh craned his neck, trying to get a better view. "Who's that stepping out?"

"Albert Speer, Minister of War Production. Well 'ello, there's the man

The wide span of Westminster Bridge.

himself, Adolf Hitler! Have a nice birthday, Sisera?"

"I hope so for your sake: it was your last. He's even punier than I imagined."

"Those SS bodyguards are giants in contrast, all more than six feet tall," observed Sylvia. "There's no hope of a clear head shot."

"Stick to the plan!"

"Who's the ranking officer here?"

"You, of course, but..."

The clanging drowned out his response. "Damn bells! Say again, please?"

"You, Captain, are in charge," he repeated.

"I know it's tempting to alter our plan, but I'd rather not make a muck of things at this late hour. Do you have everything ready for a fast exit, Herr Doktor? Maps, sidearms, radio, et cetera?"

"I do. I've smashed the radio and have the crystal in my pocket. I'll dump it in the first sewer."

"Make sure you do. Damn, where's that muzzle flash suppressor? Here, twist that on the end of the barrel. That's it; good. The procession is now at the edge of the parade grounds. I'm counting on Cliff and friends being down there, where and when. You're quite certain that you've scouted the back stairwell? Whatever show the Air Force has planned, it had better be spot on, to the second." Hugh could hear the rising tension in her voice as she continued. "Sorry, I'm just blathering on. Less than five minutes. Wish us luck! Damn, the sun's in my eyes!"

The motorcade crawled to a halt at the base of the reviewing stand. Hitler and Speer emerged, almost concealed inside a moving phalanx of black-uniformed SS and SIPO Security. They led the parade of dignitaries onto the temporary scaffolding and remained standing until the band had played the final chords of *Deutchesland Über Alles.* In unison, obeying an invisible command, the platform party was seated, leaving only the Führer standing in front of a microphone on the dais. He stood silently, hands on hips, glaring sullenly into Sylvia's range finder.

"Perfect!" Sylvia whispered. Hugh didn't comment. Hitler continued to stand and stare passively at the mass of upturned faces. "Who does he think he is, Larry blinking Olivier doing Hamlet?" she hissed. "Get on with it, you stagy bastard! Damn it, Hugh, I'm shaking!"

Suddenly, the Führer raised his right arm. He held the position for thirty seconds, then began to speak in English, in a hypnotic, guttural drone, all the while slowly lowering his arm. His amplified words drifted up.

"Citizens of the new British Protectorate and Fellow Aryans. I welcome you to the comradeship of our glorious Reich. You have made the wise choice: capitulation or destruction to the very last village. Your government and its armed forces have been turned over to German authority. I congratulate you on your wisdom and proclaim this land as the English Territorial Protectorate, and all of its inhabitants subjects of the Greater German Reich. Your well being and that of your families and relatives will be ensured by your total co-operation with, and steadfast loyalty to my Deputy, the Reich Protector Albert Speer and to your Führer, myself, Adolf Hitler. Seig Heil!"

"Seig Heil!" roared the assembled troops as with one voice, their right arms extended in the Nazi victory salute. The civilian VIP gallery was utterly silent.

"I'll be damned!" Hugh muttered.

"He obviously had it memorized phonetically. Quite a propaganda trick," Sylvia observed dryly, "that fizzled completely with the intended audience. Damn..."

"Syl, are you okay?"

"Yes, thanks...just a case of last minute jitters...seeing him at last, in the flesh, after the months of planning, the nightmares."

"You never told me about those, Syl."

"There's a lot I haven't told you, dearest. Are you certain there's a spotter on the ground to vector in the RAF?"

"Absolutely. Me!"

"Well, call them, dammit. It's almost over! Hurry!"

"I did, five minutes before the Fieseler touched down," he responded calmly.

"Why didn't you tell me?"

"Don't you believe me?"

"Yes, Lieutenant, I do believe you. Where is it coming from?"

"Scotland. The pilot's stooging around, waiting for Cliff's people to send the final word when the ceremony is over. The Führer's guard dogs may be a little less twitchy then."

"Well, it's happening...now. God forgive me, but I'm going to enjoy this!"

Big Ben and St. James Park

A display of acrobatics and gymnastics had begun. Sylvia trained her rifle on the Führer's chest. "Steady, now. Ready! Come on you RAF blighters!"

Out of nowhere, a hail of cannon fire danced along the grass, approaching, and then raking the parade stand, sending up spouts of earth and splinters.

'Professor Barns, look at your friend, Juli, now!' "Stay, stop moving...steady, steady!" She drew her breath and squeezed the feather-light trigger. The report was muffled. Hugh picked up the hot shell casing.

"Just a memento of the shot heard 'round the world" he commented sombrely.

"He's down! Send the wire and let's get out!" The dais erupted in a cloud of dirt, wood splinters, and body segments as a Mosquito fighter-bomber buzzed the parade ground. It then rose, banked, and climbed vertically to evaporate into the sun. The silvery Thames had become a river of blood. Blackish-grey airburst clouds from a fierce artillery barrage tracked upward, seeking to destroy the now invisible intruder.

"Holy smokes, it's a Canadian! Message sent:
TALON TO STALWART: RE: TENT PEG STOP
JAEL HAS SPIKED SISERA STOP'
"Okay, done. Follow me!"

Sturmbannführer Johannes Bosch recovered from his private musings as the Hitler Youth and Bund Deutscher Mädel dancers and athletes dashed onto the field to begin their performance. The sight of scores of supple young athletes swaying and leaping in breathtaking displays of youthful exuberance was overwhelming.

'Strength through joy,' Bosch reflected, 'is truly a symbol of the might of the new Order'. He stopped mid thought. 'Now I sound like the Party propaganda posted every morning in the barracks kitchen!'

He glanced over at the Führer and the Reich Protector who seemed engrossed in the display. Hitler occasionally glanced up, shielding his eyes from the sun, searching for something to appear out of the almost cloudless, clear, blue sky. The podium newsreel cameras recorded his expression of obvious delight.

The display was nearing the climax when Johannes began to feel uncomfortable. The young female dancers' movements began to take on an almost pornographic intensity. He looked away. 'This is music hall *kitsch*...not called for, or am I a prude?' His eyes shifted upward in an attempt to determine what it was that was pre-occupying the Führer.

'The clock tower!' He had seen the glint of metal. 'My God it's a gun barrel!' Suddenly, the world exploded in a maelstrom of bullets and flying debris. As the reviewing stand disintegrated, those dignitaries not lying in the wreckage or killed by the shrapnel were scattering aimlessly. It was a massacre, a blood bath. One glance told him that scores of his Standarten Wiking comrades were lying on the grass, dead or wounded, while others, running in disarray for cover, had leapt into the river and were being churned up by cannon fire in a sickening crimson foam.

The Führer was nowhere to be seen. Speer and at least one other official were draped backward over the stand's rear railing. An enemy Mosquito let loose with another burst of its .50 calibre cannons, catching some of the children now frozen in terror. Johannes felt that he would vomit as red-drenched silk pennants and shattered limbs flew through the air, fragments lodging in the sheltering tree branches. The agonising shrieks, screams, and moans of the wounded and dying swelled above the thunder of the fighter's single engine now flying into the sun, all melding into a cacophony of horror.

'The plane is a ruse! Son of a bitch! There's a sniper in the clock tower!' Sturmbannführer Bosch broke and ran at full speed toward the entrance. He pushed with his shoulder against the cumbersome wooden door, but it resisted, wedged closed from the inside. Leaning his special issue GEW 43 Mauser semiautomatic rifle against a column, he drew his SS Luger 9mm Parabellum revolver then turned, and in two savage blows with the heel of his left boot, dislodged the obstruction. Facing the door, he slammed it wide with his left hand and thrust the elongated barrel of his weapon through the opening.

He peered into the dark entryway, and then cautiously stepped inside. It had the acrid smell of his father's first factory: dust and stale air mixed liberally with industrial lubricating oil. Suddenly, he froze. Two distinct, separate voices were echoing in the stairwell overhead. Both were masculine. One was older, and English. The other was possibly American. They were close now, approaching the final landing. Bosch drew back, crouching in the darkness under the staircase.

"Damn fine piece of shooting, Sylvia! He went down like the proverbial ton of bricks!"

Now a woman's voice responded. "Thanks, Cliff. Hugh and I do make a wizard team. Let's hope it did the job, one hundred percent."

Johannes Bosch was paralysed with shock. Sylvia? No, that was the unmistakably sultry voice of Juli. They were coming around the corner. 'Decide!'

He lunged from his hiding place, confronting them. Blocking the narrow hallway, he aimed his pistol at the armed man in the centre of the trio. He, the younger of the two men, held a crude piece of weaponry that looked to Johannes like a starting pistol, or flare gun. The woman was very blonde and definitely Germanic.

"Halt! Drop the weapon. Hands up or I'll shoot the woman!" he ordered.

"Oh, God! I knew it!" she shouted in perfect English. Hugh fired first, from his hip.

"Juli..." he whispered. A second shot rang out and Sturmbannführer Bosch crumpled sideways onto the wooden floor.

"Are you all right, Hugh?" asked Cliff.

"Yes, okay, it just grazed my shoulder. Shall I finish him, Syl?" Hugh turned to Sylvia for confirmation. "What the hell...?" his voice trailed off.

She was kneeling, bending over the handsome SS man, holding his hand as he tried to speak. She bent closer, pushed back her hair, and placed her ear close to his face.

"You, Juli...?" he whispered.

"Yes, Johannes, it's Juli."

"You came to assassinate...my Führer?"

"Yes. Yes, I did."

He struggled to raise his head, and then lay back. "I never thought he could be so evil...where is our...baby?"

"Safe," she answered softly, then repeated, "Safe."

"Good. Go now. God bless!"

She sighed, then stood, avoiding eye contact with Hugh. Cliff motioned both of them to a side door, and three 'German sightseers' exited from the base of the clock tower, walking neither quickly nor slowly, but deliberately, in the direction of Downing Street.

Confusion bordering on a state of mass hysteria reigned in the streets. It was a city under siege, Hugh thought to himself. German armour and armed personnel swarmed the city. They waited at an intersection for a white-gloved field police sergeant to wave them across, then, on his signal, threaded their way between rows of strange-looking armoured vehicles.

When they reached the opposite sidewalk, Hugh broke the silence. "What in blazes was that all about? What's going on?" he demanded, testily. " 'Juli' would be you, I figure, right? And what's the connection with.... Wait. Now, I get it...your kid. He's the father! Is he dead?"

"How would I know?" she remarked coldly, her eyes glistening. "You're the one who shot him in the chest! And keep your voice down, please!"

"What did you expect, that I'd shake his hand?" he hissed.

"Pipe down, not so loud. Now, look straight ahead, shut up, and keep walking as though we're sightseeing VIP's. Let me do the talking at the checkpoint. I'll explain it all when we're clear of this town, I promise."

"In here!" Cliff led them into the doorway of an unpretentious row house. Putting his finger to his lips, he softly called, "Claymore." There was no response. "Claymore?" he repeated, now louder.

"Lord man, I'm not deaf!" Down the stairs lumbered Andrew. "Come up." He hugged Sylvia warmly, and then clutched Hugh's hand.

"Oh my, are we glad to see you! First you're there, then here, everywhere!" Sylvia exclaimed.

"A toast to your success! Verily, Jael, you have pegged Sisera, the evil Canaanite."

"Is he dead, Andrew?" asked Sylvia, anxiously.

"No, I'm sad to report. Although he was critically wounded, he's clinging to life by a thread. Your bullet was deflected by a medal, of all the bloody bad luck."

"Damn it!" Hugh exclaimed. "Are you certain? How do you know?" A long-forgotten line from *Macbeth* suddenly came to mind: "You have scotched the snake, not killed it."

"I have my ways. Sorry. You canna' linger here. The Nazi's are turning the city inside out. It will be hell. The goons have already taken fifty hostages, men and women. You can be sure that it's only the beginning."

"Is there a description of the shooter yet?" Cliff asked.

"No, but I can guarantee that there will be a country-wide police bulletin within the next hour, two at the outside. Did you encounter any resistance at the tower?"

Hugh hesitated, "Yes, an SS Sturmbannführer. And...."

"And? And what, lad?"

"We shot him!" Sylvia volunteered.

"Lord, they'll be like flies to a piece of rotting meat. You must go. I have everything ready. Clifford, you're done for now. A threesome will attract too much interest."

"Okay, we're ready. Where's our next stopover? Are we going back up to Scotland?" Hugh asked.

Andrew shook his head. "No. Southward. These instructions are to be read and memorised now, before you depart. You'll rendezvous there with a Royal Canadian Navy submarine in three days. If you miss it, I'm afraid there won't be a second chance. Are you willing to have a go?"

"You're damn right we are!" Hugh affirmed.

"Aye, I never doubted that. Now come down and have a bite. You can check your travel gear and study your orders. Then, you're on the train to Watsmede. Another dram for luck, either of you? Clifford, I know I don't have to ask you twice, old son!"

CHAPTER 9

HOTEL
GESTAPO

Lieutenant General-SS Walther Lange suffered no illusions about his future, neither the immediate nor longer term. He glanced at the ornately framed tinted photograph sitting on his desk and felt momentary pangs of guilt and nostalgia. As an SS officer, he had always known that the well-being and security of his family were contingent upon his superior officers' approval or displeasure with his performance; the sight of the trusting young faces smiling at him made him almost nauseous with dread.

He knew that his fate dangled by a tattered thread, well before his receptionist, Frau Bernt, put through the phone call from RSHA (Reich Security Service Command) headquarters in Berlin. He drew a deep breath to steel himself as he raised the handset. At the same time, he wondered if he should also be reaching into his bottom left desk drawer for his service revolver and the half-empty bottle of Polish vodka for which he had acquired a weakness while serving in Lodz.

Before the receiver even reached his ear, he could hear his chief and mentor, Obergruppenführer Reinhard Heydrich's blistering rage, railing with a litany of venomous attacks on his personal integrity and professional aptitude. The Chief of Reich Security Services began his tirade by making it clear that he and Reichsführer-SS Heinrich Himmler, both placed the responsibility for the British assassins' nearly successful attempt upon the Führer's life on Lange's head, and on his alone. In particular, his outright rejection of the obvious threat posed by the clock tower as a sniper post was not only reckless dereliction of duty under the military code, but might also be construed as criminally negligent conduct. Furthermore, Lange's incompetent bungling of Case Eagle Day was evident from the outset, Heydrich asserted testily in his peculiarly high-pitched, nasal twang. Lange knew that SD Chief Heydrich, Himmler's dreaded deputy, could squash him like a cockroach, under his heel, without a second thought, or remorse. Lange held his tongue, then reconsidered and, setting caution aside, counter-attacked, "Am I to assume, Obergruppenführer, that I wasn't considered up to this assignment, and yet I was posted...?" He let the thought dangle. There was silence at the other end. "Am I to be recalled to Berlin?"

"Did I say that, Walther?" Heydrich icily countered. "Tell me, did I say that?"

"No, Obergruppenführer Heydrich, you didn't. I only assumed from..."

"Exactly! That is a major part of your problem, Walther. You always have presumed too much," he paused, and then continued only slightly more pleasantly. "I personally put your name forward to the Führer and arranged that you be awarded this highly significant post. Now, I intend to make certain that you remain to see it through, with conditions..."

Lange hesitated to ask the question, until the silence became unbearable. "Conditions, Obergruppenführer? What must I do, Sir?" He was mildly encouraged by the fact that his superior had actually addressed him by his given name.

"You must follow my orders to the letter, that's what you must do, Walther. That is what you will do. Perhaps, you may yet escape our Führer's and Reichsführer's wrath, insofar as you can assist me in tracking down and bringing these thugs swiftly to justice. I will come down there and personally direct the investigation. I may also bring along Gestapo Chief Müller to beef up security and to handle some of the more delicate interrogations. Yes, I will definitely ask him to accompany me. You can expect us tonight. Have your car waiting for us at your airfield at nineteen hundred hours. Heil Hitler!"

"It will be there. I am very grateful to you for this opportunity, Herr Obergruppenführer. I will not disappoint you again. Heil Hitler!" He hung up the phone and looked across his desk at the little ornithologist. "Hans von Tresköw, you're not going anywhere! I have a career to salvage and you're going to help me do it, by God, starting now!"

No train was permitted to leave London until it was thoroughly searched inside, outside and underneath, and until every passenger's credentials were checked, re-checked and verified against a master list by a team of twenty uniformed Criminal Police and trench coated security specialists. The delay was agonising, a ninety-minute test of nerves for Sylvia and Hugh. Andrew had thoughtfully provided them both with German books, which they delved into in an attempt to remain as inconspicuous as possible. Hugh's was a thick volume of insurance actuarial theory complete with life-expectancy tables, and Sylvia's was a piece of

Nazi-approved fluff, a puritanical 'SS hero and the virtuous maiden' romance novel.

When the whistle finally blared, announcing their departure, Sylvia looked up to take a furtive look at the rest of the passengers. There was no one either immediately behind or in front of them. She looked to her right and suddenly felt a chill run down her spine; the railway security Hauptsturmführer seated across the aisle was the same cocky, young captain who had tried to impress her with his gallantry on the trip from Newcastle. She slumped in her seat, burying her face in her book, hoping to avoid his notice. She was unsuccessful.

"So, Frau Doktor Kortner, we meet again. How did you enjoy your stay in London? Dreadful turn of events, was it not?" He was obviously pleased to see once again the attractive object of his earlier attention.

"Very much, thank you, Captain. Yes, it was shocking, a terrible finale," she added, shaking her head and considering the irony of her answer.

"Were you close enough to see the Führer? I saw the whole thing; I'm still not sure that I believe it happened. A bloody massacre; bodies were flying everywhere. Two of my comrades were wounded: one quite seriously."

"I'm so sorry. We were quite far away from the stand. It wasn't until that airplane plunged down that we knew things were amiss."

"Did you see its markings? It was a Canadian bandit! But thanks to the Führer's luck, he's alive!"

"Yes, indeed…how fortunate! My husband and I dove for the ground and stayed there until we were told it was safe to move," she said, struggling to bring closure, to disconnect, but realising that he was drawing her in expertly.

"You're not returning to Newcastle?" he continued pleasantly, then added, "Obviously."

'Oh Lord. Would he never shut up?' She thought of fifteen ways to kill him right there and then, without a peep from his scrawny throat, courtesy of Robert Samson. "Not immediately, no."

"I don't remember if you were staying with friends in London or…"

"No, hotels."

"Honeymoon suite and all of life's little luxuries, I'd bet, no? May I get you and Herr Dr. Kortner something to drink? I'm going forward to the Club Car."

"Thank you, no, we're fine, Captain." She smiled, thinking of Samson's method sixteen.

"For certain? Very well, back in a little while. I must do my rounds while I'm up." He rose, smoothing his uniform, then, adjusting the tilt of his hat, leaned toward her, "May I be curious and inquire where you're bound?"

"To the south. My husband, Franz, has some meetings...."

"Business and pleasure!" he enthused. "I can only imagine how agreeable that would be!" He winked, salaciously. "I envy you both!" His face was now so close that she smelled the stale odour of tobacco on his breath.

'This is a one hundred percent smarmy creep, and very dangerous! Rescue me, Hugh!' "We are fortunate to be able to spend so much time together," she stated softly as she averted her face in an attempt to continue reading.

"I want to invite you and your husband to join me for dinner. I insist...simply won't take 'No' for an answer."

"That's very thoughtful of you..."

"Good, it's a date!" Reluctantly, the policeman removed his left hand from her high seatback cushion, breaking the circle of imposed intimacy, and sauntered arrogantly toward the end of the car.

"Why didn't you help me, darling?" she purred when the policeman had gone through to the adjoining car.

"You had him under control," Hugh whispered, without looking up.

"You don't give a toss, do you? Keep that in mind tonight when he's reaching under the table for his napkin for the third time."

"Don't be crude!"

"Go to hell!" she hissed through her teeth. "We have to get rid of him or get off the train. I smell trouble. Get thinking!"

"I already have. Please, calm down. And listen."

"Frau Doktor and Herr Doktor Kortner, may I present my old friend, Lieutenant Colonel Max von Roseteufel. Max and I were classmates at the Academy. He is with the Protectorate's Special Investigation Branch, and I might add, one of the senior officials assigned to probe yesterday's terrible incident."

Sylvia looked up as the debonair SD officer held her extended hand lightly, brushing it with his lips. "A pleasure, Obersturmbannführer," she smiled. "And tell me, are you making progress?"

"Yes, although it has been slow, Frau Doktor. We are expecting additional assistance from Berlin, as early as today: forensic specialists, counter-intelligence, special weapons experts, police interrogators, Gestapo..."

"What is our Führer's condition?" Hugh interrupted.

"He was flown immediately to the best SS hospital in Berlin. The surgeons and authorities are only now releasing the briefest of bulletins. However, from what little that I do know, the prognosis for his full recovery is very favourable."

"Rumour has it that he was saved by his Iron Cross medallion. It deflected the .303 rifle slug," interjected the railway police major.

"Really? A .303? A sniper? I assumed that it was a bullet from the aircraft that struck him, during the strafing attack. Do they have any suspects?" she asked, feigning astonishment.

"Naturally, I can't comment upon any specifics, Frau Doktor, but there are several leads being actively pursued. It's likely that one or more sharpshooters, British-trained, targeted him. Reich Protector Speer is personally co-ordinating the inquiries. Of course, our most-experienced criminal and counter-intelligence specialists are actively assisting him.

"But I must not spoil our dinner with such unpleasant business. Doktor, order a magnum of champagne to celebrate your recent marriage...on my tab of course. Excuse me, I'll be back in a moment."

After dinner, the liqueurs and conversation flowed until the Doktors Kortner became Ilse and Franz, and the increasingly well lubricated German officers insisted that they be called Karl and Max. Hugh glanced through a crack in the dining car's blackout shades and noted that it was now quite dark outside. Off in the distance, he thought he could make out the angular silhouettes of Stonehenge in the moonlight. They were traversing the Salisbury Plain. When the train made its fourth stop, Hugh commented absently, "I thought this was only a two or three-hour run!"

"Normally, but these are not normal times, are they?" Karl answered.

"So, Franz, Captain Karl here informs me that you have business meetings in the south. Exactly where, if I may ask? I'm relatively unfamiliar with our new territory, but I do know that there are some well-regarded vacation spots, almost tropical, with palm trees, if one can believe it!"

"Watsmede, a small resort town south and west of Plymouth, Max," Hugh replied. "And your destination, Obersturmbannführer?"

"Southampton. With so many slowdowns and delays, I'm wondering when and if I'll ever get there. The delay, of course, is completely necessary, as Karl has said; these are not normal times, as recent events indicate. This country is far from pacified, I'm afraid. Threats would seem to be lurking everywhere."

Hugh began to rub his eyes. "Would I appear rude if I were to excuse myself? I'm rather sensitive to alcohol, even apparently to such fine champagne, but in the spirit of the moment, I quite forgot. I seem to be developing those annoying bright spots, like fireflies, in front of my eyes and a rather strange, bitter taste."

"It's your migraine coming on, my darling. Go, lie back, before it does you in completely and you have to miss tomorrow's opening address."

"Thank you, Ilse, dear. Please, you are welcome to stay and entertain our friends. But don't drink too much more," Hugh added in mock seriousness as he kissed Sylvia on the cheek. "Good night, Max, Karl. It has been a real pleasure. Best wishes for a speedy conclusion to our present difficulties."

Hugh was no sooner gone than Captain Karl slid over into the vacant chair beside Sylvia. "Well, let's hope he feels better...charming fellow, he is. Can I pour you a little more of the champagne, Ilse? There's just a drop or two left and it's too good to waste. Max, you too?"

"No, thank you Karl. I've had enough for tonight. I'm off to bed. I have reports to read. You two finish it up." When Max had departed, Karl motioned to the waiter to clear the table. He continued, "I've always had a weak spot for highly intelligent, achieving women. What is your area of responsibility in your company, Ilse?"

"Hydro electrical generation: waterpower for our nation's vital war industries. I'm a dam designer." She laughed inwardly at her little quip, which meant nothing in German. "Tell me, Karl," she murmured, carefully placing her hand close to his on the table, "What else can you say about the incident at the Führer's reception? I'm very interested in police work. I think it suits my plodding, analytical mind. I've been considering applying to the SD for the last while, but I haven't told a soul, not even my Franz."

"They'd likely take you tomorrow, Ilse, and you'd make lieutenant in a blink. Well, I do know this much; mind you, Max would have me arrested if he knew I'd breathed a word of it." He lowered his voice, conspiratorially. "He said that they have a witness, a gallant SS officer who was shot by one of the gunmen."

"I see. And what is the witness's condition...?"

"Critical," he said, "but they removed the bullet and the fellow has since come out of a coma. The police now believe that there were three conspirators. One of the accomplices is a woman."

"Good for them. Is there a description? Has a reward been posted?"

"Oh, yes, the Reich governor has offered one hundred thousand marks for information leading to the arrest and conviction of the perpetrators. That should start the avalanche of informers! The descriptions of the woman are spotty, but it is likely that she was of medium height and stature, early twenties and blonde."

Sylvia glanced around the club car and noted that it was empty. "Hmm, that only describes several million. Max certainly does confide in you a great deal. A sum of money that large should draw out all the crazies and head cases," she laughed. "Karl, would you mind if we moved to the armchairs over there? I'm afraid that my back is protesting..."

"Poor dear, I can fix that, of course." When she stood up, his hands strayed to the space between her shoulder blades, rested there lightly, and then began something between a caress and a light massage. After what seemed to Sylvia an eternity, he asked, "Better?" Taking a slim, sterling silver case from his pocket, he removed a cigarette and tapped it delicately on the lid. "Ilse, I must say that you and your husband's, shall I say, liberal, attitude to marriage fascinates me deeply. I don't think there would be many newlywed wives permitted...."

"Permission has nothing to do with our relationship," she smiled. My husband and I believe strongly that we are all agents of free will. I've always done as I wish, within limits...as does he. It makes for a stronger marital bond."

"And does that include flirting?"

"That depends. It can be quite a harmless diversion, a little spice, one might say..."

He leaned toward her. "It can also be quite a dangerous game...Doktor."

"Mmm, perhaps. How so?"

"It involves deception, which is always very tricky, Ilse."

"Deception, Karl? You surprise me. Let me understand. Are you in the habit of calling near strangers two-faced? Would you care to give an example?"

"Everything!" he snorted, exhaling a stream of smoke in her face. "It is all deception! To begin with, you and your husband do not exist on your so-called company's employee roster. Max made some rapid inquiries when he went out of the coach, before dinner. He is in direct contact by field telephone with SD HQ at all times. He is not asleep, or reading papers at this moment, let me assure you. He is keeping a close watch on your partner.

"Secondly, you are not Doktor Ilse Kortner, nor is he Doktor Franz Kortner. As much as it pains me to say this, you are both impostors."

"How interesting!" she remarked casually as she reached up to smooth her carefully coifed upswept hairdo. "Any more, Hauptsturmführer?"

"Yes. You have been in my mind since I first set eyes on you. You fascinated me, and I wanted you. I still do. Unfortunately, I now believe that you are a British-trained secret agent from Camp X in Canada, and that you, Frau 'whoever the hell you are', are the blonde assassin. I am placing you under arrest. Please, do not make a scene. Max will take your accomplice into custody the moment I pull the emergency cord. The train will stop and will be surrounded by Gestapo and SD."

He stood to unholster his service revolver, simultaneously reaching for the pull cord with his left hand. Seizing her opportunity, Sylvia's right hand swiftly flashed out and upward. A stunned Hauptsturmführer Karl Oster dropped his gun on the rug, clamping both hands to his face in agony, desperately trying to wrench out the steel needle from his eye socket. Within seconds, he lay lifeless, splayed in the armchair. Sylvia scooped up his Walter PPK and dragged the inert body into the washroom cubicle, propped it on the toilet, then shut the door and silently exited the club car. 'Thank you, Robert! Now, Hugh, do your part!' she breathed.

"You misbegotten, utter cretin!" shouted Obergruppenführer

Reinhard Heydrich, flinging a large SS eagle paperweight at Lange's head. It narrowly missed, shattering the glass on the Führer's portrait hanging behind the cowering Gruppenführer's desk. "I should be done with it and just shoot you like a dog, but that would be far too humane. No, I'll hand him over to you, Müller, you and your tender mercies," he shouted.

Gestapo Müller glared balefully at Lange; "We are always delighted to co-operate with you, Obergruppenführer."

"Get out of my sight, before I change my mind and have your miserable body hanged from this window ledge!" Heydrich turned his back, glaring out the window, his slim, feminine fingers twitching on the riding crop behind his back. "I said, get out! Do something useful!"

Aware of the legion of whispered rumours inside the Service regarding the destructive effects on furniture, careers, and lives of Heydrich's legendary rages, Walther Lange did not wait for further prompting. He had reason to fear for his life; the Security Chief's sinister nickname, 'The Hangman,' was well earned by this fanatical bureaucrat, the ruthless architect of Nazi rule in eastern occupied Europe. Lange, fancying himself an iron-willed disciplinarian, admired his leader's callousness. Although not certain whether Heydrich had ever actually assaulted, much less murdered, a fellow officer, Lange decided to avoid becoming the first field commander of the new Reich Protectorate to test the limits of this man's fearsome reputation which regarded him to be the devil himself, a pitiless, and malevolent psychopath.

"Yes, Obergruppenführer, immediately!" Lange whispered as he and von Tresköw backed out and closed the door. "Frau Bernt," he shouted, "don't you have some filing to do in the basement?" Startled at the outburst, she looked up, and quickly vanished.

"That bastard! As if I'm the only one to have screwed up!"

"Settle down! Do you want to be hanged? He's probably listening."

Five minutes after Heydrich and Müller had stormed out without a glance, Lange and von Tresköw re-entered the inner office. "So, how would you react, in his boots, Walther?" queried Hans. "His reputation has not exactly been that of a choirboy, and now, thanks to your men fouling up..."

"Help me gather up this glass, Hans," Lange demanded testily, "please."

"Damn, Walther, I've cut myself! Can you imagine the reaction of Himmler and the big party boys like Dr. Goebbels and Bormann back home? I'm surprised the telephone lines haven't melted. Where are your plasters?"

"In my top drawer. Has it stopped bleeding?"

"Almost."

"Good, then you can take your feet off my desk, Hans," Lange snapped as he straightened the Führer's damaged picture. "Those English bastards got clean away. They murdered two of my very best, young Karl Oster and Max von Roseteufel, both exceptionally clever men of great promise, experienced and unquestioningly loyal, devoted to the Service."

"That sounds like stock funeral oration drivel. Face it, Walther, my friend, those two SOE brigands were either more clever, or incredibly lucky, or both. You tried, and you failed. Trust me, their luck can't hold forever. They'll slip up somehow; maybe make an impression on someone who'll turn them in for his thirty pieces of silver. We have to be patient, smarter...and luckier."

"So? What do you suggest? We've dispatched every available piece of equipment and the south is crawling with troops and cops. Five hundred hostages have been rounded up. Twenty are to be shot tomorrow morning, another twenty the next day, and so on..."

"What good will that do? It will only serve to alienate the general population, exactly the people we should be trying to win over. Listen to some common sense. Get down there yourself. Show your superiors that you're still the courageous, fire-in-the-belly, flesh eating, front line commander, capable of taking charge and getting results, fast. Lightning warfare, Walther, just like the glory days, not so long ago," he mused reassuringly. "Tell you what old man, I'll come with you...for moral and logistical support."

When Sylvia returned to their car, Hugh appeared to be asleep: a small pillow covered his eyes. She sat down and leaned toward him affectionately. "We've less than an hour to Watsmede. Where's Max?" she whispered.

"Taken care of. And Karl?"

"Likewise. We have to get out of here. Now. Where did you leave the Obersturmbannführer?" Sylvia asked. "Is he dead?"

"You don't want to know. I'm ready. Have you ever jumped off a moving train?"

"No, it wasn't on the Beaulieu curriculum. You?"

"Nope, I guess there's always a first time. I'll get up and walk to the end of the car. Wait for a minute, then follow me, strolling as though you are just stretching your legs. I'll be waiting between the cars."

"Can we jump from there?"

"How would I know? I saw it done once, though...in a movie."

"That's just marvellous. Quiet, here comes the conductor."

"Neatham, next stop. Arriving Neatham in five minutes. All passengers departing please remember your personal items and have your papers ready for inspection on the platform." The white-haired conductor ambled to the end of the car, opened the door, and went through, slamming the door on the way. They listened intently to try and hear the sound of the adjoining car's connecting door being closed.

"Perfect. It's slowing down, a bit. I'm off...one minute! Put on your sweater. It could be a bumpy ride!" He squeezed her arm as he stood up and eased his way past.

Exactly a minute later, she followed. As she stepped through the door, the sudden blast of cold air, combined with the nearly deafening rumble and high-pitched groans of steel wheels on steel rails took Sylvia aback for a split second. Hugh reached for her arm, "Just remember Parachute Jumping 1, 'tuck and roll'," he shouted.

"I should know. I taught it," she yelled.

"Is there anything you can't do?"

"If we survive this, you may just be unlucky enough to find out!"

"I can wait. Look out for telegraph poles."

"...And the rocks!" Sylvia answered, pointing towards the faintly distinguishable and rapidly passing ground. "Let's do it!"

"Give me your arm! Ready, set, go!" Hugh shouted above the din, and then they launched themselves into the darkness. Hugh's only recollection of the next five minutes was a sickeningly dull thud when his right kneecap struck hard against something solid, followed by the sensation of sinking helplessly, head first, into a bottomless pit, filled with a foul soup of thick slime and evil-smelling, brackish, cold water.

He was disoriented and fought rising panic. For one moment his mind flashed back to the night of his dreadful discovery of Tom's mutilated body in Rice Lake. Suddenly, his head hit the muddy bottom. With a racing swimmer's somersault turn, he righted himself and let his natural buoyancy float him upwards. With a practised kick, he broke the surface, spitting water and gasping for breath.

All was dark. The only sounds to be heard were his splashing and, in the distance, the faint whistle of the receding train. Treading water, he looked around for Sylvia, then stroked his way to the bank to haul himself out. He kept sliding backwards as his fingers clawed at the greasy mud. With a huge effort, he lunged once more towards the edge and managed to grasp a handful of long sedge grass. He was halfway out, crawling crab-like, when a vice-like force gripped the back of his jacket collar.

"'Ere now, what's this I've snagged this time? Another one!"

Hugh rolled over and looked up at an elderly, weather-beaten man with a great shock of unruly white hair poking out from underneath a tweed cap. He wore dark coveralls with knee-high rubber 'wellies' and a red and white bandanna around his neck. In his arms was cradled a double-barrelled antique shotgun aimed directly at Hugh's head.

"Thank you!" Hugh sputtered. "Don't shoot, please. Thank you." He stood up very slowly, palms outward, shoulder high. '*Déjà vu.*' The vision of an angry Colonel Graham flashed into his consciousness. "Have you found a woman, sir, by any chance?"

"Aye, if you mean the frow-lein, Lili Marlene over yonder, I have, Sir. She's wet as two hens, she is. Keep your hands well out in view, Sir. I am arresting you in the name of the British Citizens' Defence League."

"The what? Excuse me, I'm a Canadian, which makes me British, too, kind of."

"And I'm the Queen of the May, begging your pardon. Please be co-operative, Sir. It will go easier on you and your mate. Now, no funny business. Hands in front, wrists tight together." Holding the gun under his right arm, he pulled a leather thong from his overall pocket and with a few expert flicks and twists had securely fastened Hugh's hands. "Now, march!"

With the end of the barrel making an indent in the small of his back, Hugh was prodded around the edge of the marsh to a sodden and sullen Sylvia, huddled under a brown duffel coat, bound hand and foot.

"Hi," Hugh said,

"Hello," she sniffled.

"Aren't we a couple of drowned rats," he muttered.

"Quiet, please. Stop right there, Sir. Turn around. Now, crouch down...easy! Now sit. Good. I'll be taking you to HQ. Blindfolds will be necessary. I'd not like to have to gag you, but that depends on your..."

"Heads down! German patrol!" Hugh muttered. Three field police motorcycles with sidecars, led by an SS personnel carrier, appeared on the ridge, and stopped. A carbon arc spotlight on the front of the armoured car slowly swept over the surface of the marsh casting grotesque shadows. The edge of the beam reached within a foot or two of where they stood and paused tauntingly. "Stay perfectly still! Look down! Don't let the light hit your face!" Hugh whispered. The area was enveloped again in darkness as the search lamp swung away. They could hear soldiers chattering until the engines revved in unison and the vehicles inched forward once again. Quietly, Sylvia offered their captor an explanation. "In case you're wondering, they're looking for us!"

"Really, now. And why would that be?" he asked softly.

"We're wanted for questioning," she whispered.

"Listen, lassie. I may be old and I may look stupid, but I can assure you I didn't fall off the back of a turnip truck. So far as I'm concerned, you're enemy aliens and anything else will have to wait until we get down to headquarters. Shake a leg. I'm unfastening your ankles, frow-lein. Now, stand yourself up...very slowly. You, sir, put your left arm against her right one. Hold them tight, now...tighter...that's it." He expertly undid their individual restraints and lashed their wrists together. "This here piece has two twelve-gauge heavy game shells in its chambers." He cocked his head vaguely, indicating over his shoulder, " And, my friend out there is a sharpshooter, so any monkey business and he'll blast you both to kingdom come!"

"And you? Listen, about your invisible friend...that trick's as old as the hills, mate."

"Frow-lein, if you expect to see the sunrise, I ask you again to button your lip."

"Listen, please, for one minute, then I promise we'll shut up," Hugh interjected. "My name is Lieutenant Hugh Miller, and hers is Captain Sylvia Smith. We are both British officers. We were sent here to England on a covert mission. May I ask your name?"

"Gord. If your story's true, then why are you dressed like blinkin' German tourists? I checked her papers while you were flailing about in the pond and she's a Doctor Ilse something-or-other, a bloomin' electrical engineer. You Germans are a clever lot, like you two strange ducks with your perfect command of the King's English, and Lord knows what else you've got tucked up your sleeves." For emphasis, he let the gun swing back and forth between his prisoners.

"Pond scum's about all I've got up mine, Gord. The false identities are part of our mission," Sylvia explained tersely. "Really!"

"That may be, but I haven't the authority to decide one way or another. Step lively, please. I suppose next you'll be wanting to try and convince me that you shot Herr Hitler!" He emitted a low, shrill whistle.

"Where are we going?" Hugh asked.

"Where I say we're goin'," Gord replied abruptly, as a gangly youth stepped from the gloom, and into their pathway. Hugh judged him to be about eighteen years old. "Meet Trevor, my invisible friend." Trevor smiled fleetingly at Sylvia as he adjusted his rifle's shoulder strap. "Right, we're off. Where are your papers, Miller? Trevor, reach into his jacket and get them. That's a good lad. I'll cover you. Now hand them here. You follow, I'll lead."

"What's wrong with your leg, Miller?"

"I banged it on something hard, a rock, maybe, when I hit the ground. Feels like a bad bruise. It's okay, just not quite so fast, please."

They walked in silence, without pausing, for over an hour. Hugh managed to turn his wrist so that he could see his watch hands glowing: 4:25. The unmistakable odours of tar and salt water filled his nostrils. Through the darkness, Hugh was able to make out the shapes of dwellings.

Without warning, Gord turned and held up his hand like a Native American guide. "Halt. Wait here. Trevor, take cover; not one peep from the lot of you." They stood quietly in a grove of ancient trees that looked to Hugh as gnarled and twisted as theatre props made of plaster and papier-mâché.

Sylvia had sized up Trevor and decided that he wasn't terribly bright, and that he was nervous, a dangerous combination for someone carrying a weapon. She knew that she could take him down, but had no inclination to test his physical limits. Convinced from early on that he and Gord were patriotic members of some splinter Resistance group, she decided to play him and try to ease his anxiety. "Excuse me, Trevor. We're quite close to the sea, aren't we? What town is this?" she asked timidly.

He looked at her blankly, and shook his head.

She continued, a bit bolder now. "My wrist is sore. See how red it is and how it has swollen. Could you loosen the bindings...just a bit?"

"You 'eard Gord, shut your gob, woman!"

Hugh felt a spasm of laughter coming on and coughed to suppress it.

"You too!" Trevor muttered, swinging his rifle threateningly in Hugh's direction to emphasise his point.

"Careful with that damn thing!" Hugh objected.

"Look you, I've just about had enough...."

"All right. What's going on?" Gord had returned.

"They were annoying me, Gord!" Trevor whined, sheepishly.

"Untie them."

"What? Why, Gord?"

"Because I said so! The boss say's they're bloody well who they say and as close to heroes as we'll likely get to see in this lifetime or next. Now get on with it, lad!"

"My apologies Captain, Lieutenant, if I was a little harsh."

"Gord, it's all right," Silvia smiled reassuringly. "You did as I would have expected you to, had I been your CO. No harm done. No lasting damage," She rubbed her wrist, "and no hard feelings, Trevor. Right, Lieutenant?"

"None at all, water under the bridge, all's forgiven. Is there some-place up ahead with a short-wave radio, Gord?"

"Aye, indeed, Sir, one of those clever battery-powered devices, you know, that fits in a wee suitcase. Our HQ's a bit primitive, but we can muster up a cuppa hot tea with sugar, or grog, whichever's to your lik-ing? There's warm dry clothes, and food, plain fare but substantial. The area for miles around is crawling with Jerries. I'll lead off. Wait for my signal. Keep low and stay close to Trevor. You'll have to cover five hun-dred yards, in a dash. Can your leg take it?"

"Yes, I think so, Gord." Hugh managed a wan smile, glancing side-ways at Sylvia. She touched his arm reassuringly as Gord vanished again into the mist.

The approaching ominous clanking of heavy metal plates striking the cobblestones and the throaty diesel roar of a heavy vehicle at close range, caused them to freeze, motionless. The pitch of the engine rose then fell abruptly as the driver shifted into neutral. The motor throbbed in the background as an authoritative voice called out in German, "Has this place been thoroughly searched?"

"Yes, Gruppenführer Lange, frequently."

"How frequently?"

"Nearly daily, Gruppenführer; nothing suspicious, Sir. Just the usual collection of locals: toothless veterans, town sots and village idiots."

There was no response.

Trevor whispered into Sylvia's ear, "The lazy bastards are in there swilling like pigs at the trough every day."

"Where?"

"Over there," he gestured, "at the local, *The Ploughman and Scythe*. The goons act like they ruddy well own it."

"Good thing for us they do!" Hugh muttered hoarsely.

"Remount! Onward!" The engine coughed then revved as its drive mechanism clashed into gear, moving the vehicle's track plates forward.

"A bruiser that one, full track panzer, likely a Tiger," Trevor stated with confidence. Seconds later, they heard Gord's whistle. "All clear! Single file and run like the devil's gaining ground!"

Crouching low, Hugh and Sylvia ran, trailing Trevor down High Street, now pockmarked with bomb craters. They followed when he turned right, opened a rusted green iron gate, and loped along a narrow lane leading to the rear of a three-storey building where Gord was waiting, holding a door open for them. "Straight down...have a care...watch your heads...left at the bottom, then wait!" Gord gave their directions softly, indicating a wooden stairwell. Once downstairs, Trevor took the lead along a low-ceilinged, gloomy passageway, which led through the cellar beneath the public house.

A typical English pub as the 'Ploughman and Scythe' might have appeared.

Unaccustomed to the darkness, Hugh and Sylvia were even more perplexed when the stairway ended abruptly at a pale grey masonry wall. Neatly spaced rows and columns of wood-lined circular hollows ran from bottom to top and side to side, each containing a dark glass cylinder which, they supposed, were bottles of wine and sherry. As they waited, Trevor reached up and carefully removed the first bottle in the uppermost row and handed it to Gord. He inserted his right forearm deep into the cavity, fiddled briefly, and then pushed forward. Almost silently, the cement wall slowly opened inward as though on invisible hinges, revealing a cavernous, stonewalled chamber.

"'Cor blimey! Downright eerie!" Sylvia whispered.

"Come in, it's quite safe," Trevor assured her. Once they were all inside, he leaned against the wall and, as it closed, his entire demeanour seemed to alter. Gone was the oafish lout, now replaced by a calm and articulate guide. "This room was built for the dry storage of sherry and wine casks. It dates well back, at least to the seventeenth century. During the Civil War, the Inn's proprietor let it be used as a lair for Roman Catholic priests and wealthy Royalists hiding out from Oliver Cromwell's troops, the first Lord Protector of The Realm.

"It wasn't long afterwards that the new Roundhead owners converted it into a smugglers' den. The Revenuers never found it. Most of these villages up and down the seacoast did very nicely, thrived actually, by carrying on a roaring trade in contraband cargo, goods plucked from the sea's leavings. Shipwrecks yielded French brandy, Belgian lace, Virginia tobacco, German muskets; the list goes on and on, until the water receded in the nineteenth century," he chuckled. "By the by, there's another way out. I must remember to show it to you."

Hugh and Sylvia stared at Trevor in astonishment. He acknowledged their scepticism with a charmingly naïve smile. "I only play the fool. I apologise for misleading you, but it seems to have kept us out of trouble to date. Gord and I have worked up this little routine...a bit of amateur theatrics here and there in the provinces, you know.

"I'm District Commander of the CDL, sorry, the Citizen's Defence League. Oh, yes, we were expecting you. Your friend Claymore and another chap, who goes by 'Pendragon', a flaming 'Wales for the Welshman' it seems, have been in communication. That's why Gord and I were on patrol out there, but we had merely the vaguest notion of where or when you might be popping up. I had to be very certain that we had the real Jael and not some Gestapo fraud. I sent Gord back to proof your vitals. Even when you seemed to come up four-square, still we had to be cautious."

"Hugh and I shall be eternally grateful, Trevor, for all of your trouble. And to you, of course, Gord, as well. I've never heard of this Pendragon chap; or perhaps it is a woman!"

"That's quite possible, given the number of crack female agents, like you, who are active in the field. Picture a kind of romantic throwback, a renegade Celtic chieftain, and somewhat of a mystic. It isn't hard to imagine, if you've ever experienced the magical spell cast by Wales. I gather that Pendragon and followers firmly believe that King Arthur, the original Pendragon, their once and future king, will rise again. Then, with trusty Excalibur in hand, he and the resurrected Knights of the ruddy Round Table will turf out the Nazis once and finally.

"He runs his own show up in the mountains with the blessing of Special Ops. He is a reliable, decent sort, and has done us some good turns. Not to worry. Gord and the rest of us are honoured that were able to play a part. Your exemplary courage and outstanding dedication will serve as beacons to inspire all Britons. What may I get you?"

"I rather fancy a warm bath, a tea biscuit, a cuppa, and an eight hour sleep," declared Sylvia. "If you and Merlin here can't come up with the first three, I'll settle for forty winks on a plank."

"Well, all things are possible when you believe," he remarked, smiling warmly, "and for you, Hugh?"

Hugh awakened to the muffled sound of creaking floorboards and heavy footsteps overhead. The scraping of chair legs being dragged over a hard surface grated like chalk on slate. He sat up, stretched, and leaned over to kiss Sylvia's bare shoulder.

"Good morning, or good evening, darling, I'm not sure which," he whispered in her ear.

"Mmm. Do that again." Yawning, she took his hand and kissed his fingers. "That was definitely a memorable reunion, Lieutenant Mason! I'll mention it in my report. Let's go back to the beginning for a review, shall we?"

"Don't I wish? I hate to spoil the moment, but from the sound of it, I'd say the saloon up there is infested with either giant termites or German soldiers."

"The saloon? 'Pub', you colonial! Actually, it's a cross between the two: big, insect-like supermen prancing about in their shiny black jack-boots."

"Syl, I have a question. That SS man, your…you know, the one at the clock tower, what exactly did he say to you?"

"My ex-lover, you mean? His name is Johannes Bosch. He's a medical doctor, the father of my baby and not a bad sort. He simply wished us good bloody British luck."

"No kidding? An honest-to-God SS Sturmbannführer actually said that?"

"That was the gist of it. Sssh, someone's knocking! Hello?"

"It's Trevor here. I have some food. There are two people here who you'll want to meet."

"Just a moment, Trevor."

"To be continued, my love. So much for fun and frolic," she added under her breath. "Kisses for luck then get yourself dressed. Quickly!"

"Yes, Captain," he replied, saluting, with a wry grin.

Sylvia and Hugh blinked as they came out of their small, dark sleeping quarters into the brighter main chamber. A table with six place settings was prepared in the centre of the room. Trevor introduced two women: Gloria, Gord's wife, and Jenny, a slim, vibrant young woman with sparkling black eyes. "Ladies, I give you two extraordinarily courageous Officers, Captain Sylvia and Lieutenant Hugh."

Taking them each by an arm, Trevor escorted Sylvia and Hugh to their chairs at opposite ends of the table. Gord rose to propose a toast. With glistening eyes, he spoke quietly, "To Captain Sylvia and Lieutenant Hugh, two very special people," he paused to wipe away a tear, then continued. "Because of your valour, Britain has shown the oppressor that we can and will rise again. On behalf of all Britons, May God bless you both and...God bless Great Britain. God save the King!"

Subdued applause followed, then Gloria, seated on Hugh's immediate right and Jenny, on his left, got up together, as though on cue, and kissed him on either cheek, Gloria motherly, and Jenny, rather more emotionally. Embarrassed, he looked down the table to see Sylvia being treated in a similar fashion by Gord and Trevor.

Together, Hugh and Sylvia briefly told the others of their mission and the escape from London, without mention of the three German casualties for which they were personally responsible. During the conversation, it became apparent that not only Trevor and Gord were key officers of the local Resistance, but Gloria and Jenny were as well; Hugh guessed that the four held responsible positions in CDL's central command.

Jenny told them she had become *The Ploughman and Scythe's* proprietor by default, shortly after her parents were arrested, "Why, I'll probably never know. For treason? Perhaps some malcontent in town had it in for one or the both of them. I can't imagine it happening, but you can never tell what greed or envy will do to a person. They were snatched out of bed at bayonet point in a Gestapo night and fog operation and carted away by the bully boys in black."

"They'll pull through, dear," Gloria added, softly. "Phil and Kate are tough nuts to crack, real troopers they are, from the old school."

"Thanks, Glor. I do know that they're still alive, in the Nazi detention camp near Wales, right Trevor?"

After offering and pouring after-dinner brandies, Trevor called quietly for attention. "We're all honoured to have been able to host this little celebration, but now, we have business to discuss. As far as security is concerned, all of us here are foursquare, fully trustworthy, as I think you will agree.

"You do know, Captain, that you and Lieutenant Hugh must be at your rendezvous by 11:05 tomorrow evening. It's our job to ensure that you're there, safely and on time. There is no alternate or backup plan. Therefore, should we run into soldiers, or encounter some other unforeseen spot of bother, I'm afraid you'll be stuck here, with us, for quite some time, possibly for the duration. You'll be leaving with me, by fishing dory, from Somerset Beach, at 10:15 p.m. exactly. Your rendezvous point is a channel marker buoy in the Mede estuary, one point five miles out. Here's a map. Keep the damn thing hidden, or even better, memorize, then burn it. Any questions?"

"Is it safe for you, and for us, to remain here, while we're waiting?" Sylvia inquired, her voice reflecting her concern. "What I mean is, it sounds like a hive of activity up there. How much at risk are we all?"

"And we're already much too indebted to you to endanger you further," Hugh added. "Perhaps we should bail out...."

"This is the busy time of day, routinely," Jenny sighed, looking at her watch. "I must get back upstairs. Now pay attention to me, please. Assuming no one saw you come in, you're perfectly safe here, so long as you keep your voices down, and stay out of sight. None of the other staff knows this room even exists and no one, no one but me, has had permission to come down to the wine rack since Mom and Pop found a half case of sherry had gone missing. Right mysterious it was, until ... not now," she smiled, shaking her head. "I hope the bed is big enough for you two. Good night, then, 'til morning! Sleep tight!" she added. Then smiling at Hugh, asked, "May I hug you?"

" 'May I hug you?' 'I hope the bed is big enough..' "

"Don't be a witch, Syl. Jen's just a starry-eyed kid."

"I see. Tell me, when did 'Jenny' become 'Jen'?"

Hugh stared moodily at the ceiling, counting knotholes in the overhead beams.

"Oh, lighten up! I'm only pulling your leg. Heaven knows we need a laugh!" she giggled.

"Then try this for a lark, luv!"

"God in heaven! Slow down you fool! Let them by! I'll tell you when it's time to speed!" Walther Lange shouted at the driver. 'Who is this maniac? I need Otto. Why now, of all times, has my chauffeur been removed from my service?" He had specifically arranged to have his prized, private automobile shipped from London to Watsmede on a flatbed railway car, but Heydrich had appropriated, or more appropriately shanghaied, Otto, for his own personal use, at the last moment.

Walther sat back testily, then turned to von Tresköw and asserted, "I know they're here, Hans, somewhere. I can smell the bastards," he paused to return the salute of a Wehrmacht sergeant and twenty soldiers in a troop carrier as it pulled around the eight cylinder Horch. "Where are they hiding? With whom? Where? There, in that house, or that one?" he gestured with his riding crop. "We have five thousand men ferreting here and there, and they've come up empty handed; not a whisper, not a trace! How many of these English wretches have been brought in so far for questioning?"

"More than three hundred. Nineteen of those have died as a direct result of the Gestapo's interrogation methods; fifteen have been executed for lying or to set an example. Two had seizures. Müller's methods are most distasteful to me personally; he may uncover a gem or two, but it's nearly always too late. These birds will fly to safety within a day, if they haven't already. I'll wager a month's wages. Walther, listen, my experience with security has taught me one thing."

"Yes, what's that?" Lange asked distractedly.

"It's like birding. Where is the most obvious hiding place?"

"Do you mean in a tree?"

"Tsk, tsk. The trick is, you see, to become the quarry, and think like the quarry. Figure that out, and then concentrate your energies there. It's certain that these criminals are not holed up in the countryside. We've slopped through every marsh and bog, ransacked every farmhouse, barn, and poked every haystack..."

"Stop playing games, Hans. Dammit, my career, perhaps even my life, may be over if I fail to come through this time. Heydrich is coming and I'll be mincemeat if I come up empty-handed. Just where, precisely, do you suggest they might be?"

"Did you inspect the inn when you were out patrolling at dawn with the panzer crew?"

"Not personally. They were regular Wehrmacht, battle-hardened sluggers, the lot, not Gestapo pretend coppers. The sergeant swore on his mother's grave that the place is an open book. It's like a second home for many, too many, of our fun-loving officers and enlisted men."

"I think he may have been wrong; 'Hide in plain sight', the crime novelist's old standby. Poe, the American, used it in *The Purloined Letter*. Fine piece of writing, for a drug addicted degenerate."

"Please, spare me the literary lecture. All right, I agree. We'll go back there, carry out a lightning raid, and rip it apart, board-by-board. I'll need at least twenty-five SS to do it properly."

"Round up the very best right away; we can't waste any more time fumbling about. Leave the briefing regarding security measures and other such details to me. This operation has to be executed brutally, quickly, and with surgical precision. All the elements must be synchronized exactly so that there are no rat holes left open for retreat. British Commandos and SOE are the masters of the lightning raid, and I've made it a hobby to study their manuals and even improve on their methods. It appeals to my engineer's brain.

"And, Walther," he continued, "we're fortunate that it's going to happen at the most ideal time: late at night. Professional policemen have long realised that people tend to be more vulnerable, confused, startled, and defenceless when they're taken swiftly and by surprise, in the dark of night. Of course, the top brass will see you as the mastermind of the entire shakedown, Gruppenführer. I'll stay well back in the shadows, so, naturally, you'll get the credit and the medals."

'Or the garrotte, my friend,' he thought. "Right, Hans, I'll order up the troops and transport immediately! I'd better notify Müller that we need police vans with Colonel Greilwitz' best team ready on standby at Gestapo Harmony Club HQ. It's now twelve forty-five. We must be on the road by two-fifteen. The assault commences at 0300 hours, sharp! Put on your combat gear, Colonel. You and I are going in a Tiger; I'll blow the goddamn place to bits if that's what it takes!"

"Very good, Gruppenführer. Have no doubt, we'll nail that English bitch, Sylvia, and her Canadian crony this time."

Lange looked at the uncommonly prudish little fussbudget, birdman, engineer, and security meister, with shocked surprise and a fresh sense of comradeship. 'He curses like an SS-man; I guess the twittering little sparrow really does believe we can pull it off in time!'

"Hugh, Hugh, wake up! It's a raid!" Sylvia whispered hoarsely.

"I heard. They'll soon be all over us. We're done for if we hang around!"

"We sure as blazes can't get out through the wine wall. We'd walk right into their waiting arms. Do you remember what Trevor started to say; something about another passageway?"

"Vaguely, yes. Wait, you're right! He said, 'There's another way out'. Definitely!"

"What are you doing?"

Sylvia was on her knees, groping on the floor beneath the bed. "Where's that torch that Gloria left for us? Damnation! I hit my head. Here it is. My God, what's going on upstairs?" she murmured, pointing the light beam upward through a fine shower of dust descending from the stuccoed ceiling. It sounded as though a wrecking crew were ripping the pub apart, piece by piece.

A sudden shriek pierced the air; a male voice shouted furiously. The jarring blow of a body being hurled against a wall made Sylvia reach out to grasp Hugh's hand. "My God. Jenny!" She paused with her eyes shut as though in prayer, then opened them and raised both hands, placing them gently on either side of Hugh's face. "They'll find this place," she whispered. "We might well be done for. We can't be taken here. They'll torture her and force her to give up everyone in the Resistance. I can't live, or die, with that on my conscience, can you? I'm going to clean up every trace; you look for the passageway. We have only minutes. Take the torch. Now please, hurry! I love you."

A deafening concussion rocked the building, throwing them both to the floor. Groggily, Hugh struggled to recover his balance. He saw Sylvia sprawled motionless, face down five feet away. Horrified, he dropped the flashlight as he crawled over and felt for a pulse on the side of her pale neck. Moaning, she turned slightly, revealing a deep gash above her right eyebrow. "Are we still alive?" she murmured.

"Yes, I think it was an intentional near miss... a shell, maybe a rocket," he replied, gently touching her cheek. "Can you move your head? Let me have a look at that...." He froze. Shouted commands and curses punctuated with the pounding of hobnailed boots approached on the wooden cellar steps.

"They're coming down the stairs," she whispered. "I don't know if I can get up."

A curt voice ordered, "Sergeant, have your men use sledge hammers and pickaxes to break through every one of these walls!"

"Including the one with the wine, Gruppenführer?"

"Yes! I said every one! First, you idiot, you remove the bottles very, very carefully, then you smash the wall to bits."

The violent pounding of steel tools on the thick concrete basement walls made the room reverberate. Then, just as suddenly, it ceased.

"What the hell's the problem, Sergeant?"

"Gruppenführer Lange, the corporal says it's rock solid, a centuries-old cement and rock mixture, hard as granite and at the very least, four centimetres thick. We can't get through it without a pneumatic punch, or another rocket volley!"

"Son of a...! Standartenführer, von Tresköw, come here! I need your opinion!"

"We'll simply blow them with RDX British explosive, Gruppenführer," von Tresköw uttered quietly. "I found cases of it in the Arsenal."

"Good, then do it, and hurry goddamn it! I know they're hiding like the vermin they are, somewhere in this cellar!"

"Assuming you want them alive, it will take a little time to place the charges, Gruppenführer. I'll get started right away! Heil Hitler!" He barked out orders, and the activity recommenced with an immediate flurry of footsteps on the stairs, and the clinking of glass bottles being pulled out of their racks.

"Let's get the hell out of here! Put your arm around my shoulder...easy does it, kid...good. That secret entrance has got to be right under our noses," Hugh stated with equal parts assurance and frustration.

"I know! It's under the bed!" she blurted, adding, "I felt one of the edges when I was fumbling around for the torch, but it didn't register then."

"How do you know?"

"Trust me, female intuition, whatever. Besides what have we got to lose? Help me, for heaven's sake!"

While Hugh was tugging and lifting the ancient oaken bed frame away from the wall, slowly, trying not to make a sound, Sylvia sat on the floor holding the flashlight.

"Your eye's still bleeding, and you may have a concussion. I should...."

"I'm fine. Keep working. Listen, do you hear anything?"

"No, do you? This bed's almost clear."

"No. I don't either. That worries me! Wait, what is that chinking sound? What do you think they're doing?"

"They're tapping holes into the cement wall to insert the RDX charges! If we're lucky, we've got about fifteen minutes, if they're even remotely as adept as Hamish is. Is Trevor's revolver loaded?" He lay down on the floor and pried at the near edge of the trap door using the tip of Andrew's knife blade. "It won't...wait, it's...it feels as though it's spring loaded!" Pressing down on the edge, he released it quickly and it sprang open half an inch.

"That's it! Those old guys were pretty damn smart. May I have the light?" He raised the lid without much effort and shone the flashlight down into the darkness. "Well, look at that, a perfect stone stairwell. Are you game?"

Sylvia was leaning against his shoulder, peering down. "You're damn right I am. Smells a bit fishy...must lead to the river. I have the revolver. Where's the map?"

"Memorised and burnt."

"Good. One more thing: if we're captured, and if we survive, no heroics! Remember what they taught you at Camp X! A dead hero's of no use at all. Got that? Promise? Now go!"

They descended the steep, narrow, and twisting steps and reached a dank and musty landing. A low-ceilinged but level passageway led off into total darkness. "Hold my hand. Duck, and watch your head!" Hugh warned. "Those old-timers must have been shorter than we are. Goddamn cobwebs!

"Are you okay? Don't let go of me." They felt their way along the corridor, following the beam of light from their flashlight, for about five minutes. "Stop." He switched off the light. "Sylvia, do you see light...up ahead, maybe fifteen feet, like a small crack in the stone?"

"Whew, this is cold and clammy...really slippery! No, I don't, but I believe you! I know we can make it!" she stated, just as a massive explosion rumbled through the tunnel.

"They're through! Hurry! Keep coming! That has to be the opening!"

A voice shouted down the stairwell. "Halt!" A pistol shot followed; the bullet seemed to ricochet endlessly, like a pinball.

"In your dreams, Jack!" Hugh retorted, defiantly. "Just a little further, Sylvia, only another ten feet!" He could now clearly hear the pursuers' shouted threats, and oaths, along with the clatter of boots and metal objects on stone. A fusillade of shouts and shots rattled through the confined space. They had reached the tunnel's end. A dead end.

"There's no exit!" Hugh cried in frustration. "Hand me the gun! At least we can take some of them out." As he swung about, the beam from their light glanced over the ceiling. "No, wait! Look up there!"

Overhead, a wooden board rested neatly in a frame built into the rock ceiling. "I can't reach it!" Looking around for an extension, he gripped the end of the long flashlight in both hands and used it as an upward pile driver to force open the cover.

On the fourth blow, it moved slightly. On the sixth, it opened. "Hallelujah. I don't know what's up there, but anything's better than being shot like rats in this cesspool! You first! I'll hoist you up. Here, just step on my hands and grab the lip when I lift. Careful. I'm going to give you a big boost. Grab the edge, and haul yourself up. You're doin' great, keep going, you're almost there!" Three shots rang out in quick succession, followed by a cry of pain. "I'll bet someone got hit by a ricochet!"

Using every ounce of effort to overcome her dizziness and fatigue, Sylvia wrenched herself up and through the opening, driven equally by hope, fear and sheer determination. She raised her head and looked up at the high-vaulted ceiling of a church. The trap door entrance was a foot away from the base of a high pulpit. 'Sanctuary' flashed into her mind. 'Not bloody likely!'

"Okay, Hugh, I'm going to reach down. Take my hands. What the...?"

A gleaming black boot pressed down firmly on her right wrist. She twisted her head and looked up, directly into the barrel of a 9mm Luger, held by a one-armed, black-uniformed Gestapo Colonel. "A very commendable effort, Sylvia," he spat her name. "Too bad it didn't work out! The games are finally over. You are caught in what the Americans call a 'tight spot', a 'squeeze play', no? You see, either way, you lose.

"Now, tell your companion, Lieutenant Mason, to hand up his

weapon, handle first, then come up slowly or the Gruppenführer's men will shoot him on the spot. If he doesn't comply, I'll shoot you in the back of the head. Tell him! Now!" He pressed the barrel hard against her temple. "Do as I say, or I will kill you both!"

"Lieutenant!" she shouted.

"I heard. I'm coming. Hold on." The Colt clattered onto the wooden floor. Next, Hugh's fingers appeared, clinging to the wooden frame. Within seconds, he emerged.

"Hands behind your head, Sylvia. Lie there, face down. You, Lieutenant! There. Do not move." He called down the shaft. "I have them both, Gruppenführer Lange."

"Excellent, work Colonel!" Lange replied. "Is there a ladder?"

"No," he laughed. "But it's not that difficult. They did it!

"It's a shame the Most Reverend Gray isn't here to offer you Christian comfort, although you, Sylvia, could not appreciate that, could you, my little Jewess? Unfortunately," he sighed, and paused dramatically, "he is most dead. I had to hang him last week for speaking out once too often in front of his flock against our beloved Führer and Reich Protector Speer. Ah, Lange, meet our Camp X celebrities! Stand up, you two! Face us. Eyes front! Careful, none of your dirty SOE tricks!"

Hugh counted thirty men in assorted uniforms, and their one-armed Gestapo captor, the Colonel. Hugh glanced at Sylvia, earning them each a stinging blow in the face from the tall, silver-haired Gruppenführer's riding crop. Hugh realised there was no hope at this point of pulling off any manoeuvre. An SD sergeant patted him down and found the knife, which he handed to the bald Gestapo Colonel.

"Hmm, only a frog sticker. No Sampson dagger? Pity. I need one for my collection. Open your mouths!" the Gestapo Colonel commanded. "Gruppenführer, if I may borrow that? Sergeant!" The braided leather butt end of the riding crop was suddenly forced roughly into Hugh's mouth. Hugh reacted by biting down. "Bite on that again, you bastard, and I'll crack off your teeth. I said, 'open'!" Hugh complied.

The SD sergeant pried open Hugh's mouth like a prospective buyer at a horse auction. He jabbed and prodded with a gloved hand. The Colonel then handed over the knife, which the sergeant used to tap Hugh's molars. "No hollow tooth, no capsule, Colonel." Hugh, nauseated at the invasion, spat out blood-flecked saliva.

"Now, the woman...her mouth, you pervert! The female guards will look after the rest, at the Hotel."

"You know, Colonel Greilwitz," intoned the Gruppenführer, "these two assassins have many, many interesting tales to tell us...so many German lives taken and with such unmitigated brutality. I'm sure that they will resist, perhaps even fiercely for a while, true patriots that they imagine themselves to be. But you and your officers are welcome to use whatever methods you find most effective to break down their resolve.

"Of course, I will be dropping by frequently for updates I and ask that you send me a verbatim transcript of each day's, ah, 'interrogations'. Perhaps Obergruppenführer Heydrich himself will grace us with his presence, shortly. I understand that Gestapo Chief Müller is with him. In the meantime, I am releasing twenty of these men from my command to guard them in your premises. Once they are convinced that resistance is futile, foolish, and counterproductive, I will be happy to arrange their transport to the Fatherland.

"The Fuhrer will be informed immediately that they are safely in custody. He may well want to personally decide how best to ultimately deal with them. Take them, Colonel. Sergeant, take twenty volunteers and do as commanded by Colonel Greilwitz!"

Hugh and Sylvia's legs were manacled. Once they had also been handcuffed, they were frogmarched down the church aisle and out the entrance to the open rear door of a waiting police van, all the while surrounded by a moving phalanx of ten guards. Two burly SS corporals tossed them sadistically onto the cold metal floor, then hopped in after them, pulled the door shut and sat down on the low benches on opposite sides of the van. The doors were latched and locked from the outside.

The vehicle jolted forward abruptly, throwing Hugh and Sylvia backwards. Both guards glowered stonily at them, swaying in silence with the van's motions. In less than ten minutes, the vehicle slowed to a stop, its motor idling unevenly. The exhaust fumes from a leaking tailpipe began to seep into the compartment and mingled with the already-stifling odours of old sweat, stale urine, and vomit. Sylvia began to gag.

One of the guards, a blonde teenager, kicked the side of her head with his heel, just missing her wound. She grimaced and groaned slightly with the sharp new jolt of pain. Hugh raised his head to protest and the butt of the older guard's rifle glanced off his right temple. He drew in his breath in an effort to suppress his rage.

The driver ground the gears into reverse and the vehicle moved backward at a high rate of speed, then stopped abruptly. The engine was shut off and both guards crouched with their backs to their captives, waiting for the rear doors to open. Hugh considered making a last ditch attempt to create some unpleasantness for the Standartenführer's two henchmen, but a furtive glimpse of Sylvia's imploring glance told him to let the idea slide.

Watsmede's Harmony Arms Hotel, the once pleasant, near-luxury class, and 'almost seaside' spa, now renamed the Harmony Club, was anything but that. Seized and systematically looted by Gestapo Standartenführer Waldemar Greilwitz after the fall of Great Britain, it was now his own residence, and served as the district Gestapo and SD headquarters. It was also used by the secret police as southwest England's dreaded central lockup and interrogation centre.

Hugh and Sylvia were brought into the foyer, and then directed to what once had been the main desk, now attended by two immense Gestapo guards. After their wristwatches were removed, Sylvia and Hugh were prodded, at rifle point, towards the electric lift, a cage-like device complete with a manually operated sliding metal gate. The operator was a brawny, sullen female Gestapo corporal with coarse hands. Hugh knew that she could effortlessly strangle them both, simultaneously, and would probably relish the opportunity.

The cells, located two levels down, were laid out in two rows, separated by a narrow concrete corridor which was brightly lit by three shaded light bulbs, each suspended on a long wire. The doors of two cells, at opposite ends on the right side, were ajar. Two female warders in SS regulation black uniforms with silver death's head adornment seized Sylvia's arms and marched her to the farthest cell at the end of the corridor, next to a room with a windowless steel door and a sign which read, **Interrogation Chamber - Keep Out!** The unintentional gallows humour of the message was wryly amusing, 'As if...!' she thought.

Hugh tried furtively to make eye contact as Sylvia was flung inside and was swallowed up by her cell. He heard her door slam shut with a final metallic clang as two male turnkeys shoved him into his own cubicle then slammed and locked his solid metal door as well.

He attempted to acclimatise himself to his cell in the darkness, but was distracted by the high-pitched screams and weeping piercing the silence. They seemed to come from further down the corridor. After a momentary respite, the otherworldly sounds resumed, followed by pleading, in English.

'My God, they've got Jenny!' He lowered himself awkwardly onto the ice-cold, rough concrete floor, horrified in the certain knowledge that he and Sylvia had thoroughly compromised and brought down the local Resistance.

As sleep was impossible, he chose to stay alert by taking stock of his surroundings and considering the options. In leg irons, he found it was only possible to take a half pace. Slowly, he hop-stepped as quietly as he could manage, leaning his shoulder against the walls as he estimated the length and width. With a little mental arithmetic, he calculated the space to be eight by ten feet with an eight-foot ceiling. The only 'windows' were a peephole with a sliding cover, and a slightly larger opening, also covered, lower down in the door.

Tired from the exertion, he sat down on the foul and dank, thin straw tick. As he tried to stretch out, his feet struck a metal container, releasing the revolting odour of liquid human waste. He was overcome with disgust. 'Reminder: slop bucket needs to be emptied. Am I losing my mind? Get a grip. Pay attention, goddammit Hugh; you were trained at great expense by the best in the world to deal with this sort of situation. Think! You can bet your socks that Sylvia is!'

Loud screams and pleadings interrupted his train of thought. 'Is that Sylvia's voice? Is it Jenny's?' He forced his mind to concentrate. The Gestapo Standartenführer had made it very clear that he knew a great deal about their backgrounds, details including their names and their Camp X training. He even knew that Sylvia was Jewish. 'Maybe she should never have been sent here'.

He and Sylvia had both realised from that first incident in his bedroom in Newcastle, that they had disobeyed one of the cardinal rules of espionage: 'never sleep with or become romantically involved with a partner.' It wasn't some rusty Puritanical ethic, but rather it was simply preventive, to eliminate the possibility of the enemy exploiting and using that attachment as a powerful lever to extract confessions from either or both parties. What few engaged or married client couples there were, were rarely sent together on missions by SOE. 'But how could I resist Sylvia?' he thought, as he drifted into something fitfully resembling sleep.

He awoke the next morning and did his best to relieve himself, handcuffed and hobbled by leg irons. The cover slid open and a metal plate was inserted through the lower slot in the door. It fell, clattering to the floor, upside down. Using a motion similar to Robert Samson's speciality sit-ups, he rowed himself over to and upturned the plate. Lying underneath it was a pool of slop, a mucous gruel surrounding two small chunks of greyish green vegetable matter, perhaps potato. He scooped as much as he could back into the plate, and then tipping it awkwardly, drained the contents.

He had barely finished wiping his hands on his trousers when a key rattled and twisted in the lock. A Totenkopf Verbande-SS Death's Head Division warder stood backlit by the glaring hallway light pouring in through the open cell door. A glowering Standartenführer Waldemar Greilwitz, standing, feet apart, with his one hand on his hip accompanied him.

"Good morning, Mason. Your lady friends are dying to see you! Remove the fetters! I have him covered." The warder bent over, gingerly unlocking and unfastening Hugh's leg irons. "Get up! Walk, to the end of the hall." The Colonel indicated the direction with his drawn Luger. The handbook rule, 'Pay attention to, and remember every detail of your surroundings,' had paid off. He realized from the Colonel's 'greeting' that it was indeed the morning of the day originally slated for their escape.

'If only...'. In his resolve not to show how much pain his swollen ankles were causing, Hugh kept pace with the guard down the hallway to the metal Interrogation Room door. He drew in his breath as his SS escort knocked at the door, steeling himself. It opened; Hugh was unprepared for what was inside.

He had obviously been hallucinating during the night. 'The cries....' Sylvia and Jenny, wearing plain grey cotton prison shifts, were seated on wooden chairs in the middle of the room, facing one another. They turned their heads as he entered. Although their hands were tied tightly behind their chairs, neither woman's face showed evidence of any physical assault or abuse. Sylvia bit her lip and shook her head slightly, almost imperceptibly.

Three uniformed Death's Head males and two females, all non-coms, stood expectantly, their backs against the wooden counter that ran the length of the far side of the room, like science teachers about to supervise an experiment. The objects on the counter top were grouped neatly, much like instruments prior to a surgical procedure. Another uniformed male sat before a stenographer's desk with a typewriter, situated halfway between the two female prisoners. A fourth chair was placed squarely facing him.

"So, Gruppenführer, may we begin the session?" Hugh noted that Colonel Greilwitz was speaking to the SS General who, along with his shorter companion, were almost hidden at the far end of the room under two large, blood red Nazi banners bracketing the ubiquitous portraits of Führer Adolf Hitler and Reich Protector Albert Speer.

"Proceed, Standartenführer," the General replied, "bearing in mind please, that Hans and I have just finished breakfast."

"Naturally, Gruppenführer, we are civilised; our counter intelligence and state security services are among the most enlightened and advanced in the world, despite what these two SOE buccaneers may have been led to believe. Believe me, I adhere to the philosophy of force only if necessary, and then, only necessary force."

Turning, he addressed Hugh. "I am a reasonable man. Co-operation will gain you consideration for leniency. Resistance, refusal to answer, lying and fabrication, insolence or impertinence, I caution you, will have the most unwelcome, unpleasant, and, I must say, entirely preventable side effects, for your comrades and for you. We are very much like a court of law, dedicated to the pursuit of truth, the whole truth...no less, no more!" For emphasis, he tapped his riding crop on the side of Hugh's head.

"Corporal, place the subject in the chair and fasten his wrists securely." To the 'court reporter', he continued, "Make a note of the starting time, 0935, and record each attendee's name and rank. Very good, are we comfortable, Mason? Now, in that we know that your mother is German-born, from Hamburg, and that you speak the language fluently, as does our Sylvia, Jael, here, the proceedings will be conducted in German. My secretary will keep my young Jenny fully informed as we proceed. So, let us begin, shall we? First, a review of the facts."

'My young Jenny? My?' It dawned on Hugh that this beautiful, courageous young Englishwoman and Gestapo Standartenführer Greilwitz had a history. Although Hugh was far from comfortable and his shoulders ached, he was confident that he would be able to withstand the impending inquisition.

He had been subjected at Camp X to one unforgettable night of shockingly realistic and intense 'mock' interrogation by a trio of genuine German officers, PoW's from Camp 30 in Bowmanville. He was prepared for a carefully orchestrated increase in the level of physical discomfort. A continuous barrage of rapid-fire questions intended to wear down his resistance, undermine his confidence and probe to uncover and then exploit his deepest fears and human weaknesses would continue until his defences were destroyed, and he was 'broken', reduced to a babbling state of helplessness, a psychological wreck.

Threats of torture would be thinly veiled, beginning with subtle hints and intimidation, and escalating to the most brutally medieval techniques. The pending administration of the new, so-called truth serum, Scopolamine, would continue to play upon his fears. He knew what he had to do to ensure his own survival. He could endure, for weeks, or perhaps months. But the element that he had not been prepared to deal with was the implications of his responses on the lives of Sylvia and Jenny.

"I don't understand the questions, Colonel. I am Lieutenant Hugh Miller, Royal Canadian Corps of Signals," he responded for the fifth time, in English. The crop swung again, catching him this time across his mouth.

"You do speak German, very well, indeed. It is fully documented, here, in this dossier," the Colonel asserted, while picking up a grey folder from the secretary's desk. "Now, I insist you stop playing these games!" He slammed down the folder forcefully, startling the stenographer, who dropped his fountain pen on the floor.

"Your information is incorrect, Sir. I am Hugh Miller, born in Canada, Lieutenant, Royal Canadian Corps of Signals. I do not understand, nor do I speak, German." Hugh did understand, however, that this little Colonel felt it imperative to demonstrate his superiority and control over his prisoners to the General, as well as to his Gestapo underlings. 'Show respect, and don't be flippant. It will go easier for you.' He realised that it was important, at least for the present, not to jeopardise his safety with a heroic but foolhardy show of defiance for its own sake.

Standartenführer Greilwitz nodded to one of the female guards who calmly stepped in front of Jenny and administered a vicious backhand blow with a gloved fist to her face. Jenny gasped and choked as a river of blood trickled from her nose.

Greilwitz continued, in German, "Your British betters taught you all about games, eh, Mason? Life is one big game to them, a game that they lost, incidentally. This is my game, and these are my rules. Play, and you win, otherwise, you will all lose. Simple enough?"

Hugh looked at him in silence. Sitting on the edge of the desk, Greilwitz leaned toward Hugh and repeated, more loudly this time, "Simple enough?"

Hugh shrugged uncomprehendingly, and then spoke, in English. "Please do not hit her again, Colonel."

A blow struck his left kneecap with the force of a jackhammer.

Hugh looked up to see the Deaths' Head sergeant holding his service revolver by the barrel.

"Now, the Jew!" The female guard who had assaulted Jenny now hit Sylvia with a chopping blow to the back of her neck. "And again!" Silently, Sylvia slumped forward. "Look at me!" he ordered as the guard jerked her by the hair, forcing her head backward. "Not at the ceiling, Jael, at me! That's better!"

Hugh lurched as far forward as his restraints would allow. "Please, leave her alone!"

"How gallant! You would just love to kill me, yes? Try to understand what both you and I are up against, Mason. Gruppenführer Lange and I expect two very important visitors; you perhaps have heard of our Obergruppenführer Heydrich? Or of Gestapo Chief Müller? They are very, very anxious; no, let me correct myself, determined, to take you back to Berlin for an extended examination by some of their most expert and experienced counter-intelligence specialists. Of course, the General and I will personally receive the Führer's accolades for capturing you, but we want this matter to be resolved here first, in the Reich Protectorate, where it occurred. I can guarantee that you will all receive, at the maximum, a life sentence, if you co-operate. I do have that power. As a matter of fact, the papers are right here, all prepared, just awaiting my signature," he declared, brandishing another file folder. "I can guarantee nothing, if you refuse to see things my way. Be reasonable and help us to help you. Do I make myself clear?"

Hugh didn't answer, shrugging as much as he could manage.

"Very well. I have been patient. You, on the other hand, in your own badly misguided Commando-thug mind, have not seen fit to comply with me. I have no other choice, until you decide to co-operate. Any penalties that the women receive will be as a direct result and in proportion to your own stubbornness. Therefore, you see, you are the author of their fate. Private, take this younger Englishwoman to the table, strap her down and then...yes, Gruppenführer?"

Lange and his strange, bird-like companion stood up. "Excuse us, Standartenführer Greilwitz, but von Tresköw and I have some pressing business which requires our presence."

"Very well, as you wish, of course, Gruppenführer Lange," he fawned. Hugh knew immediately that Greilwitz' intentions had overstepped the bounds and that he had lost his audience. "Go if you must. Another time, perhaps? Do feel welcome to come back, gentlemen!" he added for good measure, and saluted the back of the departing hero of Lodz.

The door shut. "My goodness, it's lunchtime" remarked Greilwitz to no one in particular. "We shall have to have a bite, then we will continue in an hour, at one fifteen. Helga and Viktor will remain on duty. Leave the young one in the chair, for now. The other two can use the facilities at the end of the room...one at a time. Keep them apart. Do not allow them to speak. You will both accompany them. Then, use those leather belts on the hooks to secure their feet. Allow them to eat. There is a guard outside, should you need anything else." He turned, strode briskly to the door, and exited.

'Lunch' consisted of thin, watery cabbage soup with a generous, crusty piece of black bread. Afterwards, the three prisoners were seated back to back to prevent eye contact, each facing a different hospital green wall. Hugh estimated that perhaps two hours had passed when the door opened and the Colonel, with the Death's Head guards and the secretary, re-entered the chamber.

"Did they eat and behave themselves? Good, very good. Helga and Viktor, you are dismissed. Please send in your replacements.

"Now my friends, we have some business to conduct this afternoon. Indeed, I shouldn't be surprised if it runs into or beyond the dinner hour. Translate this please. As these two continue their reluctance to admit their fluency in German, it is imperative that I know they understand every word of what I have to say."

'This guy is a certified egomaniac!'

"First, I must give you some very bad news, which came in over the wires less than an hour ago. British Security Operation has written you off. You Sylvia, Juli, Jael, you, are unfortunately officially listed as KIA: killed in action, not missing, mind, but dead. Pity. So, it really doesn't matter what happens here, does it? You no longer exist. Stalwart and Warden are grieving I'm sure, as are your Camp X Colonel Gordon Graham, Robert Samson, Hamish Findlay, your parents and that baby daughter. Mason, you are missing and presumed dead."

He paused. "Second, we have successfully penetrated Andrew's Claymore circuit and have all of his collaborators from Scotland, Manchester and London in custody. They have sung their hearts out, including Annie, the beautiful red-haired woman, your colleague from the thug academy, Beaulieu, Juli. Yes, it is so! You are of very little value at this point, worthless, of no use at all. Disposable waste. I can think of only one thing..."

As he meandered on, Hugh tried to digest this information. 'How in blazes does he know so much. Is German intelligence that good? On the other hand, is ours that bad? It must be insider knowledge. Tom? Was he the traitor, their reliable source? Of course he was, and someone at Camp X figured it out and executed him. The wounds bore the mark of a professional. Hamish?'

"...And as Tent Peg's W/T operator, you could perhaps arrange to keep everyone here, under my protection, away from the certain unpleasantness at Security Services headquarters in Berlin. Of course you will be punished and will serve your time, but humanely, and in relative comfort. You, Jenny, I just don't know. You really have no bargaining chips. A shame, because one should always leave one card left to play, up the sleeve, as they say. And you seem to have none. Not one that I can think of."

'I hate to admit it, but he's good, in a twisted, sadistic way. But how in the devil does he know so much of Tent Peg's details? There must have been another source placed at the Camp, after Tom was killed!' "What do you expect me to do, Colonel?"

The interpreter was keeping pace with the Colonel's patter. "That's the spirit, Hugh, old man, as the English say. I want you to send an OU to Hydra. Through Yorkie, let Colonel Graham and the group at Casa Loma know that you're safe, in hiding and doing everything you can to return."

"Why?"

"I am conducting this interview, you impertinent, hopeless moron!" he screamed. "The woman!" The new female Gestapo corporal struck Jenny's right ear a heavy sideways blow with her clenched fist. Her head swayed with the violence of the impact. "Again, the other side!"

"Wait, hold on, Colonel! I don't understand exactly what you want me to do!" he lied, playing for time.

Greilwitz lowered his voice, as though explaining the rules of a schoolyard game to a young child. "It's very simple, Hugh, really," he said, with exaggerated patience. "You send the message and then I sign your pardons. Like that," he snapped his fingers, "you're off to prison, in the Protectorate, not the Reich. I hear that the only way out of those places is through the chimney!"

Sylvia stole a sideways glance at Hugh, ever so slightly shaking her head. Colonel Greilwitz saw and reacted, lashing her across her face with the tip of his crop. "You are already officially dead! I will make that doubly dead, slowly, using the most agonising methods at my disposal, if you try to interfere again. Corporal, you and the private strip and blind-fold her, then chain her tightly to the hook!"

Hugh stared in silent and helpless horror, as Sylvia was kicked and dragged, naked, to the far wall where the Colonel's orders were carried out. When the guards had finished, her handcuffs' chain had been secured to a moveable metal hook, which was then drawn up slowly, leaving her feet barely in contact with the floor. 'At least she's facing the wall.'

"A delectable specimen!" Greilwitz commented. The two female guards smiled appreciatively. "Now, I think it's time to let our subjects think about their choices. Anything to say, Hugh?"

'Don't fall for it! Keep your head.' Despite his resolve, he blurted, "Yes, you truly are a foul bastard. Sir!"

"Really, Lieutenant Mason, how predictable. Are you truly so naïve, so juvenile? Now how do you suppose that your British intelligence snobs would deal with war criminals: thugs, common murderers, like you, SOE scum? Shoot them, hang them? You have no rights! You wore no uniforms! You have no combatant status under the Geneva Convention. None! You are fodder for German justice, however I see fit to administer it! I'm tired of your posturing." Hugh thought he detected foam at the corners of the Colonel's small mouth.

"It's time to put my better nature aside and allow my specialists here free rein in their methods of persuasion. You will send the radio mes-sage, that I can guarantee! Right, all but you two, come! Keep them silent. Tighten their restraints. She can be raised up higher yet!" The typewriter stopped its incessant clattering and the chamber closed.

The winch turned agonisingly slowly, its grating sound almost more than Hugh could bear. Sylvia did not make a sound. He steeled himself and looked in her direction. Her toes scarcely touched the concrete; her shoulder blades stood out like axe blades. The young male Gestapo pri-vate walked over and casually inspected her breasts, eyes assessing and probing them lewdly, while Hugh gritted his teeth. Jenny appeared to be semiconscious, barely responding as the bleached blonde, paunchy female corporal cinched her handcuffs. The corporal, reeking of body odour, wine, and cigarettes, then turned and attended to Hugh. He tried to expand his wrists, for which he received a curse and sharp cuff.

Time took on a surreal quality as Hugh, dazed and exhausted, slipped in and out of the present.

"All right! Let her down!" Their lord and master had returned. "Give them each some water and a trip to the toilet. When I come back, I want them fresh and alert!" Sylvia was ratcheted down, her shift replaced, then was led by two guards to the bathroom. When she was brought back to sit on her chair, she toppled heavily onto the floor, where they left her.

Hugh remembered a colourful lecture by an Australian SOE field agent at Camp X who stated emphatically that the SD and Gestapo rarely interrogated their subjects during the first week to ten days of imprisonment. "Not out of kindness, mates," he had remarked, "but as a ploy to scare the life out of you. A poor bloke's imagination runs riot, unnerving him, and pretty well destroying his blinkin' self-esteem. Your mind can be your worst enemy, when you're faced with uncertainty, day after bloody day." 'So, why the rush? To get the glory, to break us and prove his mettle, before the boys from Berlin get down here and get their hooks into us.'

His thoughts were interrupted by the sounds of several approaching voices. A squad of four guards carried in a rectangular table and two metal chairs, setting them down against the nearest wall. They placed a British W/T radio in the centre of the table. Another guard brought in a field telephone and a table microphone, put them on the table beside the radio, then retreated, trailing wires across the room. He fed the wires under the door, then closed it behind him as he left. Colonel Greilwitz, appearing refreshed, began his dissertation anew as he removed and polished his steel-rimmed spectacles, his riding crop tucked under the stump of his left arm.

"Tie her upright in the goddamn seat, if you have to! Now, Lieutenant Mason, we talk turkey. Here's the radio; here's my ultimatum. You will send your code, then this message. My radioman is no fool and will be monitoring everything." He repositioned his glasses then reached into his breast pocket.

"I have no code!"

"We have though of that little detail. See this? What is it?"

'Damn, a one-time pad. How the hell...'

"What is it?" he repeated, approaching and flicking it against Hugh's cheek.

Hugh shrugged. "It might be a scrap of yellow paper or a parking ticket."

"You are an obstinate bastard! It's a one time code pad, as if you've forgotten!"

"If you say so, Colonel." Hugh knew he was treading on very dangerous ground. He couldn't wilfully cause Sylvia or Jenny further grief. 'Doesn't he realise that I have to send my personal identification code first?'

"I say so. Now, because it was recently captured, it's current and authentic, so, you can use it to establish your *bona fides* with BSO."

"My what?"

Greilwitz ignored this insolence. "You will send it, exactly as I have it written, or, and I did say this is an ultimatum, I will take out my considerable disappointment, first on Jenny, then on the Jew. You do understand that much, don't you?"

"Yes. I understand."

"Good. "Bring him here and pull the girl Jenny's chair closer." Her eyes were shut. Hugh hoped she was blessedly oblivious to the events. When all was ready, the technician handed him a headset. "Here it is, written out clearly in English," Greilwitz asserted impatiently. "Use the top page of the code pad and transcribe it exactly. No errors, no omissions, no tricks. Begin."

"Can we have some real food, please, Colonel? Something to drink...tea? And the women need something warmer to wear."

"Yes, yes" he responded, exasperated. Private, look after it!" he ordered.

The first part of the signal was brief, a straightforward confirmation to BSO HQ that the sender was legitimate, and not operating under duress. Hugh converted its characters methodically using the code pad while Greilwitz looked over his shoulder.

They were each given a plate with a bread roll, two thick slices of sausage, and a metal cup of weak, but warm tea. The warders tended to Sylvia and Jenny, both now responsive.

Hugh knew that he had two factors in his favour: his personal group was an essential marker in the message header to validate his, the sender's, ID, and a transposed group in the message body was a signal of distress, if he could slip it in. If he was careful, and a bit lucky, he knew Yorkie and the other Hydra operators at the Camp would smell a rat and immediately voice their suspicions to Colonel Graham.

Graham would alert Stalwart, who would then order them to play along in a radio game. Hugh figured it was worth the gamble, as they had nothing else going for them. He set down the pencil and pushed the message pad over to the young SD signal lieutenant who examined Hugh's work, carefully comparing the message with the encoded version.

"So, how has he done, Lieutenant?" inquired Greilwitz.

"Perfectly, Sir."

"Ready, Mason?"

"Yes, I'm ready but it's been months. I'm out of practice, Sir."

"Just spare me the excuses and get on with it. Lieutenant, see that he transmits it, precisely as is. Now, please!"

"A question, Sir? Why is this microphone here?"

"A technicality. Get on with it!" By this time, the technician had everything ready. He handed Hugh a headset.

The radio experts at STS 103 had demonstrated a captured piece of Danish-German electronic technology, a wire recorder. They had a great time showing the Advanced W/T Class clients how a voice, music, rude noises, or any other electromagnetic signal could be recorded on the loop of fine silver wire. "Crude, but damned effective," was the verdict.

It occurred to Hugh that Greilwitz was picking up his signature by using a wire recorder to make a facsimile copy of his personal Morse 'fist' with its highly personal, unique characteristics. With enough recorded samples, a competent signalman could learn to duplicate another's style precisely. And after sufficient practise and effort, he, Hugh would be expendable. He was well aware of this, but he also realised that he had no option.

He was out of practice. It would be too risky if he attempted to modify his 'fist'. He knew there would be hell to pay for Jenny and Sylvia, if Greilwitz caught on. "Ready," Hugh announced. He felt something burrowing under his scalp: reaching up to adjust his earpieces, his fingertips grazed his head. When he placed his right hand on the key, he saw a smear of fresh blood, 'Lice!'

"One moment!" Greilwitz walked over to stand beside Jenny's chair. He drew his .9mm Walther revolver, cocked it, released its safety catch, and placed the end of the barrel firmly against her left temple. "You may proceed now, Mason," he instructed flatly. "I've always believed in insurance, as a policy, eh, Lieutenant?" The signals man smiled disdainfully at the Colonel's weak pun and nodded, "Yes, always, Sir!"

Hugh began tapping out the OU level transmission. It took less than thirty seconds to send. A split second later, he received a confirmation. "BSO OU request confirmed. Please stand by. Please repeat." 'Thank God, nothing out of the ordinary.' Hugh responded with a duplicate of the message and received an almost instant confirmation, then silence.

A minute later, an SD signalman rushed into the room. "Excuse me, Standartenführer Greilwitz, but he has screwed us!"

"What do you mean?" he shouted angrily.

"I have the entire exchange recorded, just as you asked. He substituted a key group and his personal identifier as well! I'll play it back for you," he offered, highly agitated.

"You are certain of this?"

"Positive, I've played it back twice, Sir. Joseph and I can both confirm that it was irregular. There's no question that he sent a distress signal."

"Why didn't you notice these irregularities, Lieutenant?"

"I, I...don't know, Standartenführer..."

"Are you stupid or were you asleep? Get the hell out of here! I'll be dealing harshly with your incompetence, believe me!" The SD technician fumbled with his headset, removing it hastily, and stumbled out, his face ashen.

"You're quite certain you didn't misinterpret...?" Greilwitz continued to the other signalman.

"I swear, on my honour, as an SS man and on my blood oath of loyalty to our Führer, Standartenführer!"

Hugh sat in silence, staring straight ahead. He knew that he had underestimated the enemy and someone would pay, dearly. Suddenly, the room resounded with the ear-splitting report of a single gunshot. Hugh turned to see Jenny lurch sideways, a bullet hole in her left temple. She toppled off the chair, a twitching heap. Red and greyish-white spatters flecked the face and white shirtfront of the Gestapo sergeant who had been standing on her right, five feet away. The stench of cordite was overpowering. Sylvia bowed her head. Hugh fought a strong urge to vomit.

Calmly, Greilwitz removed the clip, examined it, and replaced his weapon in its holster. He removed his eyeglasses and proceeded to polish them awkwardly with a white handkerchief. "I did warn you about heroics, didn't I?" he asked grimly. "She's next." He indicated Sylvia with the stem of his spectacles. "Take them to their cells. Strip them. Manacles, leg restraints, I'll give you detailed instructions later. Kindly get that out of here," he nodded at Jenny's now motionless body, "and clean yourselves up. Dismissed."

Hugh knew that they would be tortured brutally and eventually turned over to the authorities in Berlin for final disposition. It was unlikely that they would be executed immediately. Robert Samson had emphasised that German Intelligence usually opted to keep high-profile SOE agents alive, so they could be exploited 'for future consideration'.

He knew that his chief responsibility now was to do anything to divert their attention from Sylvia, for as long as possible. Sooner or later, he would make a full confession confirming that not only was he the killer of the three officers, but Tent Peg's designated assassin. 'Greilwitz already knows about Sylvia's Jewish identity, but has that been passed along to his superiors?' Hugh wondered as four strapping warders seized them and began dragging them by their arms out of the chamber.

A young orderly met them at the door. "Heil Hitler. Excuse the interruption, Herr Oberst, there are two very senior SS officers waiting upstairs. They say that you're expecting them, from RSHA HQ, in Berlin. They insist upon speaking with you immediately, Sir."

"Ah, good, it must be Obergruppenführer Heydrich and Gruppenführer Müller! Please, see to it that they're made comfortable. Tell them I will be there momentarily!" he smiled.

'Christ! How much worse can this get?' Hugh thought.

"I believe they're on their way down now, actually." The orderly startled, coughed, and fell to the floor as a bullet passed through the breast of his uniform. The crackle of small arms discharging outside electrified Hugh. The twin doors swung open. He could see the floor of the corridor, littered with at least six black-uniformed bodies lying in grotesque disarray. Three SS officers entered with Thompson machine guns.

"SOE! Down!" shouted a familiar voice. Hugh and Sylvia wrenched themselves free of their escorts, and dropped face down onto the concrete. A fusillade of bullets took out the guards. The radioman who had detected Hugh's deception tried to reach for the Morse key, and was shot twice, in the face. He slumped, streams of his blood quickly covering the radio.

"Here Hugh, catch! We're taking that bloke with us!" A Colt .45

Special slid across the floor. Hugh picked it up and looked around. Greilwitz had hidden under the table beneath the portraits of Hitler and Speer."

"Hurry. Ten seconds. Sylvia, come over here. You're covered."

A lone gunman sprayed semi-automatic rifle fire at three SD men rushing down the stairs. Two plummeted over the banister, landing heavily in the stairwell. The third slowly collapsed, like a deflated balloon, sprawling vacant-eyed on the landing.

"Hurry, lad! Who's she?"

"A friend. She's dead!" Hugh fired the revolver, missing Greilwitz' now hatless head by a centimetre. "Get up! Throw out your gun! I said throw out your gun!" He fired again, shattering the Standartenführer's glasses that lay at his right hand. "Now, come out! Hands out in front! Faster or I'll polish you off like a dog, just like you did Jenny!" Hugh ordered in German. The Colonel, trembling, did as Hugh commanded.

"Got him? Here, cuff him. Tell him to him take off his boots. Quickly! Now drop them! That's a good little weasel. Okay...nine, ten. Let's move! Hugh and Sylvia, follow Robert. Heads up. Up the stairs."

"Hamish...is it you?"

"The same, lad. Now get your Royal Canadian butt up there. Come Sylvia, I'll help you, lass. Be ready for some fancy footwork! We've less than ten minutes to meet the sub!"

CHAPTER 10

ATTENTION TO DETAIL

Half-carrying, half dragging Sylvia between them, Hamish and Hugh charged wildly up the three flights of stairs, their revolvers blazing. Ahead of them, they prodded a sullen and barefoot Colonel Greilwitz, using him as a human shield. After the third guard had crumpled on the stairs, the number of Nazi defenders they had overpowered or killed outright blurred into a haze in Hugh's mind. Moreover, the image of Major 'two-gun' Hamish Findlay, in full flight, sporting the dress uniform of an Obergruppenführer-SS, would be forever etched in his memory.

They paused on the main landing to get their bearings and catch their breath. Crouching, Hamish peered cautiously into the foyer. A voice from behind shouted, "Lieutenant, head down!" as a bullet whined within a hairsbreadth of Hugh's right ear. It caromed off a large brass candelabrum shattering the plaster forehead of an ugly gargoyle ornament squatting on the newel post.

Another shot rang. Hugh turned as the peroxided head of the stout female Gestapo warder who had so obviously enjoyed tormenting Sylvia and Jenny exploded like an overripe cantaloupe. She staggered, and then toppled backwards slowly, hands flailing the air, then landed heavily on the lower landing. Her Luger clattered loose, bouncing crazily down the metal staircase.

"Good shot! Thanks, buddy. I owe you," Hugh acknowledged, half-whispering. "Who are you?"

"Andy, Sir!"

'Andy! Yes, the bartender from the Camp's mess', he recollected.

Hamish called to a Gestapo Gruppenführer standing at the front desk in the lobby. "Rob, all clear below? What's your situation?" The two bear-like Gestapo guards which Hugh and Sylvia had passed coming in were now nowhere to be seen. Instead, two other men in SS uniforms were covering the front entrance with German machine pistols.

"Come ahead. Stay low and be ready for some fireworks outside! Run when you hear the horn blow twice!" Robert ordered.

"Okay, you can set me down, boys. I can manage on my own,"

Sylvia said, adding, "Thanks."

"Good to hear that," Hamish affirmed.

"Who did in that buzzard, Brünnhilde?" she queried.

"He did. Andy," Hugh answered, pointing to the young agent in the Gestapo uniform.

"Thanks, Andy! Hip shot, good show! If I'm to survive this, somebody had better hand me a revolver!"

"Okay, are we ready? It's a flat-out dash to the auto!" Hamish cried, passing her one of his two Army Colts. "Wait for Robert's signal, then we go like bloody blue blazes. Hugh, fetch the prisoner. Shoot him if he gets any fancy ideas!"

Suddenly, there was the crackling of more small arms fire at the hotel doorway, followed by the insistent blare of a car horn. "One...two, duck and run!" Hamish yelled. As they bolted for the car, Hugh wondered how nine people would be jammed into one automobile. They ran down the front steps, jumping over or dodging around five rag doll bodies. Hugh guided the stumbling Greilwitz by his good arm.

"Get in!" he ordered in German. To Hugh's astonishment, he saw Robert, his Gruppenführer's hat jauntily backward, seated at the wheel of the massive, black Horch limousine, its headlights dimmed by blackout covers, rendering it all but invisible in the darkness. Out of nowhere, a middle-aged SD lieutenant lunged at Robert through the open driver's window with what appeared to be a dagger. A split second later, he recoiled. Dropping the knife to grasp his throat with both hands, he dropped beneath Hugh's sight line. "Now, get in or I'll bloody well have to take off without you!" Robert shouted.

Grabbing the little Gestapo Colonel by one shoulder and the back of his trousers, Hugh shoved him headfirst through the vehicle's rear door, and then pushed him onto the floor. He turned to Sylvia, took her arm, and they jumped in, narrowly avoiding kicking the Colonel's head as they struggled to find space to sit.

Andy and Hamish rode standing on the running boards, clutching the window posts. A young SS trooper lying on the front grass, rose on his elbows, took careful aim, and then fired his revolver at the fast-moving vehicle. "I've got him. Heads down!" Hamish yelled. The slug grazed Hamish's left hand then skittered noisily across the metal roof: instinctively, he swung his right arm in the shooter's direction and fired his Colt twice. The two bullets found their mark, tearing open the soldier's neck, his expression frozen in surprise. His head lolled to one side and the

Luger toppled out of his hands onto the ground.

"Bravo!" Sylvia shouted. "Is your hand alright?"

"No worse than my leg, m'dear!" he retorted, leaning through the window.

She glanced inquisitively at Hugh, who shrugged in reply. "What happened to your leg?" she yelled to Hamish, at the top of her voice.

"Just a minor mining accident!" he called back. "Hold, steady...steady, Rob. Now, hard right here! Gun this blighter! She's going to blow!"

"What...? Good Lord!" Sylvia shouted. She and Hugh turned to look through the car's rear window just as the front wall of the Harmony Arms Hotel buckled outward, collapsing in the pathway of a raging firestorm. Seconds later, another violent explosion tore away the gabled roof, as a huge fireball engulfed the wooden structure, vividly illuminating the night sky.

"Very impressive, Hamish!" Hugh called. "Too bad Heydrich and Müller missed it!"

"The grenades did add a dramatic touch. Andy's contribution," Hamish replied, grinning.

The V12 engine accelerated with a neck-snapping burst of power, hurtling the heavily armoured car at top speed down High Street. Looking around at his comrades, Hugh squeezed Sylvia's hand. She smiled and winked. Hugh counted five heads in the car, not including the outriders, Andy and Hamish, the wide-eyed Colonel Greilwitz on the floor, and himself.

Suddenly, Andy pointed ahead, and shouted excitedly, "Panzers! Troop carriers dead ahead!" Robert turned the wheel sharply left, and touched the brake pedal, swinging out the speeding car's rear end to the right in a tire-screeching racing manoeuvre, then headed west on a narrow, rutted laneway.

The lane ended abruptly at a drainage culvert beyond which lay an unploughed cow pasture. "Hang on!" Robert shouted as he pressed down the accelerator pedal to launch the mammoth automobile over the ditch. "The tach needle's past the red line! We're coming in for a landing!" The Horch thudded heavily on the other side, no longer airborne, its engine screaming in protest. The rear tires spun wildly in the mud, then finally gripped, sending up twin rooster-tails of muck, as the car suddenly lurched forward across the uneven terrain, careening precariously. Hamish and Andy, hatless and gritting their teeth, had somehow managed to hang on.

"Can someone please tell me where we're going?" asked Sylvia of no one in particular.

"Over there, just beyond that barn!" Robert replied.

"Why? What's there?" she asked.

"Our way out!" Just to the north, the tanks began firing, their muzzle blasts briefly illuminating the hovering clouds in the darkened sky. The column of German armour had mobilised rapidly and was closing at flank speed on their right, in an attempt to 'cross the T', thereby cutting off any possibility of escape. A shell burst less than twenty feet in front of them, throwing up chunks of rock and pasture, immediately followed by a second explosion. Undeterred, Robert swerved to avoid the two craters.

"They're ranging their guns, bracketing us!" Hamish shouted. "They likely want us alive. Either us, that is, or 'His Nibs', there, cringing on the floor." He indicated the cowering Colonel. "He must be some sort of fancy bloke! What d'you think, Rob?"

"Could be both! My guess is that we're about to be buzzed by the whole blinking Luftwaffe and forced to run for it. Either that or we're done for." Another shell burst with blinding intensity directly ahead. Unable to see through the rain of debris, Robert jammed on the brakes. The car veered drunkenly and came to a stop as earth and metal rained down onto the roof like hailstones, shattering the windshield. Sylvia looked anxiously for Hamish and Andy. Both had vanished into the darkness.

"Out! Keep low, follow me and cover your ears...." Robert's instructions were drowned out by the concussion of another shellburst just as two aircraft thundered overhead out of the clouds. "Here's Jerry! What did I just say? Hit the ground!" They spilled out the doors and rolled, Hugh dragging out the miraculously revived Colonel Greilwitz.

Wingtip to wingtip, an RAF Spitfire and RCAF Mosquito swept down, their machine guns and cannons blazing. With a resounding 'whump', the front end of the lead Tiger leapt upwards. The tank exploded mid-air in a brilliant orange and oily black fireball, scattering flaming shrapnel, and debris.

An armoured personnel carrier approached the Horch menacingly, then rose slightly as though being levitated, and flipped upside down, pounding its occupants headfirst into the ground. It shuddered convulsively, then erupted in a pyrotechnic fury as its fuel tank and ammunition simultaneously exploded.

A second tank slowly halted, attempting to sight in and return the aircrafts' fire. It's cumbersome turret swung around and the cannon barrel rose, and then discharged a shell. For its effort, the panzer received a direct hit on the turret, shearing off its formidable 'eighty-eight'-artillery barrel and hurtling it skyward. Infantry squads, advancing closely beside and behind the panzers in orderly groups, broke off into disarray when the Spitfire peeled off and began a devastating strafing run.

"Hugh, that's our friend, again! Thank you, thank you, whoever you are!" Sylvia shouted, waving at the Canadian Mosquito, with tears streaming from her eyes.

The pilot waggled the plywood fighter-bomber's wings as it peeled away.

"Hugh, look, over there, thank God! Hamish and Andy are safe!" she cried.

"All hell's broken loose. Hightail it to the aircraft!" shouted Hamish, hatless and dishevelled, but still brandishing his Colt. Beside him, Andy, frantically waved his arms, pointing in the direction of the old barn. They all ran madly.

Hugh stopped to help Greilwitz who seemed about to faint. "Nitro!" he panted, gesturing feebly toward his breast pocket. Kneeling, Hugh fumbled, trying to undo the silver button, then ripped it off, and reached inside the pocket, retrieving a vial marked "Nitro-glycerine." He pushed one of the small white pills into the terrified man's open mouth, jamming it under his tongue and clamping the man's mouth shut. Then, dragging Greilwitz by the back of his tunic, he continued toward the plane.

As soon as they rounded the barn, they let out a collective cheer. A Special Operations Mosquito was waiting, sitting primly in the darkness on a grass strip. Immediately, its engines coughed, belched dark smoke, and then caught. The pilot opened the cabin door. "Get in! Quickly!" Hamish exclaimed.

The other Mosquito was making lazy eights overhead. Hugh and Greilwitz were about to board the aircraft, when the Nazi stiffened, shaking his head. Speaking sharply in German, Hugh ordered him inside. The Colonel balked. Hugh drew his revolver, thrusting the barrel against the man's left temple, and repeated his command. Greilwitz shut his eyes in resignation and grimly shook his head.

From the aircraft's side window, Sylvia shouted down to him, in

German so Greilwitz would understand, "Lieutenant! Throw me your gun. I'll finish off this murderous Nazi vermin myself, right now!"

Looking venomously up toward her, Colonel Greilwitz obediently stepped forward, smashing his head on the doorframe in his haste. Robert pulled him inside by his lapels and took him aft.

In less than two minutes, the loading operation was complete and the plane began to taxi into the wind. Sylvia sat on Hugh's lap beside the young pilot, who, after welcoming them aboard, introduced himself as, "Kaz, Polish-Canadian, with the RCAF, from Oshawa, Ontario; I'm on 'special operations' duty with SOE and the RAF.

"We're a little over capacity! Cross your fingers!" he gestured emphatically, jabbing a thumb backward over his shoulder. At full throttle, the twin Merlin engines' high-pitched sounds drowned out any further discussion. Sylvia pinched Hugh's arm, staring mutely into the darkness through the canopy as the little airplane struggled heroically to attain lift. Its wheels lifted, and then bumped the ground with heart-stopping hesitancy.

Hugh cast a sideways glance at Kaz for some reassuring sign. There was none. Just when it seemed that they were about to become a part of a rapidly approaching gigantic oak, Kaz applied full stick and the labouring aircraft shuddered, and its undercarriage skimmed the uppermost branches. Miraculously, they were airborne.

Kaz shouted above the din, "Welcome aboard Special Ops Whiteknuckles Airline!" He expertly trimmed the Mosquito. "Now, we're in deep trouble if I cruise above three hundred feet. The coastal...!" He stopped suddenly, and placed his left hand against his earpiece listening intently. Seconds later, he smiled, making the universal 'thumbs up' signal. "Friends...twelve Canadian, British night fighters upstairs! Chukka, chukka, chukka...bye, bye, Fritz!" Sylvia thought that with his sparkling blue eyes, puckish boy's grin, under his leather flyers' helmet, he was adorable.

Kaz settled into his job of piloting the plane. He spoke little during the remainder of the flight, but generously shared his thermos of tea. Robert and Hamish came forward to briefly update Sylvia and Hugh. "The Colonel's a cardiac case. He may not make it," Robert announced. " I have been closely monitoring him; he's sweating, complaining of chest pains and shortness of breath."

"Roger, I'll alert ground control when we're about to land," Kaz responded.

Kaz became quiet once again, concentrating on flying them safely below the German radar. Some time later, he announced that they had crossed over the border into Scotland. He detached an earphone from his headset and handed it to Sylvia. She and Hugh leaned in to hear the terse exchange.

"Blue leader...six bandits, FW's...Galland's Squadron markings...have an eye, gentlemen...heading 1 8 5'er, at nine o'clock. This is Red leader... clear now, Alpha Bravo Foxtrot...you've shaken your tail...! Pull out of there, you lucky bastard! Roger, he's in my sights!" Although garbled and distorted, the accents were unmistakably Canadian and British. Hugh looked at Kaz, "Where are they?"

"Dogfights," he shrugged. "I don't know exactly, somewhere close by!" Kaz pointed his left thumb upwards. "The guardian angels are on patrol, flying cover in honour of you heroes! And by God, you all deserve it!"

Small aircraft training over Camp X, 1943.

In sharp contrast to the hair-raising takeoff three hours earlier, Kaz expertly guided the Mosquito on a gentle descent over water to touch down in the pitch darkness on a makeshift airstrip, nestled amid jagged crags. When Hugh opened the cabin door, four men, three jeeps, and a small Red Cross lorry greeted him. Two of the four, British paratroops officers in khaki and green battle dress instructed the medical attendants to remove the Gestapo Colonel on a stretcher. As Greilwitz was being taken off, Hamish winked, and cautioned the two orderlies "Don't drop the little blighter on his head, at least if you can help it!"

The two medics tugged and tightened the straps to secure the bare-foot, perspiring Colonel. Squinting, Greilwitz struggled to sit up. Through the darkness, he sighted two menacing figures in paratroopers' boots, camouflaged khaki battle dress and berets. Fearing that they might well be dreaded British Commandos, he shut his eyes and lay back glumly, to await his fate.

With a booming voice, and a huge smile beneath the bushiest moustache that Sylvia had ever seen, a bear-like paratroops Colonel came to the cockpit door to introduce himself. "Jack Blackmore here, Special Air Service, and SAS Chief Warrant Officer Ronald West. Our apologies for the delay in getting you off! We wanted to secure your 'precious cargo', first." He turned away and ordered the drivers to bring the jeeps up snug with the Lysander. Sylvia and Hugh stepped down and both men snapped to attention, saluting. Embarrassed and slightly amused, they smiled back courteously and returned the salutes before getting in the jeep.

"Can you say where we are, Colonel, other than that it's in the north of Scotland?" Sylvia inquired.

He laughed, "Yes, you could say that, Captain, jolly well north. 'Course, it's highly hush-hush, classified, and all that, as you might expect. Let's just say that we're only one of several installations, strung out, as the Prime Minister stated, 'Like precious pearls on a necklace that will tighten inexorably to strangle the interloper by the throat.' "

"That's certainly descriptive! I'm sorry to have missed it. I must have been out of the country!" she chuckled.

"He was in rare form, that time. Addressing the Canadian Parliament. About all I can say, Captain, is that we're located on a non-existent, flyspeck of an island, above the sixtieth parallel. The closest ... here we are! May I help you out? Gentlemen, this is the end of the road."

The base was a collection of five tents, one small, wooden hut, and a huge underground cave. Sylvia was immediately reminded of photographs that she had seen of Arctic and Antarctic expeditions, but without the usual backdrop of sled dogs, snow drifts and icy glaciers.

Warrant Officer West led the party on a tour, explaining that the base was well concealed from the air by camouflage netting, and, "tucked away as it is, under this bleeding massive rock overhang. Charlie Four comes over daily for a bit of a look, but he's just wasting his time." Noting their puzzled looks he elaborated, "Dear old Charlie Four, that's his insignia, C 4, the official eyes of the Luftwaffe. Charlie's an observer bloke in an Hs 123 biplane...gives us the once-over every day, same time. So, since we always know when to expect him, we lie low until he finishes doing his business, then carry on."

In his command HQ, a large, high-vaulted cavern dug into the mountain, Colonel Blackmore presented each SOE agent to the Camp's 2

IC, Captain Keith Latham. Before starting dinner, the Colonel insisted that they pose for a group photo before Robert, Hamish, Andy, and other the members of the team removed their SS uniforms. After the meal, the two SAS officers paid lavish tributes to each of their guests with a toast. Before the serious drinking began, Sylvia begged off, asking to be shown to her cot.

By five thirty the following morning, as the other group members struggled to get up and ready themselves for the next leg of their journey, Sylvia and Robert had already prepared a large pot of strong, hot coffee, but without the Camp's customary 'eye-opener' or 'wee nip'. Quietly, Sylvia asked, "Who are they, Robert, these SAS? Are they 'special ops' Commandos?"

"Not exactly Commandos, but very similar, Sylvia. They're superbly prepared, and undeniably among the world's crack fighting forces, made up of the cream, the élite. They are all volunteers from Britain's para-troops regiments. The SAS can afford to be choosy, so typically one is 'invited' to show up for a go while in basic training.

"Shock troops, rapid deployment specialists, call them what you will. I've had the pleasure of working with both the SAS and with Comandos. I would have to say that there's little to choose between them in terms of sheer courage under fire, raw intelligence, wits, and bloody-minded obsti-nacy in adversity. They are the world's fiercest, toughest, and canniest warriors since Ghengis Khan was a Boy Scout. However, SAS types tend to have more in common with SOE Secret Agents, in terms of their in-depth intelligence training and knowledge of the nefarious arts of espi-onage."

"But you handled them both equally well, of course?"

"I managed you, didn't I, dear girl? By comparison, they were a piece of cake."

Sylvia bent close and kissed his cheek. "Thank you again, my dear Robert...for everything. You'll have to excuse me, please. I feel a touch nauseous."

Things were not going as well for ex-Gruppenführer Walther Lange, or, ex-Standartenführer Hans von Tresköw. The morning after the gang of SOE assassins escaped from custody, Lange and von Tresköw were recalled to Berlin. At RSHA Headquarters, Prinz – Albrecht - Strasse, fol-lowing a fifteen-minute hearing by a panel hastily convened and co-chaired by Obergruppenführer Heydrich and Reichsmarschal-SS Himmler, they were both formally charged under several articles of the General Code of Conduct and summarily reduced in rank to junior lieutenant. Immediately after, they were escorted from the hearing and taken to five - by – eight - foot basement cells at the notorious Flossenbürg Prison, where they were stripped of their uniforms, handcuffed, shackled, and placed under twenty-four-hour guard, to await Court-Martial tribunals.

It was widely known that the convalescing Führer, in a characteristic fit of rage, had directed the Adjutant General to deal with both cases with dispatch. Upon pronouncing them guilty, he was to impose the death penalty by hanging, for both dereliction of duty and treason. Further, Hitler had ruled that the wife and two young children of Colonel Greilwitz be ineligible for the continuation of pay and benefits normally due families of captured SS officers.

In order to save face, Himmler and Heydrich publicly reprimanded their Gestapo Chief, Heinrich Müller, for his recklessness in posting a second-rate bureaucrat as station chief in the Protectorate where experience in security, counter-intelligence methods, and operations were paramount.

Three days later, Reichsführer-SS Himmler flew to London to represent the recuperating Führer at the memorial service for Obersturmführer Max von Roseteufel and Haupsturmführer Karl Oster. The SS Chief lauded the two men for their noble sacrifices and devotion in service to the Führer and Nazi ideals, and vowed to double his efforts to mercilessly rout and eliminate all those who sought to challenge the legitimate authority of the Reich.

Then Reich Protector Speer spoke, announcing that the heroic deeds of the two men would be immortalized by the immediate consecration and dedication of Grosvenor Square as Roseteufel-Oster Platz. Echoing Himmler's sentiments, Speer calmly reassured the gathering of more than a thousand mourners that he had instituted immediate measures designed to frustrate Allied gangster murderers intent on 'challenging the just and historically inevitable upward march of Nazi Germany to its rightful supremacy in the new world order'.

At that precise moment the bomb exploded, spraying a lethal shower of metal fragments and flaming petrol, narrowly avoiding injury to members of the official party, but killing or mortally wounding six officers and thirteen others standing by. The service was plunged into chaos, as fire crews arrived to fight the blaze and SS medical field specialists were rushed in. A steady stream of ambulances transported the injured and dying to St. Pancras Hospital.

Once the tumult died down, Heinrich Himmler, stunned but uninjured, regained his composure and ordered that the doors of the room be sealed so that every person in attendance could be searched, and detained for further questioning, if deemed necessary. Four senior officers who had collapsed from shock or smoke inhalation were hospitalised during the two-hour investigation.

In swift retaliation, the outraged Nazi leaders ordered that fifty English males be arrested at random in London and held as hostages. They were subsequently publicly hanged, under Himmler's orders. At 7:00 that evening, a broadcast on the BRPBS announced that these executions heralded the imposition of a harsh new regime aimed at discouraging any future Resistance efforts to subvert the new Protectorate. The broadcast concluded with a reading of the names of each casualty of this latest outrage, the intonation accompanied by a recording by the Berlin Philharmonic of the Funeral March from Beethoven's *Eroica* Symphony.

Of the eight fatalities, Himmler remarked that he, personally, deeply regretted the death of Sturmbannführer Johannes Bosch, the highly decorated SS officer. Bosch had been confined to a wheelchair since bravely confronting the Führer's would-be assassins at the clock tower.

Turning command over to Speer, Reichsführer-SS Heinrich Himmler then quietly departed for the airport. There followed a two-hour holdover, during which, at his insistence, a team of explosive experts meticulously combed his Junkers 52 'Iron Annie' transport for time-fused or air-pressure-activated bombs. Satisfied that the plane was safe, he returned to Berlin.

The month-long inquiries were inconclusive, but all evidence suggested that the incendiary fragmentation 'bottle' bomb, though styled after a British design, which employed an acid-activated time-delay fuse, had modifications that only a sophisticated knowledge of chemistry and the physics of explosives could have produced. The few remaining shards and fragments of the glass vial that had housed the detonator were examined; it was confirmed that the device was definitely not manufactured in England.

Despite the more than five hundred arrests, and the intensive interrogations carried out around the clock, no prime suspect or suspects could be uncovered. Over the course of the month, two hundred fifty men and women were executed in retribution, while more than two hundred others, detained for questioning, disappeared.

It was rumoured, though quickly dismissed, that a high-ranking German officer, acting on behalf of an Abwehr-funded anti-Nazi conspiracy, might have slipped past security by dint of his status or rank, and placed the device in the hall prior to the ceremony, thereby committing murder and suicide. The act was finally attributed, however, to the work of an unknown agent or agents of British Intelligence, in collaboration with a member or members of the criminal underground organisation known to police as the CDL, the Citizen's Defence League.

Former Untersturmführers Walther Lange and von Tresköw were found guilty on all counts. Stripped of their lowly ranks along with their membership in the élite 'black order', by order of Himmler himself, they were hanged on the basement gallows of Flossenbürg, back to back, their bodies cremated, and their ashes scattered ignominiously on the River Thames.

Under the leadership of Colonel Blackmore and Captain Latham, the group set out at six thirty in the morning, the wide-eyed Colonel Greilwitz swaying in a makeshift litter. As they proceeded, Latham explained that they had learned from SOE never to use the same temporary airstrip more than once a fortnight, to allow the ground cover time to grow and erase any trace of an aircraft's wheel tracks.

When they reached the water, they boarded a Danish fishing-trawler, which rolled violently and yawed wildly, ploughing through the heavy sea, and finally deposited them on a windswept shore twenty miles northeast of their point of departure. They rested briefly, then resumed, hiking through the ruggedly beautiful terrain toward their rendezvous. Twice on the journey, Sylvia fell behind, violently ill.

Worried, Hugh approached her. "What's wrong, Syl? Seasick?"

"Nothing that a premature delivery won't take care of," she gasped, retching.

"A what?"

"I am 'with child,' preggers, my dearest."

Hugh was speechless. When he found his voice, he stammered, "Are you sure, Sylvia? I mean, it's been quite a strain, what with the Gestapo's mistreatment and the boat ride just now..."

"Believe me, I'm quite certain. A girl knows these things. Now keep it under your hat, don't gloat, and don't coddle me in front of the others. Hurry along or we shan't catch up!"

Dutifully he followed, vowing silently to abide by her every wish.

Exhausted, they reached their destination, which the CO, a Commando Captain, described as a combined forces W/T and airbase operation. He led them a short distance to an airstrip.

"Hamish, I thought you said we were going by submarine?" Hugh asked.

"Ours is not to reason why..." he replied grimly. "This'll be a damn sight faster, lad."

After brief farewells with their SAS and Commando hosts, they boarded a new Special Operations DC-3 just as night was falling. Only five rows of the original seats remained in place. Flight Captain Samuel Mercer explained in a slow, west Texas drawl that the other nine had been "hauled out in order to stow a ton or two of cargo." Indeed, Hugh looked aft and saw an aircraft engine tied with ropes to the rear bulkhead amid a jumble of large wooden crates and metal canisters.

As Captain Mercer and his First Officer continued their pre-flight check, Hugh sat down beside Hamish, directly behind Robert and Sylvia, as per her instructions. Andy and his quiet companion, John, sat farthest back in order to keep an eye on Colonel Greilwitz, who, as Andy commented, "Looks about ready to croak, if he hasn't already." Overcoming the heavy payload, the twin 1,000-horsepower Pratt and Whitney engines lifted the big aircraft effortlessly and they settled back for the long flight. Hamish attempted to organize a singsong, but soon surrendered to the calls for quiet from his fellow passengers who said they simply wanted to sleep.

They landed for refuelling at Ferry Command Base, Gander, Newfoundland, in a driving rainstorm. Captain Mercer announced that there would be a one-hour stopover, enough time, "For the world's best beef burgers, exceptin' 'José's Hacienda' in San Antonio, and hot java that'd like to melt the spoon. Enjoy yourselves, y'all!"

When the DC-3 finally landed at Oshawa Airport, they were met by Colonel Gordon Graham and were immediately whisked away in two Buicks to Camp X, with the exception of Colonel Greilwitz, who was rushed by ambulance, under guard, to hospital.

Before long, the two cars pulled up at the Commandant's Residence. As the car doors opened, they were met and greeted by Erik Williamson, General Constantine, and Robert Brooks. After chatting briefly, Erik announced, "There's someone waiting to express his appreciation for your extraordinary accomplishments. Please, all of you, come inside."

Hugh and Sylvia followed Stalwart down the hallway to the French doors of the Colonel's study. As they entered, they were stunned to be met by a smiling Winston Churchill, Prime Minister of Great Britain. He hugged Sylvia warmly and shook Hugh's hand, insisting that they sit with him. Two mess orderlies poured champagne and served shrimp and lobster canapés as they chatted.

After a short while, Churchill rose and the room fell silent. Everyone turned toward Warden. "General Constantine, Sylvia, Hugh, and gentlemen. Rarely, indeed, if ever in one's lifetime, can one state, without the slightest doubt or hesitation that he, or she, has been privileged to walk in the company of heroes. Today, I can assure you, we do." Raising his glass, he concluded, "Sylvia, and Hugh, a grateful nation thanks you for your courage and fortitude in the face of the darkest adversity. You have made a difference. The enemy has been served notice that we Allies possess not only the will but also the means to launch the final battle, both from within, and without, which will utterly and decisively destroy him. Robert, Hamish, Andrew, and John, through your pluck and determination, you have brought Sylvia and Hugh safely back from the brink, to fight, perhaps, another day. I salute each one of you."

Taking Sylvia and Hugh's hands, he smiled delightedly as he raised their arms together in jubilation, while stating under his breath, "Your families send their love. You will be able to join them shortly."

Colonel Graham ended the celebration by announcing that they were all granted a two-week leave effective immediately upon completion of their debriefing. As they were about to leave, the Colonel asked that the Mission Tent Peg team members stay behind for a moment.

"I just wanted to add that your accomplishments have done you great honour; not only have you made a significant contribution to our war effort, as the PM has remarked, but your distinguished services as members of Special Operations Executive are already the stuff of legend. As Commandant of STS 103, I want to say how delighted I am personally that you have returned and I congratulate and thank you for your outstanding service.

"Unfortunately, it's the inherent nature of our trade that few if any persons can ever know or appreciate the sacrifices and triumphs of the secret war, made through the contributions of persons such as yourselves." He saluted them, and added, "Dr. Miller will be here to check each of you, here, at 0930 tomorrow. I've requested that he warm his stethoscope! Good evening."

Sylvia and Hugh were interviewed, first separately and then together, over a two-day period. A tall and distinguished English gentleman, in a Savile Row pinstripe suit, as Sylvia noted immediately, was introduced to them as Commander Lawson. He assisted Colonel Graham and Erik in the debriefing.

When they had finished reading over and signing their typed declarations, Colonel Graham, Erik and Commander Lawson each thanked Sylvia and Hugh for their patience and co-operation, then Graham asked Betty to notify the garage that their two passengers would be ready for pickup in one-half hour.

"Well, that's over, thank goodness. Did you say anything about us?" she asked as they walked along the gravel pathway to their quarters.

"No, did you?"

"No."

"You're sure, Hugh?"

"I swear."

"They already know...that's the impression I got from a few subtle comments by Erik."

"Yes, I think so. Who was that bird, Lawson? Didn't have much to say, wrote a lot..."

"Only Admiral Sir Will Cunnington, Chief of MI-6, the British Intelligence Service! "

"Notice that I'm not asking how you knew that. So, now what, Syl?"

"Well, for now, I'm going to smother my little Sarah with long-overdue love and affection, and my parents... I assume you're going to spend time with your Mom?"

"I am."

"Is there someone you'll be...calling upon?" she queried, beginning to walk more slowly.

"Sylvia. Stop. Listen to me, please. First, to answer your question: there is absolutely, categorically no one else. Second, I love you and want to marry you, expecting or not. Got that?"

"And our careers with SOE? What about them?"

"I have the feeling that Erik Williamson intends to keep us both here, on staff, at Camp X. I can't believe how much it has expanded since we left. It's as though it's poised to launch the invasion of Great Britain."

"I hope you're right, Hugh. The PM referred to the 'final battle'. I want us to be part of that!"

"Amen! By the way, do you know what he meant? Of course not, so I'm going to tell you. Some diplomat said that Britain loses every battle but one, the final battle."

"I'm impressed. Will you come for dinner to my parents' home? Oh, I keep forgetting, I don't even know where they live! But come, anyway, please? We'll need some time to break these concepts to them gently. Poppa will be able to handle it. Momma will be a bit more of a challenge...but not to worry. I love you, too, and I accept your offer."

"My mom will be so thrilled that I've finally found a wife and religion, any religion! You'll bring them all to meet her next week, okay? We can make the arrangements on the way...oops; we're going to miss our ride to Toronto. See you back out here in five! Oh, one other thing, permission to call you by your real name...Juli, Julienne?"

"Try Rebeccah...with an 'h'", she smiled.

"Rebeccah...? Just how many names do you have, woman?"

"Rebeccah is my name, Hugh! If you hurry right back, I'll explain, promise."

"Wait, Rebeccah. Rebeccah: I like that!" he stated, reaching down to pick up a piece of gravel. "One moment." Reaching into his pocket he retrieved a small object, which he then proceeded to scrape with the stone. "Rebeccah Weiss: darling, I have a little something to make this an official proposal. Please don't be offended. Here, take it please; it's genuine silver. We can have a jeweller melt it down to make an engagement ring."

"Where did you get this?" she asked examining the button bearing a defaced Death's Head insignia.

"Call it the spoils of war."

"You romantic fool!"

Commander Lawson rose, excusing himself as he left Colonel Graham's office. He closed the door gently.

Robert Samson waited expectantly for Graham to continue. Clearing his throat, the Colonel resumed, "Robert, old man, how long have we known one another? Beaulieu, I suppose, when you were my..."

"Gordon, I appreciate your tact, but I believe that I can save us all a great deal of time and bother. No need to beat around the proverbial..."

"Then, you know what I am about to say?"

"Yes..."

"Very well, let's begin with Tom. Did you kill him?"

"Yes, I did."

"Why, if I may ask?"

"He was a plant. One of them. A Nazi agent."

"I knew that, and I was handling it. Why in heaven's name didn't you confide in me?"

"I had my suspicions from the day he arrived. He stuck his beak into places where he had no business, and he asked questions, which were obviously based on prior knowledge. Someone was feeding him. I acted on my own."

"So, you suspected that he was gathering very specific information regarding subjects about which a raw recruit wouldn't have the foggiest notion. What led you to conclude that your suspicions were correct?"

"I decided to follow him to Rice Lake. When he wandered off, I shadowed him for over an hour. He met another fellow. I know I had him dead to rights: I assumed he was trading secrets and I guess I overreacted."

"Yes, he was. The other fellow was one of Robert Brooks' men...an American OSS chap, actually."

"How do you know this?"

"Because, my friend, Tom, was a double agent. Our double agent. He was an Abwehr V-Mann, code name: 'Oscar'." Erik knew this and turned him, rather persuasively, as only he can. SIS and Erik were sending me false intelligence reports that I was providing him, all tripe, extremely credible tripe, but tripe nonetheless."

Visibly shaken, Robert sat, silently. "I am so very sorry."

"Next, the client Marco. You did him in also, am I correct?"

Pausing, then looking directly at Graham, Robert spoke, "Yes. He was too obvious to be successful for long. I trailed him, after dropping him off at the depot, on his bus excursion to Highland Creek. I witnessed him giving information to a person of very questionable loyalties."

"How did you do it?"

"It was a set-up. I arranged that he should be given an assignment in town. No one else on staff was party to the deception. I was waiting for him in the closet of the hotel room, and strangled him with piano wire. Then I left. Was he a...?"

"Actually, no. We discovered that he was a spy, after we found the body and started to investigate. It's almost certain that the information he passed along to his contacts in that factory compromised Tent Peg severely. There is no question that, as a direct result of his actions, the Abwehr and SD knew something major was brewing, aimed at one or more of their top dogs."

"Wouldn't it have made more sense to catch him at his game, and then put him through the wringer, Robert? He might have given us much more information."

"I did it for England. Therefore, Sir, I now am a liability. What's going to happen?"

"It's up to GHQ, now. You are definitely finished here. In the meantime, you are being shipped off to deskwork with Erik at Casa Loma, thanks to your superb contributions to the Service and daring operation overseas. Questions?"

"Yes, Gordon, but more in the form of a favour."

"I'm listening, Robert."

"Sir, I'd like to offer my services..."

"Go on..."

"Please, don't think me mad as a hatter, Gordon, but I believe that I would stand a good chance of finishing the job."

"Job...do you mean, Adolf Hitler?"

"Yes, I do. I mean the Führer, Gordon. I am convinced that I could get into Germany...parachute, a cold drop of course, and find a way to get close enough to do him in."

" 'The hands of death' method, I presume? How is your German?"

"Better than passable...I'll need some tutoring. The rest...disguises, field craft, radio procedures..."

"You essentially wrote the book," he reflected, rubbing his chin pensively.

"What do you say, Colonel? One more wicket for the old boy?"

"I'll run it past the brass."

"Thanks. By the way, Warden thinks it's worth a capitol idea!"

"You've mentioned it to Prime Minister Churchill? When?"

"After the reception. He's anxious to hear what you and Erik think."

"Robert, you never cease to amaze me. I'll be in Toronto tomorrow and make an appointment to discuss it. Of course, you realise that this is likely a one-way ticket you're proposing."

"Not a shred of a doubt."

"Very well. Damn, I'm going to miss having you around here, but then again, I'm on my way, too."

"You are? To where?"

"Hamish and I are off to beautiful British Columbia. Roger Stedman, the last 2-I-C at Beaulieu is coming to take over as CO. Say's he's eager to get back to active status with SOE, after six months of making the rounds of the diplomatic cocktail circus, or circuit, in Ottawa and Washington. By the way, Robert, and off the record, thanks..."

"For what?"

"Marco... Pardon me, Rob, but I must catch those two before they leave."

Mac was nearly at Highway 2. He slammed on the brakes when the Colonel's jeep pulled up beside him, honking loudly. Mac pulled off the road and stopped. "Yes, Sir?"

"Excuse me Private. I'd like a moment with your two passengers."

"Certainly, Sir. I'll just go for a stroll."

Graham leaned into the back window, smiling at Hugh and Sylvia. "So, you two are off, eh? Hearth and home...Good, well deserved."

"Yes, thank you Colonel," Sylvia replied. "Is there something we've forgotten, Sir?"

"No, something I forgot, Colonel, Captain."

"Excuse me, Sir, did you...?"

"Congratulations to each of you" he beamed. "GHQ has just confirmed that you, Sylvia, are now Major Weiss. You have been appointed Chief Small Arms Instructor at Camp X...quite a stroke really, as the only female SAI in an SOE Special Training School and may I add, richly deserved. And Hugh, old chap, you are now officially Captain Mason, Assistant Small Arms Instructor, and Special Liaison Officer - Communications, at Camp X. The General, Erik and Winston are arranging a little ceremonial 'champers and signing' at the Castle."

"Really? But Sir, what about you?"

"I'll fill you in when I see you in Toronto on Wednesday. Now, I think you have more than this news to celebrate, or so a little bird tells me! Godspeed! Very well, Mac, they're ready; do drive carefully."

"On my word Sir, I'll take it as carefully as...."

"Spare us the particulars, if you don't mind Private. Please be aware that you are solely responsible for the safe delivery of your future leaders!"

"Yes, Sir!" he grinned gunning the Buick's V8. "Attention to detail!"

CFC Contact
Friday, June 01, 2001 .

Hi Lynn:

Funny that your announcement of the victory dinner should arrive right now (I am afraid that I won't be attending). I have just gotten off the phone with my aunt (Charles Constantine's daughter) in Kingston. She has now read your book, "Inside- Camp X', and tells me that she has quite a few more pictures of CFC than those I sent to you and she also has a fair amount of stuff (papers and letters) from his time in the Toronto office. She says you are welcome to come and see what she has any time if you feel like trekking over to Kingston where she lives. Or you are welcome to phone (or write) her and ask her questions about him if you like. If you give her some warning she can gather it together for you to see. She had no knowledge about his involvement in Camp X, but does know other things about him. If it helps you at all, she gave me a bit of information on the phone but I didn't know what all you really wanted to know. He went to RMC in 1902 for three years and then to the RCHA after that. He was District Officer Commanding in Kingston in the early part of WW2 and then later sent to Halifax. One of his duties was being the contact for the British Government when they decided to send all their gold to Canada on board ship. She would, of course, know much more about his life than those bits there. As always, I will help with what I can from here.

Regards,

Elizabeth

Professor Beaker's Learning Labs
Science & technology for primary grades Sudbury Ontario CANADA
Tel: 1-888-839-2153
e-mail: pbeaker@vianet.on.ca
webpage: http:llwww.professorbeaker.com

Abwehr (Ger. 'protection')	German Military intelligence and counter-intelligence service
DFC	Distinguished Flying Cross (Great Britain)
Gestapo (Geheime Staatspolizei)	Secret State Police, formed in Prussia, by Hermann Göring, 1933, which became Amt IV of the RSHA (see below) with Headquarters at No. 8 Prinz-Albrecht-Strasse, Berlin.
Kreigsmarine	The German Navy, formed in 1935
Panzer (Ger. 'armour')	Armoured vehicles; usually used in reference to tanks: Panzerkampfwagen (PzKpfw) - Panzer Battle Tank
MD2	Military District 2 HQ, Toronto.
MI-5	British counter-intelligence service
MI-6	British secret intelligence service (SIS)
OKH (Oberkommando des Heeres)	High Command of the Army
OKW (Oberkommando der Wehrmacht)	High Command of the Armed Forces
OSS	Office of Strategic Services, USA; precursor to the Central Intelligence Agency
Réseau	Allied resistance organizations behind enemy lines
RSHA (Reichssicherheitshauptamt)	The Reich Central State Security Bureau which was divided into seven 'Amter' - branches - including the Gestapo, KRIPO and SD
SAS	Special Air Service (Great Britain), an élite combat unit frequently deployed behind enemy lines
SD (Sicherheitsdienst)	Security Service (intelligence and counter-espionage) of the SS, formed in 1932, by Reinhard Heydrich
SOE	Special Operations Executive (Great Britain), formed to co-ordinate 'special warfare' in German-occupied territories
SS (Schutzstaffel-'protection squad')	The massive and overwhelmingly complex Nazi political-police-military service ruled by Reichsführer-SS, (Rf-SS) Heinrich Himmler. The Allgemeine-SS (General SS) was the main branch; it served a political and administrative role. The SS-Totenkopfverbande (SS Deaths Head Organization) and later, the Waffen-SS (Armed or fighting SS), were two other branches which made up the SS.

SS Ranks

Untersturmführer	*junior lieutenant*
Obersturmführer	*lieutenant*
Sturmbannführer	*major*
Standartenführer	*colonel*
Gruppenführer	*lieutenant general*
Obergruppenführer	*general*

SIM	Italian secret service
KRIPO (Kriminalpolizei)	Criminal Police branch of the SD
SIPO (Sicherheitspolizei)	Security Police, comprised of the Gestapo and KRIPO
V-Mann (Ger. 'trusted person')	Abwehr secret agent
Wehrmacht	Literally, Armed Forces;'The Wehrmacht' is the English equivalent for 'German Army'

PHOTOGRAPH CREDITS

Lynn-Philip Hodgson	*13, 18, 255, 257, 277*
Mac McDonald	*111*
Town of Whitby Archives Brian Winter	*54, 226, 227*
Hans Boldt	*23*
Hamish Pelham Burn	*22, 26, 67, 222, 311*
Jane Wilson	*78*
Harry Smith	*44, 91, 221*
Bill Hardcastle	*181, 230*
General C.F Constantine/Elizabeth Ginn	*95, 152*
The Thomas Bouckley Collection, *The Robert McLaughlin Gallery, Oshawa, Ontario*	*235*
John O. Kellam, Funeral *Director, McIntosh-Anderson Funeral Home*	*246*

Lynn-Philip Hodgson has dedicated the past twenty-five years to bringing to light the tales of brave and courageous Canadians who fought in World War II's secret war. Their stories need to be told and he has done this in his best seller, **'Inside-Camp X'**.

A businessman for over thirty-five years, Lynn is a proud Canadian, born in Toronto, Ontario. He has dedicated himself to assuring that the next generations will be aware of Canada's remarkable contributions to the successful outcome of WW II. As research consultant in the publication of Joseph Gelleny's biography, **'Almost'** and as co-writer with Alan Longfield for, **'Camp X The Final Battle'**, Lynn continues to work toward this goal.

Alan Longfield, B.A. (Queen's), M.Ed. (Toronto), a retired Elementary School Principal, has been researching and writing about Camp X with Lynn-Philip Hodgson, since 1977. With Joseph Gelleny, a Canadian SOE Secret Agent trained at Camp X, Alan wrote **'Almost'** (Blake Books, 1999). Alan was the Editor of **25-1-1**, the Journal of the Camp X Museum Society, (1977-'80). He is currently Past President and a Director of the Camp X Historical Society.

Alan, born in Toronto, is a resident of Whitby, Ontario. His wife, Judi, is the MP for Whitby-Ajax. Their son, Michael, is a documentary film director. Alan can be contacted at: *alongfi@home.com.*

'Camp X The Final Battle' is Barbara Kerr's third editorial project in the Camp X series. Beginning with the first book, Lynn-Phillip Hodgson's best-selling **'Inside – Camp X'** and continuing with the second, Joe Gelleny/Alan Longfield's **'Almost'**, she has worked with Lynn and Alan to assure that this most important part of Canadian history is presented in an accurate, informative and highly readable format. It is her continued wish that these stories earn the courageous but heretofore unknown heroes, the respect and gratitude that they so richly deserve. Barbara can be contacted at barbarakerr@look.ca